Troll Mountain Tales

A Novel By
Buz Swerkstrom

*How Trolls Became Ugly, Toller's Neighbors,
Hildur And The Giant Troll, Olafur And The Trolls,
Bergthor of Black Mountain* and *The Shepherd of
Silverbrook* are all traditional Scandinavian troll tales,
retold, some with different titles and character names.
Kravig And The Field of Flowers is an adaptation of an
Irish dwarf story, *The Talking Eggs* an adaptation of a
Louisiana folk tale. *The Splinter Cat Tale* is based partly
on a Scandinavian troll tale. The splinter cat is a creature
from North American lumberjack lore. *The Seven Labors
Of Lars Halvorstol* borrows a little from the Hercules myth.
"Stone cheese" is featured in several traditional troll tales.
All of the other tales in this book are from the author's
imagination.

Full Court Press
Atlas, Wisconsin

Contents

6

1 ▪ Sounds

Awakened barely an hour after falling asleep, Haar's mind was in a stupor as he shambled from his communal cave and cocked one of his large, red-tinged ears down Troll Mountain, trying to decipher the whines and growls floating faintly in the morning breeze. He had never heard such peculiar, pestiferous sounds emanating from the base of the heavily wooded mountain, or from anywhere else on the mountain, which was soft green with young, growing leaves and filigreed with Spring freshness this mid-May morning. Needless to say, he did not think of the sounds as "pestiferous," for he was as oblivious to the existence of that word as cats are to the concept of continents. And he had no idea what was causing the noises. He knew he didn't like them, though, not merely from an aesthetic standpoint but also due to the fact that the strange sounds, faint as they were, stung his ears like a swarm of wasps, for like all trolls he had an enhanced hearing capacity, compared to humans, that seemed to intensify unpleasant sounds in a particularly acute manner.

Less than a minute after Haar emerged from the cave a fellow tribe member, Rnobrna, a resident of the same communal cave, joined him outside, beneath the slab of stone that extended out eight feet, at about a thirty degree angle, from the cave opening. A jagged rock four feet high and four feet wide stood five feet in front of the cave entrance, making the opening difficult to discern from the other side of that obstructive rock. "What in the world is that?" Rnobrna growled, his voice coarse as oak bark. Like all trolls, the two were as ugly as distored mirror images, as judged by human beings. By human standards, Rnobrna was the uglier. While his ears were similar in shape and color to Haar's, which is to say pointed and reddish, his eyes were rounder, his skin more mottled and warted. His stooped posture gave him almost a humpbacked appearance. Both he and Haar had the sort of thick cucumber-shaped nose as

8

characteristic of trolls as a conical shape is of pine trees. Each also sported a generous, bushy tail, as most trolls do.

"It's awful," Haar said of the sound. "It's horrible."

"I've never heard anything like it," Rnobrna said. "Have you?"

"It's horrible!" Haar repeated, contorting his face as though the noises were painful enough to wrench his facial features out of shape in the way something sour causes someone to pucker his lips.

"Where's it coming from?" Rnobrna asked.

"From down there, isn't it?" Haar replied, pointing down the mountain with a thick, stubby, hairy finger.

"It seems to be," Rnobrna agreed after several seconds of consideration. "I wonder what the devil is making such noises."

Haar held his right hand up to block sunlight from shining in his eyes, and both trolls squinted in the morning light, for daylight is to trolls what extremely high altitude is to humans. They disdain sunlight as much as they do soap and combs. It is not true, though, as human beings widely believe, that too much sunlight—or *any* degree of sunlight, it is sometimes said!—will turn a troll to stone. This is something troll parents tell their children to keep them inside as much as possible, for sunlight does dissipate a troll's great strength, and it can inhibit a young troll's physical growth. Trolls venture out of their caves in the daytime if a situation demands it, though rarely do they venture very far from home when the sun is shining. For some strange reason, even people who generally think logically and know there are many tales about daytime encounters between humans and trolls continue to embrace the erroneous belief that exposure to sunlight is fatal for trolls. No doubt many people take comfort from such a belief because trolls are physically stronger than humans to such an extent that trolls seem a little less frightful when they are thought to have a fatal vulnerability

Haar and Rnobrna, both of whom had greasy, tangled hair and wore ragged, stained, smelly clothes, listened intently as the dull, piercing whines and growls continued.

"Ort should be told about this," a female troll behind them said. This was Rnobrna's wife, Utrud, who was standing just inside the cave entrance, which was a scant two inches higher than the top of her head, listening to the conversation between

Haar and her husband. Utrud had close-set, black eyes, bushy eyebrows, pointed ears, a lopsided mouth, and a mop of medium length coal-black hair partially covered by a stained red-and-white checkered kerchief tied beneath her pointed chin.

Rnobrna glanced back at his wife. "You're right," he agreed, standing there puzzling over the noises.

"Well, why don't you go and *tell* him then?" Utrud nagged.

"I could, I guess," Rnobrna said languorously.

"Well, go then!" Utrud snapped. "Do it!"

"I'm going already!" Rnobrna snapped back, perturbed by Utrud's provocation. "Do you want to go with me over to Ort's cave and tell him?" he asked Haar.

"Don't you think it's awful early to be waking him, if he isn't up?" Haar said. "Why don't we wait a while."

Had Haar been Utrud's husband she may well have slapped him upside his head. Instead, she squealed: "This might mean danger to all of us! And here you two hem and haw around like a couple of dumb clucks who couldn't get out of the way of a boulder if someone didn't tell you to jump. I think the king should be told about something like this right away. Now, are you two going to tell him or do I have to go over there and do it myself? I will, you know. Don't think I won't."

Rnobrna knew she would; he had no doubt about that. "Don't get yourself all worked up," he said to her in a needle-sharp tone. "We'll go tell Ort about the noises, won't we, Haar?"

"I guess maybe we better," Haar said, glad Utrud wasn't his wife. Haar's wife had died quite a number of years back.

Ort, king of the tribe of Troll Mountain trolls, lived in a large, deep cave with eleven chambers and three trickling waterfalls, as well as an underground stream. That same stream passed through the smaller of the two multi-channeled communal caves, the one in which Haar and Rnobrna lived. A different stream passed through the larger communal cave. Except for Ort and five others, all of the Troll Mountain trolls lived in the two communal caves, eight in one and twelve in the other. Ort's wife, Tattra, and their grandson, Rott, lived in Ort's cave, a wizard named Kravig and his daughter, Tala, had their own cave, and Guggle, a troll witch, preferred to live in an old, ramshackle cabin in the densest part of the forest, near the base of Troll Mountain, which is a name people gave the mountain. Trolls, even those who lived there, did not know it or call it by that name. People took to calling it Troll Mountain when the legend grew that many trolls displaced by human settlement and development fled northward to that particular secluded mountain to get away from people and their churches, which had ringing bells that jangled trolls' nerves and could drive them to madness, or even turn them to stone. All of the occupied caves were rather high up on the mountain, near the line where the forest thinned and mountain's face—its forehead, so to speak—was more grey rock than green vegetation.

To put it mildly, Ort was grumpy when Haar and Rnobrna roused him from a snoring sleep. Ort tended to snore as loudly as hogs grunt. "What is it? Whadaya want?" he growled at his two visitors.

Rnobrna quickly explained about the strange sounds. Reluctantly, fumingly, Ort agreed to go outside for a listen. His tangled, matted, scraggly, bug-infested hair looked even more disheveled than usual in the morning. He scratched himself all over, without embarrassment, as he led the way outside, cursing all the while this better turn out to be something important or somebody was in big trouble. He hated having his sleep interrupted.

Ort was in the neighborhood of 550 years of age, which was getting up there in years even for a troll. He didn't know exactly how old he was, as most trolls don't. Other Troll Mountain trolls were more aged than Ort, though; there was no doubt of that. Old Fungus was believed to be close to 900 years old, and at least three others, including Guggle, had been around longer than Ort, who had been a troll king for more than two hundred years.

Besides being older than most of those in his tribe, Ort also was, at four-feet-eleven-inches, shorter than the average male mountain troll, by about five inches. His arms were abnormally long for his height, though, which accounted, in part, for his tremendous strength. He had a barrel-shaped body and an enormously large head, which appeared to be even larger than it actually was because of the way his black hair stuck out in matted spikes. His red nose was rounder than the normal cucumber-shaped—and cucumber-complexioned—troll nose, and his small green eyes, which had an intense glow, were set close together. Having led a cattle-rustling expedition the previous night, through brushy country, his mixed dark brown and black body hair, as well as his short tail, was full of burrs, stickers and tiny twigs this particular morning. Of course, his bushy tail had been full of such substances forever, it seemed. Trolls don't put much stock in personal grooming, or in bathing or washing. In a troll community it is a point of honor to be dirty and smelly, and few trolls lack for such honor. Ort did not have to take a secondary position to any troll in either department, dirt or odor, which was part of the reason why he managed to retain his power and high standing for such a long time.

When Ort emerged from his cave, followed closely by Haar and Rnobrna, his two companions immediately began jabbering about what Ort was supposed to listen for.

"Shut up, you two, so I can hear something!" Ort growled. Haar and Rnobrna, who were both younger than Ort, by the way, obeyed the order and ceased talking. While the whines and roars were less distinct from Ort's cave than from Haar and Rnobrna's cave, it took Ort only a short time to deduce the source of the sounds. "People!" he said, spitting a plum-sized glob of saliva onto the ground, as though even uttering the world "people" was distasteful. The glob barely missed Haar's bulbous right foot, which was sheathed in an old, wrinkled leather boot caked with dried mud.

Haar and Rnobrna seemed surprised. "People?" Haar said. "Are you sure?"

"I'd stake your life on it," Ort said. "Only people could make such strange sounds. You've both heard cars passing on roads."

"But. . ." Haar started to protest, wanting to point out these sounds didn't seem to be made by cars, and that car noises *passed*, they didn't linger in one spot.

"This sounds something like that," Ort went on, verbally crushing Haar with his booming voice. "I'm sure there's some kind of connection."

"I don't know," Haar argued. "They don't sound like car noises to me."

"Do you think it means danger to us?" Rnobrna asked Ort.

"I don't know," Ort said. "Not for the time being, I don't think. Those noises are quite a ways away. It might well mean trouble in the long run, though. It's hard to say. For the time being, I suggest we all go back to sleep. Tonight some of us can take a little trip down the mountain to take a look around and see what we can see." Haar and Rnobrna needed no more of a hint than that to let Ort return to his sleep and return to their own cave to sleep themselves.

2 ▪ Investigating

When darkness descended that night Ort rounded up a group of male trolls to go down the mountain and have a look around the area where the strange noises had come from that day. The whines and growls lasted most of the day, from early morning until late afternoon. Although the trolls hadn't heard any strange sounds for several hours, Ort thought it would be wise to investigate the matter, to see what there was to find. Several of the trolls saw no point in making such a trip when the sounds had ceased, but they did not voice their opinions to Ort. They could tell Ort had his mind set on the outing and knew that anyone who said anything that even hinted of dissension, under the circumstances, did so at his or her own peril. Ort had been known to cuff someone simply for asking something as seemingly innocuous as "What way do we go now?" on a trip through the forest, as though the question implied Ort didn't know where he was going, or that he was not a fit leader. Besides Haar and Rnobrna, Ort also took Gangl, Traug and Drulle with him on this night's mission. Lantern-jawed Drulle was the youngest and largest of the group. His slanted forehead, hunched shoulders, long arms and hirsuteness gave him a Neanderthal appearance. With the possible exception of Ort, he also was the strongest member of the tribe. Gangl's most distinguishing physical feature was his droopy eyes, which made him seem dull and uninvolved. Given his tendency to let his mouth hang open, and breathe through his mouth, his entire face had a droopy, drowsy, lumpy look to it. Thin, stringy, black hair framed that face, and contributed to his overall languid demeanor. By contrast, Traug's oval-shaped face was a study in blankness. It was so pale and plain that it almost disappeared against any background. His eyes and mouth were but barely noticeable slits. Only his protruding potato nose gave his face any character whatsoever. Like Gangl, he had long stringy hair that was parted, in an uneven line, from the middle of his head.

His hair was a bit thicker than Gangl's, though, and more grey than black. Even for a troll, he had an abnormal abundance of body hair. Besides Ort's group, two other groups went out in other directions at approximately the same time to hunt for food.

There was an overcast sky that night, which blocked what little moonlight there would otherwise have been, with a slivery moon. This, of course, did little to hamper the trolls' vision. Through millenniums of optic evolution, trolls see in the dark almost as well as they do under lighted conditions. They are nocturnal creatures as comfortable, confident and surefooted in the dark as fish are in water.

Following a switchback route down the forested mountain, in single-file orderliness most of the time, it took Ort's group well over an hour to reach the bottom of Troll Mountain, on the side of the mountain where that day's sounds originated. The forest was an old, mature forest dominated by pines and birch trees, with oaks, ashes, alders and other hardwoods present in lesser numbers. The height and density of the trees made the rocky, mossy, forest floor virtually pitch black. The Troll Mountain trolls used this side of the mountain far less frequently than they did the other sides, so there was no established trail to follow; consequently, it took them longer to descend this side of the mountain than it would have to descend other sides. There were many rock outcroppings to go around and over—seemingly more on this side of the mountain than on other sides, which was one reason they ventured down this side less often. Once the group of six reached the bottom they split up and combed the area in search of anything unusual or out-of-place. After fifteen minutes Traug came upon an opening in the forest where the ground was upturned and freshly uncovered rocks and boulders lay strewn about, along with downed and squashed tree trunks and branches, and aromatic tree stumps. Two large machines loomed almost two hundred feet ahead of him. Instinctively, he drew his six-inch-long knife from its case to have it at the ready, in hand. All five of the other trolls carried knives as well. Traug hooted to summon the others to the spot. In a few minutes the five others were gathered around him, staring at the large objects, the upturned ground and the scattered rocks and tree limbs, murmuring amongst themselves as to what the objects were and why the ground had been ravaged, and why in the world everything looked such a mess. Their caves weren't that messy, and that was saying something.

"Let's take a closer look," Ort said, boldly leading the way out into the clearing. "Everybody be on your guard," he cautioned the others, drawing his knife. "This could be some sort of a trap."

Ort decided the first order of business was to investigate the large, looming objects.

"They look like some sort of machines, I'd say," he said as they drew nearer to them and could make them out more distinctly. One of the objects was, in fact, a bulldozer, the other a skidder-loader. None of the trolls had seen either before, though, so they didn't know exactly what they were, or what function they served. Ort approached the bulldozer cautiously, as the others held back, and kicked it in a couple of different places, thinking that might make it produce a sound. Nothing happened—it didn't explode, or convulse, or make any noises—so the others all went up to it as well and began touching it, and poking at it, and sniffing it. Rnobrna held an ear close to it to see if he could hear anything. "I can't hear it making any noise," he reported.

Most of the others followed his example and tried listening closely themselves, with some also doing the same with the skidder-loader.

"What kind of machines do you think they are?" Haar asked Ort.

"Who knows," Ort said. "This one might be some sort of a big car. It looks like some sort of a big car. I can't figure out why it has these big belts rather than wheels, though."

"This one has the same thing," Haar noted, for the skidder-loader also had belts rather than tires.

"Do you think this is what was making the noises?" Rnobrna asked.

"They must be," Ort answered.

By this time Traug, Gangl and Drulle had drifted away from the bulldozer and were looking over the plowed-up earth.

"What in the world is going on here?" Traug said, loud enough for everyone to hear. "Do you think it's possible that those machines have been digging up the dirt?"

Ort went over to check out things. "Look," he said, pointing to the ground, "the tracks in the dirt match the tracks on those machines. They've been moving around all right. I'd be willing to wager a chest of jewels that people were here today running those machines, just as they do cars. *People* are the only ones who drive cars, aren't they? And we've all seen what they call tractors on farms we've visited. This looks a lot like what people do on a farm."

"You mean people are farming here?" Drulle asked.

"I don't know," Ort said. "They might be starting. You never know what people might do. I don't like the look of things, I can tell you that." He spit on the ground. "I don't like the look of things at all."

"But if there was a farm here we wouldn't have so far to go to round up sheep and cattle," Traug said, thinking of the situation in practical terms. "We'd have easy pickings. It looks to me like this might be a good thing for us."

Everyone looked at Ort to see what he would have to say to that. He pondered Traug's point a few seconds, then shook his head. "No, there's just something about it that doesn't seem right to me," he said, drawing from both instinct and experience. "I can't quite put my finger on what it is, but I have a bad feeling about this. Besides, I don't like the idea of people being on our mountain, even way down at the bottom here, even if they are starting a farm. It's an intrusion is what it is! An intrusion!" he repeated thunderously, incensed by the thought of people living so close to their caves after all the years they had had the mountain all to themselves.

The trolls wandered about the area where the bulldozer and the skidder-loader had operated that day, amazed at the amount of disturbance and destruction the machines had done. They discovered the stumps of more than twenty trees, and sawed-up parts of the downed trees, off to one side of the scraped dirt area.

"Look at all of these!" Gangl said in amazement. Every one of them had been cut off perfectly flat. "Do you suppose those machines did that too, Ort?"

"It's mighty strange all right," Ort said, reaching down a hand to scoop up a small handful of sawdust near one of the stumps, then sniffing the sawdust. "Smells like regular sawdust, as far as I can tell," he said. All of the others smelled the sawdust as well, and agreed there seemed to be nothing unusual about it, except for the great amount. The trolls produced far less sawdust when they felled trees and cut them up with axes and crosscut saws for the firewood they burned in their fireplaces and in open fires.

After examining the cleared area and the downed trees for some time the trolls returned to the bulldozer and the skidder-loader to give the two machines a more thorough inspection. This time Ort boldly climbed into the cab of the bulldozer. The others looked on in rapt attention as he felt all of the levers, buttons and dials. As much as he tried, Ort could not make the machine produce the least little sound, much less the rumbling roars and piercing whines that had been audible most of the day.

While walking around the bulldozer in search of any sort of clue that would make things more understandable, Haar discovered, a short distance from the machines, a path through the forest that seemed to be the same width as the bulldozer. "Come and look at this!" he shouted to the others. In great anticipation, the five others hastened to where Haar was. "Look! Look there!" Haar said, pointing down the path, some of which was merely matted undergrowth, part levelly scraped dirt.

The trolls stood there dumbfounded for thirty seconds before Traug spoke. "What do you suppose it is, Ort?"

"It's a path, obviously," Ort said. "You can see that as well as I can."

"What it *doing* here, though?" Traug said. "How did it *get* here? What *made* it?"

"Do you think that machine made it?" Haar said, pointing at the bulldozer. "It looks like it's about this wide."

"And here are some tracks like the ones we saw over there," Rnobrna said, kneeling on the ground, on one knee, to take a close look.

"So there are," Ort said. "It looks like that machine has been here too all right."

"There are some other tracks here too, though," Rnobrna said after looking around some more. "These look like car tracks, if I'm not mistaken—tracks of a very big car."

Ort took a close look at the tracks Rnobrna pointed out. "They look like car tracks all right," he agreed. "Let's follow this path and see where it leads."

Ort led the way as the six trolls followed the path through the thick forest in a southwesterly direction. The terrain was relatively level, although the trolls encountered a couple of gentle rises. The path twisted to avoid large trees, but was arrow-straight for more than three hundred feet at one stretch. Ort stopped occasionally to check the tracks on the path, and the squashed tree roots, and to listen for any unusual sounds. Neither he nor any of his companions heard anything out of the ordinary.

After twenty-five minutes of stop-and-start walking they came to the other end of the trail, in a clearing off the side of a dirt road.

"It's people all right," Ort said upon seeing the road, for he knew wherever there was a road there were bound to be people connected to it in some way. The trolls knew of the existence of the dirt road before this time. It had existed for only twelve years, having been created to serve the growing number of families that had moved to the vicinity of Troll Mountain. None of those families lived nearer than a mile from the base of the mountain, but Troll Mountain was not quite as secluded as it had been only a few decades previously. The fact that only people used the road and that the cleared path they followed connected to the road made it obvious the cleared path was connected to people as well.

"What do we do now?" Rnobrna asked.

"I don't see that there's a whole lot we *can* do," Ort said. "We might as well go back home."

"But what about the noises?" Haar said. "We still haven't figured out what caused all the noises."

"We know that those machines have something to do with them," Ort said. "Other than that, I don't see that there's anything else we can do tonight."

"But what if we hear the same noises again tomorrow?" Haar said.

"Well, what if we do?" Ort said.

"What will we do then?" Haar wanted to know.

"We'll decide that when the time comes," Ort said, with an authority that made it clear to Haar and all the others that that was how the situation would be handled; there would be no more discussion of it this night.

There was already a murmur of dawn light in the sky by the time Ort's group returned to their caves. Most of them were so tired that they gulped down some food and went straight to sleep. Ort's stout, grey-haired wife, Tattra, whose upturned chin nearly covered her mouth, fried him some snake and crow meat, which she spiced with ants and flies. After his meal Ort opened one of his chests of stolen jewelry, coins, treasured trinkets and other prized objects and ran his fingers through the riches for close to an hour, until he grew very tired. While all trolls revel in running their fingers through their treasure, Ort did this more often than most, not only for the pure pleasure but also to continually reassure himself his treasure was still safe at hand. The tale of how another troll king, Fritjof, had once lost all of his accumulated treasure sent shivers of anxiety through him whenever he thought of the tale. He couldn't imagine a worse catastrophe than the loss of his treasure. He didn't know the full story of how Fritjof's treasure was stolen from his cave, for no troll did. All trolls had no doubt that tricky humans were behind the dastardly deed, though.

3 ▪ Written On Stone

A particularly acquisitive troll king named Fritjof stole so many coins, jewels, rings, silver goblets, gold candlesticks, amulets, swords and other treasures from people that the residents of the province where Fritjof and his minions operated rose up and demanded that the lord of the province do something to put a stop to the troll king's long crime spree. Being the concerned, caring ruler he was, this lord, who was named Erik, sent out a notice declaring that anyone who could recover the treasures the troll king had stolen would be rewarded with a huge estate and a luxurious stone mansion staffed with a large number of servants who would administer to his every need.

Soon a strong, strapping young man named Lute showed up at Erik's palace to offer his services.

"I feel it is my duty to make you aware of what you will be up against," Erik said to Lute. "It is believed that Fritjof, the troll king, lives in a cave high up on Cloud Mountain and that his chests of treasures are well guarded every hour of the day by two giant trolls."

"I'm not afraid of any troll, no matter how big he is," Lute said with a confident swagger.

Erik raised his eyebrows. Courage was one thing, after all, but foolish courage was mere folly. "You are aware of the fact, aren't you," he said, "that trolls are much stronger than humans?"

"I, too, am much stronger than most humans," Lute boasted. "I daresay that no troll has ever had to deal with any person as strong as me. Trolls don't scare me."

And so the young man named Lute set out for Cloud Mountain, where Fritjof, the troll king, lived and hoarded his stolen treasure. Lute climbed the mountain and searched for Fritjof's cave for four days. Finally he found a small cave entrance and walked toward it. As he did so, a large, hulking troll with expressionless eyes, mop-like black hair, and smelly rags for clothes stepped out of the cave entrance and stood there with his hands on his hips, blocking the entrance.

The sudden appearance of the large troll surprised Lute, who stopped in his tracks. Lord Erik certainly knew what he was talking about, Lute thought to himself. Maybe no troll had ever had to deal with a person as strong as him, but he had to admit that he had never had to deal with any creature as muscular and menacing as this troll either. Lute was nothing if not determined, however. He lit into the giant troll for all he was worth, swinging his fists and kicking his feet with abandon. As great as his strength was for a human, though, it was no match for that of the giant troll. Suffice it to say that the fight lasted but a brief time and ended with the giant troll tossing Lute aside as he would a big bone after gnawing off all the meat. Lute slid down the mountainside headfirst for a couple of hundred feet before he managed to latch on to the trunk of a small tree and stop his painful slide. Bruised, battered, and sore from the top of his head to the tips of his toes, he slinked home, humbled and humiliated by what happened outside the troll king's cave.

The next person to volunteer to try to recover the stolen treasure from the troll king was a notorious criminal widely known as Peter the Pest. Next to Fritjof, Peter the Pest had been the most active thief in the entire province. He had only recently been released from prison.

"It takes a thief to steal from a thief," Peter the Pest reasoned to the province lord.

"How do I know that if you somehow manage to succeed in your mission," Lord Erik said, "that you won't simply keep all of the stolen treasure yourself instead of bringing it to me so that it all may be returned to the rightful owners?"

"I am not like that anymore," Peter insisted. "I realize how I harmed other people in the past with my own stealing. Now I would like to use the skills of theft I possess to help society, as a form of repayment for my past misconduct. If I was interested in stealing the goods from the troll king in order to keep them for myself would I first come to you to inform you of my plans? Certainly not! I would simply go ahead and try to steal them on my own. I am interested in doing this so that I can be rewarded with a mansion and an estate and be able to live an honest life from now on."

While not entirely convinced that Peter didn't have some sort of shady scheme up his sleeve, Lord Erik had offered the generous reward to anyone who could procure the stolen objects, and as a free citizen Peter the Pest was eligible to claim the reward, so Erik assured Peter the reward would indeed be his if he could somehow get the items away from the troll king.

Peter had the advantage of knowing where Fritjof's cave was located, since Lute had been able to find it. Peter fared no better than Lute, however. After the two giant troll guards were finished with him one of his arms was shorter than the other, various bruised body parts were swelled to the size of small pumpkins, and he had absolutely no further desire whatsoever to ever again try to steal anything from the troll king—or any other troll, for that matter.

Soon after Peter the Pest's failed attempt, a third volunteer stepped forth when a wispy young man as pale as a bleached seashell and weak as a wet piece of paper showed up at Lord Erik's castle gate asking to be granted an audience with Lord Erik. The young man's name was as short as he was: Bo.

When the guard at the gate asked what business he wished to discuss with the lord, Bo said he was there to offer his services to recover the treasures the troll king had stolen.

"The lord is much too busy for such foolishness," the stern, stolid guard said. "How could a runt such as you be of any help in recovering treasure from trolls who are far stronger than even the strongest person? Be gone with you!"

"Strength is not everything," Bo said, in his feathery voice. "It is possible to reach a destination by more than one path. There is more than one way to cook an egg. The same plant may grow in more than one type of soil."

"What are you, a philosopher?" the guard replied.

"I'm someone who can think on his feet," Bo said. "And that's exactly what is needed here. Now, I repeat: I would like to see Lord Erik."

"You're a determined little rascal; I have to give you that," the guard said. "Hold still and I'll see what I can do." The guard summoned a second guard from in front of the castle and whispered to him briefly. The second guard disappeared into the castle for a short time and reappeared with instructions to allow Bo to enter the grounds. Soon Bo found himself standing before Lord Erik.

"What is your business here?" Erik asked from his high, padded chair.

"I have come to offer to go to Cloud Mountain to recapture the treasured objects the trolls have taken," Bo explained. "First, though, I want to make sure that your offer of a mansion and a large estate to whoever recovers the treasure still holds."

A small smile slowly spread across Lord Erik's face. He looked over at four aides standing in a line off to one side to see if he could detect the hint of a sly grin on any of their faces. None of the expressionless faces revealed anything to him. Like a kettle of water over a fire, which bubbles at first and then builds to a raging boil, laughter erupted from Lord Erik in the same manner, building from a chuckle into a full-blown belly laugh.

"That's a good joke," he said to Bo, still laughing. "Who put you up to it?"

"It's not a joke, your lordship," Bo said. "I'm as serious as rock is hard."

The king eyed the young man more closely. "If you're serious, then I'm afraid you must be deranged," he said. "Perhaps you haven't heard what happened to the first two men who tried to recover the stolen treasure from Fritjof? The first man was twice your size, and ten times stronger, and yet his strength was as one pail of water against a raging forest fire. The second man was the craftiest human thief who has ever plagued this province, and yet his craftiness could not recapture the treasure from the trolls. If those two could not recover the objects, what chance does someone of your size and meager strength stand?"

"Strength is not everything," Bo said, repeating what he had said to the guard at the gate. "It is possible to reach a destination by more than one path. There is more than one way to cook an egg. The same plant may grow in more than one type of soil."

"Meaning what?" Lord Erik said.

"Meaning, your lordship," Bo said, "that I intend to use my brain rather than brawn to recapture all of the stolen objects from the troll king."

"And exactly how do you intend to do that?" Lord Erik asked.

"I haven't decided yet," Bo said. "But everyone knows it is easy enough to fool trolls, considering how gullible they are. I will study the situation and formulate a plan.".

"You will, will you?" Lord Erik said. "What's your name, anyway?"

"Everybody calls me Bo," Bo answered.

"Well, Bo," Lord Erik said, "I admire your courage, and your apparent determination, but I feel obligated to discourage you. I doubt that you are aware of the dangers that await you and the enormity of the challenge that confronts you. I strongly urge you, with every ounce of persuasive power I can muster, to abandon this foolhardy notion of yours and return home before you become so entangled in trouble and adversity that you will be like a fly trapped in a huge spider web."

Bo was not to be dissuaded. Assured that the reward of a mansion and a large estate would be his if he recovered the stolen treasures, he was soon hiking up Cloud Mountain in search of Fritjof's cave, the approximate location of which was known through Lute's efforts. Once in the vicinity of the cave, he moved about stealthily, hoping to spot the cave entrance or a troll or two before a troll could spot him. When he caught sight of a giant troll seemingly on guard duty he felt confident he had found the troll king's cave. Surveiling from a concealed position some distance away, he watched several trolls congregate in front of the cave entrance as a film of dusk grew darker and darker. He could barely discern Fritjof when the troll king emerged from the cave. Bo knew it must be Fritjof, though, because of the strutting, self-confident demeanor he displayed. Almost immediately, Fritjof and the five other trolls who had congregated set off down the mountain, into the night, leaving the giant troll standing before the cave entrance. Since it was believed two giant trolls guarded the troll king's treasure chests, Bo assumed another giant troll was inside the cave. He also assumed that Fritjof and the other trolls were off to raid more houses and farms, to steal more treasure.

Bo remained where he was, observing the cave entrance. The giant troll left his post for only a few brief periods, entering the cave on most of those occasions. The eastern sky displayed hints of dawn before Fritjof and two other trolls returned. The two others immediately set off elsewhere—to their own caves, Bo assumed—as Fritjof entered his cave. It seemed likely to Bo that the other three trolls who were part of the group that departed from in front of Fritjof's cave probably returned to their own caves on a more direct route.

As the degree of daylight increased, Bo used a spyglass to scope out the layout of the landscape around the cave entrance. He was glad to see a lot of lichen growing on the rock, for he believed he could use that lichen to his advantage. He also scouted around a bit, careful to be as quiet as possible and remain unseen.

Bo continued his scouting the next several nights and mornings. The same pattern repeated each night, with Fritjof heading off with five other trolls and returning before dawn broke. Some nights a different giant troll guarded the cave entrance, so Bo now was sure two giant trolls guarded the stolen treasure. Confident he had enough information, he concocted a plan and set about carrying it out.

With everything in place, Bo watched Fritjof and the other trolls leave one night, waited a half-hour to allow the trolls to get some distance from the troll king's cave, then went moseying down a path toward the cave entrance, pretending to be preoccupied with the rocks along the path.

"Stop where you are!" the giant troll in front of the cave entrance bellowed, advancing toward Bo with huge strides.

Bo looked up, pretending to be completely surprised.

"What are you doing here?" the troll demanded.

"I'm afraid I've become lost," Bo said. "I was just reading the rocks, hoping they would tell me which way I should go to get back home."

"Reading the rocks!" the troll thundered. "What in the world are you talking about?"

"I've been blessed with the ability to interpret lichen patterns," Bo said. "I can look at lichen and know what it means."

"What's lichen?" the troll asked. "I've never heard of it."

"It's this colorful mossy stuff that grows on rocks," Bo explained, pointing to a patch of it as he spoke. "If you have the gift to read it, as I have, it can tell you all kinds of things, such as the shortest path to a certain place, or what your future holds, or where buried treasure is located."

The giant troll perked up at the mention of treasure. "Treasure!?" he practically squealed. "It can tell you where treasure is buried?"

"Indeed it can," Bo said. "In fact, I thought I may have detected something along that line right when you interrupted me."

"Where? Where?" the giant troll not so much asked as demanded.

"Right in this area here," Bo said, drawing a circle in the air above some grey and pale green patches of lichen. A full moon shone in the sky, bathing the landscape with soft moonlight. "Um huh, um huh, it's coming to me now!" Bo said with rising enthusiasm. "I'm almost certain the pattern means there is buried treasure nearby."

"Where? Where? Tell me," the giant troll demanded.

Bo pretended to study the lichen patterns more closely. "Well, it's pointing to this direction," he said, pointing that direction himself. "The lichen pattern seems to be continued on these rocks over here." He moved over to those rocks as the giant troll hovered over him, all but salivating at the thought of there being buried treasure nearby. "Um huh, we're getting closer, I'm sure of it," Bo said. "The lichen seems to be telling me that there is treasure buried between two round rocks about this big around." He indicated the size by holding out his arms as far as he could spread them. "And if I'm not mistaken," he went on, looking to his left, "it's a very good chance those two rocks over there are the two rocks the lichen pattern is talking about. Luckily, I have a little spade with me so that I can dig there."

Bo reached into a pocket for a small hand-spade and began digging. It took him but a minute to find a small buckskin pouch containing a half-dozen coins—coins he buried there a couple of days before.

"I'll take those," the giant troll said.

"How about if we each take half?" Bo proposed.

"I said I will take them all," the troll said. "You should consider yourself lucky if I let you live."

"Here you go; they're all yours," Bo said, handing over the pouch with the coins inside. "You don't want to harm me, though, or I won't be able to lead you to more treasure."

"What treasure?!" the troll said. "Is there more buried treasure around here?"

"Well, it's very possible," Bo said. "I need to read the lichen patterns to find out."

"Well, get to it," the troll ordered. "I'll be right with you every step of the way to take all of the treasure you find."

"Will you let me go on my way, then, if I do that?" Bo said.

"Of course I will," the troll lied, having no intention of keeping that promise.

"Well, okay, let's have a look around then," Bo said, and led the way back toward the cave entrance. As they approached the cave entrance, the second giant troll was there, outside the cave.

"Where did you go?" the second troll asked the other. "And who's that skinny little person with you? Where did he come from?"

"I found him snooping around," the troll with Bo answered.

"I got lost," Bo explained to the second troll. "I mean no harm.

"Turns out he can tell where buried treasure is," the troll with Bo said. "Look here." He held out the buckskin pouch with the coins in it. "He found these coins buried over here. He says he knew they were there by the way moss grew on some rocks."

"What do you mean?" the other troll asked.

"I happen to have the rare gift of being able to read moss patterns on rocks," Bo said, thinking it best to avoid using the word "lichen" with trolls, since the first had not been familiar with the word. "I can look at moss patterns and know if there is danger at hand, or tell what the weather will be like tomorrow, or know if there is treasure nearby. We're looking around for more treasure now."

Not wanting to be left out, the second giant troll joined Bo and the other troll as they ambled along, Bo pretending to study lichen patterns every few feet.

"Oh, this is bad!" Bo exclaimed as he looked at one patch of lichen. "This tells me that a boulder is about to fall right where we are! Jump out of the way!" Bo looked up the cliff as he jumped out of the way. The two trolls also looked up, just in time to see a large boulder crashing down the cliff. They jumped out of the way as well, as the boulder landed with a thud two feet behind one of them. Big as the giant trolls were, the boulder was large enough that it would have caused severe damage to either of them, or possibly killed one of them. Bo actually was in little danger, for a friend of his, Alfred, pushed the boulder over the edge of the cliff at Bo's "Jump out of the way!" signal. "It's a lucky thing for you two that I was here," Bo said to the trolls. "That boulder could have killed either one of you."

"That was a close call all right," one of them admitted. "You sure know how to tell what the moss is telling you."

"It's a gift I have, like I said," Bo said.

The three continued on, and in short order Bo told the two trolls he had found another lichen pattern that revealed the location of nearby buried treasure. This time Bo dug up a silver platter, several silver cups and two horseshoes he had buried there. The trolls, of course, greedily grabbed the treasure from Bo and demanded that he continue looking for more treasure.

"Oh, this is interesting," Bo said as he examined a fairly large area of lichen. "It's telling me there's a sack of garden goods beneath a pine tree about fifty feet or so up ahead of us here." Sure enough, Bo found a sack of garden produce his friend Alfred had deposited there. The two giant trolls were just as amazed by that as by the treasure finds.

Bo led the trolls to another cache of treasure he had buried before pulling the most audacious ruse from his bag of tricks. Not far from the troll king's cave entrance, he exclaimed "Oh, no!" and feigned something approaching horror. "This is awful! This is terrible! This is terrible!"

"What is it?" one of the giant trolls asked with great concern.

"We better get away from here as fast as we can!" Bo said.

"Why?" the troll asked.

"Because a rockslide is about to come down the mountain and bury everything in its path!" Bo said, speaking in exclamation points to make his sense of dread seem more believable. "We'll all be buried alive! We have to get away from here! If you have anything valuable in the cave you should carry it down the mountain if you don't want it buried forever. Is there anything in the cave you want to save?"

"There are some chests with things in them," one of the trolls revealed.

"Valuable things?" Bo asked. "If they are, you better grab them and run. I'll lead us all to safety, but we have to act as quickly as possible."

"But the chests belong to the king," one of the trolls said. "We only guard them."

"In that case, the king will be very proud of you for saving his valuables," Bo said. "I wouldn't be surprised if he gave you a great reward of some sort. You certainly would deserve it for saving all of his valuables from being buried."

"We would, wouldn't we?" one of the trolls said.

Having witnessed all of Bo's other predictions come true, the two giant trolls swallowed the impending rockslide warning hook, line and sinker. With that accomplished, persuading them they should save all the valuable items in the cave even though they didn't own them was as easy as making a dog bark. Without delay, the two trolls rushed into the cave and emerged with four chests stuffed with stolen items, each troll carrying two chests. Following Bo, they carried the treasure chests away from the cave, down Cloud Mountain. Bo paused every few minutes to look over some lichen, each time assuring the trolls the lichen was telling him they were headed in the right direction to avoid the devastating rockslide.

On they went, to the foot of Cloud Mountain, where Bo conveniently knew about a cave where the trolls could store their treasure chests in safety. The trolls deposited the four chests in the cave before Bo led them on a search away from the cave, reading lichen patterns as he went, telling the trolls he wanted to try to make sure the cave was a safe place. Bo took his time reading the lichen, several times pretending to be confused or confounded by what he saw. This went on for more than an hour, to allow his friend Alfred time to remove all of the valuable items in the chests and hide them in a far side chamber in the cave, then put rocks and dirt in the chests. Once he was confident Alfred had had sufficient time to take care of his part of the plan, Bo suddenly found some disturbing lichen patches that told him the four chests weren't safe in the cave where they were, after all, and must be moved to a different cave immediately.

And so off they went again, Bo leading the way and the two giant trolls each carrying two heavy chests. After a half-hour, they came to another cave entrance. Bo cautioned there seemed to be something odd about some of the lichen pattern outside the cave and said he better go into the cave first to see if everything was all right. Once inside, he squeezed through a narrow opening that led to another entrance to the cave, which he used to exit the cave. He then ran as fast as he could back to the cave where Alfred had loaded all of the recovered valuables onto a horse-drawn wagon. Bo and Alfred wasted no time in taking the wagon back to Lord Erik's castle. It was mid-morning when they arrived there, driving the wagon into the courtyard amidst cheers and shouted compliments. Soon all of the recovered items were returned to their rightful owners and Lord Erik made good on his promise to reward Bo with a mansion and a large estate. Of course, Bo shared the mansion and the estate with Alfred for his invaluable help in the recovery scheme.

The few coins and other items he planted to convince the two giant trolls he possessed the rare gift of being able to interpret meaning from lichen patterns was little enough payment for his mansion and grand estate.

As it turned out, the estate contained a lot of lichen-covered rocks and rock formations. Bo studied lichen quite extensively—what is was, exactly, and how it grew, and how people perceived it down through the centuries. Lichen became so fascinating to him that he sometimes thought there must be some message or symbolism in the colorful patterns the delicate plants presented. As hard as he tried, though, he never was able to crack the key, if there was one.

4 • The Noises Continue

As Haar had more or less predicted, the strange sounds did indeed resume the next morning, at the same time they started the previous day. The same raspy whines and undulating growls resounded across the face of Troll Mountain for hours on end.

When Ort awoke in the middle of the afternoon and heard the noises again he cursed human beings and sent his grandson, Rott, to order three members of the tribe—Hlauka, Gangl and Scurf—to go down the mountain to spy on the people making the noises. Given that Gangl had been down the mountain with Ort the previous night, he knew exactly where to go, not that locating the people would have been any problem for anyone, what with the volume of noise being generated.

As alluded to previously, it is unusual for trolls to venture very far from their caves during daylight hours. Ort believed the present circumstances called for certain risks, however, for he wanted to try to solve a mystery.

The noises ceased when Hlauka, Gangl and Scurf were still several hundred yards from where the bulldozer and the skidder-loader had been the night before. The three trolls briefly discussed whether or not they should continue on, given that the noises had stopped. Gangl was in favor of turning back and returning to the caves; he saw no point in investigating noises when there were no longer noises to investigate. Hlauka and Scurf pointed out to Gangl that Ort would likely receive them rather gruffly if they reported back to him that they had aborted the mission, though, so the three continued on. When they reached the place where the two large machines had been the night before they found the bulldozer and the skidder-loader parked in slightly different spots. There were no people in sight. The area of scraped earth had nearly doubled in size since the previous night, and many more trees were down, with all of the remaining stumps flat, or nearly so, on top. Several of the downed trees had trunks nearly three feet in diameter. Some had been cut into lengths and stacked.

The three trolls weren't sure what they should do next. They had gone to the site to investigate noises and now there were no noises to investigate, or any people around to observe. They decided they better look around to try to see what they could find in the way of clues. Gangl found a few red and white candy wrappers. Hlauka, who was paunchy and had springy, splotchy hair and simian facial features, found a two-thirds-full five-gallon gas-can near the bulldozer. Given that the trolls occasionally found cans of gas in sheds and garages, they knew what gas was. Gangl wanted to follow the path through the forest again, believing that was what Ort would want them to do. Hlauka and Scurf, who was as paunchy as Hlauka and had a blocky head that looked like one of the caricature trolls human woodcarvers like to chisel from a chunk of soft wood, with an expanded space between the nose and the mouth, outvoted him on that suggestion, though. They didn't see any point in doing that, since it had proved fruitless, or nearly so, the previous night. They wanted to simply return to the caves and report to Ort exactly what had happened—that the noises had stopped before they made it all the way down the mountain and that they had not seen any people. And so the three trolls headed back up the mountain, taking a twisting route that included only small sections of the route they had taken down the mountain.

It was after eleven o'clock when they reached Ort's cave. Not that time meant much to the trolls. Outside of daylight and darkness, trolls know next to nothing about time. Ort had left with a small group to look for a farm or a house to raid, so Hlauka, Gangl and Scurf waited outside Ort's cave. To pass the time, they wrestled, horsed around and stared into space, for several hours, before Ort returned.

Luckily for the three of them, Ort was in high spirits when he returned. He had happened to raid the house of a man who repaired clocks and watches in his spare time. Despite the fact trolls cannot tell time, they treasure clocks and watches because of their tick-tock sounds and mesmerizing movements. Ort had taken seven clocks and three watches. The three other trolls with him also made a good night's haul.

Ort was eager to go into his cave, sit by the fireplace, and admire his new acquisitions. He was so intent upon that, in fact, that the three trolls waiting for him had to practically shout at him to draw his attention. Even then, he was so excited about the timepieces that he didn't recall sending the three on a mission until they started telling him about it. After they finished their account of the mission Ort looked at the crescent moon and pondered.

"If we hear the noises again tomorrow," he said after a considerable period, "we'll just have to go down there earlier in the day and see if we can spot anybody."

With that, he sent Hlauka, Gangl and Scurf on their way so he could admire his newfound treasures in peace, in the company of his wife, who gave him all the praise a king deserves for his bravery and savvy in securing such precious valuables.

5 ▪ A Discovery

When the same sounds resounded from the bottom of the mountain the next morning Ort dispatched Traug, Dau and Brine to check out the situation. Brine was a young troll, comparatively. He was in his early forties, relatively tall, with long legs, long arms and long, slightly webbed fingers. He had curly, birds-nest hair, caterpillar-like eyebrows, and large, oval ears, which were tinged with red, of course. Had any of the trolls in the tribe been clever enough to tag others with nicknames, Puffy would have been a perfect nickname for Dau, for he had puffy cheeks, puffy lips, and even a puffiness around his bulging green-black eyes. This time the noises did not cease when the three trolls neared the area where the noises originated. Small clouds of smoke became visible as Traug, Dau and Brine drew nearer. The odor of burning gasoline permeated the air, which the trolls found delectable. Approaching cautiously, the three trolls frequently stopped behind tree trunks to listen. When they spoke, they did so at a lower than normal volume.

All at once Brine caught a glimpse, through a fence-like row of towering tree trunks, of the yellow bulldozer moving about. He scurried behind the trunk of a large white pine and frantically motioned for his two companions to do the same. As Dau and Traug tried to figure out what Brine was trying to communicate to them, they also caught sight of the bulldozer in motion, growling like a headless dinosaur, which sent them jumping for cover as well. All three watched in fascination as the bulldozer moved about, approximately three hundred feet away. Satisfied that the machine was not moving toward them, to try to run them over, they ventured closer.

After advancing about a hundred feet they stopped to look and listen. Dau caught sight of a man some distance off to their right and pointed him out to Traug and Brine. The trolls' eyes nearly popped from their heads as the man, who wore a silver hardhat, a plaid shirt, and suspenders, which held up a pair of olive-green pants cut off so that the leg bottoms reached only the top of his leather boots, toppled a twenty-inch ash tree in less than twenty seconds, with a chainsaw, the tree creaking, crackling and then thumping to the ground as it fell. The way the man felled the tree so quickly seemed like magic to them, for this was the first time they saw a chainsaw in action. They were familiar with logging only as it was done with axes, crosscut saws and workhorses. Indeed, axes and saws were vital tools for the trolls' primitive lifestyle.

"We're going to have to tell Kravig about this," Dau said to the other two. As mentioned, Kravig was a troll wizard. "He must be using magic of some sort. Maybe Kravig will be able to explain it."

The man with the chainsaw appeared to be so engrossed in his work—he was then trimming off the branches from the felled tree—that the three trolls felt safe in approaching nearer to the action. Spotting a second man with a chainsaw, they hid behind a convenient knoll, which afforded them a fairly good view of the goings-on. Branches and forest undergrowth still obstructed their view, but they did not dare venture any closer, not when men they were spying on seemingly had magical power to fell large trees with amazing ease. Who knew but what they could not dispatch trolls with the same swiftness, they reasoned. While the trolls knew they were far stronger than people, physically, they feared their strength might be futile when matched against magic.

Dau, Traug and Brine watched the men work for well over an hour, from behind the knoll. Two men wielded chainsaws, one scurried around moving tree branches and generally helping the two working with chainsaws, and another man operated the bulldozer. The three trolls whispered amongst themselves occasionally, trying to puzzle out what the people were up to. While this activity seemed related to logging, whining chainsaws and the large, rumbling bulldozer were peculiar to them, particularly the bulldozer, which not only knocked down objects but tore up the earth as well. Dau, Traug and Brine could think of no explanation that made sense to them as to what the bulldozer was doing.

Then they caught sight of the skidder-loader in action, with two other men, also wearing hardhats and suspenders, scurrying about around it, seemingly hooking heavy chains to large logs, which the machine grasped with lobster-like claws at the end of an enormously long mechanical arm, swung the logs around and deposited them elsewhere. The trolls had never seen anything like this machine either, and they found it even more fascinating than the bulldozer, for it was able to make more movements, and movement is always more eyecatching.

At noon the men shut off all of the machines, stopped working, and gathered in a shady spot to eat lunch. This was of great interest to the trolls, and made them more aware of their own hunger. While this was not a normal mealtime for trolls, for they generally were asleep at this time of the day, the hike down the mountain had made them hungry. Traug wanted to return to the caves immediately and gorge himself on bat ears and mushrooms, which were plentiful at that time of the year. Dau, on the other hand, argued they should stay and see what the people did next. Despite his gnawing hunger, for he was large, Brine reluctantly agreed with Dau that the best course would be to remain there for a while. And so they remained where they were. They could tell the seven men were talking to each other, but couldn't make out what the men said.

After what seemed to the trolls an interminably long time, but actually was only about a half-hour, the men resumed their work. The trolls watched for another hour and then headed back up the mountain, to eat and report their discovery, since the men seemed to be doing pretty much the same things over and over. Dau weighed in with a half-hearted protest that they should stay until the people left so they could give the others a complete report, but he was secretly glad the other two insisted on returning to the caves.

"We're leaving," Brine said to Dau. "You can stay here if you want. I need food."

"I'll go back with you then," Dau said. "We might as well all go together."

In addition to wanting food, the three trolls were anxious to get back and share news of their discovery, for they knew something of this magnitude would bring them a measure of glory, and they were eager to bask in that prestigious spotlight as soon as possible. Dau wasn't about to let Traug and Brine hoard that honor all to themselves. It didn't occur to him that by staying longer he might have the opportunity to discover something more to reveal.

When they reached the caves, boiling with excitement and practically panting from exertion, Traug, Dau and Brine headed directly to Ort's cave, to tell him their news first. Tattra, however, insisted, in a voice as husky as molasses, they had to wait until Ort was awake unless their news was a life-and-death matter, for she knew how much Ort hated being disturbed from his sleep.

Traug, Dau and Brine were so intoxicated with excitement that they felt they would explode if they didn't share their big news with others, so they began telling other tribe members about the people and the machines they had seen, and the odd things the people had done. The news spread like spilled water. Those who heard it secondhand went to Traug, Dau or Brine to ask for a firsthand report. As it turned out, Ort slept so long that day that he was the last tribe member to learn about what Traug, Dau and Brine had discovered.

6 ▪ The Good Luck Stone

"Would you like me to read you a story?" Anders Branstad asked his nine-year-old son, Andrew.

"Yes!" Andrew said.

"How about a troll story?" Anders said. "You like troll stories, don't you?"

"They're my favorite!" Andrew said. "Yes, read a troll story!"

"All right," Anders said. "Let's see now. . . Where did I put that book?" The book he meant was *A Treasury of Troll Tales*, which one set of his grandparents gave him as a gift one Christmas. Anders searched the parlor with his eyes and quickly spotted the book. "Ah, here we are!" He picked up the book, settled into his favorite chair as Andrew settled into another chair to listen to a story, and scanned the table of contents for the title of a tale he thought Andrew would particularly enjoy, deciding to read one titled *The Good Luck Stone.*

▪

When Goddard Christianson visited the seashore with his parents and his older sister, Cairn, he found a pretty, marbleized, bluish stone the washing surf had polished to a splendid sheen. The rectangular stone was three-quarters-of-an-inch thick, three-and-a-half inches wide and more than six inches long. Obviously, it had once been part of a layered rock formation, as evidenced by its geometric shape. It was by far the prettiest stone Goddard had ever laid his eyes upon.

It was such an exquisite stone that Goddard had no doubt whatsoever that it was a good luck stone. Like most eleven-year-old boys whose imaginations have harbored tales of magic and adventure, Goddard believed that fortune was a fate that could be contained in a charm, manipulated through magic, and sealed in a special stone. And if ever a stone was a good luck stone, Goddard knew it was the distinctive stone he found at the edge of the ocean.

At first Goddard's parents indulged his passionate conviction that the beautiful bluish stone he had found was a good luck stone. While neither his mother or his father believed the wonderful stone was a good luck stone, they thought it was a harmless enough notion for their son to embrace.

As time went on, though, Goddard's parents became concerned with what they regarded as their son's obsession with his special "good luck" stone. Goddard carried his good luck stone with him everywhere he went, despite the fact the stone was rather large for a good luck charm to be carried on one's person.

"Maybe I should split it into a few smaller pieces," his father suggested. "That way you could carry one of the pieces in your pocket and keep the rest in your room."

Goddard was aghast at that suggestion. "But then it wouldn't be a good luck stone anymore," he said. "It has to be whole to be a good luck stone. If it were split into pieces it would be ruined. Splitting it into pieces might even bring *bad* luck."

And so the stone remained unsplit, intact, whole.

Goddard's mother took a different tack. "As beautiful as the stone is," she reasoned, "maybe it's not really a good luck stone. You've had it for more than a month now and it hasn't brought you any great good fortune, has it? You haven't found any buried treasure. You haven't been saved from any injury by what would seem to be a miracle. No one has given you an unexpected gift. Just because the stone is beautiful doesn't necessarily mean it will bring you good luck, you know."

Goddard was not persuaded. He held firm to his conviction that the beautiful bluish stone would, in time, bring him good luck. There was absolutely no doubt in his mind about that. If others couldn't see that, that was their problem, not his. And so he continued carrying the good luck stone with him wherever he went.

One day, as summer waned, the Christianson family decided to take advantage of what might be one of the last sublime days of the season by going for a picnic in the mountains. After their picnic lunch, Mr. and Mrs. Christianson and Cairn wanted only to prop their heads against rocks and lie in the sun for a while.

The energetic Goddard, though, wanted to explore the area to see what he could find. His parents allowed him to do so after he promised he would wander only a short distance from where they were.

Not surprisingly, Goddard's curiosity got the better of him. He kept seeing things he wanted to explore, and told himself that it wouldn't hurt to go just a little bit farther. Every time he reached a place he wanted to explore, something else a little farther away caught his eye and he hiked to that place, where another enticing spot would catch his eye. Soon he was quite a distance from where his parents and his sister were resting. He was so far from them, in fact, that when he shouted to see if anyone could hear him there was no response. Worse than that, he had failed to pay close attention to the zigzag path he had taken to reach the spot where he was, so he was disoriented. With a sheet of clouds now blocking the sun, he had no idea which direction he should walk to find his family.

His good luck stone felt like an anchor in one of the back pockets of his pants. *Some good luck stone!*, he thought to himself. It certainly hadn't prevented him from becoming lost. Maybe his parents were right after all; maybe the beautiful stone was just that: simply a beautiful stone, not a good luck stone.

With panic beginning to set in, Goddard started walking. He walked to see if he could see anything that looked familiar. He walked to see if he could pick up his footprints anywhere, or see anything that seemed familiar. He walked because he had to do *something.*

Eventually he found a path that followed a rock ledge. One edge of the narrow path was mere inches from a precipitous dropoff. Goddard walked along this path until he came to a cave entrance. Of course, a boy as curious as Goddard could not pass a cave entrance without entering the cave to have a look around. Stepping into the dank, mud-floored cave, Goddard looked around in the dim chamber and saw a dark human-shaped form against the far wall. He stopped to listen. He could hear breathing—the sort of deep, slow breathing that suggested someone was sleeping. Stepping slowly toward the sleeping form, he drew close enough to dimly make out some facial features. At that point, he knew immediately that the sleeping form was not a human but a lumpy, hairy, smelly troll. Recognizing what the creature was, Goddard let out a frightful scream. That awoke the troll, who opened his eyes and sat up with a start, seeing somebody in his cave.

For a moment, Goddard was immobilized with fear. It was as though his feet were stuck fast to the muddy clay in the cave. When the troll emitted an angry growl and began clambering to his feet, though, Goddard regained his wits and started running from the cave. He popped through the cave entrance and ran back along the narrow path along the rock ledge. Glancing over his shoulder, he saw the troll—who looked even uglier in daylight than he had in the dark cave—running after him. So he tried to run harder. When he glanced back over his shoulder again, though, the troll was gaining on him. What a perilous predicament this was! An angry troll who could run faster than he could, and was more familiar with the terrain than he was, was chasing him, and would surely do terrible things to him if he caught him.

Goddard ran as if his life depended on it. No matter how fast he tried to make his legs move, though, the troll ran faster and continued gaining ground. As he ran, Goddard felt his good luck stone slip from his back pocket and heard it fall on the path behind him, so he slowed down, wanting to retrieve the stone. That allowed the troll to gain even more ground. Goddard knew that if he took the time to retrieve the good luck stone the troll would have a better chance of catching him. Balanced against his personal safety, the stone seemed comparatively unimportant at that moment. He knew he would have to let the stone lay where it was if he had any chance whatsoever of escaping the troll. And so he turned away from the stone and churned his little legs as fast as they could churn.

All at once Goddard heard a yelp on the path behind him, so he turned around just in time to see the troll flying over the edge of the cliff, with Goddard's good luck stone sailing out over the cliff behind the troll. Obviously the troll had slipped on the good luck stone. Since stone upon stone produces perilous footing, the troll was sent completely off-balance. A bloodcurdling scream pierced the air as the troll fell over the cliff.

Goddard couldn't restrain himself from going back to the site of the accident to find out what horrible fate had befallen the troll. Looking over the edge of the cliff, he discovered that the troll had not been killed. While falling, the troll managed to grab ahold of a gnarly old tree growing on the side of the cliff. He was far down the cliff, and it would take him quite a long time to either climb up the cliff, if he was able to do so, or climb down and walk back up another way. Whatever the troll decided to do, Goddard had plenty of time to make his escape.

The good luck stone was nowhere in sight. It had gone over the edge of the cliff and now no doubt rested somewhere in the valley below. If Goddard had to lose the beautiful stone, he could think of no better way to lose it. Truly, he told himself, it *was* a good luck stone. Maybe it had brought him only one piece of good luck, but what a magnificent piece of luck that was! The good luck stone may well have saved his life. He doubted that many stones ever contained more good luck than that stone did.

Goddard could hear the troll muttering to himself and cursing his fortune as he hurried away, trying to find his way back to his family. After walking through the forest for more than a half-hour he heard his father's voice calling his name, for when Goddard hadn't returned within a reasonable time his father went looking for him.

Back at the picnic site, Goddard told the others the amazing story about how he happened upon a troll's cave and how the troll chased him and slipped on his good luck stone and fell over the edge of the cliff.

"I *told* you it was a good luck stone!" he said in the most satisfied I-told-you-so voice anyone has ever used.

7 • A Sign Of Things To Come

When Ort learned of what Dau, Traug and Brine observed, he decided immediately to lead a group back down the mountain that very night. Every single male troll wanted to go along, but Ort decided only seven should go. First of all, there were other tasks that needed doing. Food had to be gathered, for one thing. Secondly, Ort did not want all of the male members of the tribe to participate in a potentially dangerous mission; in case anything untoward should happen the tribe would not be wiped out.

The trolls scoured the area where the bulldozer and the skidder-loader were parked for the night without finding much. The path leading out to the road had been widened and leveled further, so Ort decided they should follow that path again to search for clues. This time the hike proved to be a fruitful exercise. A large sign had been erected at the end of the path, just off the dirt road. The brightly colored sign had drawings of buildings, trees, roads, and other indecipherable—to the trolls—things on it. Strangest of all, there was an image of a cute troll skiing down a steep, snow-covered hill.

"What's that all about?" Rott, Ort's grandson, asked him. Rott was several inches taller than Ort. His eyes were orangeish-red, his large, pointed ears stuck out sideways, and he had a sinewy physique that gave him an imposing appearance.

"Is that supposed to be a troll?" Gangl asked, scrunching his face as he pointed at the image of the skiing troll.

"I guess so," Ort said, quite puzzled by the image himself.

"I've never seen a troll that good-looking," Haar commented.

"Why is he skiing?" Gangl said. "What's going on here anyway?"

"I bet it has something to do with all of this work that's going on," Ort said. "Anybody have any ideas?"

All of the trolls stared at the sign, trying to solve the visual puzzle.

"Look at this at the bottom here," Haar said, pointing to the image of a road. "Isn't that shaped a lot like the path we just followed from the big machines?" Others strained their brains trying to match reality to representation. "And look here!" he went on excitedly, pointing at the map. "This big building here seems to be where the earth is all dug up and all the trees have been cut down."

"How can that be?" Drulle said. "There's no building there."

"But maybe people are planning to build one there," Haar said. "Do you think so, Ort? Is that possible?"

Ort studied the sign. "It could be," he mused. "That just could be. People are always putting up buildings, I know that. They're a lot like ants that way. They have to be doing something all the time."

"But if that's a building, then there are other buildings all over here," Dau said, referring to the sign. "Do you mean that people are going to build all of these somewhere?"

"Not just somewhere," Haar said. "If this big building is going to be built where people have been working, then, if I'm not mistaken, all of these other, smaller buildings are going to be all over the face of this side of the mountain."

The others buzzed like maddened insects at the thought of that. "If that's true, I'm thinking these might be houses," Ort said of the smaller structures on the billboard.

Once Haar pointed it out, a few could see the map was a representation of part of Troll Mountain. Others, who could no more grasp the concept of representation any better than they could the idea of galaxies, pretended they also understood so as not to appear stupid.

In addition to the images, there was writing on the billboard, most prominently: Site of the Troll Mountain Ski Resort. None of the trolls had an inkling of what the words said or meant. Had they been able to read the writing, and better understand the images, they would have known the biggest building was to be a large ski lodge and the smaller structures luxurious mountainside cabins and chalets. Had Ort understood the full extent of the development he would have been even angrier than he was simply about what he suspected may be houses.

"We're not going to let them get away with this!" Ort thundered. "We trolls have run from people long enough. I remember, long ago, how the Great Forest was all ours. The forest and the mountains were full of wolves and bears and deer and foxes and creatures of all sorts, and every day we had a feast to eat. Then people started moving into the forest and setting traps and snares for the animals and before long all of those animals were a lot harder to find, not to mention the fact that all of those traps people put out made life very hazardous for us. Why, Feirn got caught in a fox trap once and nearly lost a leg because of it. Even to this day you can still see the scar, and she has never walked exactly right since. You've all seen it. Then after most of us moved farther north, to this mountain, and there was only one family left on Great Mountain, people started setting off explosions there. Drulle can tell you about that, for it was he and his father and mother who stayed at Great Mountain. When the first explosion went off Drulle's father became so angry that he exploded too. Isn't that right, Drulle?"

The other trolls started clamoring, for all of them knew the story.

"That's what my mother always told me," Drulle said. "I wasn't there when it happened."

"And we all know the story of how Resvar guided a tribe of trolls away from intruding people and their infernal church bells," Ort went on.

8 ▪ The Tale Of Resvar
The Cloud Reader

Like puffs of popcorn, white clouds floated in a sky as deep blue as a clear lake in autumn. Resvar, a troll wizard, lied on his back, his head resting on a rock pillow, looking up at the passing clouds. Skoug, the king of Resvar's small tribe, went and sat beside the wizard. Skoug, too, cast his eyes skyward to see if he could see any obvious shapes in the clouds, for he knew Resvar was looking for clouds that resembled something. Everyone knew Resvar was a master cloud reader who could discern shapes others did not recognize until he pointed them out, and that he had the ability to decipher what it meant when clouds shaped in certain forms passed over.

"The clouds are certainly traveling fast today, aren't they?" Skoug commented.

"It is a busy day in the sky," Resvar responded. "Do you see those two clouds coming from over there?" he asked, pointing to the two he meant.

"Uh huh," the king said.

"I'm afraid they may mean trouble," Resvar said. "I want to wait until they get closer to say for sure."

"What sort of trouble?" Skoug asked.

"Wait until they are directly over us and I will let you know," Resvar said.

When the clouds in question were closer, Resvar pointed to them again and said, "There! I feared as much! Do you see what I see?"

"Nuggets of gold?" Skoug guessed, forgetting for a second that in Resvar's eyes the clouds were a troublesome shape. "But that wouldn't mean trouble, would it?" he quickly added.

Resvar propped himself up on his forearms. "It's two people," he said. "See how the one on the left is using a scythe to cut some sort of crop and the one on the right seems to have part of a workhorse beside him?"

Skoug studied the clouds with these new clues in mind. "You're right!" he said. "I can see them clearly now."

"And look over there!" Resvar said, pointing to another cloud farther away, a timbre of alarm in his voice. "If that doesn't look like a church steeple, then teasing a gnome is no fun."

"What does all of this mean?" Skoug asked.

"It means," Resvar explained, "that many people will soon settle in this area and erect a church that will have a bell."

"A bell!" Skoug yelped, as if poked in the ribs with a sharp stick. "Church bells can cause death to us. We can't have a church close to us."

"If as many people as I think will come, and if they build a church, we will have to leave here," Resvar said.

"But this is the best home we've ever had," Skoug said. "We have gardens here with fertile soil. We have nice dry caves. We have springs with such good water. Perhaps you are wrong. Maybe people won't come and spoil everything for us."

"I hope I *am* wrong," Resvar said. "But I'm afraid I'm not. I've never felt more sure of any cloud reading in my life than I do about this one."

As Resvar foretold by his reading of clouds, so many people soon settled in the area near Resvar's tribe that a small village sprung up in the midst of those homesteads, with a church with a tall steeple in the center of the village. It was, of course, impossible for trolls to live so near so many people, much less a church with a bell. The trolls had no choice but to leave. So they set out in search of a new home.

It being a drought year, food and water were scarce. When none of them had had any water to drink for two days, Resvar saw a cloud that resembled a waterfall. A few minutes later he saw a bird-shaped cloud. After pondering about what he had seen, he announced: "If we see a large bird fly overhead I think we will find a waterfall if we follow it." Not long after, a large hawk flew over. The trolls followed it until the bird disappeared from sight.

"I don't see any waterfall anywhere," one of the trolls grumbled. "It looks like you were wrong this time, Resvar."

"Be quiet," Resvar said. "Listen."

Everyone listened attentively.

"It sounds like falling water!" Skoug whooped.

"It sounds like a waterfall!" Resvar said triumphantly. "In that direction."

Guided by the sound, the tribe of twelve trolls soon found a waterfall, where they drank water out of cupped hands until they nearly burst, and stood under the waterfall as it showered them with a refreshing spray.

The following day Resvar noticed a strange cloud that somehow appeared to be whiter than all of the other clouds in the sky. Its shape resembled nothing so much as a tubby troll with a pointed head and very large ears. Resvar had a strong sense in his heart that the cloud meant something, but he had a difficult time reading exactly what it was. He pictured the image over and over in his mind's eye as the tribe continued on in search of a new home.

As nightfall approached, Resvar noticed a rock formation that looked very much like the troll-shaped cloud he saw that morning.

"We must go to the rock and have a look around," he said to the others. "I feel in my bones that this rock is important to us."

When they climbed the mountain to the troll-shaped rock formation, they discovered two small caves at the base of the rock.

"The clouds have led us to shelter," Resvar proclaimed.

The caves were nowhere near as nice as the caves the trolls had left, and as they scoured the area in the following days they discovered that food and water were scarcer than where they had lived as well. In fact, food proved to be so hard to find, and hunting so poor, that none of the trolls had enough to eat to satisfy their hunger.

Most members of the tribe agreed the tribe should set out again in search of a better place to live. While others argued about which direction they should go, Resvar scanned the sky for a vaporous omen. A cloud of a most peculiar shape caught his attention. It was a long cloud with a general oval shape, except that it was sort of squared-off at one end and had two fin-shaped wings at the other end. Resvar pointed it out to the others and asked if the cloud reminded anyone of anything.

"It looks a little like some sort of fish, almost," one of the trolls said. "But not exactly like a fish."

"That's no fish!" another disagreed. "It looks more like a bird than it does a fish."

"Do you think it means something?" Skoug asked Resvar.

"I think it might," Resvar said. "I'm not sure."

Resvar studied the cloud until it drifted so far away it was only another white blob to him. He felt certain the cloud was significant because of its odd shape, but he didn't know what its significance was.

He found a chalky stone and sketched the shape of the cloud on the blunt face of the mountainside, then sat and looked at the drawing and thought about what the shape might mean the rest of the day and most of the night. Eventually he nodded off to sleep where he sat. He dreamed of a sea, and of a rocky coast, and of the cloud shape on that coast. In the morning he told the others he thought he knew what the cloud he saw the day before meant.

"I think it did represent some sort of a fish," he said. "I remember my mother and father telling me tales of giant sea creatures called whales. I'm willing to bet that a whale looks a lot like the strange cloud we saw yesterday."

"If that's true, what does it mean?" Skoug asked.

"I think it means that we're supposed to go live next to the sea," Resvar said. "I think it means that if we do that we will have plenty to eat. The whale image means abundance for us from the sea."

The trolls were more than a hundred miles from the ocean. Traveling there would mean a long, strenuous journey. That prospect did not sit well with several members of the tribe.

"Why go so far?" one asked. "It sounds to me like a trip that could be dangerous. If we were sure we would find a wonderful place to live there it would be one thing, but Resvar isn't even sure we will be better off by the sea than somewhere we could reach in much less time, it seems to me."

"We've done all right by following Resvar's cloud readings up till now," Skoug said, scanning the faces of the other trolls as though daring anyone to challenge that statement. "He told us that many people would move in near us and build a church, and that happened. He told us we would find a waterfall by following a bird, and that happened. He led us to these caves through his cloud reading. If his reading of clouds causes him to believe it would be best for us to journey to the sea and make our home there, then I'm ready to go with him."

That pretty much settled the matter. The tribe would make a journey to the sea, and that was that.

And so they set out in search of a seaside home. Searing sun, pouring rain, boggy bottomland, swarms of pesky insects, thick underbrush, a shortage of food, and other obstacles and hardships made the long journey an extremely difficult undertaking. Those who were against the trip to begin with began grumbling that they must have been out of their minds to take such a journey rather than go somewhere else on their own.

"Turn around and go back then, if you don't want to go on," Skoug said to the complainers. No one turned back.

Eventually the unmistakable scent of sea air could be detected. Soon the trolls caught sight of the sea itself. As they walked over the crest of a rocky bluff they were startled by the sight of some huge black creature lying atop some rocks on the shore a few hundred feet away. Part of the creature was in the water. As they ran toward it they saw it was a whale that had washed ashore.

"It looks just like the cloud did!" one of them said as they drew nearer.

"What did I tell you?! What did I tell you?!" Resvar boasted, proud that his cloud reading had been so accurate.

None of the trolls, not even Resvar, had imagined a whale could be so very large. When they found the whale was dead, they wasted no time in hacking pieces of flesh from it and boiling up a huge feast for themselves.

None of the members of the tribe ever again doubted Resvar when he told them what cloud shapes signified. As Resvar had foretold, seaside living served them well. There were plenty of fish to catch, birds' eggs to be found, and game to hunt in the nearby forest. With food gathering so easy, Resvar had plenty of time to relax in the sun by gazing into the sky and reading clouds.

9 ▪ Drench's Tale

"Things turned out all right in the end for Resvar and his tribe, even though they had to make a long journey to find a new home," Scurf said.

"They were lucky," Ort said. "They wouldn't have thought of leaving in the first place if people hadn't intruded on their territory and created a village and built a church. We should be inspired by the story of Drench. Does everyone know the story of what Drench did when people started crowding him?"

Only two of those with Ort knew Drench's tale—or remembered it, at any rate. Those who didn't know the story, or could not remember hearing it, urged Ort to tell them the story, which he did.

▪

"Drench was a giant troll who lived with his wife and his two children in a large cave along the edge of the ocean on the southern shore of the Skaanstad Fjord," Ort began. "At that time, that was far from any area where people had yet settled, which meant that Drench and his family had a wonderful life. They spent their days fishing, and hunting, and playing by the water during the summer, and playing in the snow in the winter.

"Drench and his family had the fjord all to themselves for many years. One day early one summer, though, a fishing boat entered the fjord. The fishermen aboard the boat were amazed by the bounty their nets hauled in. The Skaanstad Fjord was one of the best fishing spots they had ever found.

"After that the fishing boat began showing up in the fjord several times a week. Soon word spread about what great fishing was to be found in the Skaanstad Fjord and other fishing boats headed there as well. Some days there were as many as four or five boats fishing in the fjord.

"All of this human activity did not please Drench, of course, to put it mildly. In fact, it greatly displeased him. He considered the Skaanstad Fjord to be his family's personal playground, and his personal fishing lake.

" 'People have no business being here,' he said to his wife. 'Why don't they stay where they belong and leave us alone?'

" 'If you don't want them here, do something to make them leave,' his wife said to him.

" 'Like what?' Drench said. 'What can I do? How can we make people leave now that they're here? If there was only one boat, maybe. . . But there are so many of them to deal with now, the fjord entrance has become like a gate that has suddenly swung open.'

" 'That's it!' Drench's wife said. 'That's exactly what it is. The fjord entrance is like a gate. The thing for us to do is to close the gate so that humans cannot enter the fjord with their boats.'

"Drench asked her what she meant, and how they could prevent people from entering the fjord with their boats.

" 'We can do it by blocking the entrance to make it impossible for boats to pass through,' Drench's wife explained.

" 'Block it with what?' Drench asked, still not completely understanding the plan his wife had in mind.

" 'With anything and everything,' his wife said. 'Look around you. There are a lot of downed trees around that you could push over that big cliff or drag out from shore. There are big rocks and boulders all around that you could roll into the water, or even toss them in, with your strength. Once the entrance is clogged enough with all of those boulders and trees, boats won't be able to enter the fjord and we'll have it all to ourselves, just like we like it.'

" 'You know, I think that just might work!' Drench said.

"That very night Drench began dragging trees out into the fjord entrance, where they sank to the bottom. He dislodged huge boulders from the mountainside, sending them splashing into the water. He worked feverishly for two full weeks to block the narrow fjord entrance to the passage of boats, working at night, when the fishing boats were gone.

"One morning, after Drench worked particularly hard one night, a boatload of fishermen sailed their boat back and forth across the fjord entrance several times, looking for a safe path into the fjord, and they couldn't find a safe path anywhere, for Drench had accomplished his task well. Drench and his wife and their two children watched this with pleasure, and they celebrated their success with cheers and dancing as the fishing boat sailed away back out to sea.

"Later that morning another boatload of fishermen approached the blocked fjord entrance and retreated after concluding that it was impossible to pass into the fjord. Drench and his family celebrated their frustration and their departure as well.

"Just as news had spread like wildfire about what a great fishing spot the Skaanstad Fjord was, the news now spread just as quickly that it was now impossible to sail a fishing boat into that fjord. It wasn't long before no fishing boats even approached the fjord entrance any longer. That meant that Drench and his family had the fjord all to themselves once again. They were able to live there in peace for many long years."

■

"We're drawing the line right here, just like Drench did!" Ort thundered, startling several of his companions with his outburst of passionate defiance. "Us trolls have run long enough, and been driven from our homes far too many times. This time we're going to make the people leave. Come on!"

10 ▪ Taking Action

With that, Ort stormed back up the path, back toward where the bulldozer and the skidder-loader stood. The others exchanged puzzled glances, wondering what Ort had in mind.

"I said come on!" Ort barked over his left shoulder, though he had merely mumbled his "come on" the first time, so none of the others understood what he said. Now they all scurried to catch up with him.

When Ort and the other six trolls reached the work site, where people planned to construct a ski lodge, Ort zipped around as hyperactively as a mosquito inside a glass jar, trying to think of something to do to retaliate against the people who were working at Troll Mountain, scarring the mountain, making irritating, nerve-piercing noises, and intruding on territory the trolls considered theirs, which had the trolls worried about their future on the mountain. The other six milled about, waiting to see what Ort would want them to do next. Unable to come up with any plan, Ort gave the bulldozer a kick, cursing as he did so. Pain shot up his short leg, but he did not allow his face to reveal that pain to the others, for he believed showing pain was the same as revealing a fissure of weakness, and he didn't want anyone to have a dint of doubt about his stony toughness. All at once a thought flashed through his mind.

"I know what we can do," he announced to the others. "We'll tip over this machine! We'll see how much damage they can do then."

The others looked at each other with puzzled, dumbfounded expressions that indicated they believed Ort might be out-of-his-mind crazy, nutty as an acorn. "*That* machine?" Dau said.

"Of course this machine" Ort answered. "What machine did you think I meant?"

"We're just wondering *how* we'll be able to do it, is all," Scurf said. "After all, none of us are giant trolls."

While trolls are extremely strong, each troll, save for Ort, was thinking the bulldozer was probably more weight than he could handle. Only Ort grasped the multiplication factor involved, and understood the cumulative power of several pushing simultaneously.

"How?" Ort said. "I'll tell you how: Three or four of us will all get on one side and lift it and push it over, that's how. Now, if no one has any other questions, three of you numskulls give me a hand." Ort took a pushing position on one side of the bulldozer. None of the others moved. "Well, what's everybody waiting for?" Ort snapped, then ordered three of the others to help him. Those three joined him, despite the fact they thought even trying to move the hulking bulldozer was sheer foolishness, for they still didn't understood how much power they would be able to generate by pushing as a team.

"Okay, everybody get a good grip," Ort instructed. "I'll say 'ready, set, push!' and we'll all push at the same time." He paused a couple of seconds, then said: "Ready, set, push!"

They all heaved with all their might, pretty much in unison. To the astonishment of most of the trolls, those pushing as well as those watching, the side of the bulldozer lifted off the ground. The four trolls pushing against the bulldozer grunted and snorted like hogs as they groped for better grips and lifted as they shoved, trying to outdo the powerful force of gravity between the heavy machine and the ground. Ever so slowly, the four trolls gained leverage. They lifted the side of the bulldozer further and further off the ground until the big yellow machine reached a tipping point and gravity pulled it in the other direction. The bulldozer became but a bundle of feathers as gravity joined the trolls' cause and the enormously heavy machine tipped to its side and crashed to the ground with a quivering thud, causing the ground to cough up a puff of dust.

All of the trolls jumped for joy and shouted with spiteful glee as the bulldozer landed on its side with that echoing thud.

"There! That oughtta teach 'em a lesson," Ort said, heaving his words with satisfaction.

"That was beautiful!" Traug said. "It looked just like when the people cut down trees with those strange little machines they have."

"Don't mess with trolls!" Haar exuded. "Don't mess with us! You hear that, people?" he shouted into the grey night.

"Are we going to tip over the other machine too?" Dau asked Ort.

"Nah," Ort decided after a few seconds' thought. "One's enough for tonight."

Fired with excitement, the trolls hung around the bulldozer a half-hour longer, gloating about their achievement and reliving, over and over, the thrilling seconds of the bulldozer's fall.

11 ▪ Retta's Revenge

Back at the larger of the two communal caves, the seven trolls who tipped over the bulldozer regaled other members of the tribe with their story and talked over other ways of wreaking revenge on people.

"We should chop down a lot of the trees before they get the chance to do it," Rnobrna suggested. "They'll come, and all the trees they want to cut down would already be cut down. I bet they wouldn't like that one bit!"

"We're trying to stop them from cutting down so many trees, not help them do it," Ort pointed out with more than a hint of exasperation. "Try to *think* a little, will you? Am I the only one capable of thinking around here?"

"We should kidnap a human baby," Utrud suggested.

Others liked the idea, for despite their avowed hatred of people, trolls also envy people, particularly their looks. Old Fungus, however, waved a caution flag, both figuratively and literally, for he used a knobby walking stick that had a small, tattered piece of dirty once-white cloth attached to one end, and whenever he was agitated or wanted to make a point forcefully, as he did then, he jabbed the air with his walking stick and the piece of cloth flapped.

"Many of you are too young to remember, but a troll couple named Retta and Otmer once found out the hard way that taking a human baby does not always work out well," Old Fungus said in a wizened, croaking voice, the lines on his forehead as furrowed as mortar scraped with a deep-notch trowel. As usual, the oldest troll was wearing old, odorous overalls, which had a slot in the back for his stubby, bushy, grayish-white tail. His head was bald on top. A semi-circular ring of fairly long, straight white hair framed the sides of his face. His mouth contained only a few yellow teeth, his large eyes bulged like big convex buttons, and his cucumber of a nose, some six inches long, was thick and pimpled. His thin arms were twice as long as his stubby legs, and his potbelly hung out like a sack half filled with sand. His withered, pockmarked body had only patches of hair remaining, leaving a leathery, mottled skin that gave him a reptilian appearance. Still, as the oldest troll in the tribe, and quite possibly the oldest living troll, the other trolls looked up to him for his breadth of experience and his knowledge of troll history. So everyone listened closely as Old Fungus proceeded to tell the tale of Retta's revenge, the human version of which is this:

■

One evening a troll named Retta was wandering about a woods that bordered the tiny village of Findestol when she caught sight of a large garden full of ripe vegetables. As she crept closer to the garden, darting from tree trunk to tree trunk, she saw a young woman gathering vegetables from the garden.

While Retta was stealthy enough to avoid drawing the woman's notice, a large dog sitting at the edge of the garden perked up its ears, sensing or smelling the presence of someone or something near the edge of the woods. Noticing the dog's sudden alertness, the woman in the garden said to the dog, "What is it, Falun? Do you hear something?" The dog stood up and began barking, keeping his eyes trained on the place in the woods where he had sensed either noise or odor. "What is it?" the woman again said to the large dog as the dog started walking toward the woods, where Retta was hiding.

Dogs being nearly as frightening as chiming church bells to trolls, Retta acted on an impulse to run away. As she bolted, both the woman and the dog spotted her, with the woman having a good enough view to be able to determine she was a troll. "Get it!" the woman ordered the dog, though the naturally aggressive dog needed little encouragement to pursue the fleeing stranger.

The race was on, with Retta trying to get away and the dog barking up a storm as it chased after her. Of course Retta was no match for the dog when it came to running. Before long the dog caught her and clamped his mouth around the lower part of her left leg. Retta barely managed to stay on her feet as she grabbed a handy stick and started swinging it at the dog. While she was able to wield the stick deftly enough to slowly slip away, Retta left the scene with a bleeding, aching leg, and a pretty sizeable patch of her dress the dog ripped away was lying on the ground. This was the last straw for Retta. People had been nothing but a nuisance for her and her husband, Otmer, since they started settling in the region. Having lived in a cave on a nearby mountain long before people came, Otmer and Retta felt besieged.

"We need to do something to get back at people," Retta said · to Otmer, determined to exact some sort of revenge for the dog attack a woman had encouraged.

"Like what?" Otmer responded.

Having considered the matter, Retta was prepared with a suggestion: "We should take one of their babies."

"A human baby, you mean?" Otmer said, wanting to be sure he understood what Retta was suggesting.

"That's what I mean," Retta confirmed. "And not just any baby. I have heard that the parson's wife had a baby a few months ago. We should steal it and raise it as our own. After all, who among people are more loathsome than parsons?" From their perspective, trolls considered Christianity the worst thing about humans, so Otmer instantly perceived how kidnapping a parson's baby would be such a satisfying action.

And so shortly after midnight one very dark night Retta snuck into the parsonage while Otmer waited outside. It took Retta but a minute to locate the baby, who was sleeping in a bassinet, snatch it up—bassinet and all—and carry it outside. Then she and Otmer walked away with the baby, at a brisk pace.

Retta was barely outside the house when the baby's mother awoke and went into the next room to check on her infant, worried by a maternal instinct. When she saw that both the baby and the bassinet were not there she screamed, awakening her husband, the parson. As though by intuition as well, the mother glanced out a window and glimpsed two figures seemingly fleeing, for they were walking at a faster than normal clip.

Learning that the baby was gone and that his wife had glimpsed two fleeting figures, the parson, still in his nightshirt, hurried next door to ring the church bell, for the villagers had decided the church bell would be rung thirteen times in an emergency as a signal for everyone to gather at the church.

Hearing the church bell toll, a miller who lived a little more than a half-mile from the village began hurrying to the village, along a road, when he happened upon two trolls—Retta and Otmer, of course—forzen in place, like statues, with a bassinet containing a baby on the ground beside the female troll. Understanding that church bells can be fatal to trolls, the miller immediately surmised the tolling bell had turned the trolls to stone. He also knew the baby must belong to the parson and his wife, so he picked up the bassinet and walked briskly the rest of the distance to the village, where there was a joyous reunion of the baby with his parents and the miller told the others about the two "frozen" trolls he had encountered.

All of the village men returned with the miller to the spot where he had seen the two trolls. The trolls were no longer there, though, so the people concluded the tolling bell must have immobilized them for a time without turning them to stone, and that after the miller left they regained consciousness and fled. That seemed to be the most logical explanation anyway.

12 ▪ Sleeping Troll Rock

"**I** tell you right now that if we were to kidnap a human baby it would be sure to lead to big trouble, and probably misery," Old Fungus said, pounding his walking stick on the ground to emphasize his point. "I'm entirely against the idea!"

"Church bells!" a female troll named Skimpa spat with distaste. With a melon-round head atop a round body, she resembled a snowman—or snowwoman, if you will. She had short arms, squat legs, plump, sausage-like fingers and toes, a smaller-than-average upturned nose, and a flow of stringy black hair she brushed straight back from her forehead and temples. "How I detest church bells! They have been a curse for us trolls for centuries. More than anything, they have been responsible for forcing us to move from our homes time after time after time."

"And some have not been as lucky as Retta and Otmer when church bells rang," Feirn reminded everyone. Feirn was a female troll with a round face and a wide mouth who gave the appearance of being downcast and preoccupied with worrisome thoughts because there was a thousand-yard-stare in her dark round eyes most of the time.

"Indeed!" Old Fungus croaked, thumping his walking stick. "My friend Edda was one of those. I still think about her from time to time. Poor Edda! What a way to end up! What a fate to befall anyone, just for falling asleep!"

Though everyone had heard the story of Edda more than once, Old Fungus proceeded to tell it again. The way he told it contrasted considerably with the human version of the tale, which people know as *Sleeping Troll Rock*.

▪

One summer night a troll named Edda and her son, Ravh, went to the fjordside village of Lonsund with thoughts of thievery foremost in their minds. Staying to the outskirts of the small village, the two trolls made off with quite a haul, stealing sacks of food, metalware, tools, two medium-sized wooden barrels, and other items. When they had accumulated all they could carry they began the long walk back to their mountain cave. While they were still within the village, though, Edda spotted a small boat pulled up on the shore. .

"What's the use of us walking all the way around the end of the fjord when we could just as well make use of this boat to carry our goods to the other side?" Edda said to her son.

Indeed, by taking a direct line across the wide fjord the two trolls could save themselves nearly two miles of walking. And so Edda and Ravh loaded all of their stolen items into the small boat and shoved the boat into the water. The load was so heavy that the boat sank deep into the water, with the top of the sides only a couple of inches above the surface of the water. When Ravh stepped into the boat water came to within a fraction of an inch of swamping over the sides. As Edda started to step into the boat water *did* begin streaming over the sides, for the boat was extremely overloaded, so she quickly jumped back onto the shore.

"It's too heavy with both of us in the boat," Edda said. "The boat would sink before we got ten feet."

"So what do we do now?" Ravh asked, befuddled as he would be if asked to multiply double-digit numbers.

"Let me think a moment," Edda said, sitting down on a nearby boulder to contemplate the dilemma. After several minutes of thought she jumped up and said, "I've got it!," and proceeded to lay out a plan to her son: "You take the goods across in the boat and unload them on the other side of the fjord while I wait here. After you have all of the goods unloaded on the other side, you row back across to this place again and I will get in the boat and we can cross the fjord safely."

It never occurred to either Edda or Ravh that they could lighten the boat's load by leaving behind some of the stolen items. Greed is an ingrained characteristic of all trolls, so no troll would leave behind something he or she had just stolen any more than a hungry dog would sniff a juicy cooked steak and not eat it.

And so Ravh set out for the other side of the fjord in the loaded boat while Edda remained behind to wait for his return. She sat down and rested her back against a bank, for she was extremely tired. Soon she fell into a sleep as deep as doom.

Ravh rowed the boat across the wide fjord as his mother slept. By the time he reached the other side a soupy fog had rolled in. Ravh quickly unloaded the boat and set out again for the opposite shore, where his mother waited for him. The fog was so thick that Ravh became confused and lost his bearings, for although trolls see perfectly fine in darkness, thick fog is quite another matter. While Ravh thought he was rowing in a straight line, in actuality he was curving off toward the sea, down the length of the fjord. He rowed and rowed, engulfed by the clingy, white fog.

Meanwhile, Edda slept as soundly as a statue. The hours passed, dawn arrived as subtly as the scent of sage on a soft breeze, and still Edda slept and Ravh rowed in circles on the fog-shrouded fjord. Because of the fog, the morning wasn't as bright as most mornings are. That dimness contributed to Edda's ability to sleep so long.

Suddenly, for it was a Sunday morning, a church bell peeled. The sound awoke Edda. No sooner had she opened her eyes, however, when the church bell peeled again, which caused Edda to immediately turn to stone, for church bells have that affect on trolls, who are non-believing heathens. As the church bell rang several more times, Edda was unable to ask for whom the bell tolled, for she was solid stone.

Today the troll-shaped rock that was once Edda still stands on the eastern shore of the fjord at Lonsund. Weather has worn it smooth over the years, and made the facial features indistinguishable, but the rock is still clearly the shape of a sleeping troll.

13 ▪ A Tale of Tears

"**M**aybe we don't have to kidnap a baby," Scurf suggested. "Maybe we could kidnap someone a little older."

"Why would that be any better?" Utrud asked him. "What's the difference?"

"I don't know," Scurf admitted, not having thought through the idea. "I guess I just thought that if kidnapping a baby was likely to bring bad luck, maybe we wouldn't have such bad luck if we kidnapped someone older."

"It's *people* that are the problem, not how old they are!" Old Fungus declared as forcefully as he was able to do, then proceeded to tell another sad tale:

▪

One day, a long time ago, a troll named Swerd was out searching for mushrooms when he ventured farther from home than he ever had before. He was picking mushrooms at the edge of a forest when a young human woman with golden hair and skin as smooth as fresh cream walked over a footbridge nearby.

Swerd was instantly entranced by the woman's beauty. He thought she was the most beautiful woman he had ever seen.

The next day Swerd returned to the place where he had seen the woman cross the footbridge, which was built over a small river, hoping to see her again. He was thrilled when the woman appeared again, at the same time as she had the day before. His heart beat at twice its normal rate as he watched the woman from behind a tree.

For the next several days, he returned to the bridge every day, and at precisely the same time every day his waiting was rewarded when the golden-haired woman appeared, walked across the bridge, and then disappeared.

Swerd was not satisfied with merely admiring the young woman's beauty from a concealed vantage point, though. He felt his heart would break unless he talked to the woman and told her how beautiful he thought she was. So one day he cranked up his courage and emerged from his hiding place as the woman walked across the bridge. The golden-haired woman caught one glimpse of Swerd, who was hunchbacked, and took off running, terrified by what she saw.

Swerd was still determined to meet the woman, though, so he returned the next day and hid under the bridge until the woman appeared. When he heard her walking across the bridge, Swerd scrambled up onto the bridge and stood in her way.

"You're beautiful," Swerd said to her, and told her he wanted to marry her.

The woman shrieked and ran for home as though her very life depended on her getting home as quickly as possible.

Despite the fact that the woman obviously thought Swerd was repulsive, seeing her at such close range made her even more captivating to Swerd. He wanted her for his wife at any cost.

The next day Swerd hid under the bridge again. This time when the woman came he waited until she was nearly across the bridge before he jumped out from his hiding place and covered the woman with a large sack before she had time to run. He then tied up the sack, flung the sack over a shoulder, and started for home.

The woman in the sack cried and cried, just a torrent of tears. She sobbed so loud that the ground shook under Swerd's feet. She wept like a human waterfall. Her crying continued nonstop nearly the entire journey to Swerd's home. She didn't stop crying until Swerd had a few steps to go.

When he arrived at his home, Swerd quickly untied the sack and held it upside down to free the golden-haired woman. The only thing that came out of the sack, though, was salty water. The woman had cried so hard that all there was left of her was a big puddle of tears.

■

"Falling in love with a person is never a good thing," Ort declared when Old Fungus finished telling the tale. "People think they're too good for trolls. Trying to make a person return a troll's love is like trying to catch a snowflake in your hand. Human beings make love melt and disappear just like warm flesh melts snowflakes."

14 ▪ Consulting Kravig

Peace prevailed on Troll Mountain the following morning. No discordant, irritating sounds emanated from the worksite. Quiet—blissful quiet—was the order of the morning. So, that was that, most of the trolls thought. It appeared to them they had put an end to the noise and would no longer be bothered by people.

Their delusions of triumph were just that, though—delusions. Noises resumed late in the morning, from the same area. So a three-member scouting team went down the mountain to check out the situation. Those three were surprised to see people working there again, and even more surprised to see the big yellow machine that had been pushed over on its side back in operation. When they reported back to the others in the early evening, Ort could not understand how people, who were far inferior to trolls in terms of strength, could have righted the big yellow machine—and so quickly, at that—what with the level of effort it took him and three others to tip it on its side.

"They might have a powerful witch, or a wizard, working for them," Ort speculated, seeing that as a distinct possibility. "If that's the case, it's time to have a talk with our own wizard."

That wizard was named Kravig. Kravig was less social than the other members of the tribe, not that many trolls are particularly gregarious and convivial. He and his daughter, Tala, lived alone in their own cave, which was a fair distance from the other caves, and kept pretty much to themselves, especially Kravig. Most of the unmarried, young male trolls tried to court Tala, one of the tribe's least ugly members; she didn't even have a tail. She had long, bouncy, light brown hair, fetching—to trolls—chocolate-colored eyes, and washed both her body and her clothes far more frequently than anyone else in the tribe. Unattacheed male tribe members took her on walks to special places and presented her with gifts—items they found and stole. And more than a few fights were fought over Tala.

One of the reasons Kravig kept to himself is that he thought he would possess a greater air of authority if he cultivated something of a mysterious image—a mystique, as it were, though he of course was not familiar with that word. And, indeed, the other trolls held him in higher regard because of his aloofness. Trolls who would not back down an inch to an angry bear quivered at the thought of Kravig's perceived powers. Those who courted Tala were careful to try to avoid offending her in any way, for fear of raising Kravig's wrath. Other trolls had a certain level of respect for Kravig because of their disquietude about what powers he may possess and have the ability to use against them. Kravig's singular appearance helped him cultivate his air of mystique, for it helped set him apart and make him seem different, which was not a good thing for most trolls but *was* a good thing for someone special, such as a wizard. The best word to describe his physical appearance is spindly. Kravig was by far the thinnest member of the tribe, with arms and legs so slender it seemed as though a fierce wind might snap one of them like a dead tree branch. He had enormous hands, with long, bony fingers that made his hands resemble large, flapping leaves. While he was only slightly taller than average, his leanness caused others to perceive him as being taller than his actual height. In contrast to his spindly body and limbs, his face was full and fleshy, dominated by a broad, four-inch-long nose that was nearly as wide as it was long, and almost flat on top. His beady black eyes seemed to almost penetrate whoever he was looking at. His mane of tangled black hair covered his ears and made his head appear larger than it was. The longest strands of his hair sprouted from his temples and hung to his waist. His hair was shorter at the back, as though it had been chopped off, but still draped his shoulders.

Ort went to Kravig's cave alone to consult with the wizard, who was gazing into a fire and snacking on sugarcoated flies when Ort arrived. Tala wasn't around; she was out somewhere. Kravig's cave had an entry door made of thick pine boards and a narrow, eight-foot-long entryway section with a ceiling so low that Kravig had to lower his head slightly as he passed through. Given Ort's shorter stature, he didn't need to duck to avoid scraping the top his head, though. That entryway led into a crescent-shaped chamber with smooth rock walls about twenty feet long and nine or ten feet wide, on average, though the width varied. The roomy chamber had an eleven-foot-high ceiling, smooth as the walls, which made the chamber resemble the inside of an eggshell. A hearth was situated about six feet from the west end of the chamber, which was furnished with several wooden chairs, a wooden table, and a wood bench, all of which Kravig built. Blankets and pads covered the chairs and the bench. Another low-ceilinged passageway, this one wider than the entryway, led to several other smaller chambers deeper in the mountain, one of which was Kravig's sleeping chamber and one Tala's sleeping chamber. Ort wasted no time in telling Kravig about people doing things at the bottom of the mountain, and the two big machines, and how quickly people had the big yellow machine running again after he and others tipped it on its side. Then he asked Kravig if he thought they had accomplished that through some sort of magic.

Kravig, who was older than Ort, pondered the question while staring at flames licking logs in the fireplace. "I think you're on to something," he said at last. "It's hard to think of any other way that could happen, except through magic. People can be very powerful in ways we do not yet understand. We must never make the mistake of underestimating them."

"Can you do something to wipe away what they've done?" Ort asked. "Can't you cast some sort of spell on them and on their cursed machines?"

"Possibly," Kravig said, as much to himself as to Ort. "First, though, I must know more about these machines and the people involved with them. I must get a look at them for myself. I propose that if the noises can be heard again tomorrow that you and I, and a couple of others, go down the mountain and have a look for ourselves at what is going on, while it is going on. Do you want to that?"

Ort said he was agreeable, and left Kravig's cave soon after.

15 ▪ Lundehund Legerdemain

"**Y**ou won't believe what happened last night," Anders Branstad said to his wife, Emma. "The bulldozer got tipped over on its side."

"What do you mean, it got tipped over?" Emma said. "You mean at the worksite?"

"That's what I mean," Anders said. "When we got there this morning the bulldozer was lying on its side. It was very strange. We had to get another machine out there to right it, and it took a while to get it running again."

"How did it get tipped over?" Emma asked.

"Well, we don't know for sure," Anders said. "We don't know what's going on, exactly. There were a lot of footprints around, but we didn't see any signs of any other machine, which you would think it would take to tip over a bulldozer."

"Maybe trolls tipped it over," Emma quipped. "You *are* working at Troll Mountain, after all, and trolls are supposed to be very strong, aren't they?"

Anders chuckled. "Yeah. Or maybe it was aliens from outer space. That seems just as likely."

"You never know," Emma said.

"Will you read me another troll story tonight?" Andrew asked his father, excited by the mention of trolls.

"Oh, I guess I can," Anders promised.

The tale Anders selected to read to his son this night was called *Lundehund Legerdemain.*

▪

Once upon a time a group of trolls kidnapped a human boy named Ivor and chained him up because the boy's father had refused to give the trolls water when they asked for it.

Ivor's small dog, a lundehund named Strykar, missed its master and went out searching for him. The dog came upon the spot where the trolls had kidnapped the boy, sniffed around, and recognized Ivor's scent, along with the scent of trolls, though of course the dog didn't know it was troll scent. With his nose to the ground, Strykar trailed the two distinct scents until he came to the mountain caves where the trolls lived.

"Strykar!" Ivor called out to the dog when he saw his white and reddish-brown friend, and the dog barked with joy at seeing Ivor.

Normally trolls are as fearful of a dog's barking as they are of ringing church bells, but that is mainly because a barking dog alerts its owner that a stranger may be around, which makes it more difficult for trolls to steal animals and things. While Strykar's barking grated on their nerves, they knew his barking wouldn't bring them people trouble by their own caves, so the trolls were less fearful of Strykar than of most dogs.

"So, that's your dog, is it?" one of the trolls said, then attempted to grab the dog, which stood little more than twelve inches high and weighed less than twenty pounds. The dog scurried about, barking angrily at the troll.

"Run away, Strykar!" Ivor shouted to his dog. "Run home and get help!"

Strykar didn't understand that command. He continued barking at the trolls, who now surrounded him. Eventually one of the trolls was able to get close enough to the dog to snatch him up.

"Now we have two prisoners," one of the trolls gloated, as the trolls chained up the dog next to Ivor. While looking over Strykar, one of the trolls suddenly jumped back as though he had been poked with a sharp stick.

"What's wrong?" another troll asked. "Did the dog bite you?"

"Take a look at the dog's paws," the startled troll said to the others, who all crowded close to see what was so special about the dog's paws.

"Why, it has six toes on each foot!" one of the trolls gasped.

The trolls were stunned. Like the first troll, they all jumped back, unsure what to make of this strange small dog, for this was the first lundehund they had ever seen and they did not know that while most dogs have five toes on each foot all lundehunds have at least six toes on each foot.

"It must be a devil dog," one of the trolls suggested.

All of the others agreed that seemed to be the most reasonable explanation.

"Is your dog a devil dog?" one of the trolls asked Ivor in a gruff voice, trying to scare the boy into revealing what all of the trolls suspected.

Ivor saw that it might be to his advantage to let the trolls believe his dog was a devil dog; somehow, he might be able to use that belief into frightening them into letting him go, although he wasn't sure exactly how. Then again, he considered, maybe if they were too frightened by having what they thought was a devil dog in their midst they may possibly kill both him and Strykar. He was in a difficult dilemma. What was he to do?

"Let me go and I'll tell you if he is or not," Ivor said at last.

"No, you answer first, then we'll let you go," one of the trolls said.

Ivor wasn't about to trust the trolls to keep their word. Suddenly a plan popped into his head. "I guess you'll just have to find out the hard way," he said mysteriously.

"What do you mean by that?" one of the trolls demanded.

"Watch closely," Ivor said, taking Strykar in his lap, scooping dirt into one of his hands and blowing the dirt across the top of the dog's wedge-shaped head. Strykar's pointed, foxlike ears closed up like the petals on many flowers, only much more rapidly. The trolls were startled by this demonstration, for they had never seen any animal that seemingly had hinges on its ears. There were a lot of surprised yelps, and oohing and aahing.

"What are you doing?" one of the trolls demanded of Ivor. "Is that some sort of magic?"

"I'll let you know tomorrow," Ivor answered, and would say no more.

That night there was a terrible thunderstorm. Lightning licked down from the sky like tongue-thrusts from a giant snake. Thunder cracked with such force that it split enormous boulders. Raindrops the size of fingers and hailstones as large as fists pounded the ground until ponds formed where the land dipped.

"Would you like me to bring another thunderstorm tonight?" Ivor said to the trolls in the morning.

"Are you saying *you* made it storm last night?" the trolls asked.

"I told you yesterday that I would tell you why I made my dog close his ears," Ivor said. "Well, that was to make it storm." The trolls were divided over whether or not to believe Ivor. "It could merely be a coincidence," one of them reasoned. "How do we know that what he did really caused it to storm?"

"So, you're still not convinced, are you?" Ivor said. "All right, I'll give you another demonstration of what my dog and I can do. Watch this." The trolls watched as Ivor bent back Strykar's head until the tip of the dog's nose touched its back. The trolls found this even more alarming than what the dog did with his ears. It was unheard of for a dog to bend back its head so far.

"Now what's going to happen?" one of the trolls demanded of Ivor.

"I'll let you know when the time is right," Ivor answered, and would say no more, though the trolls tried their best to pry out an answer.

While two of the trolls were out hunting that morning, a large tree limb that lightning had struck the previous night fell on one of them, knocking him to the ground and leaving a gash across his back. When Ivor learned of the accident, he said to the trolls: "Well, is that proof enough of the powers me and my dog have, or do you want us to do something a little more destructive?"

"You mean *you* made the tree limb fall?" one of the trolls asked Ivor.

"Oh, I can't take all the credit," Ivor said, smiling at Strykar. "I couldn't have done anything without Strykar."

"He's a devil dog all right!" one of the trolls said.

"They're both devils!" another said. "Let's kill them both before they have the chance to kill us."

As the trolls closed in to seize Ivor and Strykar, Ivor picked up Strykar and spread the dog's two front legs flat out against the ground at right angles to his body. The trolls had never seen any dog perform such a gymnastic maneuver, so once more they were startled and frightened.

"You're all going to die of a terrible disease before the sun comes up tomorrow unless you let us go right away," Ivor said. "I brought you a storm and I brought you a bad accident. I don't want to bring you death, but I will unless you let me and my dog go."

"Will you promise you won't kill us if we let you go?" one of the trolls said.

"I promise I won't," Ivor said. "I won't have any power over you unless I am on your mountain."

The trolls couldn't unchain Ivor and his dog fast enough to calm their fears. "Get away from here!" they shouted at Ivor as he and Strykar ran for their home.

Ivor smiled and laughed most of the way home, for his escape plan had worked to perfection.

The trolls who kidnapped Ivor and Stryker never found out that all lundehunds have the ability to close their ears to protect the insides of their ears from dirt and moisture, bend their heads backwards one-hundred-and-eighty degrees, and spread their forelegs at right angles to their sides, and so they never understood how Ivor had tricked them.

16 ▪ Kravig Takes Action

When the trolls heard the noises again Friday morning Ort, Kravig, Rnobrna and Scurf went down to check out the situation at the worksite. They watched from a safe distance for a couple of hours, fascinated by what the people were doing. All four agreed the noises were irritating and the destruction maddening, but they enjoyed the gaseous odors that wafted their way. Eventually Kravig said he wanted to sneak closer for a better, less obstructed, view. Ort wanted to go with him, but Kravig insisted it would be safer if he went alone. And so Kravig crept as near to the people working as he dared and sated his sight with their actions before sneaking back to where the three others were concealed.

"I have a plan that just might rid us of those big yellow machines once and for all," Kravig said, sparking excitement in the other trolls. "We must wait until dark to put it into action, though. I have no power over people in the daylight, away from my cave. Besides, what I have in mind can be accomplished only when the people are not around." With that, he added: "I don't know about you three, but I'm going back to my cave and catch some more sleep right now, and come back later. I don't think we can do anything more hanging around here."

The others agreed, and made the winding, relatively lengthy journey back to the caves with Kravig.

At dusk that night, which was near midnight at that time of the year, those four and several others, including a few females, started down the mountain to carry out Kravig's plan, which he had not shared with anyone, even Ort.

The bulldozer and the skidder-loader hulked in the thin moonlight at the worksite. All of those seeing them for the first time marveled at the two machines, and touched and smelled them. Two of the trolls were openly skeptical anything of that bulk could move around, as others said they did.

"It would have to be by magic, if those things can move at all," Utrud said, not one to hold her thoughts to herself.

Eventually Ort asked Kravig what sort of plan he had up his sleeve, and all eyes focused on the wizard.

"Some of us have seen with our own eyes how these big machines can move around," Kravig said. "Well, if they can move around here, it would seem to stand to reason they can also move around elsewhere. I propose to move these machines to a place where people will not be able to find them. Then we will be rid of the noises, and rid of the people."

"But how are you going to move them?" Llop asked, as a small glob of snot fell from his hooked nose and he scratched his head just above his right ear, his hand brushing against the tattered hat he wore most of the time.

"People move them, don't they?" Kravig said, adding: "With the help of some sort of magic, no doubt. Well, with this magic potion I've mixed up for the occasion," he went on, brandishing a small leather pouch, "I'm confident I can get the job done."

With that, he opened the pouch and began sprinkling pinches of a powdery substance on the bulldozer, chanting this incantation as he did so:

Biscom, bascom, buscom, broo ...
Biscom, bascom, buscom, broo ...
Biscom, bascom, buscom, broo ...

The last word of the incantation rhymed with new.

"I don't see it moving," someone remarked.

"Quiet, you ninny!" Kravig hissed. "I must have silence. I must not be interrupted." He continued chanting the incantation, in a solemn, drawn-out manner, and tossing his powder on the bulldozer.

Biscom, bascom, buscom, broo ...
Biscom, bascom, buscom, broo ...
Biscom, bascom, buscom, broo ...

After dispersing half of the powder, Kravig mounted the machine and climbed into the cab, where he plopped down on the padded leather seat. Having watched a man operate the bulldozer the previous day, he was confident he, too, could make it run. That's what he was counting on, in any event. He knew he would have to first make it produce noise before he could move it anywhere; that much was obvious. But just how was that noise produced? That was a huge dilemma. Reasoning that all of the buttons and levers must have something to do with it, Kravig began pushing, pulling and turning everything within reach. He did not understand a key was required to make the bulldozer run, or that even if he had a key that making a bulldozer move involved precise actions. Outside, the others mused among themselves as to what Kravig was doing, and whether or not he would succeed in moving the machine. Doubt grew as minutes mounted. To most of the trolls, the massive machine seemed to be something even beyond a wizard's control.

Ort stepped up onto the bulldozer to get a closer look at what Kravig was doing. "What's the problem?" he asked.

Kravig knew he needed to do something to avoid losing esteem within the tribe. "I'm just checking things out," he told Ort. "Are you all ready to push?"

"Push!" Ort said. "You mean you want us to try to push this monster of a metal contraption?"

"That's right," Kravig said. "I'll steer it while all of you push and we'll get this thing out of here."

For one of the few times in his life, Ort seemed speechless.

"We don't have all night," Kravig said. "What are you waiting for?"

"I'm usually the last one to say something can't be done," Ort said, "but I have to admit that I have my doubts that we'll be able to move this big thing."

"The magic powder I tossed on it will give you extra strength," Kravig said. "You'll see. Just give it all you've got, and then some."

Ort stepped down from the bulldozer and revealed Kravig's plan to the others, who had even more doubts about the chance of success than he did. When he told them the magic powder Kravig cast on the machine would give them added strength, though, some of those doubts dissipated.

Ort ordered everyone to get in position to push, and the powerful trolls gave it all they had. To their surprise, the bulldozer moved forward a couple of inches, then settled back exactly where it had been. The trolls pushed harder and rocked the bulldozer forward, then back. They continued pushing and rocked the machine forward a little further. The bulldozer reversed itself nearly double that distance, which allowed the trolls to push it even further ahead. Back and forth it went, rocking like a gigantic metronome. At last there was enough forward momentum built up that the bulldozer remained on a forward roll, or skid, with the trolls pushing it. Kravig, in the driver's seat, steered the machine toward the forest path that led to a gravel road. The trolls whooped and hollered as they pushed, giddy with excitement and the thrill of their accomplishment.

Luckily, the first part of the trail either sloped downward or was flat, so the trolls were able to keep the bulldozer moving. Then Kravig, busy waving to the others as though he were a parade queen on a float, failed to negotiate a fairly severe turn at the bottom of a small hill and the bulldozer crashed off into the forest, where the terrain took a plunge. With no large trees in its path to stop it, the bulldozer picked up speed at such an alarming rate that the trolls pushing it could not keep up with it. Some of them simply stopped where they were and watched the avalanche of metal crash through the forest undergrowth. A few chased after the machine, shouting for Kravig to jump out. Kravig managed to grab a horizontal tree limb a couple of seconds before the bulldozer plunged over a rock outcropping. He hung on for dear life as the bulldozer tumbled end over end down a steep rock slope, smashing saplings and sending a wash of rocks rumbling in its wake before crashing to a stop against a row of mature oak trees, splitting the trunks of two trees.

Still clutching the limb, Kravig said to the others, who had raced to the outcropping to watch the bulldozer's demolishing tumble: "Well, that should take care of that."

"What a sight!" Hlauka said, delirious with delight. "What a beautiful sight!"

All of the trolls were ecstatic because of what they had managed to do, and lavished Kravig with praise.

"Now let's take care of that other machine," Kravig said as matter-of-factly as if announcing he was going to eat another potato.

With Ort at his side, the wizard led the way back to the other large machine, the skidder-loader, where he proceeded to scatter the remainder of the magic potion onto that machine.

"There!" he declared with a satisfied inflection. "That will give you all extra strength to push this machine too."

"Are you going to get in first?" Ort asked him.

Knowing he had done nothing to help move the bulldozer, and not eager to experience another potentially dangerous ride, Kravig answered: "Not this time, no. We'll just push this one down the same path we pushed the other one." By "we," he of course meant "all of you," since he had no intention of helping. To his way of thinking, he had given the others power with his magic potion; now it was up to them to do the rest. It was important that he stand a bit aloof, a bit to the side.

With Ort directing the effort, all of the trolls took their positions and prepared to push the skidder-loader down the same path they had pushed the bulldozer. Heaving with all their might, the trolls began pushing the machine, which proved to be even more difficult to do than it was with the bulldozer. Given that the skidder-loader was unbalanced because of its long mechanical arm, the machine began listing to one side, then tipped over, much like the bulldozer had done a few nights earlier. Llop, one of those on what turned out to be the wrong side, was nearly trapped beneath the falling mechanical arm; as it was, the machine merely grazed the side of his left leg.

"Now what?" Hlauka asked Ort. "How are we going to push it to where the other machine is now, with it laying on its side?"

"We'll just leave it here," Ort said. "Let's see how much use it is to people now."

"It would be nice to push it to where people couldn't find it, but we've done well," Kravig said. "Yes, let's just leave it here. We've done good for one night."

"This will be a night to cherish and remember," Ort said as everyone stood around looking at the overturned machine.

At the time he didn't know just how memorable a night it was. He and the others were in for exciting, pleasant news when they returned to the caves.

17 ▪ Kravig And
The Field Of Flowers

The tale Anders read to Andrew from *A Treasury of Troll Tales* this evening was called *Kravig And The Field Of Flowers.*

▪

While walking through a thick section of forest one day in search of special leaves, berries, bark, and other ingredients he needed for his magic potions, a troll wizard named Kravig detected strange hammering sounds coming from the opposite side of a hedge of bushes he was passing. Kravig spread apart some of the branches of a bush so he could peep through the barrier and discovered a dwarf with pointed ears, bony hands and hair so stiff and curly it would have made a good pot scrubber sitting on a stump hammering a sheet of metal into a small cup. The dwarf wore a pointed red cap, a green smock, a wide leather belt, brown pants, and felt boots.

Kravig pushed his way through the bushes, startling the dwarf. "My, my. What have we here?" Kravig said. "If it isn't an ugly little dwarf making a little cup may the moon fall on me tonight and strike me dead."

Despite the fact the troll was three times his size and many times stronger, the dwarf did not cower or shrink with fear. Instead, he looked disdainfully at the troll and said, "And if you aren't an ugly, smelly troll with no more brains than a pod of peas I'll eat your filthy, disgusting hat."

Kravig sprang at the dwarf and grabbed him from behind as the dwarf tried to run away. The dwarf wriggled, and squirmed, and kicked, and spat at the troll, and swung a small hammer wildly. Being much stronger than the defiant dwarf, Kravig gripped the dwarf's right arm and seized the hammer away from him, then squeezed the dwarf with a disabling clutch.

"You're coming home with me," Kravig said. "We need someone like you to fashion jewelry and trinkets for us."

Kravig's tribe of trolls had an accumulation of many gold nuggets and other pieces of raw metal, and dwarfs were well known as master metalsmiths.

"Let go of me, you brute!" the dwarf squealed.

"If you don't keep quiet I'm going to dunk your head in a stream on our way home until you do," Kravig threatened.

The situation did not look good for the dwarf. As brave a front as he put up, he was terrified by the thought of being held captive in a troll cave and forced to work for trolls, whom he detested to a degree that made simple hate seem like love by comparison.

"If you promise to let me go I'll make a deal with you," the dwarf offered.

"What sort of a deal?" Kravig asked warily.

"If you promise to let me go," the dwarf said, "I'll show you where my pot of buried treasure is and let you dig it up."

Now, here was an offer Kravig could hardly refuse. It was a well known fact that dwarfs possessed wonderful hordes of gold, silver and precious stones, and as far as Kravig knew no troll had ever seen a dwarf's pot of treasure, much less been offered the opportunity to dig it up. He also knew dwarfs supposedly kept promises, though he was skeptical of that, for he had no qualms about breaking any promise he made. Still, the possibility of gaining riches made him want to believe it.

"You have yourself a deal," Kravig said. "Let me warn you, though: If you don't keep your part of the bargain I can promise you you're going to undergo torture so painful that your shadow will scream in agony."

"Oh, I'll keep my part of the bargain all right," the dwarf assured him. "We dwarfs always do."

"Come along, then," Kravig said. "Show me the way to your pot of treasure."

Before they set off through the forest, Kravig tied a rope around the dwarf's waist so the dwarf would not be tempted to try to run away. Kravig held the other end of the rope as the dwarf led the way through the forest, across a meadow, down a rocky cliff, across a stream, up another rock cliff, around a bog, down and up the sides of a big valley, and finally to a large field of ragweed plants. The field was a blaze of yellow flowers, for the ragweed plants were in bloom.

The dwarf pointed to one of the ragweed plants and said, "Dig under that ragweed plant and you'll find my pot of treasure buried four feet deep."

"I have a way of finding out whether or not you're telling the truth," the troll wizard said, "so I hope for your sake that you aren't lying to me."

"Oh, I'm telling the truth all right," the dwarf said. "I swear I am!"

"We'll just see about that," Kravig said, taking a certain type of leaf from a pouch attached to a belt around his waist. "Here, suck on this," he ordered the dwarf.

"What for?" the dwarf asked, fearful the troll may be trying to poison him.

"Then I'll know whether you're lying to me or telling me the truth," Kravig said. "If the leaf turns yellow it means you're lying. If it turns a darker shade of green it means you're telling the truth. Put part of it in your mouth—and be quick about it."

The dwarf did as ordered. After he sucked on the leaf for about ten seconds the troll wizard held out a hand and ordered the dwarf to place the leaf in his palm. To the dwarf's great relief, the leaf had turned a deeper shade of green.

"Well, well!" Kravig said, images of gold, silver and precious stones swimming in his head like chunks of meat in a hearty stew. "It looks like you *are* telling the truth. The treasure is buried four feet deep, you say?"

"That's right," the dwarf said. "Four feet."

"In that case, I better go home and get a shovel," Kravig said. "First, though, I better mark which plant it is under so that I'll be able to find it when I come back."

Tearing a strip of white cloth from his ragged clothing, Kravig tied the strip of cloth to the ragweed plant that had the dwarf's pot of treasure beneath its roots.

"If I let you go now," he said to the dwarf, "will you give me your word that you won't dig up the treasure or remove the strip of cloth?"

"I will," the dwarf promised. "You have my word that if you set me free I won't dig up the treasure or remove the strip of white cloth."

While Kravig knew no dwarf would ever break his word, supposedly, with so much at stake he was not about to rely on the dwarf's word alone. Taking out a small packet of mixed herbs and other ingrediants, the troll wizard blew the magic mixture on the strip of white cloth and on the ground around the special ragweed plant.

"That will ensure that you keep your word," he said to the dwarf. "That is a special potion that only trolls can touch. If a dwarf such as you touched it it would melt your skin and give you a grave illness that would have you in tremendous agony for many weeks before killing you." Laughing with masochistic glee, he dismissed the dwarf thusly: "Now off with you! I have no further need of you, you worthless, good-for-nothing dwarf."

The dwarf scampered away without a word.

Kravig hurried back to his cave as fast as he was able, running much of the way. At the cave, he quickly grabbed a shovel and told a fellow member of his small tribe he happened upon to grab a pick and follow him. Then the two rushed back to the field of ragweed flowers.

Their first sight of the ragweed field brought them up short. They stared at the large field as if mesmerized by a hypnotist, for instead of seeing one strip of white cloth tied on one ragweed plant, as Kravig expected, they saw thousands of white strips tied to thousands of ragweed plants. In fact, there was a strip of white cloth tied to every ragweed plant in the field, each strip of cloth identical to the one Kravig tied to one of the plants.

"Which one is the pot of treasure buried under?" the other troll asked Kravig.

"I'm. . . not sure," Kravig stammered. He had paid practically no attention to exactly where in the field the special ragweed plant was, for he assumed that tying a cloth marker on it would be sufficient to allow him to locate it easily. "Curse that disgusting little dwarf!"

"Do you think he's the one who did it?" the other troll asked.

"Of course it was him!" Kravig snapped. "Who else would have done it? He probably had a lot of help, though, to do so many in such a short time."

"So what do we do now?" the other troll asked.

"We dig, that's what we do," Kravig said.

And so the two trolls began digging furiously, and randomly, beneath some of the ragweed plants. They dug for hours, with no luck. They were still digging when a film of dusk developed into a pitch-black picture of night. Still they dug, aided by their extraordinary night vision.

A strong storm swept through in the wee hours of the night. The two trolls took shelter under the trunk of a fallen tree as veins of lightning creased the sky, cracks of thunder resonated like cannon shots, and a howling wind drove fingertip-size raindrops sideways. Dawn was breaking when the storm abated and the two trolls felt it was safe to go out into the open field again. The storm had flattened the field. Most of the yellow ragweed flowers had been blown away. The trolls knew immediately that their chance of finding the dwarf's buried pot of treasure was now so small that it was like one grain of sand in a haystack-size pile of sand. They searched for several more hours without success.

Conceding that the dwarf had outwitted him by his sly trick, Kravig finally gave up the search. He and the other troll returned home, lugging their shovel and their pick on their shoulders as if the implements weighed a thousand pounds each, they were so disappointed and bitter.

They never did find the dwarf's pot of treasure.

18 ▪ A Prisoner

Grentd had a pit-trap set for rats and other small animals next to a walking trail. When he checked it this night, while others were down at the bottom of the mountain moving a bulldozer, he was delighted to discover there was something trapped in the hole. The first thing he saw was a glimpse of bright red, which seemed a bit strange. Upon closer inspection, he nearly fainted in a spasm of ecstasy as he realized what he had captured. Quickly clutching the prisoner in a hairy, knobby hand, Grentd, one of several tribe members with a chiseled features blockhead look, raced back toward the communal cave where he lived, which was the larger of the two communal caves. "I caught a gnome! I caught a gnome!" he shouted as he neared the cave, which had what might be called a sideways entrance, since the entrance was an opening between two parallel rock masses. That opening was only a couple of feet high when trolls first discovered it. The first trolls who occupied the cave chiseled out a larger opening, making it easy for the tallest trolls of the tribe to walk through. Like Kravig's cave, it had smooth, curvatious walls, with the high-ceilinged main chamber having many nooks and crannies. A bubbling, two-foot-wide stream maintained a continuous ambient sound near one side of that large chamber, and two natural corridors branched from that chamber and led to many other, smaller chambers deeper in the mountain. Trolls had added disorder to the cave. Objects were strewn about all over; all was clutter, disarray and dishevelment.

Other members of the tribe who were outside followed Grentd into the cave, straining to see the gnome he had captured, for this was quite a momentous event, on a par with finding a cache of gold. There is perhaps nothing that makes a troll happier than torturing—trolls prefer to call it teasing—a gnome, and it had been more than sixteen years since the tribe had had a gnome in its clutches. Gnomes, of course, are much smaller than trolls. Adult males are only about six inches tall and weigh less than a pound. Despite their diminutive size, though, gnomes are stronger than humans, though of course no match for trolls. Like most male gnomes, the one Grentd trapped sported a full beard and wore a peaked red cap, a blue smock, a wide leather belt with a tool kit attached, brown pants and felt boots.

"Get him in the cage," a fellow tribe member said to Grentd, who was holding the gnome aloft, as though it were a trophy—which in a sense it was, of course. Grentd stuffed the terrified gnome into a rusty metal birdcage one tribe member had stolen from a house quite a few years previously for just such a purpose. All of the trolls took turns poking and prodding the gnome with their fingers, often with two or three doing so simultaneously. The gnome scurried about the cage trying to avoid the pokes and prods, only to be pushed from one knobby finger to another knobby finger, first in his stomach, then in his back, then on one of his sides. The more the gnome scurried about the more the trolls enjoyed witnessing his terror and his frightened, fevered actions. They laughed uproariously while taunting the gnome with insults and harassing remarks. "People lover!" many hissed at him, for trolls know gnomes to be on good terms with human beings. Calling a gnome a people lover is a lashing insult. Given the problems people were causing this tribe of trolls, this was a particularly bad time for a gnome to fall into the hairy hands of trolls. When the gnome curled himself into a ball on the bottom of the cage the trolls used sticks to push him around until he rose to his feet and began jumping around like a mouse trying to escape from a couple of cats. One troll knocked off the gnome's red cap, then another did the same after the gnome placed it back on his head.

As if the physical prodding wasn't enough, the stench inside the cave was making the gnome sick to his stomach. The cave itself was not the problem; the air in it would have been pure and sweet without its inhabitants, for the clear mountain stream freshened the air. It was the trolls inside the cave who funkified the atmosphere, with their stinky bodies and rank clothing. The overwhelming odor was as offensive as the trolls' ugliness was repulsive. While a gnome prisoner could avoid the ugliness by looking away or closing his eyes, he could not escape the sickening smell, short of escaping from his troll captors.

When Old Fungus, who lived in the smaller communal cave, heard that Grentd had captured a gnome he at first suspected others were perhaps playing some sort of practical joke on him, bringing his passion about gnomes to a boil so they could have a good laugh at his reaction when he found out it wasn't true. Old Fungus took a back seat to no troll when it came to despising gnomes, and everyone knew it. He could imagine some members of the tribe thinking it would be great sport to tell him they had captured a gnome and then laughing at his frenetic eagerness to see the gnome when he rushed into the cave where the gnome supposedly was being held prisoner. But no! When he rushed to the other cave to have a look for himself, as much as he was able to rush at his advanced age, there was indeed a gnome there, cowering in a corner of the square cage. Old Fungus's eyes nearly popped from their sockets at the glorious sight. Having a gnome in captivity was better than finding a fist-sized lump of gold, at least to him, given the longstanding grudge he had against gnomes, which he considered ten times more loathsome than people, which was saying something.

His special hatred of gnomes stemmed from an incident that happened several hundred years in the past, after he had raided a farm. Three gnomes who lived at the farm followed him into a mountain forest, without his being aware of it. When Fungus stopped to rest and refresh himself at the bottom of a precipitous waterfall the gnomes went to the top of the waterfall and pushed a boulder over the edge of the cliff—remember: gnomes are much stronger than humans—directly above Fungus. Catching a peripheral glimpse of the plunging boulder, Fungus tried to step out of the way. While that action prevented the boulder from conking him on the head, he didn't react quickly enough to avoid the boulder entirely. The boulder landed on his tail and pressed his tail against a jagged rock beneath, resulting in the severance of two-thirds of his tail and the most intense agony he had ever endured, or would endure until this day. As he screamed and writhed in pain, the two cows he had stolen ran away. The three gnomes caught up with the cows and took them back to the farm. That was the worst night of his life. Of course, he was merely Fungus at the time, not yet Old Fungus; that is how far in the past it was.

"So, we've got you now, don't we, little gnome?" Old Fungus hissed at the gnome, pressing his face against the bars of the birdcage so that the metal mesh left impressions on his wrinkled, mottled skin. "You're not as smart as you think you are, are you, little gnome? Let's see you try to escape now, with your famous trickery and your famous guile."

While trolls are loath to admit it, gnomes are more intelligent and much cleverer than trolls. Because of that, they always seem to escape from trolls who capture them by outwitting trolls with ingenious, crafty schemes, often in distressingly—to trolls— short order. Old Fungus had had gnomes escape his clutches many more times than he liked to think about. Given that history, he wanted to tease the gnome prisoner as much as possible while the opportunity presented itself, so he went on hectoring and deriding the gnome for a good many minutes, informing the gnome as to what was in store for him in the way of teasing, by which he of course meant torture. The other trolls derived as much enjoyment from Old Fungus's relish as they did from the gnome's quivering, knee-knocking terror.

The gnome didn't say a word. He knew that shouting or screaming would be fruitless. In fact, he reasoned that dis- playing the full depth of his fright probably would merely serve to heighten the trolls' perverse pleasure. He didn't want to give the brutes any more satisfaction than they already took from his grave distress.

"Grentd caught a gnome!" a female troll named Jompa, who had a fountain of white hair, streaked with black, erupting to both sides of her head, framing her round face, informed Ort and others upon their return to the caves.

"No!" Ort said, as though the news were too good to be true, especially on the heels of what many tribe members had managed to do to the big yellow machines at the bottom of the mountain.

"It's true!" Jompa said in her scratchy, high-pitched voice, which resembled the sound of a nail scraping a sheet of metal. "We've all been having a ball teasing it, especially Old Fungus."

"Where is it now?" Ort asked.

"In the cave here," Jompa said. "We locked it in the bird- cage. You should see it dancing about! The terror in its little eyes is a sight to see!"

"I have to see it!" Ort said excitedly, rushing into the cave's large chamber. Like Old Fungus, Ort derided and terrified the gnome prisoner for several minutes, making the gnome shiver with fear with his threats, bluster and intimidating demeanor.

Given that Grentd captured the gnome, Ort allowed him the honor of torturing it first. After much thought as to just what form that teasing should take—with more than a little advice from the other trolls—Grentd took the gnome from its cage and carried it over to an old grindstone in the cave. Rnobrna cranked the handle, which turned the grindstone, while Grentd held the gnome over the revolving stone wheel so that the gnome's tiny felt-booted feet touched the grindstone, setting off showers of sparks. This brought so much delight to the other trolls that they danced joyously around the cave chamber. The gnome's felt boots provided little protection for his feet. The pain was so great that he couldn't help but shriek, which delighted the trolls all the more, for it was proof their torture was having its desired effect.

This went on for a good fifteen minutes before Old Fungus insisted it was his turn to tease the gnome, by which he of course meant torture the gnome. Since most agreed his appetite for revenge accorded him a special privilege, the others acquiesced to his desire. While it may be assumed his advanced age entitled him to special privileges as well, that was not the case, for trolls are notoriously non-sentimental concerning such matters as age. They recognize there is such a thing as age, but their extremely limited ability to count and their complete lack of calendar knowledge makes age irrelevant for the most part.

"I think I'd like to see this little fellow dance for us," Old Fungus cackled, coughing up and spitting out a gob of phlegm. "Would you like to dance for us, little gnome?" he said to the gnome, squeezing it in the palm of his left hand. "You would like to do that, wouldn't you? Say yes."

The gnome said nothing.

"Sure you would!" Old Fungus said. Without taking his eyes off the gnome, he said to the others in the cave: "I need a good-sized chain."

"I'll get you one," Scurf said, heading for the treasure chest in his chamber. In a minute he returned with a gold chain about two feet long—a chain that had once held a human pocket watch.

Rott helped Old Fungus tie the ends of the chain around the gnome's shoulders, then Old Fungus started bouncing the dangling gnome on the floor like a marionette. "Dance now! Dance!" he ordered.

The gnome was like a stiff rag, except that he flailed his arms and legs, attempting to free himself from his bonds.

"What he needs is music," Utrud said. "Let's all make some music for him to put him in the dancing mood."

Everyone thought that was a splendid idea. They gathered up pots and pans and began banging them with rocks, sticks, and any metal objects they could find. Some whistled, discordantly. Someone stretched out a long rubber band and plucked it. Dau blew into a harmonica he had stolen long before, which was now rusty from prolonged exposure to dampness.

The gnome wanted to cover his ears to muffle the din, but was unable to do so because Old Fungus was jerking him about, making him "dance." The chain dug into the gnome's armpits, sending a numbing pain down the length of his arms, and down his sides. Old Fungus jerked him as much as a foot off the floor at times, as he yanked him around, trying to force him to dance.

This, too, went on for about fifteen minutes before the gnome was once more shut up in his cage while the trolls discussed what the next method of torture should be, with that discussion sounding very much like a heated argument, given that the trolls had so many passionate opinions about how the teasing should proceed. Some of the trolls wanted to subject the gnome to the most horrifying forms of torture imaginable to their mean-spirited minds. Others thought the gnome should not be treated to several methods of severe physical torture in a short span of time, lest he should crumble from the torment. They wanted to space out the most severe methods of torture so they could torture the gnome for a longer period of time, feeling it was more satisfying to torture someone who had a little fighting spirit in him, to see the psychological terror it produced, than someone who had already been whipped into submission, someone to whom more torture would have little noticeable effect.

19 • The King's Crown

"I really liked the story you read last night, that had a dwarf in it," Andrew said to his father. "Are there any more that have dwarfs in them?"

"Let me think. . ." Anders said. "Oh, I know! Yes, there's a great one called *The King's Crown*. I think you might like this one even better."

And he proceeded to read it aloud.

■

Many years ago there was a troll king named Esor, who had a daughter named Tanja. A young troll named Orrick fell in love with Tanja and went to ask for Esor's consent to marry her.

"Before I give my consent you must first prove yourself worthy," the troll king said to Orrick. "I will give you three tasks. If you accomplish all three tasks you will have my permission to marry my daughter. If, on the other hand, you fail to accomplish any one of the three tasks that will prove that you are not worthy of marrying my daughter."

"What are the tasks I must accomplish?" Orrick asked.

"Return tomorrow at this time and I will tell you what your first task is," the king said. "If you succeed in accomplishing that task I will then tell you what your second task will be. If you succeed at your second task I will then tell you what your third task is to be."

As instructed, Orrick returned the following morning to receive his first assignment from Esor.

"Your first task," the king said, "is this: You must find a bucketful of gold nuggets and bring it to me before nightfall tonight."

With no time to spare, Orrick took a spade and a bucket and hiked to Sky Mountain, which was said to contain more gold than any other mountain in the region. Tromping along as fast as his legs would carry him, Orrick climbed the steepest, rockiest side of Sky Mountain, looking for a cave entrance so that he could search the cave for gold.

He was walking along a narrow ledge when all at once he caught a glimpse of something scurrying behind a jagged rock. It looked like a flash of blue, so Orrick knew it couldn't be an animal, for he knew of no blue animals, other than birds, and this was definitely not a bird. He hurried to where the flash of blue had been and looked around behind the large jagged rock. There, scrunched into a ball, was a skinny little dwarf wearing a blue, frilly smock, a dull-green vest, brown breeches, white stockings, and soft shoes. The dwarf was slightly more than two feet tall, had large, pointed ears, deep-set eyes, and a look of terror on his wrinkled face. Orrick grabbed the back of the dwarf's vest and lifted him off the ground with one hand.

"Put me down, you ogre!" the plucky little dwarf said.

"Well, well, a little dwarf!" Orrick declared with menacing glee. "Now I'll have some fun!" He held the dwarf out over the side of the narrow trail and said, "I've always wondered what it would look like to watch a dwarf tumble down the side of a steep mountain. Do you think you would splatter into many pieces or just sort of be flattened like a bloody hotcake?"

"Don't drop me!" the dwarf begged.

Orrick cackled with laughter. "I just love to watch a dwarf squirm," he said sadistically. "Maybe I'll just hold you out like this and see how long it is before my hand gets numb and I drop you. That would be an interesting experiment, don't you think?"

"I'll make a deal with you," the dwarf said in a desperate tone.

"What kind of a deal?" Orrick asked.

"Let me go and I'll grant you three wishes," the dwarf said. "All you have to do it let me live and you can have whatever you want. Even a troll should have enough intelligence to jump at a deal such as that."

Orrick knew very well that dwarfs possessed magical powers, so the dwarf probably *was* capable of fulfilling three wishes for him. He also knew that a dwarf never broke a promise. Trolls, of course, believed that was a silly dwarf ethic they were glad they didn't have to adhere to. Orrick also knew dwarfs knew where all the gold and silver was to be found within a mountain, not to mention precious stones as well. With his first assignment from the king being to find a bucketful of gold nuggets, it occurred to Orrick he could make use of the dwarf to fulfill the three tasks he had to fulfill to win Tanja's hand in marriage.

Still holding the dwarf's vest, Orrick set the dwarf on the ground and sat on a rock so that he didn't need to look down so far when talking to the dwarf. "Let me be sure I have this straight," Orrick said. "You will grant me three wishes—whatever I want—if I let you go. Is that right?"

"That's right," the dwarf said. "It's that simple. You spare my life and I will grant you any three wishes you desire. Is it a deal?"

"It's a deal," Orrick said without hesitation, releasing his grip on the dwarf's vest.

"You have made a wise decision," the dwarf said, straightening his clothing. "So. . . what will be your first wish?"

"A bucketful of gold nuggets," Orrick blurted out, answering as quickly as he would recoil if stung by a bee, failing to consider the fact he could have asked for dozens, or hundreds, of buckets of gold, given one to the king and kept all the rest himself. His mind was so focused on fulfilling the task the king gave him, and thus winning Tanja's hand, that he was oblivious to anything else. "And I need it today," he added gruffly.

"Then you shall have it today," the dwarf assured him. "Do you know where the waterfall is at the bottom of the mountain?"

"You mean the one I passed on my way here?" Orrick asked.

"That's the one," the dwarf said. "Go and wait for me there. I will take your bucket and fill it with gold nuggets and bring it to you."

Orrick did as directed. He waited at the waterfall until the dwarf brought him his bucket filled with gold nuggets.

"What is your second wish?" the dwarf asked.

"I don't know yet," Orrick said. "I should know by tomorrow."

94

"Very well," the dwarf said. "Meet me here again tomorrow morning and you may tell me then." With that, he ducked behind a tree and was gone.

Orrick went back and presented the bucket of gold nuggets to Esor, who said to Orrick, "You have done well for your first task. Come and see me again tomorrow morning and I will give you your second challenge."

The following morning Esor said to Orrick, "I have been king of the trolls now for many years, and yet I have never had a crown, as a king should have. I think it is time that I have a crown. King Alfred, who lives in the castle south of here, has a beautiful golden crown embedded with many diamonds, rubies, and other jewels. *That* is the crown that I deserve. *That* is the crown I want. If you bring me King Alfred's crown you will have fulfilled your second task."

"I will do my best to get you King Alfred's crown," Orrick said, then hurried off to tell the dwarf his second wish.

"That is a very ambitious wish," the dwarf said. "Getting a king's crown will be a most difficult challenge."

"But you promised that I could wish for anything and you would grant my wishes," Orrick said. "Are you going back on your word?" This question was asked none too kindly.

"Not at all," the dwarf assured Orrick. "I promised I would grant you three wishes, and I plan to honor that pledge. All I'm saying is that getting a king's crown is not nearly as easy as finding a bucket of gold. If it's a king's crown you want, though, then it's a king's crown you shall have. This is not something that can be done in a single day, however. It may take me a week to get you the crown that you desire."

The dwarf said that when he managed to get King Alfred's crown he would bring it to Orrick at the waterfall. Orrick was to go to the waterfall each morning.

The crown wasn't there the following morning, or the next morning, or the morning after that, or the morning after that, or the morning after that. Orrick started to worry that the dwarf might not keep his promise and grant Orrick his second wish.

Meanwhile, Esor pestered Orrick as to when he was going to get his crown. Esor had his heart so set on having a crown that he took to badmouthing Orrick for not producing him King Alfred's crown as quickly as he produced the bucketful of gold nuggets.

Finally Orrick simply couldn't put up with Esor's criticism any longer. "You'll get your crown!" he said angrily, not caring that he was talking to a king. "He promised he would get it for me, and he will!"

"Who promised you what?" Esor demanded to know.

Orrick hadn't wanted to tell Esor about the dwarf and the three wishes, believing Esor would have more esteem for him if he thought Orrick accomplished all three tasks completely on his own.

"Tell me who promised to get something for you," the king demanded, "or I promise you I will never allow you to marry my daughter."

Orrick felt trapped. Not wanting to ruin any chance he had of marrying Tanja, he told the king all about the dwarf and the three wishes the dwarf had granted him, thinking, as he related the story, that at least Esor should admire his quick thinking and keen deal-making ability. Esor was anything but admiring, though.

"You stupid, idiotic numbskull!" Esor said upon learning how Orrick had used two of three wishes the dwarf granted him. "You boneheaded, feeble-minded fool!"

No, this was far from admiration.

"What's wrong?" Orrick asked innocently, puzzled by the king's explosive reaction.

"What's wrong?!" the king fairly shouted. "You have a chance to ask for anything you want and you ask for only a bucket of gold when you could have had tons of gold, and for only a crown when you could have had a grand castle."

"But they were the things you wanted," Orrick said. "I was getting them for you."

"Can't you think for yourself at all?" Esor groaned. "I don't know if I'll let someone as stupid as you marry my daughter even if you do accomplish all three tasks. But at least all is not yet wasted. You still have one more wish. I will help you use it wisely. If the dwarf grants what we wish I will let you marry my daughter Tanja."

"What wish do you want me to ask for?" Orrick asked.

"I shall have to think over the matter and contemplate the question," Esor said. "This is a decision that requires a lot of consideration."

After hours and hours of thought Esor concluded that Orrick's third wish should be that Esor be given the same knowledge dwarfs possessed as to where gold, silver and precious stones could be found. He quizzed Orrick relentlessly as to what his third wish should be until he was satisfied Orrick knew precisely what to ask for, in precise words.

On the seventh morning after he told the dwarf that his second wish was for King Alfred's crown, Orrick went to the waterfall and found the dwarf seated on a large rock holding a gleaming golden crown. Orrick took the crown from the dwarf and admired it, explaining to the dwarf that the crown was actually for Esor, the troll king. He also told the dwarf about the way the king berated him and badmouthed him when he hadn't produced the crown as quickly as Esor wanted it.

"Boy," Orrick said offhandedly, "sometimes I wish I was the king of the trolls so that I could boss others around like Esor does."

"You do?" the dwarf asked.

"I sure do!" Orrick said.

"All right, your wish is granted, your majesty," the dwarf said, placing the crown on Orrick's head.

"What are you doing?" Orrick asked.

"I'm putting your crown on you," the dwarf said. "You said you wished you were king of the trolls, and so you are!"

"But that wasn't my third wish!" Orrick protested.

"It's too late to take it back now," the dwarf said, scampering away up the waterfall like some magic fish. "Once you make a wish it's final." With those words, he disappeared.

Orrick felt heartsick. What a tongue-lashing the king would give him now, for making such a grand blunder!

Wait a minute, though, he thought. *If my wish has been granted and I truly am king of the trolls, then Esor is no longer the king. And if he is no longer the king I no longer have to fear him.*

But was he really king of the trolls now? He decided there was only one way to find out: Return home and see if the other trolls treated him as king.

· He returned to the troll caves with the golden crown perched on his head. None of the other trolls, not even Esor, questioned the fact that Orrick was now their new king. All acknowledged Orrick's kingship as readily as if there had been a coronation ceremony.

Orrick quickly became accustomed to being king. Being king was great fun. And being king did not change his feelings for Tanja; he found that he still loved her. As king, though, he didn't need to seek Esor's permission to marry her. As king, he was free to marry anyone he wished to marry. Since he wanted to marry Tanja, he did marry her, and the two of tem lived a long, happy life together.

20 • The Prisoner Speaks

The trolls resumed torturing the gnome the next evening, beginning with a forced treadmill exercise. They set the gnome on a hand-cranked treadmill and made him run in place. Generally a treadmill operator—the trolls took turns at this—cranked the treadmill very slowly for a time, then suddenly cranked as fast as he could, trying to throw the gnome off-balance and cause him to fall. The gnome did just that several times, suffering cuts and bruises in the process. Occasionally the treadmill operator suddenly reversed the direction of the treadmill, which never failed to cause the gnome to fall on his face. At times the troll operating the treadmill simply cranked quite fast for a fair stretch of time, forcing the gnome to exert himself to near-exhaustion if he wanted to remain upright.

Ort entered the cave while the gnome was on the treadmill. He was wearing his "king's crown," which he did on occasion—the rare occasion. His crown, as he liked to call it, was not really a crown but a tarnished, battered, partial Viking helmet made of metal and meant to protect the top of the wearer's head. It was essentially a smooth metal bowl except that strips of metal criss-crossed the top from front to back and side to side, with those two strips connected to a bottom strip that ran the circumferance. The helmet had two significant crack-lines, one along the left temple and the other at the back, and a chunk in the right forehead area had rusted away. While Ort did his best to keep the helmet shined, tarnish and rust had long since set in, so it had a dull, mottled appearance. Ort told everyone he had taken the helmet from a Viking warrior after killing him in hand-to-hand combat. In truth, he found it buried among building ruins. None of the other trolls knew enough about history to understand that Ort was born long after the Viking era ended and that he knew of Vikings only through tales about them. Ort immediately took a turn cranking the treadmill, after which he put the gnome in the birdcage and began speaking to him.

"I'm the king here," he informed the gnome.

"King!" the gnome said derisively. "If you're a king, then I'm a saint."

"What's your name?" Ort demanded.

"What's it to you?" the gnome said, displaying a verbal feistiness that was part of his nature.

"Because I want to know!" Ort blustered, opening the door of the cage, reaching in a hand, and twisting the gnome's left arm.

"Lekov!" the gnome cried, in obvious agony. Ort released his grip. "It's Lekov. Okay?"

Ort slammed the birdcage door shut so hard that Lekov was knocked off-balance from the tremor.

"When I ask you a question I expect an answer," Ort said.

Lekov averted his eyes from Ort's withering glare.

"Come and get it, everyone," Elseth said, as she and Jompa carried two large iron kettles filled with food into the cave chamber, having cooked the food outdoors.

"Have you had anything to eat?" Ort asked Lekov, all pleasantness.

Lekov didn't answer right away, but when Ort started making a move toward him he barked out, "No."

"You must be hungry," Ort said. "How would you like some roasted bat ears? They're fresh. The bats were caught just last night."

Lekov said nothing.

"Or how about some boiled worms, and frosted grasshoppers?" Ort offered.

"You can't be serious," Lekov said. "I didn't think even trolls would sink so low as to eat things such as that."

Ort ignored that remark. "Let's start you out with a plate of bat ears. Rott," he said to his grandson, "bring our little visitor here a few bat ears."

The other trolls heaped food onto tin plates and gulped down food they scooped from their plates with their hands as often as with their spoons. Rott fetched some roasted bat ears, as ordered, and poked them through the bars of the birdcage. Lekov made a sour face at the odor.

"Eat up," Ort said. "Go ahead."

Lekov spat on the bat ears and folded his arms across his chest in defiance.

"Why, I oughtta butcher you alive!" Ort said. "You lousy little gnomes are just no darn good. And then you wonder why us trolls hate you so, you snobbish little twerps. You eat that right now or I'm going to hold you by your hair until you apologize."

Old Fungus charged across the cave, saying "Let me do it! Let me do it!"

Lekov fidgeted and licked his lips nervously. He made no move to pick up one of the bat ears, though.

"Well, I'm waiting," Ort said, like a mother addressing an uncooperative child.

"Eat it yourself," the gnome blurted out, giving Ort a bold look of defiance.

Quick as a whip, Ort opened the door of the cage, snatched up Lekov in his right hand, pulled him out, and held him several feet above the floor by grasping a lock of Lekov's hair between a thumb and an index finger. He then jiggled the gnome up and down until the hair was pulled from Lekov's head and Lekov fell to the dirt floor, landing with a thud, feet-first. As he writhed in pain and held a hand up to the sore spot on his head from where hairs had been yanked out, Old Fungus scooped him up and thrust him into the cage again. The trolls laughed as Lekov flexed his limbs and felt his body here and there to try to determine if he had suffered any broken bones or any other serious injury, or was bleeding anywhere.

"You're all swine!" Lekov hissed at his tormenters, his fortitude seemingly forged stronger with each tortuous fire he endured.

"You shut your face!" Grentd shouted, amidst a general uproar.

Old Fungus shook a finger at the gnome. "You better just thank your lucky stars that you weren't captured by snotgurgles," he said. "They wouldn't be as easy on you as we've been. You'd be lucky to still be alive if you were in the hands of snot-gurgles."

What Old Fungus said was true. It was a far worse fate for a gnome to be captured by a snotgurgle than a troll. Snotgurgles are larger than trolls, with six black-clawed fingers on their hands, seven toes on each foot, and hair covering their entire bodies. It is believed that trolls and snotgurgles were related in distant times. The most prevalent theory is that the first snot-gurgles were the offspring of the mating of trolls and bears. Gnomes have been known to meet their death at the hands of snotgurgles. Others have lost limbs and suffered other crippling injuries. While a few gnomes have been seriously wounded by trolls, there is not one documented case of a gnome being killed by trolls, for trolls are not as malicious as snotgurgles. Trolls do not want to kill gnomes; they merely want to torture them.

"Do snotgurgles really exist?" Jirik, one of the tribe's youngest trolls, asked Old Fungus, for few living trolls had actually seen a snotgurgle.

"Of course they do," Old Fungus said. "Or at least they did. I've laid my eyes on several of them in my time, but no one is quite sure whether or not any are still alive. If they are, they live way up north, even much farther north than we are here, in the furthest reaches of the coldest mountains."

"I've heard it said that maybe some giant trolls who lived in the past were really snotgurgles," Brine, another relatively young troll, said. "Is that true?"

"No, no, no, no, no, no, no," Old Fungus said. "Giant trolls who lived in the past were not snotgurgles."

"Tell us a story about one of the giants," Grentd requested of Old Fungus, and others added their voices to that request.

"Very well," Old Fungus said, as others gathered around where he was seated on a boulder. Thoughts of torturing the gnome prisoner were put on hold as Old Fungus told the tale about the giant troll of Thunder Mountain.

21 ▪ The Giant Troll
Of Thunder Mountain

Once, long ago, Thunder Mountain was the home of a giant troll named Snaggle. In Snaggle's time a tiny village rose up at the base of Thunder Mountain, which was hard by a small, shallow fjord. The residents of that tiny village were hard-working people who were content with their simple lives, for the most part. To most of the people living in the village, the worst thing about the place was that Snaggle went into periodic rages, which disrupted the usual peace and serenity, often put people's possessions in peril, and sometimes even proved hazardous to their physical safety. When the giant troll became angry about something, or his stomach bothered him because of something rotten, rancid or moldy he ate, or he didn't like the look of the sky, or he was simply in a foul mood for any number of other reasons, he would moan and bellow, wail and roar, and yell and blare. He would hurl and roll large rocks and boulders down the mountainside toward the village and kick angrily at dirt until he stirred up a virtual dust storm. He would barge down to the village at night and steal boats, garden produce, bricks and boards, and all manner of other items.

This sort of behavior went on for years and years and years. At first Snaggle threw one large three- or four-day tantrum, and raided the village, only once a year or so. The remainder of the year the giant troll and the villagers had a harmonious co-existence. Snaggle remained high up on the mountain, and went quietly about his own affairs, while the people strayed only short distances from the village, whether on land or on water. As time advanced, though, Snaggle grew increasingly surly and grouchy. His noisy flare-ups became more frequent until eventually his temper tantrums occurred almost on a weekly basis. The people who lived in the village lost so much sleep because of the noise Snaggle made, and were so jittery and on-edge worrying about what Snaggle might do, that the situation became intolerable. A village meeting was called so that everyone could talk things over and see if anyone had any ideas as to how they could deal with Snaggle's menacing, disquieting presence nearby. The village blacksmith spoke first.

"I can see only one solution to this problem," he said. "I think we will have to kill Snaggle."

Many of those attending the meeting gasped or lowered their heads as though ashamed by the mention of murder. While most village residents had wished Snaggle dead in recent years, talking opening about the possibility of killing the irascible troll was quite another thing altogether.

"I'm afraid it's our only way out of this mess," the blacksmith went on. "The thought of killing anyone—even an ugly, sour-tempered troll—is no more appealing to me than I'm sure it is to any of you, but if we don't get rid of Snaggle somehow things will only get worse and he might well end up killing all of us. I, for one, am not anxious to wait around for that to happen."

Others voiced agreement. A lively discussion went on for some time. Eventually there was a vote taken, with the majority voting for Snaggle's death. Then the question became how to best accomplish the distasteful task. After much discussion the villagers decided that poisoning Snaggle would be the easiest and probably most effective means of murder.

Three days later, when the wind was right, a delegation of village residents journeyed some distance up the mountain and cooked a huge vat of stew, which they liberally laced with a strong dose of slow-acting poison. The wind wafted the stew odor directly toward Snaggle's large cave. Following his nose, the giant troll descended the mountainside toward the vat of stew. When he found the food, the people who cooked the stew had fled back down the mountain to the village. Sensing nothing suspicious about the situation, Snaggle wolfed down the entire vat of warm stew and returned to his cave for more sleep.

Before long the poison that was in the stew began having its affect. The people in the village at the base of Thunder Mountain could hear Snaggle's agonizing moans of pain. It sounded as though the very Earth was in agony. It seemed as though the wind was wailing. Snaggle's anguished moans, tortured wails and rumbling grunts continued nonstop for a full twenty-four hours. The pain-wracked sounds became almost unbearable to the villagers, especially when they knew they were the cause. It was almost as though the gods were tormenting them for what they had done by making the people have to listen to the giant troll's expressions of excruciating pain.

And then, at last, the wailing ceased. After all was quiet for twenty-four hours, the villagers concluded Snaggle was surely dead.

"We should go and block up the entrance to his cave so that the stench of his rotting body will not be in the air," someone said.

That sounded logical to many others, so a delegation went up Thunder Mountain to block the entrance of Snaggle's cave. The men who went on that mission could see part of Snaggle's enormous, hairy body lying within the dark recess of the dank mountain cave, which was close by a small mountain stream. Working as quickly as possible, they rolled large rocks into the cave entrance and carried smaller rocks to stack on top of the boulders until a thick rock wall hid the entire entrance.

Six days later, on a Sunday afternoon, everyone in the village gathered for a picnic at the shore of the fjord to celebrate their liberation from the tyranny of the giant troll. While the picnic was in progress there was a rumbling, like distant thunder, far up on the mountain, from the vicinity of Snaggle's cave. Everyone stopped what they were doing and turned their attention to the sound as it grew louder, for it seemed to be headed down the mountain straight toward them.

"It's a rockslide!" someone shouted.

"Let's get out of here!" another man said.

Following the lead of a couple of quick-thinking men, every-one dashed for the boats, then rowed for all they were worth toward the opposite shore of the fjord. Meanwhile, the rockslide roared down Thunder Mountain in a blizzard of dust. It was a rockslide the likes of which is rarely seen, a rockslide of massive strength and size. The villagers watched in horror, from their boats, as the rockslide headed directly for their homes and shops and flattened and buried every building in its path. They shed many tears and uttered many words of woe as a mushroom cloud of dust rose over their buried village.

Then someone thought she detected more movement high up in the mountain, in a clearing through the trees. Others thought so as well, when she pointed out the spot.

"It looks like. . . No, it can't be! But it has to be! Surely that's Snaggle!" one man stammered, finding it difficult to believe his own eyes. Others concurred. Snaggle! Alive?!

"You mean, he isn't dead after all?" someone said.

"It surely looks as though he isn't," someone answered.

Watching from their small boats, the villagers spotted Snaggle several more times, in open areas, as he made his way down the mountain toward where the village lay buried. Indeed, Snaggle was not dead, after all. The poisonous stew had nearly killed him, but it hadn't quite done the job. It had sent him into a three-day coma, after first torturing him with pain, but it hadn't quite been able to lift the last breath of life from him. When he awoke and found that the opening to his cave had disappeared he panicked and started kicking with his huge feet and pushing at the rock wall with his huge shoulders, which started the power-ful, destructive rockslide. He literally cracked off a section of the mountain and sent it reeling toward the village.

The villagers quickly concluded Snaggle might well be out for revenge against all of them, so there was no going back to face his wrath. Anyway, with their village destroyed, there was nothing to go back for. The wisest course of action seemed to be to flee as fast as possible, to get far away from Snaggle. And so that's what they did. The oars in the boats flapped through the water like wings of fast-flying birds as men pulled for their very lives, and the lives of their families.

As the boats left the fjord and started down the coastline of the open sea, Snaggle stood on the shore where the onetime village was now buried under thousands of tons of rock rubble and shouted curses and threats at the escaping people, who had to rebuild their lives from scratch somewhere else.

22 ▪ Playing With Fire

"I love that story!" Hlauka said when Old Fugus finished telling the tale. "It's so uplifting!"

"You have to love it when people get what they have coming to them," Haar said.

"A whole village!" Drulle marveled.

"I wish we had Snaggle with us now to start a rockslide down the mountain," Hlauka said. "How great would that be?"

"What we did last night seems to have put a stop to that nettlesome noise," Ort said, for none of the trolls heard any human noises the entire past day. "People don't always get the best of us." He looked over at the gnome. "You hear that, people lover? People don't always get the best of us!"

"I'm going to have some fun with our little friend," Traug said, tromping over to Lekov's cage, where he tied the gnome's hands behind his back and proceeded to tickle his nose, ears and feet with feathers, which the others found to be amusing and enjoyable entertainment of the highest order. They cackled and chortled and chuckled diabolically.

"Let's conduct a little experiment," Traug said, like an illusionist announcing his next trick. "Let's find out if gnomes are fireproof, or if they burn. What do you say?" he posed to the others.

Everyone seemed agreeable. In fact, they all loved the idea. Calls of encouragement poured forth, so Traug untied the gnome's hands and carried him over toward the fireplace, where logs burned amidst flickering flames. Of course, all the trolls already knew gnomes were not fireproof, for nearly every time they caught one they set fire to his clothing; it was one of their favorite ways of teasing the little folk.

"No, no! Please don't put me in the fire!" Lekov pleaded, fearing he was about to be burned alive.

Traug ignored the gnome's pleas and lowered him ever closer to the fire, holding him by his legs, upside down.

"Please don't!" Lekov cried, more desperate by the moment. "Have pity! I beg of you!"

Traug cackled gleefully and continued lowering the gnome ever closer to the fire. Lekov's coat, which was hanging down nearest to the flames, suddenly caught fire and began burning. Traug pulled Lekov away from the fire and tossed him to Grentd, saying, "Put it out! Put it out! But don't burn yourself!"

Grentd slapped at the burning coat with a sweaty palm for a few seconds before tossing the gnome to Scurf, who happened to touch the burning coat and quickly tossed Lekov to Ort. This game of hot potato went on for more than twenty seconds. All the while, Lekov's coat continued burning slowly and the terrified gnome shrieked shrilly, for he was in a state of full-blown panic. The trolls tried to put out the fire without burning themselves, for the point of the game was not to burn a gnome alive but make the gnome believe that was their intention so he would be as terror-stricken as honey is sweet. Eventually Brine mishandled a slightly errant toss and Lekov plopped into a large bowl of porridge, on his side. That doused the fire.

The right side of Lekov's face was pressed against the thick porridge as Brine fished him out of the bowl and set him back in the birdcage, where Lekov curled up in mute terror and wiped the rank porridge from his face and hands.

For the time being, the trolls left the gnome alone as they relived their hot potato game, laughing until their sides ached as they tried to imitate some of the gnome's terrified expressions and describe the way he screamed in terror as his coat burned and they tossed him around. They felt as though they were on top of the world.

23 ▪ The Noises Resume

Sunday, like Saturday, was another quiet day, to the trolls' delight. Monday morning was peaceful as well. Then, like a recurring nightmare, noises resumed Monday afternoon at the bottom of the mountain. Ort sent for Kravig, in order to consult with the wizard.

"I don't understand it," Kravig said. "How can this be? I thought for sure we put one of the big yellow machines in a place where people could no longer make use of it, and made the other one useless by tipping it over."

"You know how tricky people can be," Ort said. "They have their own kind of magic at times."

"That's true," Kravig agreed. "It can be hard to counteract their magic, curse their tricky minds."

"It sounds like the same noise, doesn't it?" Ort said. "Isn't that the same noise we heard before?"

"I'm not sure," Kravig said. "I would say it sounds the same, but it's hard to say, people make so many different noises."

"We have to figure out a way to put a stop to the noise once and for all," Ort said.

"What do you have in mind?" Kravig asked.

"I'm not sure yet," Ort responded. "Me and a few others will go back down there tonight to have a look around. I hate having to keep doing that when there are so many better and more important things we could be doing."

Ort took four other trolls with him on that night's reconnaissance mission. They started out just as the moon was rising over Troll Mountain, which made the night even lighter. Fog grew thicker and thicker as they made their way down the mountain, though, and there was drizzle in the air. The moonlight gave the fog an orange tinge. Halfway down, they encountered a large owl sitting on a long horizontal branch of an oak tree less than fifteen feet off the ground, which Ort found quite odd. The owl eyed them with a cold, quizzical look that rather unnerved Ort and began hooting in a strange manner after the trolls passed its position. The story of Ulf and a strange, odd owl popped into Ort's mind, and he wondered if this owl might prove to be as ominous an omen as the owl Ulf encountered had been. The thought of turning back crossed his mind, but he quickly dismissed it, not wanting the others to think he feared anything, especially when he had but a vague sense of peril. He wondered if the appearance of the owl in such an unlikely place occasioned thoughts of Ulf's story in any of the other four. If it did, none mentioned anything about it. And he wasn't about to remind them of the story, if they had ever heard it, for he didn't want everyone worrying unduly about the possibility of trouble.

At the worksite, a bulldozer loomed as large as ever, a fuzzy blob amidst the shroud of fog and drizzle, sitting almost in the exact spot it had been when the trolls pushed it away. While this was a different bulldozer, the trolls didn't know that; they assumed it was the same one they had pushed down the path and crashed over a rock ledge. The skidder-loader also was upright, not on its side.

With Ort leading the way, the five trolls tramped boldly toward the bulldozer to check out the situation. When they were twenty feet from it, a human voice rang out from the edge of the forest behind the machine: "Hold it right there! Don't move!"

"Let's beat it!" Ort whispered loudly, making a dash for the cover of forest where they had just been. The others ran after him as three explosions split the night with ringing echoes, in quick succession. Gangl felt a sharp pain in his upper back, behind his right shoulder, which caused him to fall to the ground, unable to move. He knew right away he had been hit by a bullet, for trolls knew what bullets and guns were, and how gunshots sounded, and what power they possessed. Another bullet grazed Dau's left thigh. The third whistled over everyone's heads. Hearing Gangl's anguished cries, Haar and Scurf went back to drag him away from the open area. That drew two more gunshots from whoever was doing the shooting. One of those bullets skipped in the dirt very near them. Dau managed to hobble into the woods on his own power.

The five trolls retreated about two hundred feet into the woods, where they hid behind a knoll. They could make out a person walking around the cleared area, but the fog was so thick that even their keen eyesight left them unable to tell exactly what the person was doing. As far as they could determine, there was only one person there. Eventually that person disappeared from view and the trolls slipped away up the mountain. Gangl needed to be helped along, for his gunshot wound put him in great pain. The trolls paused at several places to allow Gangl to rest.

They heard two owls calling to each other from very tall trees much of the time. Ort wondered if one of them was the large owl they had seen sitting on a low branch of an oak tree on their way down the mountain.

Great excitement greeted their return to the caves. Everyone wanted to know what happened, especially to Gangl. Ort sent for Kravig so that he could attend to Gangl's wound. Aside from Guggle, who lived farther from the caves, Kravig was the only member of the tribe who knew anything about medicine. While he knew precious little, the others thought he knew more than he actually did, so the faith they had in him acted as medicine of a sort itself when he treated someone. He knew enough to wash and dress Gangl's wound, and he also had his patient eat an herb mixture.

"He'll be fine," Kravig assured everyone. "He just needs some good rest." He hoped that was true, at least.

All of the trolls were angry about what happened to Gangl. They vented their anger by cursing humans and their malevolent minds, and their malicious actions towards trolls.

After Kravig treated Gangl, Ort took the wizard aside and told him about the large owl he and the four others had seen on their way down the mountain, so low in a tree.

"Considering what happened tonight," Ort said, "I can't help but believe that that owl was a bad omen. Owls are such strange birds anyway, and this one was *very* strange. You know what it made me think of?"

"Ulf?" Kravig said without hesitation.

"Exactly," Ort said. "Ulf."

"Now, *that* was a very interesting incident," Kravig said. "I think about that from time to time myself, even when I don't see an owl."

The tale of Ulf and the owl both Ort and Kravig were recalling goes as follows:

24 ▪ Ulf And The Owl

One night when it was so dark it was as though the air was full of black ink, a young troll named Ulf was walking through a forest when he encountered an extremely large owl in his path. The owl was not perched in a tree, but standing on the ground. Ulf's noisy approach did not spook the owl or cause it to fly away. On the contrary, the owl stood its ground so steadfastly, and was so silent, that Ulf nearly collided with it. Ulf was only three feet away when he saw the creature and jerked to a stop, startled. More precisely, Ulf sensed the owl's presence before he actually saw it. If Ulf had been a human being rather than a troll he certainly would have crashed into the owl, for human eyesight is far inferior to the night vision of trolls. As it was, Ulf could barely make out the stock-still owl from the blackness around it, even at such close proximity that he could have reached out and touched it.

"Shoo! Get out of my way!" Ulf ordered, waving a hand.

The owl did not move. It did not flinch. It did not so much as blink. It looked at the troll as if it could see right through him.

"Out of my way, I said!" Ulf demanded, and clapped his hands together so hard it sounded like the crack of a gunshot.

The strange owl stood its ground, still silent, seemingly as serene as a flower.

Ulf stomped his feet, flapped his arms, jumped in the air several times, and made every sort of strange noise he could think of making to try to make the owl move. Nothing worked. The odd owl would not move.

Now, trolls are afraid of few things. Fear is a rare emotion for them. Ulf wasn't afraid, precisely, at this point, but it can be said with certainty that this strange encounter with this large owl unnerved him, at least. This sort of behavior by an owl was something decidedly unnatural, something akin to seeing a green sun in the sky.

As much as he hated the thought of backing down to a bird, Ulf decided the most prudent course of action for him was to walk around the owl, through brush, to avoid a physical confrontation. With an owl of such a peculiar nature, he reasoned, who knew what sort of potent poison the owl might possess and be able to inflict upon him.

For the next month, not a single drop of rain fell in the mountain region where Ulf had his cave. The drought diminished the stream that slithered down the mountain near his cave to less than half its normal flow. Another month passed and there was still no rain. By this time the stream had nearly dried up; it was a mere trickle of water.

Ulf and the other trolls who lived nearby were worried that they would soon have no water to drink if the drought continued much longer. None of the trolls had ever seen a drought last that long. A couple of the trolls spoke of looking for homes elsewhere if rain didn't soon fall and provide relief.

Ulf, who was more introspective than most trolls, thought back to his encounter with the strange owl and wondered if perhaps that event was somehow related to the drought. He brought up the issue with Gorgon, a troll who lived fairly near to him.

"Do you think we are having this drought because of how the owl acted?" Ulf asked after telling Gorgon about his encounter with the owl.

"I don't know," Gorgon answered. "That sort of thing is beyond me. Kravig is the one you should ask about something like that. He would be the one who would know, if anyone would."

Ulf had never heard of Kravig, a troll wizard who lived alone about a hundred miles away. After Gorgon explained who he was, Ulf resolved he would go to see Kravig to see what the wizard had to say bout the situation.

Ulf set out on his journey the next night and reached Kravig's cave after three nights of walking. Kravig was quite young for a troll wizard, but even much older trolls respected him for the wisdom and insight they believed he possessed.

Kravig listened attentively to the story of Ulf's encounter with the strange owl, then sat in silence for several minutes thinking over what Ulf had told him. Ulf dared not utter another word at this time for fear he would disrupt Kravig's concentration and cause the wizard to miss snaring a passing thought.

"Tell me more about where this happened," the wizard said at last. "Describe the location for me in detail."

Ulf did so.

"I know of this place of which you speak," Kravig said. "Strange, mysterious things have happened in that part of the forest. It is said that an evil human witch once lived there. It is said that several human beings disappeared without a trace in that area. It is said that the evil witch changed them into evil animals. It is very likely that it was one of these evil animals that you saw."

"Then you think that the strange owl I saw caused the drought we're having?" Ulf asked.

"That is very likely the case," Kravig said.

"This is terrible," Ulf said. "How much longer will the drought last?"

"No one can say," Kravig said. "It depends on how much evil power the owl possesses. From your description of how it acted, I think it is safe to say that is possesses great power."

"But I'm sure that you possess great power too," Ulf said. "Isn't there something you can do to make the drought end?"

"I have a potion that should work against the owl, yes," the wizard said. "In order for it to have its effect, though, you or someone else must be willing to venture into that evil part of the forest to search out this owl and toss the potion on it."

"I will do it," Ulf said. "Give me the potion and I will take it back with me and do it."

"There will be danger for you," Kravig warned. "You should understand that what you are agreeing to do is something that involves much risk. If you get near the owl and the owl senses that you are carrying this potion it is likely that the owl may direct an evil spell at you to try to prevent you from accomplishing your mission. Are you still willing to go ahead?"

"I am," Ulf said. "It seems to me that someone has to do this, and I'm as brave as anyone."

And so it fell to Ulf to seek out this strange owl and try to spray it with the magic potion the troll wizard Kravig gave to him.

Each night Ulf went to the part of the forest where he had encountered the owl the first time to look for the strange creture. Nothing happened for six nights. Ulf saw many creatures, including several owls, but he did not find the large owl he was looking for.

Then on the seventh night, shortly after midnight, Ulf caught sight of the strange owl standing next to an old oak tree. Moonlight bathed the forest this night, allowing Ulf to see the owl from fifty feet away. As before, the owl stood completely silent and still. Ulf kept his eyes trained on the owl as he pulled out the pouch containing the magic potion Kravig had given him. The owl stared intently at Ulf as Ulf began walking slowly toward the owl. Then the owl's eyes began glowing with a peculiar luminescence. Ulf could feel the strength draining from his body. He knew he had to act quickly if he was so accomplish his goal and dust the owl with the magic potion. He ran straight at the owl as fast as he could run under the circumstances. His legs felt so heavy that it seemed to Ulf as if his legs were tree trunks rooted in the ground and he had to yank out the trunks by their roots with each stride. He thought he detected an expression of surprise in the owl's eyes as he staggered forward.

When Ulf was ten feet from the owl, the owl flapped its wings and whirred into the air. Drawing upon every last speck of his dwindling strength, Ulf flung the magic potion at the fleeing owl as he leapt in the owl's direction and crashed to the forest floor face first, falling into unconsciousness.

Raindrops as large as willow leaves awakened Ulf in the morning. He was already soaked by the time he opened his eyes, and the ground around him was saturated as well. Lifting his head, he saw nothing but the trees and bushes of the forest. For a minute, he didn't know where he was or how he had come to be there. Then he remembered. He remembered how he had searched for the strange owl, found it, and flung the magic potion at it as he blacked out from exhaustion brought on by the owl's evil spell. He remembered, and he howled with manic laughter, for rain was falling—sweet, wonderful rain, a hard rain that would swell the mountain streams and make life good again. He laughed with happiness because he knew the magic potion he flung at the owl must have dusted the owl and counteracted the spell the owl had cast to bring about the drought. Nothing had ever felt better to Ulf than the sheets of rain he walked through back to his cave.

■

"Do you think the owl we saw could be a person that was changed into an evil animal?" Ort asked.

"I'm not sure," Kravig said. "Anything's possible. Of course, the owl Ulf saw was far, far away from here."

"It was not a normal owl, I know that," Ort said.

"Well, if anyone sees it again we better take greater heed next time," Kravig said.

25 ▪ Another Prisoner

"**I** caught another one! I caught another one!" Grentd shouted as he ran toward the communal cave where he lived.

"Another what?" someone asked.

"Another gnome!" Grentd crowed, the tone of triumph in his voice.

"Another gnome!" Ort said as he and others followed Grentd into the cave, the same cave where the gnome prisoner named Lekov was being held. "This is too good to be true!"

This being the night after the scouting trip where two trolls were wounded by gunfire; the trolls needed some uplifting news, and the capture of another gnome was high on the list of occurrences that would cheer them. Grentd stuffed the new prisoner into a side alcove that was four feet off the floor and only slightly larger than the birdcage Lekov was in. The alcove had a grid of metal bars across its face, and a lock.

"Tewalt!" Lekov called to his friend. "Oh, not you too!"

"Shut up, you!" Ort snapped at Lekov.

"Lekov!" Tewalt said to his friend. "Are you all right?"

"I've been tortured!" Lekov told him.

"I told you to shut up!" Ort said to him. Turning to the new prisoner, he went on: "So, your name is Tewalt, is it?"

"What of it?" Tewalt said in a defiant tone.

"What's that in the pocket of your smock?" Ort said.

"None of your business," Tewalt said.

"We'll just see about that," Ort said, and easily took a few tools from Tewalt's smock. "I believe these are goldsmith tools, aren't they?"

"What of it?" Tewalt said.

"If you carry goldsmith tools, you must be a goldsmith," Ort reasoned. "Are you?"

"Wouldn't you like to know?" Tewalt said, in such a manner as to make clear he wasn't about to divulge such information.

"Yes, we would," Ort said. "We could use someone like you, to forge gold and silver for us. We have enough work to keep you busy for a long, long time." Over the centuries the trolls had accumulated hundreds of gold nuggets of various sizes, as well as silver and copper, by both theft and luck.

"I wouldn't lift a finger to do anything for a bunch of thieves like you," Tewalt declared.

"Thieves?" Ort said. "We don't like being called thieves. One takes what one can get."

If trolls have a guiding principle, it is that: One takes what one can get.

"I think you'll soon change your mind about working for us," Ort said. "If you don't forge gold for us we'll never set you free. What do you have to say to that?"

"I spit on your stolen gold!" Tewalt said. "You don't think that stupid oafs like you can keep me captive, do you? I'll escape from here as easily as smoke escapes a fireplace."

"Oh, you will, will you?" Ort said. "If it's so easy to escape, then why hasn't your friend over there done so already? It's not as though he wouldn't like to, I'm sure. Are you saying that you are so much greater and smarter than he is?"

Lekov and Tewalt were indeed friends, close friends. Tewalt grew very worried when Lekov disappeared for several days, and when Lekov's wife pleaded with Tewalt to search for Lekov he agreed to do so. Tracing the approximate route Lekov was believed to have followed, a weary Tewalt fell into the same pit-trap just off the forest trail.

"I'm saying that you're all a bunch of ugly, no good, lousy fiends, that's what I'm saying," Tewalt said.

"Let's not give him any food until he agrees to forge gold for us," Hlauka suggested to Ort.

"Better yet," Ort said, "let's put his friend on The Line until he promises to forge gold for us."

One of the trolls took Lekov from his cage as others set up The Line, which was a rope stretched between two walls of the cave, above several burning candles. The trolls attached the gnome to the rope by a loop of twine so they could push him along the rope, through the candle flames.

"You beasts!" Tewalt shouted. "Stop it! Stop it! He'll catch on fire and be burned alive!"

"Say you'll forge gold for us and we'll stop doing it," Ort said.

"Don't do it!" Lekov managed to shout to his friend. "They're lying. They'll make you work and then they'll torture both of us."

At that instant a flame of fire licked the back of Lekov's neck, causing him to cry out in pain.

"Okay, I'll do it for you," Tewalt said. "Just let Lekov loose and stop torturing him." Although he suspected Lekov's fear may well be well founded, that the trolls would torture both of them after extracting all the work they wanted out of him, he couldn't bear to watch his friend tortured. Anyway, he was confident he and Lekov could manage to escape before the situation reached that point, for every gnome he knew about who had been captured by trolls had been able to escape through cunning and deception. The way he saw it, any gnome without wit enough to trick gullible, mush-minded trolls almost deserved whatever fate befell him.

Chuckling with glee, the trolls put Lekov back into his cage and gave Tewalt the items he needed to forge gold. Despite his weariness, Tewalt worked many hours that night, forging a number of rings, bracelets and necklaces. The trolls, males and females alike, adorned themselves with the trinkets and danced around the cave for hours on end, their dancing spastic and disjointed, so that most were covered with perspiration. They forced Tewalt to work until he fell asleep standing up. Rott poked him in the ribs to wake him and said, "Keep working, you, or we'll tease your friend again."

It was mid-morning before the trolls allowed Tewalt to sleep for a few hours. Then they rudely awakened him and forced him to forge more gold.

26 ▪ The Troll
Who Loved Harp Music

The tale Anders read aloud from *A Treasury of Troll Tales* this evening was called *The Troll Who Loved Harp Music.*

■

At first it was only a whisper in the wind, a soft breath in a summer breeze.

Bjork strained his ears to hear the flutter of enchanting sound. *Is it only the breeze?* the lonely troll asked himself. *Can a breeze sound so beautiful?* If it wasn't the wind, what else could sound so delightful out there in the forest? This seemed to be a musical sound. As far as Bjork knew, birds produced the only musical sounds in the forest, and he felt sure no bird made this strange, exotic sound.

As though drawn by a musical magnet, Bjork rose from the ground, where he was seated against a tree trunk, and began walking in the direction from which the sound seemed to emanate, stopping every ten to twenty seconds to listen. It took only a few listening stops before he could tell he was hearing music. A lilting stream of notes flowed in his direction, flooding the forest with a magical melody. Bjork had no idea what was producing such a celestial sound. Not that he thought of it as a celestial sound, of course. The word celestial was no more part of his paltry vocabulary than the concept of a century was part of his limited grasp of time. He simply knew he had never before in his life heard anything more beautiful than the music he was then hearing.

Drawn inexorably toward the music, Bjork walked faster through the forest. He *had* to find out what was producing the music that made his heart ache with its beauty. He wanted to immerse himself in the music as much as he ever wanted to splash cool water on his face on a sweltering summer day.

Eventually he came to a good-sized circular pond. A young woman with flowing blond hair, wearing a flowing white dress, was seated on a large boulder at the edge of the pond, directly across from Bjork, playing a small folk harp. Having never seen a harp, Bjork didn't know what the instrument was. Concealing himself behind a birch tree, he watched the woman strum her harp, producing music so wonderful he felt like one of those fluffy white clouds that float in the sky some days.

Wanting to get even closer to the music, so he could hear it better, Bjork snuck around the pond and came up close behind the harpist, still trying to stay out of sight behind trees. Sensing that someone was staring at her, the young woman slowly turned her head to see if she could spot anyone behind her. At that moment, Bjork poked his head out from behind a tree trunk. Repulsed by the sight of the dirty, disheveled, misshapen troll, the woman let out a piercing scream and nearly dropped her harp in the water.

Bjork rushed out into the open, where the woman could see him. "Don't be afraid," he said. "I just wanted to listen to your music."

"Don't you come near me!" the woman said in a panicky voice. "Stay away from me!"

"You have nothing to fear from me," Bjork said. "I mean you no harm. I heard your music and I came here to see what was making such a beautiful sound. You make the most beautiful music I've ever heard. What do you call that thing you're playing?"

"A harp," the woman told him.

"A harp," Bjork repeated, saying the word slowly and reverently so that the name would stick in his mind. "It is most wonderful. A harp. My name is Bjork. What's your name?"

"Serena," the woman told him.

"I didn't mean to interrupt you," Bjork said. "Please go on playing. I will just sit here on the shore and listen to you, if you don't mind."

"I really should be starting back home," Serena said, wanting to flee from the hairy intruder, but fearful that might be a fatal mistake. "My mother and father will worry about me being gone so long if I don't return home soon."

"Then they'll just have to worry this one day," Bjork said. "I'm sure that I will go mad if I don't hear more music from your harp. I must insist that you play for me some more."

"Well, I guess I could play a couple more tunes for you," Serena said, hoping she could appease him by doing so, and then be able to slip away safely.

Once again her fingers danced on the harp strings and the strings sang with angelic grace.

"I could listen to you play forever," Bjork said. "Now that I have heard harp music I will never be happy without it."

"I really *must* be going now," Serena said, the troll's stated passion making her even more apprehensive.

"I'm not sure that I can allow you to do that," Bjork said. "What if I never have a chance to hear you play the harp again? I'm sure my heart would break and I would wither away and die."

"I promise that I'll come back so that you can hear me again," Serena said.

"When?" Bjork asked. "Tomorrow? Will you come again tomorrow? I don't think I could stand it if I didn't hear harp music again tomorrow."

"Tomorrow?" Serena pondered, thinking she should tell the troll whatever he wanted to hear if it meant escaping from him to save her life. "Sure, I'll come again tomorrow." Even as she made that promise, she knew she had not managed to inject any conviction into her tone of voice. She certainly would have known it was a lie if she heard someone else say the same words in the same manner. She only hoped that this terrible troll was not attuned enough to detect her insincerity. Unfortunately for her, his skills of perception were not quite that dull.

"No you won't," Bjork said bluntly. "You're lying. I can tell that you didn't really mean what you said."

"Why do you think that?" Serena said, trying to bluff her way out of this predicament as her anxiety reached a new peak. "Of course I'll come back again tomorrow to play for you again."

"I don't think I can trust you," Bjork said. "I can see in your eyes that you think I'm ugly and that you are still afraid I'm going to do you harm. I think the thing I better do is take you back to my cabin and keep you there so that I can be sure you will be able to provide me with harp music anytime I want to hear it."

"If you kidnap me I can promise you that I won't play my harp for you," Serena said, desperate to find some way out of the sticky situation, "so you can see that would do you no good."

"Oh, I think you'll play your harp for me if I don't give you anything to eat if you won't" Bjork said confidently.

With harp in hand, Serena bolted from her boulder perch and tried to run from Bjork. The troll quickly overtook her, slung her over one of his shoulders and carried her back to his creaky, dirty cabin deep in the forest, carrying Serena's harp in his other hand. Serena screamed for help, but her cries went unheard.

Bjork chained up Serena in his cabin and tried to make her play her harp, but Serena refused to play. As he had threatened to do, Bjork refused to give Serena anything to eat or drink as long as she refused to play her harp for him. He would not even let her have a sip of water.

By the following afternoon Serena was so desperately thirsty that she agreed to play her harp for the troll if he would give her some water. Bjork kept his word and gave her water after she played two short tunes for him. That was all she would play, though.

By the following day she was so voraciously hungry that she played her harp for Bjork in exchange for some food.

All the while, Serena was trying to formulate a plan of escape. She thought of playing a lullaby over and over to put the troll to sleep, but that would have left her still chained up. She thought of smashing her harp to pieces so that it wouldn't be possible to play it, but that seemed like a perilous course of action. Bjork no doubt would be irate if Serena destroyed the harp and exact a wrathful revenge. After all, as far as Serena could tell, Bjork wasn't in love with Serena but with harp music. That being the case, she had an idea. . .

"How would you like it if I gave you my harp?" Serena asked Bjork.

The troll was stunned. "You would give me your harp?" he said.

"I will if you will let me leave," Serena said. "Just think: If the harp was yours you could hear harp music anytime you wanted to hear it; you wouldn't need me around."

"It would be great to have a harp of my own," Bjork said.

"Unchain me, then, and the harp is yours," Serena said.

Bjork took a couple of steps in Serena's direction, apparently ready to unchain her. All at once something occurred to him, though. "Wait a minute. What good would a harp do me when I don't know how to play it?"

"Well. . ." Serena said, trying to think of something persuasive to say, "I could *teach* you how to play. A harp is one of the easiest instruments there is to play."

"Do you really think you could teach me how to play?" Bjork asked.

"Of course I could," Serena said, knowing such a task would be an enormous challenge, but believing the troll might be satisfied if she could teach him the most rudimentary sort of sounds.

The first lesson began at once and lasted far into the night. After a few short hours of sleep, Serena's teaching continued early the next morning. Hard as she tried, Serena could not make the ham-handed troll produce anything resembling a sweet sound. Until hearing Bjork try to play, Serena would not have believed it was possible to produce such scratchy, discordant, harsh sounds with a harp. Whatever awful noises Bjork made with the harp—and some were so excruciating they caused Serena pure agony—Serena praised Bjork's playing and told him he was improving all the time, for her hope was that the sooner Bjork was satisfied with his own playing the sooner he would release her.

Even a naïve, gullible troll couldn't be completely fooled by totally unwarranted compliments, though. Bjork knew the music he made with the harp—using the word music in an extremely loose sense—was nowhere as nice as the music Serena made when she stroked the strings.

"I'll never make music as pretty as you can," the troll said to Serena. "I'm afraid I can't make myself happy with the music I make. It is only when I listen to you play your beautiful music that I am most happy."

"You mustn't become discouraged so quickly," Serena said. "You can't expect to play as well as me so soon. I've played the harp for many years, after all. I'm sure you'll get the hang of it. You just need more practice, that's all."

But Serena knew this avenue of potential escape was probably blocked because of Bjork's ineptitude. It was doubtful he would ever consider himself a good enough harp player to satisfy his own love of harp music and release Serena. She would have to devise another plan.

Looking around the troll's cabin, trying to spot something that would spark an idea, her eyes fell upon a handsaw amongst a tangled pile of tools.

"I see that you have a saw," she said to Bjork. "Did you know that it's possible to play music with a saw?"

"Really?" the troll said.

"Really," Serena said. "*Anyone* can make music with a saw blade. I'm sure I could teach you how to play music with your saw. I think you might like saw music even better than harp music. Bring the saw over here to me and I'll show you how to play it."

Bjork did as asked, and brought the saw to Serena.

"We also need a bow," Serena said. "Let me think. . . What could we use for a bow? Horsehair is best. Do you know where there are any horses that you could pull hair from?"

"I know where there are horses," Bjork said, "but it would take many hours to go there, get hairs from the horses and come back here."

"Then you must go," Serena said. "We must have horsehair for a bow in order to make the best music."

"But I shouldn't leave you alone for such a long time," Bjork said. "What if someone was to pass by when I was away? He might set you free, then you would run away from me and I wouldn't be able to hear your beautiful harp music, and I know I couldn't stand to live if I couldn't hear such beautiful music."

"Who could ever come upon your little cabin this deep in the forest?" Serena said, desperate to persuade the troll to leave. "I'm afraid that such an occurrence is highly unlikely. You could be gone for several months and no one would find your cabin." Pulling out all stops, Serena went on: "If you go and get horsehair for a bow I'll be able to use the bow on my harp too, and make even more beautiful music than I can play now." Fortunately for her, the troll did not have the faintest idea that was unadulterated claptrap.

"*More* beautiful?" Bjork said, startled at the thought that any music could be any more beautiful than the harp music he had already heard Serena play. "I'll leave right away and get you the horsehair you need."

"Good," Serena said, managing to hold in the grin that wanted to break out on her face.

Before leaving, Bjork checked the metal chain that held Serena captive to make sure it was secure. Satisfied that it was, he set out for a farm where he knew there were horses.

As soon as the troll left Serena picked up the handsaw and began sawing away at one of the links of the sturdy chain. Working feverishly, she pushed and pulled the saw back and forth across the metal until perspiration soaked her dress and hair, the teeth of the saw blade were worn to stubble, and the metal became so hot she couldn't touch it without practically burning herself. Eventually she managed to make a deep enough slice so that she was able to snap apart the link. Wasting no time, she grabbed her harp and fled into the forest, with the broken chain dragging on the ground behind her. Guided by the sun, she ran much of the way home, free at last from the troll who loved her harp music.

Bjork was forever sad after Serena's escape. Every day he listened closely to the wind, hoping to hear a distant hint of harp music. Several times he thought he detected harp music, but every time it proved to be either his ears playing tricks on him or some other sound. Many times he returned to the pond where he first heard Serena play, hoping to find her there again. Serena never went back to that pond again, though, and Bjork never again heard the beautiful harp music he loved so much.

27 ▪ Guggle Has A Plan

Having two gnomes in captivity raised the spirits of all the trolls. Little in their lives was more satisfying than the opportunity to tease a gnome, partly because that opportunity presented itself at such relatively broad intervals. Having two gnome prisoners at the same time was as rare as seeing a double rainbow, so such a state of affairs was to be cherished and relished. Still, there was disquiet within many tribe members, for the noise problem with people hung over their heads like looming thunderclouds. Ort was particularly worried, especially since the shooting incident occurred. He pondered over what could be done to deal with the situation and concluded it was time to consult with Guggle, the troll witch who lived in the forest near the bottom of Troll Mountain, on the opposite side of the mountain from where men were working to create a ski area.

Accompanied by Haar, Traug and Scurf, Ort left his cave shortly before midnight to pay her a visit. Guggle's dwelling was farther from the troll caves than was the ski area worksite, so it took the four a considerable length of time to make the walk to what Guggle thought of as her cottage; most people would have regarded it as a shack, or a hut. The exterior of the small building was a patchwork of various types of wood, rusty sheet metal and cardboard, with moss, mildew and other sorts of growth spattered everywhere. Overlapping pieces of thick moss covered the sagging roof. Tree branches scraped against both the moss roof and two sides of the structure. The door and the shack's two small windows were warped and lopsided. All sorts of debris lay scattered around the cabin—rusty, dented, leaky pails, pieces of scrap metal, broken tools, whole and partial bricks, broken garden tools, and that sort of thing. Many of these objects had been there so long, in one spot, that small trees and bushes had grown up through some of them. Dirt covered other objects, either partially or completely. The cottage blended so well with its forest surroundings that it was difficult to detect there was a building there from more than forty feet away, which is how Guggle liked it.

Luckily for Ort and the three others, Guggle was close to the cottage when they arrived, out gathering plants for both tea and potions. She hadn't seen any members of the tribe in more than a month. From the expressions on the faces of her visitors, she suspected this was more than merely a casual visit. After welcoming Ort and the three others she invited them into her cottage, where she lit two candles, stoked the embers in the fireplace and set several pieces of wood on the hot coals to build a fire to heat water for tea, then sat back and listened while Ort told her about the recent happenings involving people, from the initial noises to the shooting incident.

The cabin's patchwork look carried over into the interior, which consisted of but two rooms—a bedroom and a larger room that served as a combination kitchen and sitting room. That room featured a fireplace and a small, square, wiggly table with three wooden chairs around it. The room's wood floorboards were weathered and uneven. A ragged, musty quilt served as a rug in front of the fireplace. With only three chairs available, two of the trolls—Traug and Scurf—had to stand, leaning against a wall, rather than sit.

Guggle was older than Ort, but not nearly as old as Old Fungus. She had a hooked nose, a pointed chin, long, crooked fingers, more warts than a wolf has teeth, and black, greenish and magenta blotches all over her skin. Her long, once-black—and once-grey—hair was the color of dirty snow. Her clothing was patterned after gypsy fashion, for she liked the look gypsy women she once met, who belonged to a traveling band of gypsies, presented. A large red bandanna covered the top of her head, she wore a flowing print dress dominated by red, and had several necklaces, a couple consisting of animal teeth, and long, colorful silk scarves draped around her wattled neck.

"Is there anything you can do to help put a stop to what the people are doing?" Ort asked Guggle after laying out the problem to her. "We can't allow people to take over this mountain too."

"I have no power to stop bullets, if that's what you're thinking," Guggle said, her cracked glass voice high pitched and assertive. "But we trolls do have certain powers in a situation such as this. There is a certain call that young female trolls can make that has a very good chance of casting a spell on men and putting them under our power. Have four girls come to me tomorrow night and I will teach them the call, and teach them what they can do once they have a man in their power. Once the girls know the call they will be able to draw the men away from the machines and give you a chance to do something."

"Will that really work?" Scurf said. "I thought that people considered us trolls ugly—even female trolls."

"They do," Guggle said, "but this call is something it is hard for men to resist. It will work as I have told you it will work, I assure you."

"I hope so," Ort said. "I'm counting on it."

"Just send me four girls and I will do the rest," Guggle responded. "I have had many dealings with people over the years."

"People are just no darn good," Haar said. "They're nothing but trouble."

"That isn't entirely true," Guggle said. "I have encountered some good people over the years. Not all people are trouble. I have even helped some people who I sensed were good people. I have also punished some bad people, of course, when they had it coming."

"What do you mean?" Haar asked. "How did you punish bad people? And why did you help some people you thought were good?"

"Those are stories for another time, perhaps, not for right now," Guggle said, whetting Haar's curiosity.

"Good people?" Ort said with as much skepticism as the sun has brightness. "If I ever met a good person, I forgot about it a long time ago."

"You perhaps have not had the same experiences I've had with people over the years," Guggle said to him. "I agree with you, though, that what people are doing on the other side of the mountain is a disturbing development."

28 ▪ The Talking Eggs

"How would you like to hear a tale with a witch in it?"
Anders said to his son, Andrew.

"What kind of witch?" Andrew asked.

"A troll witch," Anders said.

With Andrew agreeable to his suggestion, he then read the
following tale to him.

▪

.

A widow with two unmarried daughters, Brigid and Rosetta,
once lived in a mountain foothills region.   Brigid, the older
sister, was lazy and vain.   Rosetta, the younger sister, was hard
working and humble.   Even so, the mother liked Brigid better
because Brigid was the spitting image of her.

The mother pampered Brigid like a princess, for she dreamed
that someday a rich young gentleman would come along and be
smitten by Brigid's beauty, fall in love with her, and marry her.
She knew Brigid would want to share her good fortune with her,
so she envisioned a luxurious life for herself after Brigid married
such a rich young gentleman.   In order to preserve her beauty,
Brigid wasn't allowed to do any chores.   That meant that all of
the work that needed to be done around the place fell upon
Rosetta's shoulders.   The mother doubted any man would ever
want to marry Rosetta because of her physical deformity.   As a
result of a childhood disease, Rosetta walked with a limp.   "No
man wants to marry a cripple," the mother said to Rosetta a
thousand times, well aware that the cruel remark stung Rosetta
more sharply than a slap to the face.

One day the mother sent Rosetta to draw some water from
their well.   While Rosetta was at the well, filling a bucket with

water, a troll witch named Guggle came along and said to her: "Pray, my little one, give me some water. I am very thirsty." Rosetta did not know that Guggle was a troll. To her, the stranger was merely a wrinkled old woman. So she dipped a ladleful of fresh water from her bucket and handed it to Guggle.

"Thank you, my child, you are a good girl," Guggle said, drinking the water and going on her way.

A few days later, while serving tea to her mother and her sister, Rosetta tripped on a loose floorboard and dropped her mother's prized china teapot, which shattered into fifty fragments.

"Now look what you've done, you careless, cursed cripple!" the mother roared at Rosetta, her flaming temper flaring like a forest fire. "I'm going to give you the biggest whipping you've ever had, you better believe it! I'll teach you a lesson you'll never forget!"

The mother swatted at Rosetta's head, but Rosetta ducked away and her mother's fingernails scratched down her upper arm. Fearing for her safety, Rosetta ran from the house to escape her mother's fury. Her mother chased her out the door, but even with her limp Rosetta was able to easily outrun her.

She ran into the nearby forest, and continued running until she could barely breathe any longer. At that point she dropped against a tree to catch her breath and sobbed and sobbed at the thought of what her mother may have done to her and the thought of where she could go, now that returning home would not be safe. After a time, she heard a gentle voice saying, "There, there! Don't cry. Everything's going to be all right."

Wiping away tears, Rosetta looked up to see the same troll witch who had asked her for a drink of water a few days earlier. "I remember you!" Rosetta said.

"And I remember you," Guggle replied. "Tell me, what can the trouble be that makes you cry so?"

"My mother threatened to whip me, and I am afraid to return home," Rosetta explained.

"You did me a good deed, so now I would like to return that good deed to you," the witch said. "Come home with me. I will give you supper and a warm place to sleep for the night."

Rosetta immediately accepted the invitation and Guggle led the way to her small, mossy cottage. It was twilight when they arrived there. Before they came within sight of the cottage, Guggle stopped and said to Rosetta, "I just have one warning for you: You're going to see some queer sights tonight. Whatever you do, don't laugh at or show disgust toward anything you see. None of us on this earth can help being what we are."

As soon as the two of them stepped inside the wobbly fence surrounding the cottage Rosetta spotted a goat unlike any goat she had ever seen. The goat had two heads, one at each end of its body, and silver horns that glinted in the light of a rising moon. It walked in a zig-zag pattern and sidled up to Rosetta, who nearly laughed at the odd-looking, odd-acting creature. Remindful of Guggle's warning, though, she stifled her laugh. When the goat licked the back of her hand, Rosetta scratched both of its heads, behind its ears, which the goat liked very much.

As Rosetta and her hostess walked down the stone path that led to the front door of the cottage, three blue geese waddled across the path and chickens of various colors scattered like large windblown leaves.

"I've never seen such pretty chickens," Rosetta remarked, wondering how they happened to be different colors.

Guggle smiled. "Come inside," she said. "You must be hungry. We'll cook up a kettle of stew."

Embers remained in the fireplace, so it wasn't long before they had a strong fire burning and water heating in an iron kettle suspended over the burning logs. Rosetta watched in fascination as Guggle tossed a large old bone, bits of mushrooms, and several colorful chicken feathers into the kettle. Suddenly the water bubbled and boiled. There was so much steam it was as though a heavy fog had filled the cottage. Rosetta could barely see Guggle, five feet from her. After a few minutes the steam wafted away. Guggle grinned at Rosetta and ladled out savory stew into two deep bowls—stew rich with hunks of meat, potatoes and vegetables.

After their meal the troll witch fixed a bed on the floor in front of the fireplace for her guest and retired to her own bed for the night.

The next morning Guggle said to Rosetta, "It is time for you to go home. As you are a good girl, and showed me kindness, I want you to have some of my special talking eggs. Go to the chicken coop and check the roosts for eggs. All of the eggs that say 'Take me' you must take. All of those that say 'Let me be!' you must not take. Do you understand?"

"Yes," Rosetta answered.

"Good," Guggle said. "Now, on your way home, toss the eggs over your shoulder."

Before Rosetta could ask why she should do such a thing, Guggle said, "Run along now and do exactly what I told you to do, to the very letter."

As Rosetta walked to the chicken coop, she suddenly realized she was walking without a limp. She wondered if she was dreaming. Entering the chicken coop, she found the roosts full of eggs. As she reached for a large one the egg said, "Let me be!" Rosetta pulled back her hand and reached for another. It also cried "Let me be!," so Rosetta left it alone as well. As if recognizing Rosetta's presence, all of the smallest eggs called out, "Take me! Take me!" Rosetta gathered all of the eggs that said "Take me, take me!" into a basket Guggle had given her and started home.

When she had walked some distance she remembered how Guggle had told her to toss the eggs over her shoulder. Although it seemed sinful to waste food, after what she had witnessed at Guggle's cottage it seemed advisable to do what Guggle had asked her to do. "Well, here goes," she said, taking one of the eggs from the basket and tossing it behind her. The egg landed with a splat. Rosetta turned around expecting to see a gooey mess. Instead, she saw only a pile of gold coins surrounded by a ring of silver coins.

Rosetta tossed a second egg. It cracked open to reveal a diamond pendant. The third egg contained a beautiful silk dress, the fourth gemstone jewelry, the fifth a sapphire ring, and the rest more fine clothes, elegant vases, bronze statuettes, and other treasures.

When she arrived home with her load of valuable treasures her mother and her sister Brigid were dumbstruck with puzzlement. They gawked at and stroked Rosetta's treasures for a couple of minutes without saying a word before the mother asked, "Where in the world did you get all this? Did you go and steal them from some rich folks' house?"

"You know I wouldn't steal anything from anyone," Rosetta answered. "An old woman I met in the forest gave all of these things to me."

As Rosetta carried the treasures into the house, Brigid pointed at her legs and said to her mother, "Look! She can walk like you and me! She's not limping."

"Oh, that's right!" Rosetta said. "The old woman cured my leg too."

The rest of that day Rosetta's mother and sister were nicer to her than they ever had been. All of the anger the mother had directed at Rosetta the previous day had flown from her heart as suddenly as birds flit from a tree branch. Brigid and her mother plied Rosetta with question after question about the old woman Rosetta had met, wanting to know where she lived and what she looked like. Rosetta answered all of their questions honestly, as fully as she was able.

After pulling all of the information they could from Rosetta, the mother said to Brigid, "You must go into the forest and look for this old woman yourself. You must have fine dresses and splendid jewelry too."

And so the following day Brigid ventured into the forest in search of the old woman's little run-down cottage. It took her most of the day, but she finally found it as the sun slipped behind the western horizon. Guggle was hoeing in her garden when Brigid arrived. Weeping in mock anguish, Brigid told Guggle she had run away from home because her mother mistreated her and asked if she could spend the night there.

"Why, of course you can!" Guggle said. "I'll be glad to put you up for the night. It's always nice to have some company. I should warn you, though, that you're likely to see some odd things around this place. Whatever you do, don't laugh at or show disgust toward anything you see. None of us on this earth can help being what we are."

As Guggle spoke, the two-headed goat sidled over to Brigid and licked her hand. "Eeek!" Brigid screamed, jerking away her hand. "Get that thing away from me!"

Guggle called the goat to her side and invited Brigid into her cottage.

"*This* is your cottage?!" Brigid said. "I thought it was your chicken coop. What a creaky little cottage you have! It's a wonder a strong wind didn't blow it down long ago."

Inside, Guggle said, "I was just about to have my supper. Would you like to help me make a kettle of stew?"

"I've never cooked anything in my life!" Brigid said indignantly. "I'll let you do it."

"As you wish," Guggle said, proceeding to cook up a kettle of stew as Brigid watched her.

Try as she did, Brigid was unable to hide her true character. She couldn't contain her tongue any better than a baby is able to contain its crying. She laughed at and ridiculed nearly everything in and about the cottage. She criticized the stew and pushed it aside after taking only a couple of small bites. Every time Guggle turned her back to her she made a sour face, stuck out her tongue at the old woman, or rolled her eyes because she found the troll so grotesque.

Guggle caught glimpses of some of Brigid's disdainful actions, but she let them pass without saying a word. She had a plan of retaliation in mind for the morning, though.

Since Brigid refused to sleep on the floor, Guggle allowed her visitor to sleep on her bed and slept on the floor herself.

"**I** hate to see a mother and a daughter at odds with one another," Guggle said to Brigid in the morning. "If you promise to return home I will give you a present to take back to your mother that will make all the troubles between you disappear."

"That would be wonderful!" Brigid said, visions of fine clothes, sparkling jewelry and piles of coins dancing in her head. "You have my promise."

Just as she had explained to Rosetta, Guggle told Brigid about the talking eggs and how she should take those that said "Take me" and leave those that said "Let me be," then toss the eggs over a shoulder on her way home.

As soon as Brigid entered the chicken coop all of the eggs began saying either "Take me!" or "Let me be!," with an equal number speaking each phrase. Brigid noticed that all of the ones saying "Let me be" were larger. "I bet the ones saying 'Let me be' are truly special ones the ugly old woman wants to keep for herself," she thought. "If the ones that said 'Take me' held such treasures, I can only imagine what fantastic treasures those saying 'Let me be' contain!"

Smirking at how she was outwitting the old woman, Brigid gathered up all of the eggs that said "Let me be!" and left all of those that said "Take me."

After Brigid left, Guggle went to the chicken coop and discovered that only the "Take me" eggs remained. She cackled with delight to know she had gauged Bridgit's greed perfectly, and at the fact that Brigid had taken the eggs Guggle wanted her to take.

Brigid was no sooner out of sight of Guggle's cottage before she tossed one of the eggs over her shoulder. She didn't even wait for the egg to hit the ground before turning around to see what treasure it would give forth. When it hit the ground and cracked open, a hundred huge spiders crawled out.

Brigid screamed and tossed another egg over her shoulder. It cracked open to release a dozen slithering snakes. Brigid screamed again, terrified by what was happening. Her hands started shaking as the remaining eggs in her basket began rumbling. She threw the entire basket of eggs aside. When the eggs broke, freakish frogs and toads, monstrous rats, misshapen snapping turtles, and all sorts of other vile animals and reptiles appeared. Brigid shrieked and started running through the forest as the creatures pursued her at a speed she was barely able to match. She ran all the way home, with the reptiles and the large rats close behind her the entire distance. She arrived home nearly out of breath, so terrified she was trembling.

When her mother saw all of the snakes, giant frogs and other creatures that had followed Brigid home she was so angry that she punished Brigid by making her do all of the housework for a month while letting Rosetta take it easy during that time. After that Brigid never again received special treatment, but had to share the workload equally with her sister.

29 • The Cursed Garden

The night after Ort and the three others visited her, Guggle sat in her cottage thinking about one of her unpleasant encounters with a human being as she waited for other visitors to arrive this night. People know the tale of that encounter in the following form:

■

While planting a garden one fine Spring morning, Marja Renstrom heard footsteps approaching through the nearby woods. Looking up, she saw an ugly old woman in tattered clothing and a large bonnet emerge from the edge of the woods. At least she at first thought it was an old woman. As the stranger drew nearer Marja could see that the passerby was not an old woman, after all, but a female troll. Indeed, this was none other than a troll witch named Guggle, though Marja had no way of knowing she was a witch.

Marja's husband, a carpenter, was not at home; Marja was all by herself. Because of that, the troll's presence made her doubly worried. She was fearful of what the troll might do to her, for she had heard many stories about how trolls had tried to harm and rob people.

"Don't come any nearer," Marja said to the troll once she realized that Guggle was a troll. "What are you doing here?"

"I am a weary traveler walking from village to village looking for work," Guggle said, trying her best to conceal her face with her bonnet. "I'm afraid that I have lost my way. All of my food is gone and I have nothing left to eat. Could you spare a crust of bread and a cup of milk for an old woman down on her luck?"

"I won't spare a single crumb of bread or a single drop of milk for a worthless troll, for that is what you are," Marja said, picking up a pitchfork that was stuck in the ground close to her and brandishing the pitchfork at Guggle. "Now, be gone with you!"

"You are mistaken," Guggle said. "I am not a troll. I am a poor old woman asking for a simple kindness."

"If that's true, remove your bonnet so that I can see your face better," Marja said.

"I don't have to remove my bonnet to prove anything to you!" Guggle said angrily. "I will give you one last chance to give me something to eat. If you don't, I shall be forced to take certain measures."

"What measures?" Marja asked, strengthening her grip on the pitchfork in the event it became necessary to use it as a weapon.

"I have certain powers," Guggle stated. "I see that you are planting a garden. If you refuse me any food I will put a curse on your garden. Because of my curse your garden will be filled with weeds and thistles. If you pull out the weeds and thistles to try to get rid of them, ten times as many will grow in their place overnight. You will find it impossible to rid your garden of weeds and thistles. Any vegetables that do manage to grow amongst the weeds and the thistles will be stunted and woody and not worth picking."

"I don't believe in your silly curses," Marja said boldly. "Go away. You'll get nothing from me except contempt."

"I have given you fair warning," Guggle said. "Because of how you have treated me, I will now place a curse on your garden."

With that, she intoned these words while tossing a pinch of some ground herb mixture into the air so that the breeze blew it over into the garden:

May this garden's planted seeds
Produce an endless growth of weeds.
Thistle-do and thistle-dee,
Curse this plot of land for me.
Thistle-fi and thistle-fo,
Allow no bit of food to grow.

"It is done," she proclaimed. "'From now on this garden will be great for growing thistles, but not much else. You will learn a hard lesson because of your hard heart." She then turned her back to Marja and continued on her way.

Marja chuckled to herself at what she considered the ridiculousness of Guggle's action. She no more believed that Guggle had cursed the garden than she believed she could sit on a cloud if she could jump high enough. As she resumed planting seeds in the rich soil she resolved to work extraordinarily hard in the garden that summer so that she would have her best garden ever and be able to ridicule the ineffectiveness of the troll witch's curse.

Marja's husband, Gunnar, wasn't nearly as unruffled by the incident as Marja was when he learned what had happened that day, for Gunnar had a far greater belief in curses, charms and witchery than his wife did.

"What a terrible worry to have over us," Gunnar said to Marja. "If we get nothing from our garden how will we survive? We may have to turn to begging ourselves to get the vegetables we need."

"Now, don't go thinking that way," Marja said. "Believe me, the curse will have as much effect on our garden as one termite would trying to eat a house by itself. I am determined that we will have our best garden ever."

"Determination is one thing," Gunnar said. "A troll's curse is something else entirely, especially if that troll is a troll witch, as the troll who cursed our garden probably was. I hope for our sakes that you are right about this, but I fear deeply that the troll's curse will come to haunt us worse than any ghost ever could."

Sadly for Marja and Gunnar, Gunnar's fear proved to be well-founded. Weeds and thistles reigned in the Renstroms' garden that summer with kingly and queenly dominance. The few runty vegetables that managed to grow were either spongy or stone-like. They were all but inedible. Marja pulled weeds until her hands bled and blisters formed on top of blisters, and hacked down thistles the size of small trees. As the troll witch had warned, however, for every weed she pulled and every thistle she cut, ten new ones grew in its place overnight.

Eventually she had to admit that trying to overcome the troll witch's magic was an impossible task. Conceding defeat, she let the weeds and thistles completely inundate the garden.

Gunnar, who was quite experienced in carving decorative designs and patterns into furniture he built, decided to carve a troll from a large stump at the edge of the garden as a symbolic reminder to his wife of how their garden had been ruined that year. He worked on the carving for several days before it was finished.

"Let that serve as a lesson to you," Gunnar said to Marja, who seethed with resentment at how her husband blamed her for the weed-choked garden and seemingly wanted to rub her face in the misfortune.

When Gunnar left the following morning to do some carpentry work at a neighboring farm Marja stood looking at the troll carving for a time, growing increasingly irritated about it by the minute. Finally she simply couldn't stand it any longer. She wasn't about to put up with that accusatory troll carving for years to come. The carving would be a constant reminder that her husband had not forgiven her for something she believed wasn't even her fault. The carving had to go!

Marja brought out an axe and started whacking away at the carving. After a few blows she stopped for a breather.

"My, my! What happened here?" Marja heard a voice perhaps thirty feet behind her say. "It looks as though your garden didn't do very well this year. What a pity!"

The voice sounded vaguely familiar, but Marja couldn't quite place it. Swinging around to see who was there, Marja immediately recognized Guggle, the troll witch, who was once again trying to disguise herself as an old woman, as she had on her previous fateful visit. "It's you again!" Marja exclaimed. "What are you doing here?"

"Oh, I was just passing through," Guggle said, "so I thought I would stop to have a look at how your garden is coming along. Quite poorly, I see. I warned you that you would learn a hard lesson because of your hard heart."

"I may be able to teach you a lesson too," Marja said, lifting the axe and taking a couple of menacing steps toward Guggle.

When Marja moved from in front of the troll carving Guggle gasped and her head jerked backward in shock at the site of the carving. "That's Jorgum!" she said. By coincidence, the troll figure Gunnar carved from the stump looked exactly like a living troll named Jorgum, who just happened to be Guggle's son. "Is he dead? Why, I spoke to him only yesterday. Now you've gone and killed him!"

"We didn't kill anyone," Marja said. "That's a carving. My husband made it."

"What were you doing to it with the axe?" Guggle asked.

"I'm chopping it apart," Marja said.

"Chopping it apart?!" Guggle said. "But why? Oh, I see! You're putting a curse on Jorgum, aren't you?"

Marja opened her mouth to tell Guggle she was chopping apart the carving because she detested the sight of it, but then thought better of that. She reasoned that if Guggle wanted to believe she was putting a curse on this Jorgum character she might be able to use that misconception to her advantage.

"You bet I am," Marja said. "I'm putting a curse on him because he's your son and you put a curse on our garden. He's going to suffer horrible pain and suffering because of what you've done."

"Oh, no!" Guggle cried out. "Spare him! Please spare him! I'll remove the curse from your garden if you promise me that you won't put a curse on Jorgum."

"That sounds fair," Marja said, brandishing her axe. "Go ahead, remove the curse."

Guggle made a series of gestures and intoned the following words:

Garden full of burrs and weeds,
Clear the way for planted seeds.
Thistle-nigh and thistle-near,
Make the evil disappear.
Thistle-up and thistle-down,
Remove the curse upon this ground.

"It is done," Guggle then declared. "The curse has been removed. Your garden will once again be productive. All of the weeds and thistles will die out in a few days and the vegetables will grow large and sweet."

"If you are telling the truth, then you have my word that your son will not be harmed by me," Marja said.

"For your sake, I pray that you keep your word," Guggle said, "for if you don't you can be sure that I will return and put an even worse curse on you."

"If you keep your word I'll keep mine," Marja promised, setting aside the axe.

The troll witch left then.

Just as Guggle forecast, the weeds and the thistles in the Renstroms' garden all withered and died within a matter of days. The vegetable plants started growing with a vengeance, giving Marja and Gunnar a bountiful harvest that autumn.

Forever after, Marja had a warm place in her heart for the troll figure Gunnar carved from a stump. She even came to regard it as a good luck charm. It remained by the side of the garden for many years before the stump of which it was a part rotted to powder and weather elements wore it away.

30 ▪ A Chase Through The Night

The trolls kept Tewalt, the gnome goldsmith, busy to the edge of exhaustion, forcing him to forge trinkets and jewelry. Having their own personal goldsmith working for them made up for the fact they no longer had the pleasure of torturing Lekov, the other gnome prisoner. They tortured Lekov only a couple of times after capturing Tewalt, when Tewalt refused to forge any more gold. "Okay, then, we'll tease your friend then," the trolls said to Tewalt on those occasions, then took Lekov from his cage and tortured him until Tewalt could no longer bear to watch and listen and quickly relented and agreed to forge more gold. One of those occasions involved Scurf flicking a knife as near to Lekov's feet as he could, with Lekov's hands and feet tied. Tewalt begged for an end to that game when the knife blade missed Lekov's left foot by no more than the thickness of two hairs.

When some of the trolls, with Old Fungus being the most vocal, grumbled about having two gnomes in captivity and not taking the full measure of pleasure by teasing them to the hilt, Ort deflected the disgruntlement by promising that after Tewalt forged all of the gold nuggets they had accumulated they would give both gnomes double doses of teasing to make up for lost time.

Ort selected Tala, Jompa, Skimpa and Elseth as the four female trolls best suited to be part of the plan Guggle had cooked up. While Guggle had specified that she wanted young females, only Elseth and Tala met that specification, so two older tribe members would need to be involved if there were to be four. The night after Ort and three others visited Guggle, the four troll women Ort selected went to the witch's cabin to learn a special man-attracting call from her. It took Guggle much of the night to teach the four the intricate call and instruct them as to what they should do to lead a man astray after he responded to the call. "I think you're all ready!" Guggle said at last, confident the four were capable of carrying out their important assignment.

The following night Ort took Tala, Jompa, Skimpa and Elseth down the mountain to the construction site, along with three other male trolls—Haar, Drulle and Dau, who had been grazed by a bullet. This was the first time any of the trolls had returned to the site since the night of the shootings. Gangl was recovering nicely, and Dau felt no ill affects. Ort sent out Haar as a scout to find out if the site was still being guarded, which Ort assumed it was, while the others remained hidden in the forest a good distance away.

"I saw two men on guard," Haar reported when he returned to where the others were waiting.

"Well, that doesn't surprise me," Ort said. "Actually, I thought there probably would be more than two men there guarding things. Do you think there could be others around you didn't see?"

"I don't think so," Haar replied. "There seemed to be only two."

"They no doubt both have guns," Ort said. "That means we'll have to go ahead and try the plan Guggle gave us, and hope that Guggle knows what she's doing. Are you girls ready to do your thing?"

The four female trolls Guggle coached the previous night all said that they were ready, so Ort sent Tala and Elseth in one direction and Jompa and Skimpa in another direction, with instructions as to what they should do. "We're all counting on you," he called after them in encouragement, in a loud whisper. Ort and the other three male trolls then crept closer to the construction site so they would be able to see how the men reacted to the female calls and be in position to raid the site if Guggle's plan worked as envisioned.

After a time, Tala and Elseth began voicing the haunting, bird-like call Guggle had taught them. The two construction site guards, who were sitting on lawn chairs talking, perked up their ears and listened attentively, trying to figure out where the calls were coming from. As Tala and Elseth continued calling, the two men stood up, walked around, spoke to one another, and pointed off into the forest to where Tala and Elseth were producing the calls. Both men seemed to be headed in that direction when Jompa and Skimpa started calling from elsewhere in the forest. This seemed to both thoroughly enthrall and confuse the men. They twisted and swiveled their heads and started first in one direction and then in another direction, bumping into each other a couple of times in their confused, overwrought state.

The four male trolls, who had a clear view of how the two men reacted to the calling, bounced around with delight and tittered with laughter. *This* was entertainment! "The calls are working all right," Haar said gleefully. "Just look at them!"

"But why aren't they leaving?" Dau said. "I thought the whole idea of all this was that they would follow the calls."

"Give them time," Ort said. "Give them time. The poor, stupid saps are so delirious right now that they don't know what to do. I'll bet you the first stone's throw that they leave soon."

Just as Ort predicted, the two men soon abandoned their post. After conversing briefly, one of them headed off in the direction of one call, the other in the opposite direction. The two men were barely out of sight before Ort, Haar, Dau and Drulle charged out into the open and had themselves a high old time stoning machinery, ripping parts off of machines with their bare hands, and dancing about celebrating their vandalism.

In the meantime, the four female trolls led the two men on merry chases through the forest for several hours. Tala and Elseth led their pursuer through thorns and brambles, bogs and bushes. At one point the two trolls split up and drove the man half-crazy with their seductive calls. The man would follow one call and be almost to the source when the other troll called from elsewhere, causing the man to abruptly change directions. When he came near the second troll—Elseth, say—Tala, having moved to a different spot, would call again, and the man would respond to that call. Tala and Elseth kept up this game for about a half-hour, by which point the man was a nervous wreck, moving in jerky motions and unable to keep his head still. After leading him through one last bog to get him thoroughly soaked, Tala and Elseth shrieked out peels of maniacal laughter to let the man know he had been fooled, and to stop him from following them any longer. They left the man soaked, shivering, and exhausted deep in the forest. His clothes were ripped, torn and stained. Blood trickled from several of the dozens of cuts and scratches he sustained during the chase. His gun was long since lost, swallowed by moss in a bog when he tried to use the gun as a walking stick and let go of it as he lost his balance at one point.

It was much the same story with Jompa and Skimpa and the man who followed them, except that he was led through only one bog.

31 ▪ Olafur And The Trolls

"**W**hat in the world is going on there, anyway?" Emma
Branstad said to her husband, Anders, after Anders told her what
had met him and the other workers at the Troll Mountain Ski
Resort construction site that morning.

"It sure looks like some people don't want the ski area built,
for some reason," Anders said. "No one can figure out why. It's
going to be a great place, once we get it built. Of course, all of
this vandalism certainly isn't helping matters."

That evening Anders read his son, Andrew, another tale from
A Treasury of Troll Tales, this one called *Olafur And The Trolls.*

▪

Once when a group of charcoal burners went into a forest to
cut wood for charcoal they took a lad named Olafur with them to
look after their horses.

Left alone with the horses, Olafur strolled a short distance
away, investigating that part of the forest. Suddenly a giant troll-
woman swooped down upon him, seized him in her arms, and
ran off with him. She ran until she came to some great rocks in
the heart of the wilderness. The troll-woman's cave was in those
rocks, and she carried Olafur into her cave.

A second troll-woman was inside the cave when they arrived.
She was younger, but equally tall. Both were dressed in horse-
leather tunics that fell to their feet.

The two trolls kept Olafur imprisoned in the dark, dank cave.
They did not restrain him with chains or rope, but they kept
careful watch over him. While one was out catching trout for the
three of them to eat—as one or the other of them nearly always
was—the other kept an eye on Olafur so that he would not run
away. At night the two trolls forced Olafur to sleep between
them on a horse-skin bed. Sometimes the trolls lulled him to

sleep with magical songs so that Olafur would have wonderful, enchanted dreams.

Except for the fact they would not permit him to leave, the two trolls treated Olafur quite kindly. They fed him well, did not physically harm him in any way, and allowed him to go outside for fresh air every day. As time went on, they even relaxed their guard somewhat.

One day the trolls relaxed their guard to the extent of leaving Olafur by himself. As he stood outside the cave wondering if he should try to take advantage of the opportunity to try to escape, or if he likely would get lost in the thick, vast forest if he made such an attempt, Olafur spotted wisps of smoke far in the distance, across the expanse of wilderness. "It must be the smoke of charcoal burners!" he thought to himself.

His feet reacted almost instantaneously with his brain making the decision that he should run toward the smoke as fast as his little legs would carry him. He went no more than thirty or forty strides, though, before the younger troll-woman saw him, ran after him, and quickly overtook him. She slapped Olafur across one of his cheeks, which sent him reeling to the ground, then seized him in her arms and carried him back to the cave.

After that incident the two trolls never again left Olafur alone. They resumed a vigilant watch, with at least one of them remaining within sight of their prisoner at all times.

A bruise remained on the cheek where the younger troll had struck Olafur. Apparently feeling some remorse for the injury she had inflicted, the younger troll occasionally touched Olafur's bare cheek with the back of one of her corrugated-skin hands. Whenver she did, her hand seemed to burn like fire. When she asked the older troll why that happened the older troll said, "There's nothing mysterious about that. You feel a burning because of what the boy has been taught by ministers and other miserable people about prayer and faith and the Christian religion." To trolls, religious faith of any kind, especially Christian faith, is as abominable as field blight to farmers.

Three years passed, with Olafur still held prisoner, all the while trying to devise some foolproof plan of escape. Finally he thought of a scheme that he felt just might work. He waited until the charcoal burning season to put the plan into action, for he knew there would be people in the forest then, and smoke that would signal their location.

What Olafur did was pretend to be sick. He told the trolls that he could not eat any food because of his sickness. As hungry as he was, Olafur refused everything the two troll-women tried to force him to eat.

Alarmed by how his health seemed to be failing, the trolls tried chanting and sprinkling various potions over Olafur to try to heal him. Olafur only feigned greater pain and growing weakness. "You *have* to eat something," the older troll said to him, "or you'll die." She no more wanted him to die than she wanted to hear church bells peal. "Think hard. Isn't there some type of food you would be able to eat?"

Olafur pretended to think hard for several seconds. "I've always had a fancy for shark flesh that has been dried in the wind for nine years," he told the worried troll.

"We are in the middle of a forest, child," the old troll-woman said. "There is no shark flesh to be found around here."

"But you could find some in the village of Ogur, on the western coast," Olafur said. "Please try to get some for me."

"If that is what you need, that is what I will try to find," the old troll said, and left immediately to search for the delicacy Olafur requested.

Soon after the old troll-woman left Olafur pretended to fall asleep. The younger troll recognized that as an opportunity to slip away and catch some trout for herself. After allowing her several minutes to get some distance away from the cave, Olafur rose to his feet and went to the cave entrance. Pausing just long enough to assure himself that the troll was not within sight or sound, Olafur bolted through the forest in the direction where smoke rose above the trees in the distance. He never looked back. He didn't so much as pause for breath. He simply ran and ran until he caught sight of charcoal burners—a sight to him as sweet as sugar to taste buds. These, in fact, were the same charcoal burners who took Olafur into the forest with them three years previously, and so they were as glad to see him as grass roots are to feel rain after a months-long drought.

The charcoal burners gave Olafur food and water and listened to his tale of how he was captured by trolls and held prisoner for three years.   After hearing his story, the charcoal burners mounted their horses and sped homeward with Olafur, for they were worried that once the trolls discovered Olafur was missing they would scour the forest for him, with vengeance foremost in mind.

32 ▪ A Key Development

One night, when giving Tewalt some food, Gangl had a difficult time unlocking the lock to the gnome prisoner's barred alcove. As Gangl cursed the lock while trying to make the key unlock it, Tewalt said to him: "It's not working because the teeth of the key have been rubbed away, you idiot. What you need is a new key. I'll make you one. Bring me some copper." Even as a prisoner, Tewalt maintained dignity by giving trolls orders rather than meekly making requests. They might have had his body trapped, but he wasn't about to let them trap his mind or take away his dignity.

As requested, or ordered, the trolls brought Tewalt some scrap sheet-copper so that he could make a new key for the lock. Whistling while he worked, Tewalt used a special whistling pattern as a way of signaling Lekov that he wanted him to distract the two trolls in the cave. Understanding the signal, Lekov did whatever he could think of to make the two trolls in the cave, Gangl and Hlauka, take their eyes off of Tewalt and draw their attention to him. He complained, asked questions, made strange sounds, jumped around in his cage, and engaged in other actions that had the trolls focusing their attention on him. Using the original key as a template, Tewalt made not one but two duplicates, managing to do so without the two trolls noticing he made an extra one.

At one point Hlauka said to Tewalt, "Aren't you finished making that new key yet? What's taking you so long?"

"I want to have it just right," Tewalt said, hoping to allay suspicion. "I take pride in what I do. I'll let you know when I'm finished. There's no need for you to concern yourself with it."

With Lekov doing a wonderful job of making the trolls focus their attention on him, Tewalt was able to use eye and head signals to communicate with Lekov. When it came to the critical moment, Lekov raised a ruckus that had both trolls shouting at him to be quiet and settle down. That distraction allowed

Tewalt to slip one of the new copper keys into a crack in a cave wall without the two trolls detecting his action.

"Well, here it is," Tewalt said to Gangl and Hlauka, holding up the other new copper key. "Want to try it out?"

Gangl tried the new key in the lock and found that it worked as smooth as silk. "I'll take that other key too," he said to Tewalt, giving Tewalt a momentary sinking feeling in the pit of his stomach before Gangl pointed at the old key and said, "Yeah, that one."

"You can leave that one with me if you like," Tewalt said.

"Give it here!" Gangl snapped, grabbing the old key from the gnome as he grumbled something unintelligible.

"You're welcome," Tewalt said as Gangl stepped back from the side alcove where Tewalt was.

"What?!" Gangl said.

"I said you're welcome," Tewalt said. "Didn't you just thank me for making you a new key?"

"Foo on you!" Gangl spat.

"Be quiet, both of you," Hlauka ordered the two gnome prisoners, "or we'll have some fun with you. I think you know what I mean."

Tewalt and Lekov did indeed know what he meant; he meant torture. They were quiet then, for Tewalt had accomplished what he wanted to accomplish and was confident that escape was now merely a matter of time and opportunity.

That opportunity presented itself the very next night when all of the trolls who lived in the communal cave where Lekov and Tewalt were caged prisoners headed out for the night on various missions of mischief and scavenging. This was not the first time the two gnomes had been left alone, for the trolls were confident the gnomes were securely imprisoned and so believed they did not require constant watch.

Three minutes after the last two trolls left the cave, Tewalt, hoping all of the trolls had truly left and none would suddenly return for some reason, pulled the secreted key from the crack in the wall and reached through the bars to unlock the lock holding him captive. Being a skilled rock climber, he had no difficulty climbing down the rock wall of the cave to the floor. Once there, he zipped across the large chamber of the cave, to the left edge of the fireplace, and scaled up to where the trolls kept the key to Lekov's birdcage. "Catch!" he called to Lekov, tossing him the key. Pushing his right arm through bars of the birdcage, Lekov snared the key out of the air with his hand. "Hurry!" Tewalt said. "Unlock the door and climb down." Tewall then nimbly clambered down to the floor again as Lekov used the key to open the door of the birdcage.

At that moment, Old Fungus shambled through the mouth of the cave, more or less shuffling his feet and supporting himself with his faithful old, gnarly walking stick. Knowing that everyone was away from the cave, Old Fungus thought he would take advantage of that situation to torture the two gnome prisoners, and he had gone to the cave with the idea of teasing them. Ort might have thought it best to delay such torture—or teasing, as trolls preferred to call it—but he didn't agree with Ort on that point and saw no reason why he couldn't do some extra teasing when Ort wouldn't need to know anything about it.

"Hey!" Old Fungus called to Lekov, since the birdcage was the first thing he looked at upon entering the cave. "What's going on here?" He headed straight toward Lekov, without even glancing around to see if the other gnome was still locked up, as Lekov started climbing down a knobby wall. "Stop right where you are, you scamp!" Old Fungus ordered, making a beeline toward Lekov as fast as his old, arthritic legs would take him.

With Old Fungus directing his complete attention on Lekov, Tewalt was able to pick up a handy piece of iron, sneak up on the troll from behind, and use the piece of iron to knock Old Fungus's walking stick off the ground just as Old Fungus was putting the maximum amount of support pressure on the walking stick. Set off-balance, Old Fungus tumbled forward, face-first. His long, thick nose hit the floor of the cave first, which stung like the dickens. He also wrenched his right shoulder trying to brace himself against the fall. By then Lekov had reached the ground.

"Come on! Let's run!" Tewalt said to Lekov, and the two gnomes ran from the cave as Old Fungus moaned with pain that was both physical and psychic as he tried to rise to his feet. Once outside the cave, the two gnomes quickly put distance between themselves and the troll caves and wended their way through the forest toward their homes.

33 ▪ Mirror Image

"I liked that story you read about the troll witch," Andrew Branstad said to his father.

"You did, huh?" Anders said. "How about the one we read before that, the one about the boy who was captured by two giant troll women? Did you like that one?"

Andrew thought a moment. "I think I may have liked that one even better."

"Maybe because it involved a boy about your age?" Anders suggested.

"I don't know. Maybe," Andrew sort of muttered.

"How would you like to hear another story that involves a woman troll?" Anders said, with one in mind.

"Does she kidnap a person too?" Andrew asked.

"Well, you'll just have to wait and see," Anders answered. "I'm not going to tell you the ending before I read you the story. It's more exciting when you don't know where the story will lead."

"What's it called?" Andrew asked.

"It's called *Mirror Image*," Anders told him, and proceeded to read the tale.

▪

One day when Ingrid Ostland went walking in the woods near her village a troll woman named Skimpa, who was out gathering wild berries, saw Ingrid advancing along a path, hid behind the trunk of a large tree, and jumped out in front of Ingrid when she reached that spot.

"What are you doing here?" the troll demanded gruffly.

"I'm merely out for a walk," Ingrid managed to say, frightened as she was by this ogreish creature, who had stubby limbs, misshapen fingers, skin as rough as coarse sandpaper, button-like ears that stuck out sideways from her head, a bulbous nose, and no eyebrows.

"You humans are disgusting," Skimpa said. "You think you have the right to go anywhere just because you're so pretty, don't you?"

"I have to be getting back home now," Ingrid said, wanting to run to get away from this embittered troll woman, but fearing that if she tried to run the troll might overtake her and do who knew what to her. "I'm afraid I walked farther than I had planned to walk, and I'll be late getting supper started as it is."

"Not so fast!" the troll virtually growled, as Ingrid took a couple of steps back in the direction from which she had come. Skimpa scurried around Ingrid to block her retreat.

"That certainly is a lovely necklace you have," Skimpa commented about the string of turquoise stones threaded through a gold-plated chain that made up Ingrid's necklace.

"Thank you," Ingrid said.

The turquoise necklace was Ingrid's favorite piece of jewelry. She liked it for its pure beauty, and the fact that her husband gave it to her as an anniversary gift made it extra special to her. She didn't want to reveal that to this resentful troll woman, though. Knowing that trolls liked to collect such treasures, by hook or by crook, she was afraid that the more special the necklace seemed to the troll the more she would want it.

"It's not worth much, really," Ingrid said. "It probably looks prettier than it really is in this bad light."

"If you don't think much of it, then you wouldn't mind giving it to me, would you?" Skimpa said, with a forced sweetness that could not entirely mask the sneer in her voice.

"Oh, I'm afraid I couldn't do that," Ingrid said. Since the low-key approach wasn't working, she decided to play an empathy card. "It was a gift from my husband, you see, and he would be angry with me if I gave it away." Ingrid hoped that any woman, even a troll woman, would empathize with such a declared sentimental attachment.

"Would your husband be angrier if you came home without the necklace or with one eye plucked out?" Skimpa said, as casually as though asking someone if she wanted tea or water to drink. "If you don't give me the necklace I will be forced to pluck out one of your eyes and take the necklace from you."

Perspiration poured from Ingrid's forehead. This troll woman certainly appeared to be strong enough, and spiteful enough, to pluck out someone's eye. What was Ingrid to do? The turquoise necklace was one of her most precious possessions, and yet she wasn't about to sacrifice an eye in an effort to keep it. She was set to remove what was to her a priceless necklace and hand it over to the troll when a sudden thought struck her like a bolt of lightning. If the scheme she had in mind worked, she would be able to keep the necklace and all would end well. If anything was to go haywire, though, she feared the troll would show her no mercy and do something worse than pluck out one of her eyes. She had always been told that trolls are very gullible; she prayed that was true, for the trick she was about to attempt required an extremely gullible victim.

"If I gave you something much, much more valuable than this necklace would you let me keep the necklace?" Ingrid said to the troll woman.

"I really have my heart set on having that necklace," Skimpa said. "I can't imagine anything you could give me that would be worth giving up that necklace. Even if you offered me gold, you would have to offer me an awful lot of gold before I would even consider such a deal."

"What I have in mind is something much more valuable than gold," Ingrid said.

"What could possibly be more valuable than gold?" the troll asked, obviously believing someone would have to be a little crazy to consider anything better than gold.

"What if I could make you beautiful?" Ingrid said. "Wouldn't that be more valuable to you than a stack of gold, or this simple necklace?"

"Why, of course," Skimpa said. "I would give anything to be beautiful. If you could make me beautiful I would give *you* treasures. But how can you make me beautiful? I am a troll, after all, so I am what I am."

"Nevertheless," Ingrid said, "I promise I will make you look prettier than me if you first promise that you will let me keep the necklace if I can accomplish that. Do I have your promise?"

"Prettier than you?!" Skimpa squealed gleefully. "Certainly, I promise you that. But I don't see how such a thing is possible."

"It just so happens that I have a jar of magic skin cream in my shoulder bag," Ingrid said. "All I have to do is rub it on your face, let it sit for a short time, and then remove it. It will make you beautiful instantly."

Skimpa was as excited as a young child anticipating Christmas morning. As far as she knew, there had never been a truly beautiful troll, not in terms of human beauty. The thought that she would be more beautiful than most human women made her dizzy with excitement.

"Where is it? Where is it?" Skimpa asked about the magic skin cream, impatient as a hungry infant.

"I have it right here," Ingrid said, removing a small jar of skin cream from her shoulder bag. "Come over here and sit on this log and I'll rub it on your face."

Skimpa sat on the log. Ingrid removed a vanity case from her shoulder bag and opened it so that Skimpa could look at herself in the small mirror. "Here," Ingrid said, "have a look at how you look now so that you can see how remarkable the change is after I give you the treatment."

The image in the mirror was revolting even to Skimpa, especially so now that she believed she would soon be pretty.

"Take it away!" she said to Ingrid.

"Here goes," Ingrid said, spreading skin cream all over Skimpa's face. "Now you must close your eyes for one minute to allow it to set in."

"What kind of a fool do you take me for?" Skimpa snarled, her mood instantly transformed from euphoric anticipation to unconcealed suspicion. "That would give you the perfect chance to run away, wouldn't it? I'm not letting you out of my sight until you prove to me that this cream is truly magic cream that can make me beautiful."

"But you must close your eyes for the cream to work on your entire face," Ingrid said. "I promise I won't try to run away. I'll sing the entire time you have your eyes closed so that you will know I am right here the entire time."

"Well, all right," the troll woman said. "I'll close my eyes if you sing. If you stop singing for a single second, though, I'm going to open my eyes. And if you do try to run away, I promise I'll run you down and tie you to a tree and leave you there to die."

Ingrid began singing and Skimpa closed her eyes. Working quickly, and keeping one eye on Skimpa to make sure she kept her eyes closed, Ingrid took a small painting of her beautiful twenty-year-old daughter from her bag and fitted it over the mirror in her vanity case. With that done, she announced that one minute had passed and wiped the cream from Skimpa's face with a handkerchief. Breaking into a broad smile and blinking rapidly as if to blink back tears, Ingrid said: "What a change! Even I am amazed at how well the magic cream worked on you. You are so beautiful it makes me want to cry."

"Show me! Show me!" Skimpa said excitedly. "Let me look in the mirror."

"We must be careful about that," Ingrid said. "I'll let you have just a brief peek at yourself, but you have changed so drastically that I'm afraid the shock might be too much for you if you were to look too long. It could give you a stroke and you could die from it. Even women who have used this magic cream and undergone much less of a change have been shocked by how much they changed. For your own good, you will have to get used to your new appearance gradually. Get ready and I'll let you look at yourself for just a second."

Ingrid flipped open the vanity case just long enough for Skimpa to see the picture covering the mirror, then snapped it shut.

"I *am* beautiful!" Skimpa shouted, leaping up and dancing about in delirious delight. "You actually kept your word! How can I ever thank you? I am beautiful!"

"Just seeing how happy I've made you is thanks enough," Ingrid said.

"I must have another look," Skimpa said. "Let me see myself in the mirror again."

"Well, all right, I'll let you have one more quick look," Ingrid said. "A *quick* look. It would still be too shocking for you to have anything more than a quick look at yourself."

Once more Ingrid permitted Skimpa to have a brief peek at the picture of her daughter which covered the vanity case mirror. Once again the glimpse of this beautiful image she thought was her sent Skimpa into spasms of jubilance.

"It is growing late," Ingrid said. "I must be getting home."

"I must get home, too, and show the others that I am beautiful," Skimpa said. "I will be the most envied troll throughout the land. I will probably have the others waiting on me hand and foot because of my beauty. This is the luckiest day of my life."

Ingrid and Skimpa departed in opposite directions, with Ingrid fingering her precious turquoise necklace during much of the walk back to her village. Skimpa ran as much as she could to reach the mountain caves of her troll tribe as quickly as possible. When she reached those caves, Skimpa expected many of the others to flock around her, since they wouldn't recognize her now that she was beautiful. None of the other trolls even gave her a second glance when she returned, though, which seemed exceedingly strange to Skimpa. She approached Fordyce and Halva, who were cooking a pot of stew together, and asked, "Do you know who I am?"

"What are you jabbering about?" Fordyce said. "Certainly we know who you are. You're Skimpa."

Skimpa was shocked. "You recognize me?"

"Why shouldn't we recognize you?" Halva said. "Wel've all lived together forever, haven't we?"

"But I'm beautiful now," Skimpa said. "Don't you think I look as beautiful as any human woman you've ever seen?"

Fordyce and Halva exchanged puzzled looks. "What in the world are you talking about?" Fordyce said. "You look the same as you've always looked."

"What do you mean?" Skimpa said, alarmed by this observation. "A woman I met a short time ago changed me with magic cream so that I look beautiful."

"Did she tell you that?" Fordyce said. "It sure sounds like she fooled you."

"But I saw myself in a mirror!" Skimpa said, her brain feeling as though it were tied in knots trying to puzzle out this perplexing mystery. "I saw with my own eyes that I was beautiful."

"Well, unless you've always thought you were beautiful, you aren't now," Halva said.

"Where's a pan?" Skimpa said, searching frantically for a metal pan that would reflect her face.

She found a battered pan that reflected her likeness, then screamed in horror when she saw she was as ugly as ever. "I'm not beautiful anymore!" she wailed. "What happened? I *was* beautiful, I tell you!"

Skimpa examined all of her facial features as well as the dull, battered pan would allow. "*Nothing* is changed anymore!" she moaned. "The magic cream must have worn off. I was tricked."

"That's people for you," Halva said. "They can't be trusted. They're full of tricks."

34 • How Trolls Became Ugly

"How come trolls are so ugly?" Andrew asked when his father finished reading the tale.

"What do you mean?" Anders said.

"I just wonder why they're so ugly," Andrew said.

"Actually," Anders said, "there's an interesting legend about how they became ugly. There's a version of that in the book. It's a short story, so I think we would have time for that now too if you'd like to hear it. Would you?"

"Yes!" Andrew said.

Anders used the table of contents to find what page the tale began, then proceeded to read it to Andrew.

■

In the beginning of time trolls were not ugly, as they are now. Far from being the ogreish, homely, hideous, ill-proportioned, ill-mannered, graceless, gnarled, grubby, grotesque creatures of legend and lore, trolls were among the fairest living beings on Earth. Female trolls were all as exquisitely beautiful as an elegant sunset, as delicately comely as a dazzling display of blooming flowers, as charmingly well-favored as a crystalline mountain waterfall. Male trolls were as handsome as Arctic winters are long, as attractive as snow is white.

Trolls were so beautiful and so handsome that they became, in time, exceedingly vain and conceited. They gazed at their reflections in placid pools of water for hours at a stretch, admiring their graceful good looks. They preened and pranced and perfected pride to an art form. They strutted and swaggered and spoke of themselves in supreme superlatives. They were arrogant, imperious and immodest in the extreme. They were boastful, bragadocious and bigheaded. They were haughty, highly vainglorious and hopelessly egotistical.

Looking down upon all of this vanity and all of this self-glorification, the gods were greatly displeased with what they saw. Trolls seemed to think they were even more fair and worthy of admiration than the gods themselves, and this annoyed and angered the gods. Obviously they could not tolerate such a situation, so to punish the trolls for their overpowering pride and their exalted boasting, the gods sent all of the trolls into a deep, dark recess within the earth and covered over the entrance opening so that the trolls were trapped underground. The trolls were forced to live in the dirt, and the dankness, and the slime, and the mud and the mire of this deep, dark underground recess for thousands of years.

When the gods finally allowed the trolls to find their way out of this slimy underground prison the trolls had turned so ugly that they were ashamed of themselves. They could hardly bear to look at each other, much less their own reflections. They were now as ugly as they had once been beautiful and handsome. The pride and the vanity they had once felt was now transformed into shame and humiliation. Where they were once arrogant and immodest, they now felt degraded and disgusting. Shambling and shyness replaced their former strut and swagger. Their egotism had turned to ignominy.

They felt such overwhelming disgrace and degradation that they didn't want to be around other creatures, particularly human beings, who were now so much fairer in appearance than they were. And so they moved into the mountains to live in caves along the mountain streams. And that is where they have lived throughout all of the millennia since they emerged from their wretched, slimy underground exile, resenting the ancient banishment by the gods and begrudging human beings all of their wealth, happiness and grace.

35 ▪ Double Dismay

Even if Old Fungus had not been the one who had an opportunity to foil the two gnomes' escape, he would have taken their escape harder than anyone, given his deep hatred of the crafty little creatures. Although he was careful to not let anyone see him do so, he actually shed a few tears about the gnomes' escape. And now he had a throbbing, painful nose and a wrenched shoulder to add to his list of grievances against gnomes. But the emotional pain of no longer having two gnomes as prisoners, and the promise of future teasing sessions with them, seared far more intensely than his physical aches. For days after the escape, he went to where the two gnomes had been held prisoner and stared at the cages for hours as he remembered what joy it had been torturing one of the gnomes and seethed at how he and the others had been robbed of even more pleasurable torture sessions Ort had promised, once Tewalt, the goldsmith, had forged all of their accumulated raw gold and silver into trinkets and jewelry. Old Fungus then would have been able to exact a true measure of revenge for having had to live with a chopped-off tail for hundreds of years. At his age, who knew how many more opportunities he might have to tease accursed gnomes. He needed to take advantage of whatever opporunities presented themselves, and this particular opportunity had slipped away before he had a chance to take full advantage of it. That was truly a cause for mourning. And he blamed Ort for that almost as much as he blamed the gnomes' escape. Were he a couple of hundred years younger, and thus in better physical condition, he may have challenged Ort for the position of tribe king. He would handle some things differently than Ort handled them, that was for sure, and the treatment of gnome prisoners was definitely one area where that difference in philosophy would manifest itself. Ort was an okay king most of the time, as far as that went, but Old Fungus believed he had his shortcomings and blind spots.

For his part, Ort, who, as king, took the lion's share of the new trinkets and jewelry Tewalt forged, found solace from thinking about what they had been able to exert from the two gnome prisoners. On several occasions he retreated to his bedroom chamber and ran his fingers through his large chests of treasures, including the new treasures they contained. He dwelled on past exploits and acquisitions rather than on present problems and losses as he pawed and caressed his treasures. He wasn't able to put the present state of affairs out of his mind entirely, though, for that situation included not only the escape of the two gnomes but the resumption of whines, rumblings and other noises wafting up from the construction site at the base of the mountain. He and his fellow trolls had seemed to have the upper hand on both gnomes and people, and now suddenly both of those enemies had turned the tables on them, blast their tricky, deceitful, shrewd ways. As Ort's arms and fingers swam through the shiny treasures in his chests, thoughts of the noisy despoliation of Troll Mountain and the escape of the two gnomes gradually crept from the corners of his mind to the center of his ruminations. The resumption of noises particularly made his blood boil. He was determined that humans would not get the better of trolls this time, as they usually did. This, he felt in his heart, was the time and the place to make a stand, to draw a line and say "no further." But trying to put an end to the noises, and the human activity, for good was like trying to plug leaks in a porous rock wall where every time one leak was plugged two new leaks appeared. He was perplexed as to what they needed to do to force the noise and the activity to stop. Was he fated to be plagued by people forever? Would he never find refuge from their meddling ways?

With such thoughts swimming in his mind, Ort emerged from his cave and bumped into Jirik, who happened to be passing by. Jirik had very long, thin arms and legs, bulging dark brown eyes, and a tangled mop of dark brown hair that dropped over his shoulders.

"Oh, it's you," Ort said.

"You look a little worked up," Jirik commented. "What's up?"

"People, that's what!" Ort seethed. "I need to figure out a way to make people stop what they're doing at the bottom of the mountain, and put an end to all their noise so we can all go back to living in peace."

"Remember when my thinking got all twisted about people?" Jirik said. "How I thought their ways were better?"

"You were young," Ort said. "Luckily I was able to straighten you out before such thinking took a deeper hold in you."

"And I'm always grateful for what you did," Jirik said. "It made me the troll I am today."

"Yes, I've been proud of you ever since," Ort said. "You've been a good member of the tribe."

When Jirik strode off to explore the night, Ort sat on a rock and thought about the time when Jirik had doubts about the sort of life he was leading as a troll.

36 ▪ The Troll With Doubts

Jirik was not a typical troll, in that he had more of an appreciation for the natural world than most trolls have. One of his favorite activities was to sit on a boulder at the base of a ninety-foot waterfall and drink in the beauty and wonderful kinetic sound of the scene. He loved the crashing of the falling water, and how the water foamed, swirled, bubbled and rushed at the base of the waterfall.

Jirik had the place all to himself for more than a year after he discovered it one summer day. Then one evening he was sitting there quietly when a young man—a person—approximately his age, which was nineteen, appeared on the other side of the thirty-foot-wide river.

"This is a great place, isn't it?" the person called across to him, seemingly not at all afraid of him.

Jirik eyed the intruder warily and said nothing.

"I know you're a troll," the person said, "but that doesn't bother me. I don't think you're a mean troll. I just have the sense that you're a kind troll. I won't hurt you if you won't hurt me." He smiled as he said that to signal he was making something of a joke. Jirik did not catch the nuance, though.

"I won't hurt you," Jirik called across the river.

"Good," the person said. "I'm happy to hear it. I'll just sit over here and you can sit over there."

After a while, though, the friendly person waded across the shallow rapids a short distance downstream of the waterfall and introduced himself, as Sten, to Jirik. Despite what he had been taught about humans, about how he should dislike and distrust them, Jirik couldn't help but like Sten, for he was friendly and enjoyed going to the waterfall as well. On subsequent visits to the waterfall, Jirik found himself hoping he would find Sten there so he could talk with him. Occasionally he did find Sten there, or Sten showed up while he was there. As they talked and became better acquainted with each other, Sten began asking questions about why trolls did what they did—why they stole things from people, and sometimes kidnapped them, or put evil spells on them, and why they didn't bathe regularly, and groom themselves better, and celebrate Christmas.

"Christmas is the best day of the year," Sten said. "It's when everyone is kind to each other, and generous, and feels wonderful because of it."

Sten told Jirik about how humans thought and behaved, and why they thought and behaved the way they did. He seemed so happy all the time that Jirik couldn't help but wonder if he would be as happy if he thought and behaved in the same manner. Why *did* trolls steal so much, anyway? And why didn't they clean themselves regularly with soap and water, and comb their hair, and eat with knives and forks all the time? They were all good questions to Jirik, and he contemplated these matters as best as he was able to do so. Truth be told, most trolls *were* envious of the good looks and advantaged circumstances of people, after all, so didn't it make sense to try to think and act more like people? Jirik thought the question deserved attention.

Jirik's father, Nordo, found such questions and doubts so troubling that he sought help from the troll tribe's king, Ort.

"My son is all mixed up in the head!" Nordo said to Ort. "He says he doesn't want to go along on any more raiding parties because he doesn't want to steal, and he wants to know why we don't eat with knives and forks all the time, and he wants more fresh air in our cave all of a sudden, and he wants to know why we don't celebrate Christmas. Celebrate Christmas, of all things! It's like he wants to be a *person* all of a sudden. He's all mixed up, like I say."

"Obviously," Ort agreed, quite shocked by what he heard.

"I've tried reasoning with him, but I just can't seem to get through to him," Nordo lamented. "Will you talk to him and try to straighten him out? You're better with words than I am. I'm sure you can explain things to him that maybe I can't."

"It sounds serious," Ort said. "Of course I'll talk to him. People are cunning. We must never underestimate their treacherous and tricky ways, especially when it comes to someone Jirik's age. That's why it's so important that we not mix with people, that we avoid them at all costs, if possible."

"Do you think the man could have cast some sort of a spell on Jirik?" Nordo asked. "Do you think maybe we should ask Kravig if he has some sort of magic potion that would remove any spell?" Kravig was a wizard who was a member of this particular troll tribe.

"Let's hold off on that for right now," Ort said. "I'd like to talk to Jirik myself first and see if I can't straighten out his thinking. I'm interested in hearing firsthand just what sort of strange ideas he had jammed into his head. If I can't sweep all those people thoughts from his brain, then we'll have to think about consulting Kravig."

"I'd be eternally grateful to you," Nordo said. "The sooner you can do it, the better, as far as I'm concerned."

"Why not bring him over right now," Ort said. "Is he in your cave?"

"He was when I left," Nordo said. "I'll go and get him right now, and bring him over here."

"It's good to try to get something like this straightened out as soon as possible," Ort said.

A few minutes later Nordo was back with Jirik. Ort invited the two to sit with him on rocks outside his cave.

"Your father," Ort began, addressing Jirik, "tells me that you seem to have acquired some strange ideas from a person you met, and both of us would like to have you thinking straight again, because you should know that the way people think is not always the way us trolls should think. Don't you like being a troll?"

"Sure, it's what I am," Jirik said. "But why do trolls have to survive by stealing all the time? That's wrong, isn't it? Why can't we work for what we want and need, as people have to do?"

"Stealing?!" Ort said, as though shocked by the very suggestion. "We trolls take what we can get. You know that. All trolls know that as soon as they're old enough to talk."

"But isn't taking what we can get stealing?" Jirik asked. "Isn't that just a nice way of saying that we're a bunch of thieves?"

"Words," Ort said. "What do they mean? People seem to put so much stock in words. We trolls take what we can get. Why does that have to mean that we're thieves? It's all a matter of words, isn't it? 'Thieves' is such a nasty word. We take what we can get. Why not leave it at that? What gave you the idea that we *shouldn't* take what we can get, anyway?"

"Well, a friendly person I met and talked to said it makes you feel better if you work for what you get than if you just take what you want," Jirik said. "He said people don't try to steal things from trolls because bad things happen to people who do that."

"Of course it's wrong to steal things from us trolls," Ort said. "I've never thought anything else. But what does that have to do with us trolls taking what we can get?"

"I told you he was all mixed up," Nordo said.

"There are troll ways and there are people ways," Ort explained to Jirik, trying to control his irritation. "I could tell you a thousand stories about why us trolls should not try to think or act like people. That's what you're trying to do—you're trying to think like a person. Well, trolls *don't* think like people. It's as simple as that. And anyway, people aren't as honest and goody-goody as they want you to believe. All of us trolls know how people have lied to us, and tricked us, and been mean to us, and have driven us away from our homes with their church bells and their conniving behavior and their conceited attitude." He expectorated a great wad of saliva, as though simply speaking about human beings brought a sour taste to his mouth.

"I know that's true," Jirik conceded. "But can't we learn some things from people? All I'm saying is that maybe stealing so much is not right, that stealing so much is not good for us."

"Then why do us trolls live so much longer than people do, if we're as terrible as people say we are?" Ort challenged. "Answer me that!"

"I don't know," Jirik admitted. "I've never thought about it in that way. That does seem strange, now that you point it out."

"I don't see anything strange about it," Ort said. "It seems perfectly logical to me. Thieves, they call us! Pshaw! We take what we can get, that's all. At that, we have a lot less than people do. Why shouldn't we be able to take just a little bit of what they have?"

"That makes sense, I have to admit," Jirik said.

"Of course it makes sense," Ort said. "Anyway, you're fooling yourself if you think people are opposed to someone getting something for nothing. They're merely against us trolls getting something for nothing, as they see things. Have you ever heard the story of the shepherd of Silverbrook?"

"Not that I remember," Jirik said.

"Well, I'm going to tell it to you. Listen and learn," Ort said, and proceeded to tell the story—or as much of the story as he knew, at any rate. In his version, which is shorter than the version people know, the troll is much more kindhearted and much less menacing than she is in the version included in several books.

37 ▪ The Shepherd Of Silverbrook

A rich sheep farmer named Gunnar Bjornson once lived along the Bay of Torborg on a farm he called Silverbrook, for a brook of that name flowed across his property. Gunnar was married, but had no children.

One Christmas Eve his herdsman did not return to the farm at night, so Gunnar organized a widescale search for him, which proved futile; the herdsman was never found.

The following spring the farmer hired another shepherd, a man named Rendal, to replace the shepherd who had disappeared. Rendal was tall and strong, and certainly didn't lack courage or confidence; he boasted of being able to out-fight anyone. In spite of Rendal's strength and boldness, Gunnar warned him about taking any unnecessary risks. And given what had happened the previous year, the farmer ordered Rendal to drive the sheep into the pens early on Christmas Eve and return to the farm while the sky still held some daylight. Rendal did not return at all that Christmas Eve, however. Once again the farmer organized a diligent search for him, but again no trace of the shepherd was ever found.

There was all sorts of speculation in the neighborhood about the cause of the two shepherds' disappearances, with most guesses focusing on the supernatural—ghosts, witchcraft, deviltry, and the like. Given that, no one else wanted to serve as a shepherd for Gunnar, who was grief-stricken by how the two shepherds had disappeared without a trace. Running out of potential candidates for the job, Gunnar approached a very poor widow with several children who lived in a nearby village to see if she would allow her oldest child, fourteen-year-old Peter, to work as his shepherd. Gunnar offered such a large sum of money that Peter begged his mother to allow him to take the job so that the family could be much better off. While concerned about Peter being old enough to handle the job, and the unexplained disappearances of the two shepherds, Peter's mother eventually relented and allowed him to take the job.

As it turned out, Peter proved to be a very good shepherd. He did not lose a single sheep all during the spring and summer. Pleased by how Peter was handling the job, Gunnar gave the lad a wether, a ewe and a lamb sort of as a bonus to his regular pay.

When Christmas Eve arrived that year, Gunnar begged Peter to return to the farm before nightfall, since he was horrified by the thought of losing yet another shepherd after what had happened the last two Christmas Eves.

As evening approached, Peter had just finished herding all of the sheep into pens when he heard the reverberating sound of heavy footsteps behind him. Turning around, he saw a giant, menacing female troll coming straight toward him.

"Good evening," the troll growled, her voice like the sound of gravel sloshing in a stream of water. "I have come to put you in my sack."

Frightened, but determined to do what he could to avoid being a troll's meal, Peter said: "Put me in your sack! Can't you see how small and skinny I am? I wouldn't make much of a meal for you. But if you leave me alone I'll give you a sheep and a fat lamb for your pot tonight."

"Show them to me," the troll growled.

Peter showed her the sheep and the lamb, and she agreed to the bargain Peter had offered. So the giant troll carried the two animals back up the mountain as Peter headed back to Gunnar's farm, where a greatly relieved Gunnar greeted him enthusiastically, for Christmas Eve did not bring heartbreak this year.

"Did you see anything unusual?" Gunnar asked, thinking he might obtain a clue as to what happened to his two herdsmen who disappeared the last two Christmas Eves.

"No, nothing out of the ordinary," Peter replied, saying nothing about the giant troll who accosted him.

A couple of weeks later the farmer visited the flock of sheep and noticed that the lamb and the sheep he had given to Peter were missing. "Do you know what happened to them?" he asked.

"Oh, a fox got the lamb, and the wether fell into a bog," the boy answered. "I guess I'm just not as lucky with my own sheep as I am with yours."

The farmer gave Peter a ewe and two wethers to replace the lost ones and asked him to remain his herdsman for another year, to which Peter agreed.

When Christmas Eve came around again near the end of that year Gunnar again cautioned Peter to be careful and not take any risks, for by then he loved Peter as he would have loved a son.

As happened the previous year, the giant female troll showed up as soon as Peter had penned the sheep for the night.

"This year you won't avoid being boiled in my pot," the troll said. "I think you will fit quite nicely in my sack."

"I see that your eyesight hasn't improved any," Peter said boldly. "Can't you see that I'm still as thin as a rail? I'm nothing compared to even one wether. Leave me alone and I will give you two old sheep and two young sheep. No one in their right mind would turn down a deal such as that."

"Show me the sheep," the troll growled. Peter did so, and without a word the troll gathered up the four sheep and started back up the mountain while Peter returned to the farm, where once again Gunnar welcomed him grandly and asked if he had seen anything unusual. Once again Peter told the farmer he had seen nothing out of the ordinary.

"I'm afraid I've been dreadfully unlucky with my own sheep again, though," he added, telling the farmer that he had lost his sheep, but not how he lost them. The following summer Gunnar gave him four more wethers.

Peter's third Christmas Eve as a herdsman, the giant troll once more appeared just as Peter was putting the sheep into pens and again threatened to carry him off and boil him in her pot. Peter offered her the four wethers the farmer gave him the previous summer in his stead. While the troll took those, this time she seized Peter as well, tucked him under one of her arms and headed for her mountain cave. Once they reached the cave, the troll ordered Peter to kill the sheep, which he did.

"Now sharpen this axe well," the troll said, handing Peter an axe, "for I intend to cut off your head with it."

Peter did as ordered; he sharpened the axe and handed it back to the giant troll.

"Brave lad!" the troll fairly cried out, letting the axe drop to the ground. "You are too brave to kill. You deserve to live to a ripe old age, and you deserve good fortune. And I will tell you how to obtain it. Next spring, you must move from Silverbrook and go to the house of a silversmith, to learn his trade. Once you have thoroughly learned that trade you must take some specimens of your silverwork to the farm where the church dean lives. He has three daughters, the youngest of whom is the fairest maiden in the whole country. The two oldest daughters love dress and ornaments, and they will admire what you bring them, but the youngest will not care about such things. When you leave the house you must ask her to accompany you to the end of the grass field. Then you must give her these three precious things—this handkerchief, this belt and this ring." Here the troll gave Peter the three items she just mentioned. "These things will make her love you. When you see me in a dream you must return here. You will find me dead. You must bury me, and then take anything of value from my cave that you wish to take, for you were kind to me in giving me Christmas Eve meals."

At that point Peter left the troll's cave and returned to Gunnar Bjornson's farm.

"Am I ever glad to see you!" Gunnar said to him, welcoming him more warmly than ever. "I was afraid something terrible had happened to you. Did something happen to make you so late?"

"No, nothing unusual," Peter answered. "I don't think you'll need to worry about a herdsman's safety on Christmas Eve ever again." He offered no explanation as to the reason for that.

As the giant troll had urged, the following spring Peter left the Silverbrook farm and became a silversmith's apprentice, though he continued to visit Gunnar from time to time. Two years later he was a master of the trade. Making his way to the church dean's house, he showed the dean's three daughters some of his wares. While the two oldest sisters bought many trinkets from him, the youngest, Margaret, was not the least bit interested in any of the ornaments. As he was leaving, Peter persuaded Margaret to accompany him to the end of the grass field. There he gave her the belt and the handkerchief the troll had given him, and he placed the ring on one of her fingers. With that, he left.

In the days that followed Margaret found she could not stop thinking about Peter, for she felt great love for him. When she told her father about her feelings, her father told her she must get such foolish thoughts out of her head and declared he would not allow her to marry Peter as long as he was around to prevent such an action. Margaret grew so thin and forlorn from disappointment and sadness, though, that her father eventually relented and allowed her to marry Peter, fearing Margaret may be doomed to a life of misery and resentment if denied her desire. And so Peter and Margaret were engaged.

Not long after, Peter dreamed of the giant troll woman one night. Believing this meant the troll was dead, as she had foretold, he asked the church dean to accompany him as far as the Silverbrook farm. When they told Gunnar that Peter was betrothed to one of the dean's daughters, Gunnar revealed that for a long time he had intended to leave all his property to Peter, and offered to let Peter take over management of the farm the coming spring. Peter jumped at that opportunity, which pleased the dean, for it meant his daughter would be well provided for.

The next day Peter asked Gunnar and the dean to accompany him up the mountain, where he was able to find the opening to the troll's cave with little difficulty. Inside, they found the giant troll woman lying dead on the floor. Only then did Peter tell the other two about his three Christmas Eve encounters with the troll. After the three men buried the troll they returned to the cave and found a great number of precious objects, which Peter took back to the farm.

Shortly thereafter, Peter and Margaret were married, and the two of them were prosperous to the end of their days.

■

"See how good and generous trolls have been to people at times?" Ort said upon finishing the story. "And yet how many instances can you show me where people have displayed such kindness and generosity to trolls?"

Jirik said nothing; obviously the tale touched him, though.

"Listen to Ort," Nordo said. "He knows what he's talking about."

"Tell you what," Ort said to Jirik. "Why don't you come with me and I'll show you one of my treasure chests."

And so Ort took Jirik into his cave and opened one of his treasure chests, which was full of gold, silver and bejeweled items. "See what taking what you can get can get you?" Ort said as he immersed his hands in his treasures with sensual pleasure. "When you see this, you can't help but agree that getting what you can is a good thing, can you?"

"I must admit that I'd like to have this much treasure myself," Jirik said.

"Maybe someday you will," Ort said. "It doesn't just fall out of the sky, though; you have to seek it out. Tell you what: How about tomorrow night just you and me go down the mountain to see what we can get? We'll work together, and divide what we get."

"I guess so," Jirik said.

"Sure!" Ort said. "Just you and me. It'll be fun."

The next night Ort and Jirik made their way down the mountain to the outskirts of a village, where the two trolls raided a blacksmith shop. While the pieces of metal they were able to get there were not precious metals, Jirik was thrilled by the horseshoes, hinges, pans and other objects they were able to find. Just as importantly, Jirik felt special making a raid with Ort, the troll king, as his only companion. It made him appreciate his troll heritage to a greater degree, and better understand that trolls are different than people, with their own way of thinking and behaving. After that night Jirik never again questioned the wisdom that trolls have the right to take what they can get.

38 ▪ More Machines

The noises at the bottom of the mountain had not only resumed; they seemed louder than ever. Sent down to investigate, Haar and Rnobrna were appalled by what they beheld. There were more men and machines at the construction site than on past trips. In addition to a bulldozer and a skidder-loader, several other large machines, including a digging backhoe, were rumbling around like huge mechanical pigs playing in dirt. Several men dashed about with chains, rope, metal bars and other implements, helping to move logs and direct the machine operators. Haar and Rnobrna had never seen such a great degree of activity as this before. Keeping well back from the action, and well hidden, they watched the activity in rapt fascination, puzzled by exactly what the men were doing, and especially by why they were doing what they were doing. Most troubling to them was the presence of a ten-foot-high chain-link fence, topped by several strands of barbed wire, around part of the construction site. After a time, the two trolls noticed three men putting up more such chain-link fencing.

"I hate fences almost as much as I hate church bells," Haar remarked to Rnobrna. "People think trolls are ugly, and then they put up something like that that's far uglier than any troll ever was. People!"

"Yeah, *people*!" Rnobrna agreed with a sneer.

"Who can understand why people do the things they do sometimes?" Haar said. "Who *wants* to understand why they do things sometimes?"

Haar and Rnobrna watched the people and their machines work until the people finished working and left for the day. Before they left, though, three other people arrived to guard the site, so those guards remained after the workers left.

"I don't like the way things are going here," Ort said when Haar and Rnobrna reported their observations to him. "This is a bad, bad turn of events. We take care of two machines and they return with even more machines! How do we get rid of these people anyway? What do we have to do? Getting rid of these people is like trying to stamp out a puddle of water; you stomp your foot in the puddle and the water splashes all over and makes ten other puddles. We aren't licked yet, though. There must be some way to make them stop what they're doing and force them to leave!"

"What do you have in mind?" Rnobrna asked.

"I'll think of something," Ort asserted. "First, I want a look at what's going on there now myself."

Accompanied by only Scurf, Ort went down the mountain to observe the worksite the following afternoon. As Haar and Rnobrna had been, he was appalled by what he beheld. Like those two others, he was fascinated as well. Much as he did not like what was happening, with trees being felled and areas cleared, he grudgingly admired the resilience the people displayed, though of course he did not think of it as resilience, for he was not familiar with that word. He knew he and his fellow trolls would need to tap an even greater reserve of resilience if they were to save the mountain by making the people abandon whatever it was they were doing. At the moment, he was at a loss as to what more they could do to accomplish that end.

As Haar and Rnobrna had done, Ort and Scurf observed the human activity until the workers left and other men arrived to guard the site, particularly the machines.

"Look at them, with their guns," Ort said. "I hate guns almost as much as I hate people. It's not a fair fight when people have guns and we don't. If there are always people there with guns it's going to be very hard to do anything."

"Maybe if we had a giant troll or two we could call on things would be different," Scurf said.

"Maybe," Ort said. "But I'm afraid the time of the giant trolls is past, unless there are a couple left far to the north, living off all by themselves, which is not likely."

"I bet a giant troll could toss big rocks from right here and hit one of those men," Scurf said. "It would be like you and me throwing rocks at squirrels; it would be that easy for them. Boy, would I love to see that! A big rock would go flying through the air and conk one of the men right on the head and knock him out cold."

"They could do some amazing things," Ort said of giant trolls. "Of course, they weren't the friendliest trolls that ever lived; even smaller trolls were afraid of them."

"I never saw one," Scurf said. "I wish I had, just once. I've seen some trolls that were pretty big, but I've never seen a truly giant troll."

"I saw two of them in my time, when I was pretty young," Ort said. "I was in awe of them, of course, but I really didn't think too much about it at the time. Giant trolls were just part of the landscape, something that you saw once in a while. I don't think anyone ever thought there would come a time when there wouldn't be any more giant trolls, just as at one time none of us could have ever imagined how many people would move in and take over our territory and force us to move to other places."

"Well, what do we do now?" Scurf said after a ten-second interval of silence.

"Well, we're not accomplishing anything sitting here," Ort said. "Let's head back up the mountain. I need to think over the situation a little."

And so Ort and Scurf hiked back up Troll Mountain, to their caves, along what was by then a fairly well-trod, and thus defined, trail through the mountain forest.

39 ▪ The Bully And The Troll

Diverging from a string of tales featuring female trolls, the next tale Anders read to Andrew from *A Treasury of Troll Tales* was called *The Bully And The Troll.*

▪

Some time ago—quite a long time ago, in fact—a farmer named Oskar Thordal set up a farm in a green and pleasant mountainside setting called Trinity Valley. That is to say, Trinity Valley was a pleasant place from a physical standpoint. In other aspects it was not always a particularly pleasant place to live—for Oskar Thordal's neighbors, that is—because Oskar Thordal was a bully who often made life very unpleasant for people who came in contact with him.

Once Oskar cut down quite a number of trees on land that belonged to Lars Holmquist, his nearest neighbor to the north. When Lars went out to tell Oskar he was cutting trees on his land Oskar insisted the trees were on his land and threatened to chop Lars's head off with his axe if he didn't leave him alone. Since Oskar was far bigger and much stronger than he was, Lars dropped the matter and let Oskar Thordal steal his wood.

Oskar was bigger and stronger than not only Lars Holmquist, but any other man within at least a hundred miles around. And he was just as mean and ornery as he was strong. He would just as soon spit at another man as look at him, or shove him rather than say hello. He would growl "get out of my way" if anyone came close to him or accidentally impeded the path he wanted to follow. If he happened upon boys fishing along a bank of the Trinity River he would likely take the fish they had caught and warn them he would give them a good whipping if they told their parents what he had done. Not that he was in any way fearful of what their parents might do about it; he simply enjoyed putting fear into the hearts of children as well as adults.

While Oskar had no respect for the property rights of others, he protected his own property with the zealousness of a mother bear protecting her cubs. If he saw anyone—man, woman or child—take a single step on his property he shouted at the other person to get off his land and threatened that the next time he saw the person do that he would shoot to kill without a word of warning. He actually did take shots at a few people who trespassed on his land, or simply looked at his house in what he took to be the wrong way as they passed by on the public road.

Oskar Thordal was a man no one wanted to anger, for everyone knew he would retaliate against any perceived slight, whether that was a word or a deed. He could become enraged if he thought someone erected a fence along a property line for the wrong reason, or if anyone accused him of stealing anything, or even if he felt someone looked at him in the wrong way. Everyone in Trinity Valley suspected he burned down Alfred Oleson's barn after Alfred told others Oskar stole several of his sheep. The Thill family found all of their garden tomatoes splattered all around one morning, the day after one of their cows broke loose and ambled down the road onto Oskar's place. And Charles Nyberg knew it was more than coincidence that two of his wagon wheels fell off his wagon simultaneously as he was traveling back home after a visit to the nearby village, where he was telling a merchant and another man what a nasty man Oskar Thordal was when Oskar himself walked through the front door of the store. In short, Oskar Thordal was a neighborhood terror who was mean-minded, menacing and dangerous.

No one suffered more at Oskar's hands than his nearest neighbors, Carl-Erick and Nina Denstad. Many was the morning they awoke to find out some of their hay, or vegetables, or a couple of chickens had been stolen overnight, and the enormous size of the boot prints left on the ground pointed directly to a single suspect: Oskar Thordal. The few times Carl-Erick dared to confront Oskar as to whether or not he had any knowledge of a missing item, Oskar cursed him, shoved him around, and threatened him bodily harm. Once Oskar stood sharpening a large knife as he told Carl-Erick he wanted to get the knife so sharp it would skin a man as easily as it would a deer. The devious gleam in Oskar's eyes left Carl-Erick with no doubt Oskar meant he was the man the knife could skin.

Certain that Oskar would set fire to their house or their barn, or slaughter all their livestock, or possibly even murder them, if they did anything to make Oskar angry enough, Carl-Erick and Nina held their tongues and allowed Oskar Thordal to bully them. They considered moving away from Trinity Valley, as a couple of families had already done because of Oskar's presence, but Trinity Valley was such a pretty place that they hated the thought of leaving it.

One evening, in mid-autumn, there was knocking at the front door of Carl-Erick and Nina's house. Since Nina served as a midwife and nurse, it was not unusual for someone to knock on their door any time of the day or night.

"I'll see who it is," Carl-Erick said, rising from his chair, where he had been repairing a broken rope. Opening the door, he was startled to see a stumpy, hairy, pimplish, ill-proportioned troll standing on the stoop.

"I understand that the lady of the house is a nurse," the troll croaked with a frog-like voice. "My wife needs her. She's very sick. I think she might be dying."

"You've come to the wrong place," Carl-Erick said, anxious to get rid of this ugly visitor. With Oskar Thordal as a neighbor, the last thing he wanted was to get mixed up with more wicked creatures. Although he had never before met one in person, he had always been taught that trolls were vile and wicked.

"Wait! You *must* help me," the troll pleaded as Carl-Erick started closing the door.

"Who is it?" Nina called to her husband, rising from her chair and walking toward the front door.

"No one," Carl-Erick said to her. "Stay back."

"I need your help, ma'am," the troll called to Nina, trying to make himself heard past Carl-Erick, who was doing his best to block the troll's voice as well as shield Nina from the troll's sight. "My wife is very sick. I'm afraid she might die if you don't help her."

Nina moved closer to the door, next to her husband. "Why, you're a troll!" she said, getting her first look at the visitor.

"And you're not welcome here," Carl-Erick said, trying to shut the door. The troll, however, stuck a lumpy foot in the door opening to prevent Carl-Erick from closing the door completely.

"Please, ma'am," the troll said to Nina. "I promise I'll repay you sevenfold if you do me this favor. I'll cut stacks of firewood for you. I'll harvest your crops for you. I'll move boulders for you. Just please come and help my wife."

"Open the door, Carl," Nina said to her husband.

"But, Nina. . ." Carl-Erick protested, wanting to protect her from this creature at their front door.

"Carl, I'm a nurse," Nina said. "You know I have to help anyone if I can."

Reluctantly, Carl-Erick opened the door wide.

"Where's your wife now?" Nina asked the troll.

"At home in our cave," the troll told her.

"Up in the mountains?" Nina asked.

"That's right," the troll answered.

"How long does it take to get to your cave?" Nina asked.

"Not so long," the troll said. "Only long enough for the moon to travel this far in the sky." He spread the palms of his hands in a V shape so that the fingertips of his two hands were four or five inches apart.

"It must be no more than an hour's ride away," Nina said to Carl-Erick. "I better go and see if there's anything I can do."

"I won't let you," Carl-Erick said. "There's no reason why you should do this."

"Then you come with," Nina said. "I can't just let someone die if there's anything I can do to save her. I couldn't live with myself if I did that."

"Oh, all right, do it if you must," Carl-Erick said. "But I'm going with you."

Carl-Erick prepared two horses they would ride to the troll's mountain cave while Nina got her satchel with her medicinal herbs, clean pieces of white cloth, and other items and commodities. Luckily, it was nearly a full moon that shone that night, which made the ride nearly as safe as if it had been made during daylight.

When they arrived at the trolls' cave they did, indeed, find a very ill troll woman there. Her name, Nina quickly learned, was Piela. Her husband's name was Klopf. While Klopf looked on anxiously, Nina treated Piela with various herbs and potions to the best of her ability, administering to her symptoms in exactly the same way she would have for a human patient. At dawn Nina sent Carl-Erick home to attend to their livestock. Carl-Erick was reluctant to leave Nina alone with trolls, but Nina assured him she would be all right. She said Piela required her attention, so she needed to stay there to look after her. Nina sat by Piela's bedside for two days, trying to nurse Piela back to good health. Finally, on the evening of the second day, Piela showed small signs of recovery. By the next morning her health had improved immensely. She felt good enough to get up and eat solid food for the first time in several days. The crisis had passed; she was well on her way to a full recovery.

Klopf didn't forget about the promise he had made to repay Nina in some fashion if she would help his wife. He insisted he wanted to do some work for her, so before Nina left to return home it was agreed that Klopf would work at the Denstads' farm for two weeks, doing whatever chores the Denstads gave him to do.

It didn't take Carl-Erick long to learn Klopf could be most useful doing chores that involved the most muscle power. He had always heard that trolls were stronger than people, but he had no appreciation of exactly how much stronger they were until he saw firsthand what feats of strength Klopf was capable of performing. In a matter of minutes, Klopf chopped down a tree it would have taken Carl-Erick more than an hour to fell. And then he moved that large tree as easily as Carl-Erick could have moved one of its medium-size branches. Klopf dislodged boulders from the ground and carried them around with no more effort than Carl-Erick's two workhorses used to drag boulders. He carried a large bucket of water in each hand as though the buckets were cups.

"I bet he's at least five times stronger than that no-good, nasty neighbor of ours, Oskar Thordal," Carl-Erick said to Nina one night as he described Klopf's feats of strength to her. "I'd like to see Oskar pick a fight with him and see how that would come out. I betcha he wouldn't act like such a bully anymore after Klopf got done with him."

"Maybe that could be arranged," Nina said.

"How do you mean?" Carl-Erick asked.

Nina explained her idea as Carl-Erick chuckled with glee at how Oskar Thordal might get his comeuppance.

When Klopf came the next day Nina and Carl-Erick spelled out for him what they wanted him to do. Knopf was more than happy to oblige them. He was willing to do whatever they wanted him to do because of how grateful he was for Nina having saved his wife Piela's life.

With Klopf at his side, Carl-Erick drove a wagon over to Oskar Thordal's place. With Klopf's help, he started loading the wagon with firewood from a stack of wood next to one of Oskar's sheds, making sure Oskar, who was mending a fence not far away, had full sight of him.

"Hey, you! Get away from there!" Oskar shouted. "What are you doing?" He began running toward Carl-Erick and Klopf, waving his arms angrily and cursing a blue streak as he ran. "I'm going to wring your neck," he said to Carl-Erick, stopping forty feet away. "You're stealing my firewood!" He sounded as surprised as he was angry that anyone would have the nerve to try to steal something from him—in broad daylight, no less.

"I'm just taking back a little of what you've stolen from me over the years," Carl-Erick said. Turning to Klopf, he instructed: "Go ahead and keep loading the wagon."

"Who's that?" Oskar asked. "I don't recognize him."

"Oh, he's my new helper," Carl-Erick replied.

Oskar stepped closer. "Your helper!" He spit in Carl-Erick's direction, nearly hitting one of his shoes. "That squatty little thing!"

Dressed in some of Carl-Erick's old clothes, and with a large brimmed hat covering much of his head and shading his face, Klopf was disguised enough so that Oskar couldn't tell he was a troll.

"Get out of here, both of you," Oskar demanded, "before I tie you both into knots and feed you to the hogs."

Carl-Erick ignored Oskar's threat and nodded to Klopf. "Let's get this wagon loaded."

Klopf resumed his work, tossing pieces of wood into the back end of the wagon.

"Put those back, you little devil!" Oskar snarled at Klopf as Klopf picked up two more pieces of wood. Then he rushed at the troll, furious, with a fiery anger in his eyes. As Oskar drew back his right arm to punch Klopf in the face, Klopf boxed Oskar's ears with two hunks of firewood, staggering Oskar. "Now you're in for it!" Oskar thundered, scowling with menace. He lowered his head and charged at Klopf like a battering ram. With a deft uppercut to Oskar's chin, Klopf laid out Oskar flat on his back. He then grabbed the front of Oskar's shirt, pulled him off the ground with one hand, and held him in the air above his head. After shaking him a little, he tossed him against the side of the shed. As Oskar lied there in a heap, trying to regain control of his senses, Carl-Erick said to Klopf: "He looks a little droopy. I think you better drag him over to the water trough and dunk his head in water a few times." Which is exactly what Klopf did; he dunked Oskar's head in the trough of water several times, five to ten seconds at a time. By then Oskar was begging for mercy, fearing that Klopf would drown him, or kill him some other way.

"Take all the wood you want," Oskar said, his head soaked and dripping. "Just leave me alone."

"Thanks for the offer," Carl-Erick said. "I think I'll take you up on that." He and Klopf began walking back toward the woodpile, as he said over his shoulder: "We'll be back tomorrow for another load." Then they finished loading the wagon and drove home.

When Carl-Erick returned to Oskar's place the following morning, alone this time, Oskar met him on the road with a loaded gun.

"Where do you think you're going?" Oskar demanded after Carl-Erick reined the horses to a halt.

"I came back for another load of firewood," Carl-Erick said, "just as I told you I would."

"Not today, my friend," Oskar said, with his rifle aimed directly at Carl-Erick's heart. "Today you're going to leave your horses and your wagon here and you're going to walk home, unless you'd rather I shoot you."

"You didn't ask where my helper is today," Carl-Erick said calmly. "Don't you want to know where he is?"

"Yeah, where is he, anyway?" Oskar said, curious. "Was he too cowardly to come with you today?"

"Not exactly," Carl-Erick said. "Look behind you."

As Oskar turned to look, he was dumbstruck by the sight that met his eyes. Thirty feet away, there stood Klopf with a three-foot-diameter boulder held over his head. Oskar was so spellbound by such a display of strength that his mind froze with fear and he didn't even attempt to get out of the way when Klopf pulled back the boulder and flung it toward him. The boulder scraped the front of Oskar's chest, tore the gun from his hands and flattened it on the ground. Oskar ran toward his house as Klopf stepped toward him.

"Roll the boulder at him," Carl-Erick directed Klopf.

Klopf picked up the bounder and rolled it at Oskar. The big rock rolled into the back of Oskar, buckling his legs and sending him face-first into the dirt.

"Water! I need water!" Oskar said as he lied there coughing up dirt and nearly choking.

"You heard the man," Carl-Erick said to Klopt as the two of them walked up close to Oskar. "He needs another dunking in the water trough."

"No, no, not that again!" Oskar begged, still spitting out dirt from his mouth.

"Not that?" Carl-Erick said. "All right. Let's take him over to the well instead."

Carl-Erick led the way to Oskar's well as Klopf carried Oskar like a sack of potatoes by the back of his suspenders. With Carl-Erick telling him what to do, Klopf stuffed Oskar into the wooden bucket and let Oskar and the bucket fall to the bottom of the well. The bucket broke apart as it hit the water, sending Oskar sprawling.

"There's the water you wanted," Carl-Erick called down the well shaft as he pulled up the rope and what remained of the bucket.

"I'll get even with you!" Oskar threatened.

"I think not," Carl-Erick called down, his voice echoing in the circular hole. "In fact, unless you promise to move away from Trinity Valley we're not going to help you out and you'll rot to death down there."

"You won't make me move," Oskar said defiantly.

"Okay, let's get our load of wood and go home," Carl-Erick said to Klopf. Speaking down the well shaft, he told Oskar: "We'll be back again tomorrow to see if you've changed your mind."

The following day Oskar was still defiant, so Carl-Erick left him at the bottom of the well and told him he would return again the next day. When Carl-Erick came that next day Oskar was hungry enough, cold enough and tired enough to agree to Carl-Erick's demand. "I'll leave Trinity Valley," he promised.

"When?" Carl-Erick asked, as Klopf stood by his side.

"Soon," Oskar answered.

"*Very* soon sounds better to me," Carl-Erick said. "In fact, I think today would be the perfect day for you to move, and so does my friend here. Don't you?" he said to Klopf, who nodded his head. "In fact," Carl-Erick went on, "we took the liberty of packing up all of your belongings for you, and selling off all of your livestock, in anticipation of your agreeing to move. So all you have to do is come out of the well, climb on your loaded wagon and leave."

And that is exactly what Oskar Thordal did. And that is how a troll named Klopf helped rid Trinity Valley of a bully and give the pretty place the peaceful and placid environment it still has to this day.

■

"I thought trolls were only mean and nasty," Andrew said when his father finished reading the story, "but the troll in that story helped people."

"After they helped him," Anders pointed out.

"Still, he kept his word and did something good," Andrew said.

"That he did," Anders agreed. "He was a good troll in that way."

"So trolls can be good too?" Andrew said. "Are some trolls bad and some trolls good?"

"Well, I don't know about that," Anders said, "but there are some stories that tell about trolls doing good deeds for people, or helping them in some way. I guess maybe some trolls are nicer than other trolls, just as there are nice people and not-so-nice people. There are more stories about mean trolls than nice trolls, though."

40 ▪ The Strongest Troll

As he tramped about the forest by himself, in misty moon-light, Ort's thoughts drifted toward possibilities of what could be done to make people stop working at the base of the mountain, for it appeared to be the same old story: Once people started coming somewhere, inevitably more people and despoliation followed. Hard as he tried to think of clever ways to make people abandon what they had started, his thoughts always circled back to one conclusion: Physical strength was the only advantage trolls had over human beings. And now that people had brought guns into the equation that one advantage had evaporated like morning mist always does. He thought back to what Scurf said the previous night: how having a giant troll or two on their side might be their only hope. And of course that was really no hope at all, for the age of giants was past, as he had observed. Still, he couldn't suppress thoughts of how amazingly strong giant trolls were. Their feats were legend. A natural chain of thought led Ort to recall one of the most legendary troll stories of all, which relates how two giants clashed over the contention that each was the strongest troll.

▪

Gristle was a giant troll who lived on Spruce Mountain. Another giant troll, Jorgum, lived in a cave on Rain Mountain, a mere twenty miles away. Both Gristle and Jorgum believed he was the strongest troll alive, and neither hesitated to boast of that belief. Each giant frequently demonstrated his prodigious might, amazing other, smaller, trolls with astounding feats of strength and stamina.

The trolls told stories among themselves about what they had seen Gristle and Jorgum do, and what they heard the two giants had done. Not surprisingly, many of these stories were embellished with exaggeration, aggrandizement and hyperbole. Indeed, some of the stories were fabricated from mere scraps of fact, or even out of thin air.

The other trolls loved to tell and hear stories about the strength of Gristle and Jorgum, and argue about which of the giants was the strongest troll. More than a few fights erupted when they agued about which giant was stronger, as though they thought they could settle the matter by fighting amongst themselves—as combatant proxies, as it were, though of course trolls were no more acquainted with the word "proxies" than spiders are with the notion of numbers. The troll community was fairly evenly divided as to whether Gristle or Jorgum was stronger. Inevitably, the idea of a contest between the two giants, to decide once and for all which one was stronger, bubbled up, and it wasn't long before the idea flowed like a raging river. Every troll in the region, it seemed, was curious as to which giant would best the other in a test of strength. Gristle and Jorgum inflamed such speculation by scoffing at each others' power with disdain, derision and scorn even as they bragged, blustered and blew their own horns regarding their own physical prowess.

"No one is stronger than I am," Gristle said to two trolls who told him of some deed Jorgum reputedly had performed. "That is mere child's play compared to what I am capable of doing."

"Gristle may have strong talk, but strong talk is not strong action," Jorgum said to a troll who brought up the idea of a contest with him. "I would show that blowhard what real strength is."

In time, both Gristle and Jorgum agreed to participate in a competition against each other, each one eminently confident he would come out on top. A committee of four trolls worked out the details of the contest, such as where and when the contest would be held, what feats of strength would be involved, and the means by which the winner would be determined.

The committee decided the only way to have a fair contest was to hold the event midway between the two giants' caves, which happened to be a meadow beside a fairly large lake, with a large woods nearby. Trolls from a wide radius ventured to the site to witness what promised to be an event of splendorous and enthralling entertainment. More than thirty trolls were gathered and waiting by the time one of the participants, Jorgum, arrived. Most trolls had only heard stories about what feats of strength Gristle and Jorgum had performed and so were eager to witness such feats themselves. Those who had actually seen either Gristle or Jorgum accomplish some amazing achievement were curious about whether or not the other giant could live up to his reputation.

"My opponent isn't here yet?" Jorgum said upon his arrival. "I'm not surprised, actually. In fact, I wouldn't be surprised if he doesn't show up at all. After all, who wants to be humiliated in front of others, as I will humiliate him if he does find the nerve to show up."

There was murmuring in the crowd, but those who believed Gristle was stronger than Jorgum dared not speak very loudly for feat of arousing Jorgum's wrath.

Gristle was not long in arriving, from the opposite direction from which Jorgum came.

"I must say that I'm more than a little surprised to find you here," Gristle said to Jorgum, using the same derisive thrust Jorgum used. "I thought perhaps you would pretend to be very ill, or even flee to another place to avoid having to show what sort of weakling you are compared to my great strength."

"Talk is cheap," Jorgum spat back. "We will see which one of us is strongest through action."

"That we will," Gristle agreed, "so be prepared to find out what *real* strength is."

This was not the first time Gristle and Jorgum had come face to face; they had encountered each other a couple of times previously, though never at such close range. They exchanged words with each other on only one of those two previous encounters. Truth be told, both found it best to try to avoid each other, for each had a dint of doubt he was the strongest troll— merely a dint, mind you, but doubt nonetheless.

The first event was rock throwing, which began with rocks weighing about twenty pounds each and proceeded to progressively heavier rocks and boulders. Each in his turn, Gristle and Jorgum hurled each rock and boulder as far as he could across the meadow—and some, of course, landed in the woods. With each weight, there was barely an inch of difference in where the rocks and boulders landed. The spectator trolls oooh-ed and aaaw-ed with each toss, with those who had never before witnessed such awesome power particularly impressed.

"I'm glad I'm here to see this," one troll said to another at one point. "This is something we will talk about for years to come." Other trolls expressed similar sentiments.

The second event was tree pulling. Taking turns, Gristle and Jorgum ripped trees right out of the ground, roots and all. As with rocks and boulders, they started with small trees and proceeded to trees so large they could barely reach their arms completely around the trunks. Beyond that reach-around circumference, neither giant could completely dislodge a tree from the ground. As a result, they were still tied after the tree pulling competition.

The third event was log chopping. Using finely honed giant axes, the two giant trolls chopped through the trees they had ripped from the ground to create long, de-branched logs. The object was to see which one could complete the chopping in the shortest period of time. Once again the two giants performed equally, swinging their final chops at the same instant.

Next the two giants had a series of drag races, so to speak, dragging huge logs a considerable set distance. They finished neck and neck every time, neither one ever managing to out-distance the other.

Thus the contest proceeded all through the day. Gristle and Jorgum pushed and pulled and tossed and lifted various objects, one after another, each giant the equal of the other in every test. Day transitioned to evening and still they continued to match each other in everything they did, in both strength and endur-ance, as the other trolls watched in riveted fascination. Not a single troll left as the contest went on hour after hour, for no one wanted to miss seeing how the contest would eventually conclude and which giant would win.

Gristle and Jorgum were tossing boulders into the lake as the sun set and pastel patches of reflected sky painted the still surface of the water. As Gristle started to pick up another boulder to toss, all at once a boulder more than twice the size of the one he was picking up flew over the heads of all the trolls, plopped into the lake twenty feet from shore and sent water splashing over all of the gathered trolls, with the most water splashing on Gristle and Jorgum. Confusion reigned as all of the trolls looked around, trying to comprehend where the flying boulder had come from and what was happening. All heads turned in the same direction as several trolls pointed, with the faces of those pointing etched in various expressions of awe, fright, surprise and astonishment. Soon all of the trolls' faces had the same sort of surprised, startled and shocked expressions, for another giant troll was standing there in the meadow, with his hands on his hips and a sneer on his face. This giant was more than half again taller than both Gristle and Jorgum, a giant of a giant.

"I am Swerd," the newcomer announced with a thunderous rumble of a voice. "What's going on here? I have heard there is a contest to find out who is the strongest troll. Is this so?"

No one responded. Swerd took several giant strides forward, focused on one troll, who began shaking, and asked him directly: "Is this so? Is this the contest to find out who is the strongest troll?"

"Yes, it's been going on all day," the tense troll answered. "Gristle and Jorgum there have been at it since this morning."

"And who are Girstle and Jorgum?" Swerd asked.

"Those two giants over there by the shore," the troll told him.

"Those two?!" Swerd sneered. Addressing all of the trolls, he went on: "Those two are but large small trolls, as far as I can see. Does anyone here think either of them is stronger than me?"

No one spoke, though several trolls shook their heads to indicate they didn't think that.

"And yet no one invited me to take part in the contest?" Swerd said, looking about, as if to blame and shame every troll present. "If there is a contest to find out who the strongest troll is, don't you think the strongest troll should be there?"

"None of us knew about you until now," one troll was brave enough to explain. "Where do you come from?"

"That's for me to know and you to find out," Swerd thundered. Actually, he had come quite a distance from the north, having caught wind of a contest between two giant trolls he previously knew nothing about. "If you're all here to find out who the strongest troll is, then let's find out right now."

With lightning quick action, Swerd picked up Gristle and Jorgum by the scruff of their necks, one in each hand, and tossed them out into the lake as the smaller trolls fled in every direction. Gristle and Jorgum both hurried away as furiously as they could.

"Yeah, you better get away, if you know what's good for you," Swerd called to them in a jeering fashion, tossing a few boulders in their direction, not trying to hit them but merely to reinforce the reality of who the strongest troll was.

41 ▪ The Seven Labors Of Lars Halvorstol

"Can you read me another story about a troll who is good to a person?" Andrew said to his father.

"Oh, I think so, if that's what you want to hear," Anders said. "Let me see if I can remember what one of them is. I know there are several of those in the book, but it's been a while since I've read or heard most of them." He scanned the table of contents, trying to recall the plot attached to each title. "Here, I'm pretty sure this is one," he said after scanning about thirty titles.

"What's it called?" Andrew asked.

"*The Seven Labors Of Lars Halvorstol*," Anders informed him. "I think you'll like this one a lot. It's a really good story, if I remember right. It's also pretty long. Should I look for a shorter one?"

"No, long is fine," Andrew said.

▪

A king named King Thorlaug had only one child, a beautiful daughter named Anna. When Anna was eighteen the king and the princess made a trip to visit several of the villages in the kingdom. During that trip, Princess Anna happened to meet a commoner named Lars Halvorstol, who fell madly in love with her at first sight. Anna, likewise, felt love for Lars as well. King Thorlaug tried to discourage the budding romance between his daughter and Lars, however, for the king did not believe a commoner was worthy of a daughter of his, particularly his one and only daughter. Anna, though, insisted she was in love with Lars, which did not please the king.

One day Lars went to the king and asked if he could have Anna's hand in marriage. The king knew that if he simply forbad the marriage on the ground that Lars was a commoner Anna would resent him and harbor bitterness toward him for a long time. He reasoned that if he could make Anna believe Lars was not worthy of her, though, she would quickly put Lars out of her mind and be forever grateful to her father for saving her from making a huge mistake. And he had a plan in mind that would accomplish that end.

"My dear Anna is more precious to me than anything in the entire world," the king said to Lars. "The man who will marry her must first prove himself worthy by accomplishing deeds of strength, bravery, ingenuity, resourcefulness, intelligence, fortitude, and valor. To test your worthiness, I will assign you seven labors. If you can accomplish all seven tasks you may have my daughter's hand in marriage. If, however, you fail to accomplish any one of the seven labors you will promise to go away and never attempt to contact my daughter again. Do you find this arrangement satisfactory?"

Lars didn't see that he had much of a choice, for he was in no position to try to negotiate with a king. "I am prepared to prove myself worthy of your daughter's hand," he said.

"Good," the king said, stifling a laugh, for the seven labors he had in mind for Lars were tasks so difficult they would be next-to-impossible to accomplish. Lars was like a fly trapped in his intricate spider web. "The first labor you must accomplish is to take an axe I will give you and chop down one of the petrified trees in Halland Forest, then drag the tree back to my castle. After you have completed that labor I will assign you your second labor. Do you have any questions?"

Lars said he had none, so the king supplied him with an axe and sent him on his way.

Although Lars was a strapping young man who possessed greater-than-average strength, he had serious doubt as to whether or not he was capable of chopping down a petrified tree with an axe. And that seemed to be the easier part of the first labor. Hauling a huge petrified log through miles and miles of forest would no doubt prove even more challenging. His horse was strong, but Lars didn't know if it was strong enough to accomplish that arduous chore.

As he rode through another forest toward Halland Forest he came upon an ugly, old, small, shriveled-up woman lying in pain beside a path.

"Will you please stop to help a poor old woman?" the woman called to Lars.

Lars drew his reins to stop his horse.

"I tripped in a hole and sprained both my ankles and cut my arms and legs," the woman explained. "I need a ride to the next stream, where there are ten trees with magic sap that will heal my wounds."

Lars sensed something extremely peculiar about the old woman. He had seen ugly women before, but this woman was so infused with ugly that she was approaching hideousness. If she wasn't a troll, he thought, then surely the sun might set in the east someday.

"You're not a woman," Lars said. "You're a troll. I'm not about to do a troll any favors."

"You're right, I *am* a troll," the troll said. "I'm a troll witch. My name is Guggle. And if you don't give me a ride to the next stream I'm going to put a curse on you, which will bring you bad luck and misfortune. If, however, you give me a ride to the next stream I will use my powers to help you."

"I don't believe in your curses," Lars said, and started to ride away.

Calling after him, Guggle recited:

Curses, curses follow your way.
May bad luck fall on you today.

At that instant a huge limb broke from high in a large birch tree and crashed to earth directly in front of Lars and his horse. If the horse hadn't reared up on its hind legs the tree limb would have bonked Lars on the head.

"That's only the beginning," Guggle said to Lars. "Next time I'll make it a whole tree, and the tree won't miss you."

Lars turned his horse around and went back to the troll witch. "Will you still use your powers to help me if I give you a ride to the next stream?" he asked.

"I will," Guggle said.

"Very well then," Lars said. "I'll give you a ride to the next stream."

After Lars carried the troll witch to the next stream Guggle spread sap from one of the ten special trees on her wounds. Her cuts and bruises healed immediately, which amazed Lars. Guggle asked Lars how he came to be riding through the forest. Lars told her about his love for Princess Anna and his bargain with King Thorlaug and how he was on his way to Halland Forest to chop down a petrified tree and haul it back to the king's castle.

"I don't know if my horse and I are strong enough to accomplish the task, though," Lars confided to the troll witch. "I fear that I may lose my Princess Anna."

"Have no fear," Guggle said. "I promised that if you did me a good turn I would do a good turn for you. At my cottage I have an herb potion that will give both you and your horse strength enough to fell a petrified tree and haul is back to the king's castle."

Lars and Guggle rode to the witch's forest cottage at once. There, Guggle gave Lars two small packets of mixed herbs and instructed him to eat one packet when he was ready to chop down a petrified tree and feed the other packet to his horse when he was ready to have the horse haul the felled tree back to the king's castle.

"Feel free to seek my help again if you need it for any of your other labors," Guggle said to Lars when Lars was about to depart. "I know of this King Thorlaug, and he has not been kind to us trolls. He no doubt wants you to fail, and I will do whatever I am able to do to help you succeed."

When he reached Halland Forest and located a large petrified tree, Lars took out his axe and hacked a few blows at the trunk without eating the herb mixture the troll witch had given him. His blows barely chipped the stone. Praying that the witch had not given him poison, Lars ate the herb mixture and once again swung his axe. This time his axe dug into the stone column as easily as though the tree had turned to powder. He felled the tree in no time at all.

He then harnessed the huge tree to his horse, fed the horse the other packet of mixed herbs, and ordered the horse to go forward. Giving a powerful pull, the horse jerked the heavy petrified tree ahead and then trotted along at a steady pace as Lars directed it through the forest.

King Thorlaug was more than a little surprised when Lars returned to the castle with a petrified tree, having succeeded at his first labor.

Summoning Lars, King Thorlaug said: "You have passed your first test. Now I will give you your second task. Centuries ago, King Odin lost his favorite encrusted sword somewhere in this region. You must find that sword and bring it to me."

Lars had no idea where he should start looking for King Odin's sword. He feared that the king had assigned him an impossible labor this time, but he dared not make any complaint, for he had entered into a bargain and felt duty-bound to try to live up to his part of the bargain, however overwhelming the odds against him. He doubted that even a troll witch could help him this time, but for the time being Guggle appeared to be his only ray of hope, so he rode to her cabin—for it really was more of a cabin than a cottage, as she called it—to see her.

Guggle asked Lars to describe the lost sword. After listening to Lars's description, Guggle said: "I think I just might know where the sword is. That sounds very much like a sword a troll named Ravh found many years ago. If you come again tomorrow morning with a sack of potatoes, a sack of vegetables, and a sack of apples I think I will have the sword for you."

The following morning Lars returned to Guggle's forest cabin with the three sacks of produce the witch had requested.

"Is this what you're looking for?" Guggle said, handing Lars a sword.

"That's it!" Lars squealed, examining the sword, which had a bejeweled handle. "This *has* to be the sword."

"Then take it and give it to the king," Guggle said.

When Lars presented the sword to King Thorlaug the king was as excited as a child who had received exactly what he had wished for on his birthday. At the same time, it made the king worry that assigning Lars a labor at which he would fail might prove to be considerably more difficult than he had originally imagined it would be.

After some thought, the king presented Lars with his next challenge: A ferocious three-headed monster that was a cross between a wild bull and a wolf lived in a cave near a certain seacoast village. It was said that no weapon could wound the monster. Lars was to slay this beast and bring back the three heads as proof of his success.

Lars again sought Guggle's help. This time Guggle consulted her Book of Wisdom. "I must mix a potion for you," the witch said. "You must get close enough to the monster to blow the potion into the nostrils of all three of its noses. That will put the monster into a trance just long enough to allow you time to choke it to death."

Lars took the potion Guggle mixed up for him and rode three days to the seaside to reach the place where the three-headed monster lived. The monster was sunning itself on a rock when Lars first spotted it. Sneaking up close, Lars sprang at the monster. Lars and the monster wrestled around as Lars tried to pull out his potion so that he could blow it up the monster's noses. He suffered many scratches and cuts, and a few bites, before he managed to pull out the magic potion and blow it in the monster's three noses. Immediately, the monster was immobilized, in a trancelike state. Lars wasted no time in choking the monster's three necks and hacking off its three heads with a sword. He took the three heads back to King Thorlaug as proof of his success and asked what his fourth labor was.

The king was prepared with a new challenge. "In the Far North," he said, "it is said that there is an enormous wild ram that has fleece of pure gold. The ram lives in a treacherous mountain region where it is believed it is impossible for anyone to catch it. To prove your worthiness, you must capture the ram, shear off its golden fleece, and bring the golden fleece to me so that I may have a golden robe woven out of it."

Once again Lars sought Guggle's help. After consulting the Book of Wisdom again, the troll witch told Lars to return three days later, by which time she would have something that would help him. The witch needed three days to find certain special substances she needed to concoct a potion that would cause a ram's fleece to fall out.

"All you have to do," she told Lars when he returned, "is get close enough to shower the potion on the ram, then follow it and pick up the fleece that falls off."

Lars made the long journey northward, then spent two weeks searching for the wild ram with the golden fleece and another two weeks observing the ram from a distance so that he knew its routine. Once he figured out the ram's routine he was able to hide behind a rock above a canyon where the ram often visited. When he saw the ram directly below him, Lars tossed handfuls of Guggle's magic potion into the air and the potion showered the ram like snowflakes.

Then he climbed down into the canyon as the ram moved on. Just as Guggle said there would be, tufts of golden fleece marked the ram's trail. Lars gathered the golden fleece into a large sack until there was no more golden fleece to be found. Then he journeyed home to present the sack of golden fleece to King Thorlaug, who was growing increasingly worried that Lars might actually manage to succeed at all seven labors. Lars had already succeeded at four tasks; if he succeeded at three more the king would have to honor his promise and allow him to marry his precious Anna.

This was Lars's fifth labor: He was to capture a stag with solid gold horns that lived in Knorrwood Forest and bring the animal back alive to King Thorlaug's castle.

This time Guggle carved a horn from a special type of wood, aged just so, to help Lars in his hunt. By blowing the horn, Lars was able to entice the golden-horned stag to follow him as though the stag was an obedient dog accustomed to following him wherever he went.

King Thorlaug never imagined that Lars would succeed at so many of his labors, so he wasn't prepared to assign Lars his sixth task when Lars returned with the golden-horned stag. After considering the matter for two days he was ready with the next challenge. This time Lars was to find a set of a dozen diamond-studded silver goblets that had been buried deep within a mountain hundreds of years before when a large rockslide covered the entrance of the cave where the goblets were kept.

After learning of Lars's new challenge, Guggle consulted with several of the most elderly trolls in the area to find out what they remembered of rockslides. Two of the old trolls remembered a particularly large rockslide that covered the entrance of a cave that humans frequently visited. Guggle told Lars what she had learned and provided him with the directions he needed to locate the sealed cave.

By digging where instructed to dig for several weeks, Lars eventually shoveled his way into a cavernous passageway. Using a torch to light his way, he searched the sprawling cave for hours before something glinted in his light. It turned out to be the dozen diamond-studded silver goblets King Thorlaug had asked him to find.

Now Lars needed to accomplish only one more labor and he would have the king's blessing to marry Princess Anna.

King Thorlaug was well aware of that, so he was determined to assign Lars a task so challenging that he could not possibly succeed this time. He spun ideas around in his mind for a week before deciding what Lars's final challenge would be.

"Some years ago a small ship carrying a chest of coins sank in extremely deep water near Kronenberg Island," the King told Lars. "You are to locate the sunken ship, recover the chest of coins, and bring me the coins."

Could Guggle come to the rescue one last time? Lars wasted no time in heading for her cabin to find out. The witch leafed through the Book of Wisdom for a long time for a solution to the problem. Finally she said she thought she could help Lars locate the sunken treasure, but she wasn't completely confident. She needed a week to find certain roots, herbs, flower petals, insects, and other substances for magic potions Lars would need to have any chance of success.

When Lars returned, Guggle gave him a pouch filled with magic powder and a jar full of liquid potion. Lars was to secure a boat and sprinkle the powder on top of the water as he rowed about the area near Kronenberg Island. If gold coins were below, the specks of powder would be drawn together like nails to a magnet. With the sunken treasure pinpointed, Lars was to drink the liquid potion and dive for the treasure. The potion would give him the ability to fill his lungs with enough air to remain underwater for fifteen minutes, and dive as deep as necessary. It would also give him extra strength.

Lars did as Guggle instructed he was to do. He secured a boat, rowed about near Kronenberg Island sprinkling powder on the surface of the sea until he found a spot where the specks of powder congealed together, then drank the magic liquid potion and dove to the bottom of the sea. There he quickly located a well-preserved ship, which he searched until he found a chest of coins. With the extra strength the potion gave him, and the fact that objects are much easier to move underwater, Lars was able to lift the chest of coins to the surface and push the chest into his boat.

By now King Thorlaug wasn't all that surprised when Lars returned with the chest of coins from the sunken ship. Indeed, after assigning Lars his seventh and final labor the king actually hoped Lars would succeed, for he realized that anyone who could accomplish seven such difficult labors truly was someone of strength, bravery, ingenuity, resourcefulness, intelligence, fortitude and valor, and so someone worthy of his only daughter's hand, regardless of his station in life. The king was more than happy to let his daughter marry Lars.

The wedding took place in short order, with a celebration as grand and glorious as the castle had ever seen.

As a wedding gift, the king gave Anna and Lars the chest of coins Lars recovered from the sunken ship.

After Lars told Anna how the troll witch Guggle helped him accomplish his seven labors, they agreed they should give one-third of the coins to Guggle for how she had helped Lars and made it possible for them to be together for the rest of their days.

42 • Mushrooms And Majesty

The day's strong northwest wind was still singing, surging and swooping across the slope of Troll Mountain when Skimpa and Elseth, the daughter of Llop and Retta, ventured out in the early evening to hunt for mushrooms. Trolls consider mushrooms to be as tasty and delectable as people do, and so they are more than willing to expend considerable effort to find them, especially their favorite species. Mushrooms were far more plentiful at lower elevations than higher on the mountain, so serious mushroom hunting meant long walks down the mountain and back to the caves. Anticipation—going down—and gratification—returning with a nice harvest—made those long walks seem less arduous.

"I hope we find a lot," Skimpa said to Elseth this evening, soon after they started out.

"I hope so too," Elseth responded. "There's not much I like to eat more than mushrooms."

"I can taste them now!" Skimpa said, licking the lips of her wide mouth.

Elseth, more than two hundred years younger, was six inches taller than Skimpa, with arms and legs closer to human proportion than is the case with most trolls. Strands of her mop-like black hair obscured part of her pockmarked face, which featured puffy cheeks and a bulbous nose. Skimpa wore a black dress, Elseth a print, short-sleeved blouse and a long blue skirt that flared out from her waist to the ground. The skirt was too long for her legs, so the bottom part was frayed and caked with dried mud.

The two found their first mushrooms about twenty minutes into their walk—only a few small ones growing out of a decomposing log. Moving on, further down the mountain, they found others scattered here and there, which they added to their woven baskets. After more than an hour of walking they came upon a north-facing slope where at least fifteen species of mushrooms were as concentrated as daisies or black-eyed Susans often are in places. "What a sight!" Skimpa said. "Just look at 'em all!"

"How are we going to carry them all home?" Elseth said. "They won't all fit in our baskets."

"We'll worry about that later," Skimpa said. "Let's get to picking!"

And that is exactly what the two did—they began picking the mushrooms, and placing them in their baskets. Not every mushroom they picked went into the baskets, though; they ate some as well. Indeed, they stuffed themselves full of mushrooms, as though stuffing feathers and other fluff into a pillow. Twenty minutes into their picking, Elseth said: "I don't feel too good. I feel a little dizzy."

"Maybe you better sit down," Skimpa said.

Following Skimpa's suggestion, Elseth sat on a large log and set her basket of mushrooms on the ground.

"Does your stomach hurt?" Skimpa asked.

"Sort of," Elseth said. "You look a little blurry."

"I don't like the sound of that," Skimpa said. "I hope you didn't eat a poison mushroom."

"Do you think I did?" Elseth said with grave concern. "Do you think I'm going to die?"

"I don't know," Skimpa said in answer to Elseth's first question, which Elseth interpreted as an answer to her second question.

"You think I might die!?" Elseth said in a panic. "This is awful! I can't die like this, this young!"

"I mean, I don't know if you ate a poison mushroom," Skimpa clarified. "Maybe you just ate too many. I ate most of the same ones you ate, and I feel all right. Are you still dizzy?"

Elseth nodded her head. "Yeah, and it's getting worse."

Skimpa looked around, as though an answer to the problem might be visible somewhere. "If I have my bearings right," she said, "I'm pretty sure that Guggle's cottage is not too far in that direction." She pointed in the direction she meant. "I think we should get you to her. She'll be able to help you better than I can, if she's home. I just pray that she *is* home. Do you feel up to walking?"

"Not really," Elseth said. "Maybe I should just lay down here and see if it passes."

"No, we have to get you to Guggle," Skimpa insisted. "Come on, I'll help you."

"Maybe you could go and get Guggle and bring her back here," Elseth suggested. "I don't know how far I can walk."

"That might take too long," Skimpa said. "It's better that we go to her cottage. I'm sure it's not very long of a walk. You can do it, with my help. Come on, I'll help you up. Pull yourself up on my shoulder."

With Elseth relying on Skimpa for support, the two started walking in the direction where Skimpa was fairly certain Guggle's cabin stood, Skimpa hoping all the while that her sense of direction was accurate and that Guggle would be home rather than off somewhere for the night. Elseth's dizziness and stomach pain grew worse as they proceeded through the forest, so Skimpa did what she could to reassure Elseth that they would soon be at Guggle's cottage, where Guggle would know what to do to ease her pain.

"I think that's it!" Skimpa cried out when she caught a glimpse of what appeared to be Guggle's cabin. "Yes, I'm sure that's it!" she said after several more steps. "It must be! We've made it!"

The sky held only a hint of light by then, and there was only a light breeze; the strong wind had faded during their walk to Guggle's cabin, without Skimpa being aware of it. Candlelight glowed in one of the cabin windows, which Skimpa took as an encouraging sign, for it meant Guggle likely was at home. Skimpa was soon knocking at the door, which Guggle quickly opened. Instantly, the witch could tell something was wrong with Elseth.

"She may have eaten a poison mushroom," Skimpa informed her.

"Let's get her inside, quickly!" Guggle said, standing aside to let Skimpa help Elseth through the doorway. "We'll put her on my bed."

With Guggle leading the way, Skimpa helped Elseth into the small bedroom and onto Guggle's bed.

"What sort of mushroom did she eat?" Guggle asked Skimpa. "Can you describe it?"

"I'm not sure what it was," Skimpa said. "We both ate a lot of different kinds of mushrooms. Maybe she just ate too many."

"Maybe," Guggle said, then proceeded to ask Elseth a series of questions to pin down her symptoms. "I think I have just the thing for her," she said. "I'm going to brew up a special tea. You stay here with her," she instructed Skimpa.

Moving about with confident efficiency, Guggle quickly brewed a strong, dark tea of her own creation that was meant to be an antidote for mushroom poisoning, then brought a cup of it to Elseth and incanted:

Mushroom poison, out with thee,
Leave this woman drinking tea.

"Here, drink this down," Guggle ordered. "It will cure you right up."

With Skimpa's assistance, Elseth raised her head to sip the special tea from the cup Guggle held to her lips.

"Good, good; keep drinking," Guggle said soothingly.

"It's tasty," Elseth said. "I feel a little less dizzy already."

"Good, good. It's doing its job," Guggle said. "Here, take the cup and help her keep sipping it," she said to Skimpa, then went back into the kitchen and returned to the bedroom with another cup of the special tea, which she held out for Skimpa. "Here," she said to her, "you better drink a cup of it too, just in case."

"But I feel fine, really," Skimpa said.

"You better drink it anyway," Guggle said, "just in case you ate some of the same poison. Maybe you just ate less of it, or it would hit you later. Drink it up now; it won't hurt you, even if you didn't eat any poison."

Skimpa took the second cup of tea, sat back in a chair and began drinking it, for by now Elseth felt strong enough to hold her own cup. Guggle sat on the edge of the bed and asked Elseth if she felt any better.

"Some better," Elseth answered. "I don't seem to be as dizzy as I was, but my stomach still hurts."

"Keep drinking the tea," Guggle said. "That should make you feel better. You need to drink the whole cup."

Guggle and Skimpa did most of the talking as Elseth finished the rest of her cup of special tea.

"I hear that more men and more machines have come to the bottom of the mountain," Guggle said. "This is a bad state of affairs for us trolls."

"It's awful," Skimpa said. "Tattra says Ort is at a loss to know what can be done to drive them away. You know how much Ort despises people, and how much he hates them being there. Do you think we might all have to leave and move somewhere else if things get bad enough?"

"Let us hope it doesn't come to that," Guggle said. "We've been here so long now. This mountain has been our home for a long time. It's ours."

"Well, Ort is determined that we will make a stand here and not move, but. . . I just can't help but wonder if that might become impossible at some point, as it became impossible many other places we lived," Skimpa said.

"As long as the people stay where they are, at the bottom of the mountain, we won't have to move," Guggle said. "It would be better if they weren't there, so close, of course."

"Isn't there something you can do to put a curse on them and force them to leave?" Skimpa asked.

"Unfortunately," Guggle replied, "I have little power over people away from my cottage. If they could be brought here one by one maybe I could do something, but as it is. . . Well, it is what it is."

There was silence for a full minute before Skimpa said: "Look at the way the sky is glowing through that window," by which she meant one of the small windows in the cabin's main room.

Guggle swiveled her head and torso to look. "It's The Lights!" she said, meaning the Northern Lights, which are simply The Lights to trolls. "This is the best omen there could ever be. It means you're going to be just fine," she said to Elseth. "How do you feel now? Any better?"

"Much better," Elseth said. "I'm not dizzy at all, and I have no pain anywhere." She sat up, bent at the waist. "I feel refreshed, in fact."

"Wonderful!" Guggle said.

"What about The Lights?" Skimpa said to Guggle. "You said they're a good omen?"

"The best," Guggle said. "Seeing them is a sign that Elseth is completely healed."

"I like to just look at The Lights sometimes," Skimpa said. "They're so pretty. Sometimes I'll just lie against a tree or a rock and watch them for a long time."

"Let's all go outside where we can see them better," Guggle said.

Outside, the northern sky shimmered with shafts of misty green, yellow, red and soft lilac, the pastel smears of diffused color dancing and shifting shapes, washing across the sky like waves across a sea, only with much slower movements, like slow motion waves. The aurora borealis was in full luminescence, displaying its majesty as showily as a queen displaying an elegant new robe.

"Do you know that you can actually hear The Lights if you listen closely enough?" Guggle said.

"Really?" Skimpa said. "I didn't know that."

"They whoosh, like a soft wind," Guggle said. "Listen."

All three stood there as quietly as possible, trying even to keep their breathing low.

"Can you hear it?" Guggle said.

"I'm not sure," Skimpa said. "Can you?"

"Yes," Guggle said. "It's very faint, but it's there."

"A whoosh?" Skimpa said.

"Like a distant wind, very soft," Guggle said.

"Can you hear it?" Skimpa asked Elseth.

"I'm not sure either," Elseth admitted. "I'm not sure if I'm hearing the wind around us or the sound The Lights are making."

There was still a hint of wind, though the intensity was that of the green glow of The Lights compared to the verdant green of June trees.

They watched The Lights for ten minutes before Skimpa and Elseth went on their way, baskets full of mushrooms in hand.

43 ▪ The Field Of Magic Mushrooms

"Maybe it's because we had mushrooms for supper and I still have mushrooms on my mind," Anders said to his son while scanning the book's table of contents, "but I think I'll read you this story called *The Field Of Magic Mushrooms*."

▪

For several centuries, a legend survived in the province of Galveberg that a field of magic mushrooms existed somewhere within the province. According to the legend, a charcoal burner working deep in a forest saved an elf from the clutches of a wolf. To reward the charcoal burner for saving his life, the elf took him to a secret place in the deepest, darkest part of the forest where a small field of large mushrooms grew.

"This is a field of magic mushrooms," the elf told the charcoal burner.

"They look like ordinary mushrooms to me," the charcoal burner remarked. "What makes them magical?"

"Keep your eye on that mushroom," the elf instructed the charcoal burner, pointing to a particular mushroom, "and you will see for yourself."

As the charcoal burner watched, the elf transformed the spongy, fibrous mushroom into a gleaming, solid gold mushroom right before his eyes.

"It looks like gold!" the charcoal burner said in amazement.

"Go touch it," the elf invited.

The charcoal burner went over to the golden mushroom and touched it with his left hand. "It *is* gold!" he exclaimed.

"It is my gift to you for saving my life," the elf told the charcoal burner.

"You mean it's mine?" the charcoal burner said.

"It is," the elf answered. "Go ahead and pick it if you like."

The charcoal burner did exactly that, pulling the golden mushroom from the ground with ease.

"That is but the first of many golden mushrooms you shall have as a reward for saving my life," the elf said. "Return to this spot on this exact date each year and you will find another golden mushroom waiting for you to pick."

The charcoal burner thanked the elf profusely for his generosity and the two parted ways, never to see each other again.

The golden mushroom was so valuable that the charcoal burner was able to live in high style for a full year on the money he received from selling it.

The following year the charcoal burner returned to the field of magic mushrooms on the exact date he had rescued the elf from his perilous situation and the elf had given him the golden mushroom. True to his word, the elf had transformed another ordinary mushroom into a solid gold mushroom. The charcoal burner picked the second golden mushroom, sold it as he had the first one, and again lived in high style for a full year on the profit he made.

This pattern repeated itself for a good many years. On the special date each year the charcoal burner—who no longer worked as a charcoal burner, of course, for he had sufficient money without having to work—returned to the field of magic mushrooms, found a gold mushroom waiting for him, picked it, sold it, and continued to live in the high style to which he had become accustomed.

Eventually, of course, the one-time charcoal burner died. He passed away without revealing the exact location of the field of magic mushrooms to anyone. While he had told others about how he saved an elf from a wolf and how the elf had then rewarded him by leading him to the field of magic mushrooms, the most precise he ever was about the location was when he said it was "somewhere within the province of Galveberg."

It seemed logical to most people that there should be at least one golden mushroom in the field of magic mushrooms, for if there was one there every year on a certain date there should have been one there for the charcoal burner the year he died and was unable to pick it. As hard as many people looked, though, no one could find the last gold mushroom, if there was one, in the field of magic mushrooms. As the years went on fewer and fewer people searched for the gold mushroom, although the story was still widely told, particularly in the province of Galveberg.

Long after the charcoal burner who gathered the gold mushrooms died, a lad named Leif Swelander heard the legend for the first time when he was nine years old. The story stuck with Leif like a shadow, fascinating him more than any other tale ever did. Over a period of many long years, Leif hiked through the Galveberg forests at every opportunity, searching for the gold mushroom, or mushrooms. Other people said he was wasting his time and shook their heads sadly in the belief that Leif's obsession had unhinged his mind. Year after year Leif Swelander searched for the gold mushroom, without success. He found seemingly millions of mushrooms—and became a mushroom expert, in the process—but not the single solid gold one he so desired.

At age seventy-five Leif was still hiking through forests in search of the golden mushroom. One day he hiked into a part of a forest that was so thick with brushy undergrowth that he needed a large knife to clear a path for himself. After hiking for more than three hours he suddenly burst upon a small open area lit by a steeply angled beam of sunlight. When a metallic gleam caught his eye, he stepped quickly in the direction of the gleam, which arose from a small field of mushrooms. When he saw what was giving off the gleam, Leif's heart raced, for it was unmistakably a gold mushroom. Leif leaned down and touched the gold mushroom with the sort of tenderness he would use to stroke the wings of a butterfly. He tugged at the stem of the mushroom and the mushroom popped out of the ground. "It's gold!" he shouted, cackling with glee and dancing around deliriously. "Gold! I've found it at last! Gold!"

Unbeknownst to Leif, he was not alone. A squat-shaped, malevolent-minded troll had spotted Leif hacking his way through the thick forest and trailed him for two hours. Now the troll hid behind a tree trunk watching the ecstatic old man perform a dance of joy. Hearing Leif shout the word "gold" several times, and seeing how the mushroom Leif held in his hand gleamed in the sun, the troll realized that Leif was holding a golden mushroom. Since trolls adore anything made of gold, the troll wanted the golden mushroom for himself.

Before Leif knew what hit him, the troll burst into the opening and smashed Leif on the back of the head with a large rock. Leif crumbled to the forest floor, unconscious.

When he awoke—groggily—nearly two hours later it took him a minute to remember where he was and what had happened. There was a large bump on the back of his head and the gold mushroom was not there. Leif felt like crying. After searching for the golden mushroom for so many long years, then finally finding it, only to have it stolen from him. . . Well, had fate ever played a crueler trick on anyone? Leif stood up and took a couple of wobbly steps. All at once he noticed something out of the corner of his left eye: a battered boot sticking out of the bushes. Approaching cautiously, he discovered the boot was attached to a stubby leg that belonged to a troll lying flat on his back, unconscious.

He wondered if his attacker also had knocked the troll unconscious. As he searched the ground around the unconscious troll with his eyes, he beheld a sight that caused his heart to pound with excitement: The gold mushroom was laying only a few feet from the troll. Leif reasoned the troll must have been the one who conked him on the head and stole the gold mushroom. But why was the troll lying there unconscious? Had he stolen the golden mushroom and then decided to lie down for a rest? That seemed unlikely.

Leif wondered if the troll was dead. As he watched closely, he detected the troll's chest swell with an intake of air ever so slowly and ever so slightly, so he knew the troll was alive. Clearly, though, this coma-like slumber was not normal sleep. Looking around, his mind grasped what had happened. Laughing aloud at his good fortune, he snatched up the precious, long-sought golden mushroom and fled as quickly as he was able to flee, for he knew the troll probably would eventually awake, and he wanted to be far away when he regained consciousness. Before leaving the field of magic mushrooms, though, Leif said a prayer of thanks that trolls were gluttons who never passed up a morsel of food and another prayer of thanks that the field of magic mushrooms was a field of poisonous mushrooms.

44 ▪ More Activity

"**W**hat in the world!?" Haar thought as he surveyed the construction site, taken aback by the amount of activity, which had increased greatly since his last visit, like a rain-swollen river surging with a stronger current. Curious about what seemed to be an increased noise level, he had made his way down the mountain alone to investigate, not anticipating what a teeming bustle of activity he would find on display. In addition to the digging, the dirt moving and the tree cutting, and all of the attendant noise that went with those activities, a stream of large trucks arrived and dispensed mounds of potato soup-like concrete, which men with shovels, rakes and scrapers pushed and pulled about, and leveled, though from his relatively distant vantage point Haar didn't know the workers were smoothing the workable concrete into a level surface. Indeed, Haar was pretty much perplexed by everything going on in front of him. He couldn't comprehend exactly what the people were doing, or why they were doing it. Of course, as Ort was fond of saying, he knew people had different ways of thinking and acting than trolls did. Still, sometimes that divide seemed wider than usual, and this was one of those times for Haar.

Though bewildered, he was also enthralled. As though under a spell, he felt compelled to continue watching, for he found himself continually wondering what would happen next, what new machine might arrive, where all of the activity would lead, even as a competing compulsion pulled at him: a desire to let the others know about this new development, and the increased level of activity, as soon as possible. "I'll stay and watch just a little while longer," he kept telling himself, over and over, until those "little while" periods of time, put together, added up to a rather considerable length of time, links of minutes in an hours-long chain. He couldn't pull himself away until the workers left, at five o'clock, though Haar wasn't aware of the time. Armed guards arrived at that point, to stay through the night, even though the chain link fence people erected to protect the construction site now completely surrounded the main construction area.

When Haar returned to the caves and began telling others about what he had seen, before they left on night sojourns, his news was met with a mixture of anger and perplexity. Few could comprehend what Haar meant when he described the potato soup-like mounds of gray substance the men dumped on the ground and then poked, prodded, pushed and pulled with a variety of tools. Over the course of the next several days two-thirds of the tribe members went down the mountain, close to the construction site, to observe the activity for themselves. They witnessed a continuation of the concrete work, and an even more alarming development: tree cutting and earth scraping up the side of the mountain.

"Are they going to cut all of the trees on the mountain and make the mountain completely bare?" Brine asked Grentd and Rnobrna, his two companions this particular afternoon.

"This is an outrage!" Rnobrna declared. "They have to be stopped!"

"Wait until Ort hears about *this*!" Grentd said.

And Ort heard about it in short order, of course. "A thousand curses on people!" he said as an initial reaction. He went and looked for himself, and was even more disgusted by the revolting development. The distressing, maddening situation seemed to be snowballing, and the prospect of stopping that growing, speeding snowball was growing as dim as mid-afternoons in December.

The trolls discussed the construction site developments more than they had at any time since the initial discovery of the tree cutting and earth moving. The logging and earthwork up the slope was the most troubling aspect of the operation, so that was what the trolls discussed most, and most vehemently. On more than a few occasions the trolls took out their frustration and anger at what people were doing on each other, arguing and fighting with one another as a way to vent their rage and frustration. As angry as they were about what was taking place, their frustration was worse than their rage. The fact that they couldn't come up with any reasonable, realistic ideas as to what they could do to put a stop to the activity ate at them like acid eats at metal. They were all as creatively empty as Ort when it came to possible strategies or actions. They felt helpless and hopeless, and thus completely frustrated. They had the advantage of strength, and that was it; people had intelligence, powerful machinery, deadly weapons, determination and perseverance. People generally got their way and did what they wanted to do because of that.

There was talk about how bad the situation might become, with more and more tribe members growing anxious about the possibility that it may become necessary to flee the mountain and find new homes to the north. As brave a face as he put on, even Ort began having stray thoughts about whether things might come to that calamitous turn. He didn't share such dark thoughts with anyone else, though, not even his wife, Tattra. "People won't get the best of us this time," he vowed. "We'll beat them in the end. It's only a matter of time."

"But how will we beat them?" Skimpa asked during a group discussion.

"We'll figure out something," Ort said. "We have to. We just have to. That's all there is to it."

"You don't suppose they're planning to mine the mountain, do you?" Gangl said to no one in particular. "If that happens, everything that has happened up to now will seem like nothing. What a commotion their mining makes! It's maddening! *Boom! Boom! Boom!* They set off blasts that make your hair stand on end, your ears ring, and the ground beneath you shudder. That's why we left Frost Mountain, you know, because people were blasting away on the other side of the mountain." By "we," he meant himself and his wife, Feirn. "Each blast was like a hundred church bells all ringing at once. It gives me chills just thinking about it. What a horrible, horrible sound!"

"I'm glad I've never heard it, if it's as bad as you say it is," Retta said. Like Jompa, Retta had a fountainous spray of frizzy, frowzy hair, only hers was ink black rather than dirty white.

"You can't imagine!" Feirn said. "It's unbearable. We simply couldn't bear to keep living where we were living."

"Is it really possible that could happen here?" Grentd said, posing another question directed at no one in particular.

"Yeah, what makes you think people are going to start mining here?" Hlauka asked Gangl.

"I don't know if they are or not," Gangl responded. "I'm just saying that's one possible explanation as to why people are clearing away trees where they are, even up the lower part of the mountain. I think we have to be prepared for anything."

"Prepared how?" Hlauka asked.

"Well. . . I don't know exactly," Gangl said, his droopy eyes seeming droopier than usual. "I'm just saying that anything is possible when it comes to people. Isn't that right, Ort?"

"I'm afraid so," Ort said. "They're tricky devils."

"Tricky?" Dau blurted out, his bulging eyes giving his reaction added weight. "You can say that again! I found that out for myself a long time ago."

"What happened?" Feirn asked.

She was one of the few tribe members who hadn't heard the story Dau proceeded to tell.

45 ▪ Dau And The Butterfly Catcher

"When I lived on Owl Mountain, a long time ago, I was out trout fishing one evening when I spotted a man—a person—in a clearing not far away. I didn't like the idea of having a person so close to my home, so I snuck over toward where he was to try to see what he was doing there. Well, he was acting very strangely, even for a human. As I watched from behind the trunk of a big tree, he ran about in the meadow with a long net, with a handle, made out of silk or something. I mean the net looked like it was made out of silk; the handle was made of wood. Imagine the sort of cap gnomes wear, only much, much larger; that's what the net was shaped like. I don't mean he was running all the time; he would walk around slowly most of the time, or stand still, and then all at once dash this way or that way, or lunge somewhere, and then swing his net through the air or into the tall grass and flowers. At first I had no idea what he was doing, he was acting so crazy. Of course, we all know that people do a lot of crazy things that are hard to figure out, but this was extremely puzzling. As I kept watching, and the man came closer to where I was, I finally saw some butterflies flying around, and the man seemed to be swinging his net at them. Crazy as it sounds, that's what he seemed to be doing.

"Well, I guess I must have moved a little bit, and he saw me move and he froze in place, right where he was. Since he was looking right at me anyway—or at least at what part of me he could see; I don't think he could see all of me—I rushed out into the meadow and ran to where he was. He backed up and looked very frightened, but he didn't try to run away. I think maybe he was too surprised to try to run.

" 'What are you doing here?' I said to him. I was none too nice about the way I said it, of course, because I didn't like the idea of him being there, so close to my home.

" 'I'm catching butterflies,' he said.

" 'Catching butterflies!' I said. 'What for? To eat?'

" 'No, not to eat; to add to my collection,' he said. 'I'm a butterfly collector,' he said, as though that was supposed to mean something to me.

" 'What does that mean?' I asked him.

" 'It means I collect butterflies,' he said. 'I catch them and mount them in display boxes, and I want to have as many different kinds of butterflies as I can catch.'

"Well, obviously he was up to no good, so I told him he better go back to my cave with me until I could think about the situation and decide what I should do with him. I guess that must have scared him, because he *did* try to run away then. It was nothing for me to catch him, though. I got a good grip on one of his arms and twisted it, which made him fall to his knees. He was a pretty big fellow, with a big beard, but he was weak for his size, so it was easy to keep him under control. I jerked him to his feet and made him start walking toward my cave.

" 'Hold up!' he said after we had walked only a little ways.

"He stopped, and I stopped too, and said, 'What is it?'

" 'See that butterfly flying right over there, to our left?' he said. It was this large butterfly with bright yellow and green wings, with red spots on the edges of the wings.

" 'What about it?' I said.

" 'That's a very special kind of butterfly,' he said. 'I'll let you in on the secret of how it could be of great use to you if you promise to let me leave in peace.'

" 'How could a butterfly be of great use to me?' I said.

" 'If you promise to turn me loose I'll tell you,' he said.

" 'Better yet,' I said, 'you tell me the secret first, and then I'll decide whether or not I'll turn you loose.'

" 'I'm afraid it doesn't work that way,' he said. 'For the secret to work, you can't be doing something bad at the time, and holding someone against his will is a bad thing.'

" 'All right,' I said, 'tell me what the secret is and I'll let you go.'

" 'Okay, it's a deal,' he said. 'The secret is that that kind of butterfly has special magic powers, but only when they are in groups of three. It can't be one, or two, or four; it has to be three of them. Catch three of them and bring them together and they have the power to make three wishes come true for you. You can wish for anything you like—wealth, or the love of a special lady, or super powers. Anything.'

"Well, you can imagine how excited I was then. All I had to do was catch three butterflies to have three wishes come true? That sounded sort of like a wish come true itself, though of course it had never occurred to me to make that particular wish. But what did I know about catching butterflies? I had never even thought about trying to catch them, that I could remember. The man knew how to catch butterflies, though, so I said to him, 'Tell you what: You catch three of the butterflies for me, and then I'll let you go.'

" 'I would be happy to,' the man said, 'except that the three wishes come true only if the one making the wishes catches the butterflies himself. That's the only way it works, I'm afraid. So, you see, you will have to catch the three butterflies yourself.'

" 'Then give me your net,' I said, for I could see that using the net would help me catch butterflies much more easily than if I tried catching them with my hands. So he handed me the long net, and I made him teach me how to use it. Then I told him I wouldn't let him go until I caught three of the butterflies and saw that my first wish came true, so I could tell he wasn't lying.

" 'There's one other thing I forgot to tell you,' he said. 'Your three wishes will come true only if you catch the three butterflies yourself, when you are all alone, by yourself, with no one else watching what you're doing, and if you make each wish when you are all alone. That is the only way things work. You have to be all alone each step of the way.'

"Well, what could I do? I wanted to have three wishes come true, so I let the man leave—keeping his net for myself, of course—and immediately started looking around the meadow for the special butterflies with the yellow and green wings, with red spots on the ends of the wings. I found only one of them that evening, then I went back to that same meadow the next day to look for more. It took me quite some time, but I eventually managed to catch two more of those butterflies. Butterflies are not easy to catch, by the way, even with a net like I had. They're tricky little things, the way they flit around. Try catching one sometime and you'll see.

"Anyway, now I had three of what this man had told were special butterflies, and I couldn't wait to make my first wish. I had the butterflies in this little sack I had. I usually used it to put trout in that I caught, but it worked good for butterflies too. I went and sat on this rock ledge at the edge of the meadow and thought for a while about what I should wish for. After thinking for quite a while, I finally decided what I would wish for first, and I made a wish that the walls of my cave would turn to solid gold. I couldn't wait to get home to my solid gold cave! I ran as fast as I had ever run back to my cave, imagining how the inside of my cave would gleam and how everyone would envy me for my solid gold cave. Do you know what I found when I reached my cave? Nothing had changed! It looked exactly the way it had when I left it earlier that day. You can imagine how surprised I was, and disappointed. I had no doubt that I would walk into a solid gold cave. At that point I started to worry that maybe the man had lied to me and fooled me into thinking I could make three wishes come true by catching three butterflies just so I would let him go. I didn't want to believe that, though. I still wanted to believe the butterflies could make wishes come true.

"I thought maybe I had done something wrong with the first wish, that I hadn't done things exactly as I was supposed to do them. So I made another wish. I wished that a huge feast of food would appear before me. But it didn't. Nothing happened again. Then it began to look like the man had lied to me about the three wishes. I started making all sorts of wishes, to see if any of them would come true, and not one of them did. Talk about being disappointed! The man fooled me, and I had nothing to show for it. That's what people are like. They're no good."

46 ▪ Galen And His Spyglass

This evening, the selection from *A Treasury of Troll Tales* was entitled *Galen And His Spyglass.*

▪

When two of Reimer Lundborg's best cows disappeared from his pasture the farmer sent his young hired hand, Galen, to look for them. Galen found tracks and other evidence pointing to the likelihood the two cows had been stolen. He was able to follow the tracks sporadically for a short distance, then continued on in the same direction when he could no longer detect tracks. He walked through woods and mountain meadows, higher up the nearby mountain than he had ever gone. Every so often, when he came to a high spot that afforded him a vista view of the surrounding countryside, he pulled out a collapsible spyglass he carried with him and took a look around. After walking for nearly two hours he looked through his spyglass while standing on top of an escarpment and spotted what he thought might be Mr. Lundborg's cows in a distant opening. They seemed to be penned in a small area by a crude wooden fence.

Galen headed for the spot where the cows were, which was a walk of more than a mile from where he spotted them with his spyglass. As he drew closer he stopped where he could see the cows, took out his spyglass and trained it on the cows, for before taking any action he wanted to make certain these two cows were, indeed, the two lost cows that belonged to his employer. One look through his spyglass at that range left Galen with no doubt whatsoever that the penned cows belonged to the Lundborg farm, for each cow had distinctive markings Galen knew as well as he knew his own facial features.

As he stood at the edge of a woods watching the cows through his spyglass, Galen was startled by a gruff voice behind him saying, or more accurately demanding: "What are you doing here?"

It was a hostile question asked in a hostile tone.

Whirling around, Galen found himself face to face with the first troll he had ever seen. Although he had never seen one before, he knew immediately that this stout creature with a long, scraggly beard, skin as coarse as tree bark, beady eyes, rags for clothes, shoes as holey as Swiss cheese, and a tattered felt hat was a troll. It made sense, for trolls are renowned for stealing cows and other livestock.

"I'm searching for two. . . lost cows," Galen told the troll. He almost said "stolen" rather than "lost," but the troll had such a surly look about him that Galen thought it would be wise to not antagonize him if he could avoid doing so. He knew trolls are much stronger than people and that the nearer a troll is to his home the bolder he becomes when dealing with a person.

"Lost, you say?" the troll said. "No, I haven't seen any lost cows around. I think you're just wasting your time looking around here."

"Whose cows are those two cows over there?" Galen asked, pointing at the cows.

"They're mine," the troll said. "Those two belong to me."

Galen wasn't sure what to do. There was not a dint of doubt in his mind that the two cows the troll claimed were his belonged to his boss and that the troll had stolen them. Confronting the troll with that accusation didn't seem the wise course of action to follow, though, given the circumstances. He pondered how he could get the two cows back while saving his own skin. As he pondered, the troll asked Galen what he had in his hand.

"That's a spyglass," Galen answered.

"A spyglass?" the troll said, pronouncing the word slowly. "What's a spyglass?"

"You mean you've never seen a spyglass?" Galen asked as an idea jumped into his mind with the quickness of a frog jumping off a lily pad into a pond. "Well, a spyglass is like a mirror into your soul. You can look through it and know what things it is good for you to have and what things it is bad for you to have."

Galen demonstrated to the troll how to look through the spyglass.

"If you look into it and something appears to be closer than it really is it means that whatever you're looking at is something good for you and something that will bring you happiness," Galen explained. "If you look into a spyglass and what you are looking at appears to be farther away than it actually is, though, that means what you are looking at is not good for you and will bring you misery and trouble."

"Let me look through it," the troll said, more as an order than a request.

"Surely," Galen said, handing the spyglass to the troll. "Take a look at this nearest mountain peak right over here."

Imitating how Galen had looked through the device, the troll pointed the spyglass toward the mountain peak and slowly brought his head forward so that his left eye looked through the small end. Startled by how near the mountain peak seemed to be through the spyglass, the troll jerked his head backward and looked at the mountain with his bare eyes.

"What's the matter?" Galen asked.

"It makes the mountain come closer," the troll said.

"No, no, it just makes it *look* closer because the mountains are obviously something good for you," Galen said. "If living in the mountains was bad for you the spyglass would make the peak look like it was farther away than it actually is."

Galen persuaded the troll to take another look at the mountain peak through the spyglass. "Do you see the bird nest way up in this tree up here?"

The troll said he did.

"Why don't you take a look at that through the spyglass," Galen said, "and see how that looks to you."

Once Galen helped the troll locate the bird nest through the spyglass the troll looked and practically shouted, "It's magic!," for the bird nest appeared larger than life to him.

"Does the bird nest look large to you too?" Galen asked.

The troll said it did.

"That means that those birds will bring you happiness," Galen said, then used the spyglass himself to look at the bird nest.

"Does it look large to you too?" the troll asked.

Galen said it did, then asked the troll if he wanted to take a look at his cows.

This time, when Galen helped the troll focus on the two cows through the spyglass, he made sure the larger end of the instrument was next to the troll's eye so that whatever the troll looked at would appear to be far, far away. The troll, being a typical dimwitted troll, failed to notice the difference. When he looked through the spyglass this time he was more surprised by what he saw than he was by his first look at the mountain peak.

"What's wrong?" Galen asked in an innocent tone of voice.

"I can barely see the cows, they're so far away!" the troll said. "What's going on?"

Galen shook his head sadly. "It's just what I explained to you, I'm afraid," he said. "If something appears to be farther away than it really is it can mean only that what you are looking at will bring you misery or trouble."

"What kind of misery or trouble?" the troll asked, anxiousness as apparent in his voice as stars are on a clear night.

"It could be most anything," Galen said. "The only clue I can give you is that the farther away something appears to be the deeper the misery and the more terrible the trouble is likely to be."

"But the cows look *very* far away to me!" the troll said in a desperate intonation.

"That doesn't sound good," Galen said. "Let me have a look." He peered through the large end of the spyglass. "The cows look so close that it seems like I could reach out my hand and touch them. But they look far away to you?"

"Yes!" the troll said, snatching the spyglass away from Galen and taking another look through it. "They *still* look far away! What should I do?"

"Well," Galen said, "if the cows look as far away to you as you say they do I can say with certainty that they are going to bring you big trouble or grief so great that you might wish you were dead. If I were you I would get rid of the cows right away, the sooner the better."

"I know!" the troll said. "I'll kill them and eat them right away."

"Are you crazy!?" Galen exclaimed. "That would be the absolute *worst* thing you could do. If you did that, whatever unhappiness or trouble they have for you would be with you forever. You would never be able to get away from it."

"I wouldn't?" the troll said.

"Of course not," Galen said. "You wouldn't want that, would you?"

"No!" the troll said. "So what should I do then?"

"Like I said," Galen advised, "the best thing to do is to get rid of the cows as quickly as possible. You could give them to me if you wanted to; I would take them off your hands if you wanted me to. It would save you from trouble or misery."

The troll couldn't agree to that arrangement fast enough. And so the deal was made. The troll was relieved and happy to get rid of two cows he thought would bring him trouble or misery and Galen was relieved and happy because he managed to get back the two stolen cows for his employer without having to engage in a verbal confrontation or physical altercation.

When Galen returned to the Lundborg farm with the two cows and told Mr. Lundborg how he had managed to get the cows back from a troll Mr. Lundborg was so proud of Galen for how well he used his head that he gave Galen a big bonus for that week as another way of saying "thank you" to him.

47 ▪ Something New

"What's that?" Rnobrna said to Haar, at their hiding spot overlooking the ski resort construction site. An overcast sky, light mist and drizzling rain made it difficult even for trolls, with their superior night vision, to make out exactly what is was.

"Whereabouts?" Haar said. "I'm not sure I know what you mean. Point to it."

Rnobrna did so, saying "There" as he pointed.

"I don't know for sure," Haar said. "It looks like something new."

"Are the people building something?" Rnobrna said. "Is that what it is?"

"It looks like it, doesn't it?" Haar agreed.

"What is it?" Rnobrna said.

Haar squinted, trying to see it better. "Some kind of building? I bet that's what it is. People like to build buildings more than birds like to build nests."

"I think you're probably right," Rnobrna said.

In fact, the structure Haar and Rnobrna were looking at was two upright stud walls of a planned lodge.

"You don't suppose it's a church, do you?" Rnobrna said. "What a terrible thing that would be, to have a church so nearby."

"I don't know," Haar said. "That *would* be terrible. More likely it's a house or something. That wouldn't be quite as bad, but it would still be bad."

"I feel like running down there right now," Rnobrna said, "and breaking through the fence and tearing it down. It doesn't belong there!"

"Control yourself," Haar cautioned. "There are still people there with guns, you know. You don't want to get shot." Indeed, Haar and Rnobrna could see two armed guards from their vantage point.

"Curse them to pieces!" Rnobrna snarled.

The two trolls looked over the site some more.

"What's that over there?" Haar said, pointing to a spot farther away. "Could that be another building?"

"I think it is," Rnobrna said after some seconds.

There was but a wooden platform in place, the floor structure of what was to be a prototype cabin, with a partial stud wall flat on the ground beside it.

"That looks like it's a lot smaller, though," Rnobrna remarked.

"It does, doesn't it?" Haar said. "Now, that must be a house."

"It must be," Rnobrna agreed. "What else could it be?"

The trolls scoured the site with their eyes to see if they could detect anything else new, or any other construction activity. There was nothing else in progress, as far as they could see. But seeing two buildings, one as large as a church—which possibly *was* a church—was distressing enough.

"*What* is going on here?!" Haar seethed, with an equal measure of puzzlement and pique.

Every night various trolls—generally two or three—went down the mountain to have a look at the construction site as the skeletons of the lodge and the cabin came together quickly and workers began placing skin, in the form of plywood and boards, over the skeletons. The trolls were amazed by how quickly the large building was taking shape, and worried that it may in fact be a church, given its size.

At the same time, other men and machines were busily felling and removing trees from the bottom section of the mountain slope, and pushing dirt around, and engaging in other activities that left the trolls perplexed and seething.

"I wish I could see it!" Old Fungus said one night when half the tribe was having a communal meal. Arthritis and other infirmities of old age prevented him from making the arduous trip down the mountain; he didn't venture very far from the caves by this stage of life. "I'd like to see what the people are making."

"Be glad you can't," Drulle said to him. "It would only make your blood boil all the more, if you saw what was being done."

"Drulle is right," Gangl said. "You're better off not seeing it. It's enough to make you puke."

"Puke!" Old Fungus said derisively. "I remember when us trolls actually did something when people started getting too close like this! People would start to build a church and we would go there at night and tear down what they had built. Then they would start building again, and we would go back and tear it down again."

"But did you ever stop a church from being built because of that?" Utrud challenged, knowing the answer. "No! People always got it built in the end, didn't they? Never once, that I know of, did people abandon a church they were building just because some trolls tore down part of it."

"So what?" Old Fungus said. "At least we *did* something. We should be doing the same thing here."

"We've tried," Rnobrna pointed out. "The people have guns and we don't. People didn't have guns in the times you're talking about."

"That's right," Utrud said. "Do you want more of us to get shot or killed? What can we do?"

"Well, we should be doing *something*, I know that!" Old Fungus pressed.

"You can't understand how hard it is to do something because you haven't seen what's going on," Gangl said.

"Bah!" Old Fungus said disgustedly, and rapped the end of his walking stick into the floor of the cave. "I'm leaving."

"Where are you going?" Retta asked as he started hobbling from the cave, seeming to rely on his walking stick more than he normally did. He didn't respond to Retta's question.

When Haar and Scurf went to see what was going on at the construction site one night they found the skin and bones of the lodge almost finished and roof boards in place; the roof was not yet shingled, though.

"Look at the size of that!" Scurf marveled at the scale of the structure.

"If it's a house, it must be for a king," Haar said. "It looks more like a castle."

Actually, it looked nothing like a castle. The only thing it had in common with a castle was size. While castles generally are turreted, ornate, complicated structures, the lodge had an elegantly simple, triangle-like design. The two sides of the roof had shallow pitches, which gave the building a horizontal heft, particularly given the fact that the edges of the roof were only about ten feet above the ground. A full-length wooden deck facing the side of the mountain gave the low-slung lodge an architectural line that made the triangle shape stand out even more distinctly. That mountain-facing side of the lodge consisted mainly of a wall of windows, which meant the lodge was a far cry from the windowless caves the trolls occupied, or even Guggle's ramshackle cabin, with its two tiny, foggy windows.

After the two trolls stood and looked at the building for several minutes, Haar said: "I want to get a look at it from a different side. Come on."

Without a word, Scurf followed Haar as he crept through the forest, making his way around the construction site. Several times Haar cautioned Scurf to try to be quieter, for he was concerned Scurf was making so much noise that the guards might hear him and perhaps start shooting at them. Haar's movements weren't exactly cat-like either, but he didn't make nearly as much noise as Scurf did. In about twenty minutes they were almost exactly opposite—which is to say 180 degrees away—from where they first viewed the lodge.

"I can't quite figure out what's going on," Haar admitted to Scurf, in a gruffly loud whisper, when they stopped where an opening afforded them a fairly clear view of the building. "Is it a house? A barn? A castle? It doesn't look like a barn, but you never know with people."

"You don't think it's a church?" Scurf said.

Haar thought about that a few seconds before responding. "I doubt it. It doesn't really look like any church I've ever seen either. It's not good for us, whatever it is, I know that."

Impulsively, Scurf picked up a jagged rock about four inches long and hurled it toward the building. The rock landed in the dirt a good thirty feet short of the nearest side. While it failed to reach its intended target, the sound of it landing attracted the attention of one of the guards, who immediately sprang to "alert" mode, drawing his gun and looking around. "Who's there?" he called into the darkness, not sure exactly what had made the noise or what direction he should look.

"What's up?" the second guard called to the first.

"I heard a noise, like maybe a rock or something," the first guard answered.

"Come on, let's get out of here," Haar said to Scurf, bolting away. Scurf followed him, again without a word. They heard the two guards talking to each other, but could not decipher any words, as they walked through the woods at a just-short-of-running clip. As best as they could determine, neither of the guards attempted to follow them, and no gunshots sounded. Since their retreat took them further from the foot of the mountain, they had to make a big circle back through the woods, which included crossing the construction site entrance road, to get back to the part of the mountain that was most familiar to them.

48 ▪ Nils And Notch

"**T**rolls are really stupid, aren't they?" Andrew said to his father as Anders prepared to read him another selection from *A Treasury of Troll Tales.*

Anders chuckled. "Well, I guess you could say that. But it's better to say that they're uneducated, or dimwitted, or gullible."

"What's gullible?" Andrew asked, not knowing the meaning of the word.

"That means easily fooled," Anders explained.

"Stupid, in other words," Andrew said.

"It's not really nice to call someone stupid," Anders said. "Almost everyone could be called stupid about certain things, in the sense that they don't know much, or anything, about those things."

"But trolls know less about most things than people do, don't they?" Andrew pressed.

"Well, I guess that's true, according to most of the tales that have been written about them," Anders said. "No, trolls are not as smart as people, if that's what you mean."

This evening's selection was a tale entitled *Nils And Notch.*

▪

There was once a farmer named Nils Olsgaard who often pastured his cows on the far side of a river that flowed through his property. Since the river was too deep and fast for cows to wade across, the cows had to cross a narrow wooden bridge to reach the green pasture on the other side.

One winter an aged, ornery, grouchy troll by the name of Notch took up residence under the bridge. In the spring, when Nils led his cows out to pasture for the first time that year, Notch heard the farmer and his cows approaching and scurried out from under the bridge.

"Where do you think *you're* going?" Notch demanded, standing on the bridge with his hands on his hips, clearly intending to block Nils's path.

"I'm taking my cows to the pasture on the other side of the river, just as I've done for many years," Nils explained.

"I'll allow you to use my bridge on one condition:" Notch said, "That you give me something for the privilege."

Nils knew the troll possessed far superior strength, so trying to force his way past the troll would be a foolish move. He also knew that trying to reason with the troll by pointing out that Notch did not own the bridge and thus had no right to say who could and who could not use the bridge would be both futile and fruitless. For the time being, it appeared he had only two options: either turn back and take his cows elsewhere or submit to Notch's demand and give the troll something so that he could take the cows across to the green pasture on the other side of the river. He decided on the latter course of action, for it seemed the most practical.

"I'll give you this pouch of tobacco," Nils offered, "if my cows can cross the bridge."

"It's a deal," Notch said, snatching the pouch of tobacco from Nils and stepping aside so that the cows could cross the bridge.

The following day Nils took his cows back to the bridge so they could again cross over to the green pasture on the other side of the river. Once more Notch blocked the bridge when he heard Nils and his cows approaching and demanded that Nils give him something before he would allow the cows to cross the bridge. Reluctantly, Nils gave the troll another pouch of tobacco so that Notch would permit his cows to cross the bridge.

Being but a poor farmer, Nils was distressed at the likelihood the troll would demand he give him something every time he wanted to take his cows across the bridge. Not only would such extortion become a financial drain; Nils knew his self-respect would dwindle if he allowed himself to be bullied by a trespassing troll. So he determined he had to do something, and quickly, to rectify the disturbing situation. Nils knew little about trolls except that they were supposed to be dimwitted and gullible. Somehow, he reasoned, he would have to outwit the troll that lived under the bridge.

After contemplating the matter for some time, Nils came up with a plan he believed would fool Notch and buy him time.

The following day, when Notch demanded that Nils give him something before he would permit the cows to cross the bridge, Nils was prepared to implement his plan.

"How much would it be worth to you," Nils said to the troll, "if I were to give you a solid-gold brick? Would you allow my cows to cross the bridge freely for an entire year if I gave you such a present?"

Notch's eyes popped like swelling balloons, for the very thought of acquiring a brick-size block of gold is enough to send any troll into a dither.

"Certainly!" the troll said. "You have my word on it."

"Good," Nils said. "I was hoping you would say that."

"You mean you're going to give me a gold brick?" the troll said excitedly. "Do you have it with you now? Show me!"

Nils brought out an ordinary baked clay brick.

"That's not gold," Notch declared. "What are you trying to pull here?"

"It's not gold *yet*," Nils said calmly, in spite of Notch's irritation. "This is a special sort of magic brick that will turn into gold in exactly one year if kept in the cool current of a river the entire year. If you put the brick in a fast-flowing part of the river, and leave it there, exactly one year from today you will have a solid-gold brick. Do we have a deal?"

"It's a deal!" Notch said, taking the brick and setting it in a secure place in the river current while Nils directed his cows across the bridge.

All through that summer, and into autumn, Nils's cows crossed the bridge where the troll lived every day. Notch stuck to his promise and did not once bother the cows or demand any additional payment from the farmer. When winter's icy paws once again gripped the land, Nils, of course, kept his cows inside his barn. When spring arrived once more Nils again led his cows out to pasture, over the troll's bridge.

Nils had hoped Notch would have forgotten the agreement the two made the previous spring, but—unfortunately for Nils— trolls have good memories when it comes to such things as gold and greed. Notch was marking off the days to the day when he believed his common brick would be transformed into solid gold.

Knowing that the troll would be greatly angered when the baked clay brick did not turn into gold, Nils knew he had to dream up a new scheme to avoid trouble.

The day before the one-year anniversary of the agreement, Nils said to Notch: "I feel ashamed of myself for giving you such a trifle as a magic brick in exchange for your generosity in allowing my cows to cross your bridge for an entire year. I realize now that such great generosity should be rewarded with something much more special. Return the brick to me and I will give you this Jar of Dreams." At this point Nils took out an elegantly shaped jar, which was capped with a cover and elaborately decorated.

"What can I do with a Jar of Dreams?" Notch asked.

"You can wish for anything you want," Nils answered. "You can wish for a hundred gold bricks if you want to."

Put that way, Notch could not resist. After all, a hundred gold bricks were certainly much better than a single gold brick. So Notch retrieved the common baked clay brick from the river rapids and exchanged it for the purported Jar of Dreams.

"Do you understand how a Jar of Dreams works?" Nils asked Notch after the two exchanged the two items.

"I wish for what I want and receive it," the troll said.

"Yes, that's right," Nils said. "First, though, of course, you must bury the jar along with three acorns near the base of a large oak tree for exactly three years."

"You mean I have to wait three years before I can make a wish?" Notch said, his disappointment the equivalent of a deflated balloon.

"Believe me, three years will seem but a short time once you begin having your wishes fulfilled," Nils consoled.

With this new agreement, the farmer had bought himself three years, during which time his cows could freely cross the bridge under which Notch lived without any interference from the ornery troll.

When the three years were up Nils was prepared to buy more time with another proposition.

"I have been giving a lot of thought to the agreement we made about my giving you a Jar of Dreams for your indulgence in allowing my cows to cross your bridge freely," Nils said to Notch. "It seems to me that a jar that makes wishes come true is worth but very little compared to what eternal life would be worth. Wouldn't you like to live forever?"

Forever! To an aged troll, who sensed he had but a few years left to live, the thought of living forever was as appealing as nectar to bees.

"Only recently," Nils went on, "a friend took me to the Spring of Eternal Life, where I filled a large jug with that precious water. I am willing to give you half of that water if you return the Jar of Dreams to me. Drinking the water will allow you to live forever. I will give you some of this water from the Spring of Eternal Life if you will allow my cows to cross the bridge freely for as long as you live under the bridge. What do you say—would you rather have eternal life than a Jar of Dreams?"

"Certainly!" Notch said. "Who doesn't want eternal life? Trolls live a long time, but no troll has ever lived forever!"

"You are a wise troll," Nils told him, which made Notch grin with pride. "Who, indeed, wouldn't prefer eternal life to mere material objects? Dig up the Jar of Dreams and have it here at the same time tomorrow and I will bring you some of the water from the Spring of Eternal Life."

The following day Notch returned the Jar of Dreams to Nils, who had a small jug of spring water for Notch. The troll downed the water in one long swallow.

"How do you feel?" Nils asked.

"I feel young again!" Notch exclaimed, completely convinced he had swallowed magical water that would allow him to live forever.

In truth, of course, there was no such thing as a Spring of Eternal Life. Nils saw no harm in pretending there was, though. The pretense maintained peace, for one thing, and allowed his cows to freely cross the bridge. For another thing, Notch mellowed after drinking what he thought was water from the Spring of Eternal Life. After that he became friendlier and acquired a more pleasant personality, for he felt at peace with the world and was happy to live and let live.

Notch became as much a part of Nils Olsgaard's farm as particular trees and the river that ran through it. Nils actually felt a pang of sorrow when he found Notch's lifeless body beneath the bridge one morning, after the old troll died in his sleep, his body worn out from age. Nils dug a grave and buried Notch near the bridge that had been his home the final few years of his life.

49 ▪ Shelter From A Storm

Rott was headed out alone one night, with no more plan than to wander about, when he caught a glimpse of Tala striding along a path forty feet downslope from him. "I wonder where she's going," he thought, checking an impulse to call to her, or run to her, so close to the caves, fearing she would give him the cold shoulder. He decided to follow her instead. With Tala being the most fetching, and youngest, female member of the tribe, Rott was not alone in dreaming of one day winning her hand. While he had hit on her a few times, Tala never encouraged his advances. He thought that if he followed her to a remote area and then made his presence known, pretending to be in the same place coincidentally, Tala might be more receptive to his company.

Staying a good distance behind, Rott stealthily followed Tala through the forest, wondering all the while where she was headed and at what point he should show himself to her. Tala maintained a fairly swift pace, as though she had a destination in mind and had no need to stop periodically to ponder if she was still on course or decide which direction she should follow next. As far as Rott could tell, Tala did not see him, or even sense she was being followed, though of course Rott would not necessarily have known if she sensed she was being followed since there were no obvious indications of that, such as Tala stopping to listen or suddenly turning her head in his direction. The fact that Tala whistled much of the time made her less aware of surrounding sounds, and less likely to be aware Rott was following her.

In time, which is to say about a fifty-minute hike, Tala came to a mountain meadow, where she at last stopped, to look over the meadow. By this time a fairly strong wind was stirring, which also helped cover whatever noises Rott made. Rott watched from behind a tree trunk as Tala began ambling about the meadow, examining plants and flowers, occasionally picking one and placing it in a basket she carried. It appeared as though Tala would be there for a while, so Rott decided this likely would be the best opportunity he had to present himself to her. Circling around the meadow so as to approach it from a different direction, Rott went tromping up to the meadow with no concern as to how much noise he was making. In fact, he wanted to make Tala aware of him by making a clatterous entrance.

"Rott!" Tala said upon seeing him, and recognizing who it was. "What are you doing way out here?"

"Tala!" Rott said in mock astonishment. "What a surprise to see you here! Oh, I'm just coming back from a little outing. What are you doing way out here, all by yourself?" It struck him that Tala might find it a little suspicious that he knew she was alone, so he quickly added: "You are you by yourself, aren't you? I don't see anyone else around."

"I am by myself, as a matter of fact," Tala said just as the western sky rumbled like a giant's empty stomach.

"What are you doing?" Rott asked bluntly as a hammer stroke.

"Well, not that it's any business of yours," Tala said rather icily, "but I'm gathering some plants for my father." Thunder rumbled louder as she spoke the last few words.

"It sounds like a storm coming up," Rott remarked as the wind suddenly increased in intensity, a massive bolt of lightning illuminated ominous storm clouds, and thunder cracked like a huge whip.

"I think it's here!" Tala exclaimed as the sky's floodgates suddenly opened, drenching the two with heavy, cold, prickly rain.

"We better take cover!" Rott said, taking Tala's right hand with his left hand and running with her for the relative cover of the forest as rain poured down as profusely as at a waterfall and nature's fireworks blazed and boomed, zipped and cracked.

As heavy as the rain was, the canopy of trees provided little protection. Tala and Rott were in a bad place wherever they tried to find cover.

"Guggle's cottage is not far from here," Tala said after a couple of minutes. "We should go there."

"But we'll get wetter than we are, running to it," Rott said.

"We can't get any wetter than we are already," Tala countered. "Come on. I'm going. You do what you want."

With that, she bolted in the direction of Guggle's cabin.

Not wanting to miss out on any alone time he could have with Tala, even if it was time spent dashing through a thunderstorm, Rott did not hesitate in following, and quickly catching up. While there was practically no conversation between them as they ran, Rott felt a constant tingle of excitement simply being in Tala's company, alone with her. In less than ten minutes, during which time the rain, thunder, lightning and wind did not dissipate a dot, Rott and Tala were pounding on Guggle's cabin door and Guggle was asking who was there. Rott and Tala had to shout to make themselves heard above the thunderstorm's din. Once she knew who was outside in such miserable weather, Guggle quickly opened the door and ushered them inside, where a single candle glowed flickeringly on the small table, its flame wavering with wind drafts that swept through cracks in the cabin walls. Trickles of water fell from the underside of the leaky roof into several buckets and pots Guggle had set out to catch the water.

"My word!" the witch remarked, as though the sight of Rott and Tala was as amazing as a couple of wind-flatenned buildings. "I haven't seen anyone as wet as you two in I don't remember how long. You're both as wet as though you had jumped into a river ten times in a row."

"We got caught in the rain," Rott said, stating a fact as obvious to Guggle as the fact that rain is wet.

"You better stay here until the storm passes," Guggle said.

"That's what we were hoping to do," Tala said.

"Certainly you can," Guggle said. "I'm glad to have the company, in such weather. You're more than welcome. Tala, we better get you out of those wet clothes. I have a robe you can wear. Rott, I'm afraid I don't have an extra robe for you, but I can offer you a blanket for you to wrap yourself in. It would be nice to have a fire in the fireplace to dry your clothes by, but I don't keep a fire when the wind is so strong."

Indeed, inside the cabin the howling wind seemed louder than it had outside. The storm continued raging, with no evident let-up, shaking parts of the cabin. Guggle took Tala into the bedroom and left her there to change out of her wet clothes into a long pink, belted robe. After Tala returned to the main room

Guggle took Rott into the bedroom and laid out a blanket for him to wrap himself in after he removed his soggy clothes. Without a fire to help dry the clothes, Guggle hung up her visitors' wet clothes to air dry as well as possible.

"I have a feeling this storm is going to last most of the night," Guggle said. "I think you better plan on spending the night here. Are either of you tired?"

Neither one was.

"Are you hungry?" Guggle asked. "I have some lingenberry muffins I baked yesterday. Would you like some of those?"

"I would!" Rott spoke up.

"All right, I'll get them," Guggle said, rising from her chair to take some muffins from a tin container and set a plate of them on the table. Rott devoured a muffin in a matter of seconds, then took a second, which he attacked with more measured bites. Tala took one of the muffins as well, and started eating it slowly.

"It would be nice to have some tea with the muffins," Guggle said, "but I'm afraid I can't make any without a fire in the fireplace."

"The muffins are fine," Tala assured her as a particularly loud thunderclap shook the cabin.

"That was a close one," Guggle remarked. "You know, this storm, and having you two here, reminds me of the story of Tanja and Holger. Do both of you know the story?"

"No, I don't," Tala said.

"I thought your father would have told it to you," Guggle said. "How about you, Rott? Do you know the story?"

"Not that I remember," Rott said.

"Well, if neither one of you is tired yet, I think I'll tell you the story," Guggle said. "It will help the time go by faster, and it's a wonderful story."

She then proceeded to tell Rott and Tala the following tale:

50 • A Stroke Of Fortune

"A troll maiden named Tanja once happened to be in the right place at the right time to overhear a conversation between two thieves—two human thieves. The two were miles from the nearest house, so they didn't think there was any risk in talking openly about where they had hidden their loot. They were completely unaware that Tanja was close enough to hear every word they said. They also had no idea that once Tanja learned the secret of where their loot was hidden she was determined to find the stolen loot and make off with it before the two thieves could retrieve it.

"Tanja was not able to determine precisely where the loot was stolen by hearing what the two thieves said to each other, but she knew the general area where it was buried, and she knew that the three nights' journey it would take her to reach the place would be worth her while, for the thieves spoke of golden goblets, silver platters and gemstone jewelry.

"As Tanja started out on the first night, she had walked less than a half-mile from her home cave when a young male troll named Holger ran up to her. Holger, who lived nearby, had romantic designs on Tanja. The maiden, however, was not attracted to Holger.

" 'Where are you off to, with such a determined look?' Holger said to Tanja.

" 'I am taking a long journey,' Tanja said icily, continuing to walk along at a steady clip.

" 'All alone?' Holger said.

" 'You don't see anyone else with me, do you?' Tanja said.

" 'Someone as young and as pretty as you should not go on a long journey all alone,' Holger said, keeping pace with Tanja's quick steps. 'You might encounter danger. I will go with you to protect you from danger.'

" 'I don't *want* anyone to go with me,' Tanja said, not wanting to encourage Holger's romantic notions in any way, and not wanting to share the stolen loot she was after with anyone. 'I don't *need* anyone to go with me. I'm perfectly capable of looking after myself.'

" 'But I *want* to go with you,' Holger said.

" 'Well, I don't want you with me, and that's final,' Tanja said. 'Please go away.' She stopped and looked Holger in the eyes with a stern, no-nonsense expression. 'Go on,' she said. 'Get away from me. You're going to be mighty sorry if you don't get away from me right now.'

"Seeing how irritable she was, Holger slunk away as Tanja resumed walking.

"**H**olger was not easily dissuaded, though. He sensed that Tanja was up to something secretive. If she could be sneaky, then he could also be sneaky and follow her, without her knowing, to try to find out what she was up to. And anyway, he really did believe that a maiden such as Tanja might be incapable of dealing with a dangerous situation, so it was also in his mind that if he followed her and she fell into danger and he was close at hand to rescue her from the danger that Tanja might be so appreciative of his daring and his thoughtfulness that she would feel tenderness for him and love might blossom between them.

"And so Holger tailed Tanja through the forest as Tanja walked all that first night, then found a shady spot to sleep the next morning. Holger slept that day too, at a high place from where he could see Tanja.

"**I**n the middle of the second night a thunderstorm swept in. The wind howled, driving big raindrops through the air like nails. Thunder cracked as though granite clouds were colliding. Bolts of lightning blazed brilliantly across the angry sky. Tanja found shelter in a shallow cave three feet high and only slightly deeper. Holger looked around desperately for somewhere he could take shelter from the storm. But he seemed to be out of luck. There was seemingly nowhere to take cover—except for the recess Tanja had found in the rocks. He decided that heading for that small cave and revealing himself to Tanja was far preferable to staying out in the open, in the pelting rain. And so that is what he did.

"Tanja was not pleased to see Holger, to put in mildly. She fumed as Holger crawled into the stony recess beside her.

" 'What are *you* doing here?' she snapped. Then, in an instant, she realized that Holger must have been following her the entire time. 'Have you been following me? You have, haven't you? You've been following me!'

" 'So what if I have?' Holger admitted. 'I warned you that you might run into danger, and here you are, hiding from a thunderstorm in a little hole.'

" 'Yes, and doing rather nicely until you came along!' Tanja shot back. 'This "little hole" is only large enough for one person, by the way. You have to get out. Go find your own little hole.'

" 'But this is the only shelter around,' Holger said. 'There is nowhere else. I couldn't see anywhere else I could go.'

" 'Well, go look some more,' Tanja said. 'I don't want you here.'

" 'But look at how it's storming,' Holger said.

" 'You deserve whatever comes to you," Tanja said, 'because of how you've acted so sneaky and so rudely. I wouldn't care if it was raining roosters. I just want you out of here.'

"With that, she shoved Holger. Since Holger was not prepared for the push, he tumbled out into the open, where the hard rain once again pelted him.

" 'Go on,' Tanja ordered, as though commanding a dog. 'Go find your own place for shelter.'

"Had he not liked Tanja so much, Holger would have stayed and fought for his share of Tanja's place of shelter. Even if it meant discomfort and hardship for himself, though, Holger didn't want to do anything to further anger Tanja, so he resigned himself to her wish. For several seconds he stood in the rain with a hangdog expression on his face, silently pleading for Tanja to relent and agree to share her small shelter with him. Tanja simply stared back at him blankly, saying nothing.

" 'You have a hard heart,' Holger said, then turned and started sprinting away in search of any little shelter he could find to get out of the fierce storm. Forty feet away, a serrated streak of silver lightning ripped the air from sky to ground precisely where Holger was running. Tanja actually heard the lightning hit Holger, with a sharp sizzle. She thought she saw his entire body glow for an instant as a halo of light wrapped his body in an electrical current. The bolt of lightning blew Holger to the ground faster than a direct hit from a cannonball could have. He was immediately flat on his back, as stationary as a stone.

"Instinctively, Tanja ran out to see if Holger was dead. He didn't seem to be, so she dragged him back to the recess in the rock wall and provided her lap as a pillow for his head. She did what she could to nurse him as Holger remained unconscious. There wasn't much she could do except keep him out of the rain, use her lap as a pillow for his head, and hope he didn't die. She felt guilty about forcing him to leave the shelter—for actually pushing him out—and exposing him to the lightning. She knew that if he died she would feel responsible for his death, and she didn't want to have to live with the weight of that in her heart.

"Holger remained unconscious for fully half a day. Occasionally he stirred slightly, or one of his muscles twitched, or he tried to mumble words. All of that gave Tanja hope he would not die.

"Tanja's heart sighed with relief when Holger did eventually open his eyes. It was daylight then, on a grey, gloomy day. Tanja explained what had happened—how a streak of lightning had struck Holger, and how he had been out cold for many hours.

" 'What in the world are you doing way out here, anyway, so far from home?' Holger asked Tanja. 'Where are you going?'

"Feeling responsible for Holger having been struck by lightning, Tanja felt she owed him an explanation, at least. And so she told him about overhearing two men talking about where they had hidden stolen treasure and how she intended to dig it up for herself before the men could return for it. That information did more to hasten Holger's recovery than any medicine could have done. What is more bracing to a troll, after all, than the prospect of getting his hands on gold and other gleaming treasure?

"**B**y the time Earth donned its cloak of darkness that night both Holger and Tanja were hungrier than hogs. So they set off together in search of a farmstead where they could find some food. They walked for three hours before they spotted a farm. The front door of the farmhouse was unlocked, so they snuck inside and looked around for the kitchen. While they were looking about, a floor lamp near Holger suddenly switched on, flooding the parlor with light.

" 'Why did you turn on the light?' Tanja hissed. 'Shut it off!'

" 'I didn't touch it!' Holger said, pulling the lampchain to try to switch off the light. The bulb in the lamp actually seemed to become brighter, though. Holger tugged at the chain desperately as his body tingled with electricity. 'It won't go off!' he said to Tanja.

" 'Well, get away from it then,' Tanja said.

The light dimmed as Holger backed away, though the lamp continued throwing off some light. Suddenly a phonograph started playing a musical record at loud volume, right behind Holger. The sudden noise caused both Holger and Tanja to jump in surprise. Tanja actually let out a startled grunt. The two of them dashed about the room completely confused as the music continued to play.

" 'What's going on?' Tanja said to Holger, at a loss to explain why music was playing.

"What was going on was that unbeknownst to Tanja and Holger, the streak of lightning that struck Holger had electrified him. His body was now surrounded by such a strong electrical force that electrical devices reacted to his presense. In fact, he had become a walking electrical switch.

"Then Tanja and Holger heard footsteps from upstairs, above them, and a deep voice called down the stairway: 'Who's there? What's going on down there?'

" 'Let's get out of here!' Tanja said as she dashed for the front door, with Holger at her heels. The music ground to a stop and the lamplight went out as Holger left the house. The foot-steps quickened behind them, though. Then the blast of a gun sounded and pellets sprayed the air above Tanja and Holger, which caused the two to run even faster, for they were running for their lives. No more gunshots were fired, though. Once Tanja and Holger were a safe distance from the farm they stopped to catch their breaths.

" 'It's all your fault!' Tanja said to Holger, angry at him again. Her feelings, which had softened for a time, had hardened again.

" '*My* fault!' Holger said. 'Why is it my fault? I didn't do anything.'

" 'You must have done something,' Tanja said, 'because I know what happened back at the house wasn't my fault, so it had to be yours. Now look at us: We're even worse off than we were before. Not only did we fail to get any food there, but we used up energy and became even hungrier trying to get some.'

"Holger did his best to defend himself as Tanja continued insisting that he was fouling up the entire expedition and making her life miserable. She asked Holger to leave her sight again, but Holger pointed out the rather pertinent fact that Tanja had revealed the approximate location of the buried treasure to him. He threatened that if she tried to make him leave again he would do whatever it took to find the treasure before her, or even fight her for it if it came to that. 'Either we're in this together all the way now or you'll have to fight me to keep me from the treasure,' Holger said.

"In her enraged state, Tanja thought she just might be able to win a fight with Holger, even though Holger was bigger and stronger. She knew she would be risking everything if she took that course, though. It seemed wiser to accept Holger as a treasure hunting partner, no matter how much resentment she felt for him. And so Tanja and Holger continued toward their common goal together, keeping up their strength mainly with berries and bugs they found to eat along the way.

"**B**ecause of their encounter with the sever thunderstorm the second night, it took them four nights of walking to reach their destination. At last they were there, near the waterfall the two thieves had spoken about. But where was the treasure buried? They couldn't see any sign of any recent digging anywhere.

" 'What now?' Holger said. 'Where's the treasure?'

" 'How do I know?' Tanja snapped. She suggested that they split up and walk around to see if they spotted anything that looked unusual or out of place. After about half an hour Holger's body tingled when he walked over a particular spot. He felt his arms being pulled down toward the ground, as though someone very strong was pulling on them. He asked Tanja to come to that spot to see if she felt the same sensation. Tanja went over to where Holger was and didn't feel any tingling.

Holger was surprised by that, and asked Tanja why she supposed he was tingling.

" 'How should I know?' Tanja said.

" 'I feel just like I did back at that house we stopped at, when the light came on and the music started playing," Holger told her.

"Tanja wondered if that might mean something significant. It occurred to her that strange things began happening to Holger only after he was struck by lightning, which made her wonder if the lightning strike might have done something to him.

" 'I have a hunch,' Tanja said. 'Let's dig here.'

"The dirt was soft, so it was not so difficult for them to dig with their hands. Three feet down Tanja's hand scraped against something hard. It felt like wood. As she dug some more and brushed away loose dirt, she seemed to be sweeping dirt off the top of a wooden chest.

" 'I think we've found the treasure!' she said to Holger, who broke into a broad smile and danced about deliriously. 'Help me dig!' Tanja said to him, for she was anxious to raise the wooden chest out of the ground as quickly as possible so that she could see what was inside. She had no doubt in her mind that it was the treasure the two thieves had buried. Both of them dug furiously to get the treasure chest out of the ground. When they lifted it out and opened it their eyes bulged at the gleaming treasures it contained. Holger snatched up one of four golden goblets in the chest, felt a shock, and immediately dropped the goblet back into the chest.

"Tanja asked him what was wrong.

" 'It gave me a shock,' he told her.

" 'What did?' Tanja asked him.

" 'The goblet,' Holger told her.

" 'The goblet?' Tanja said. 'Try it again. Pick it up again.'

"Holger picked up the golden goblet once more, and once more he felt a shock. Tanja cackled with laughter.

" 'What's so funny?' Holger said, a little annoyed that Tanja seemed to find his pain humorous.

"Tanja wasn't laughing at his pain, though, but because she had suddenly realized something. 'Don't you see?' she said. 'I bet this is happening because you were hit by a bolt of lightning. Somehow, it made metal attract to you. You felt the tingling at this spot because you had been struck by lightning. Oh, Holger, I love you!' she said, and gave him a long kiss flat on his lips. And she truly did feel love for Holger now, for he had helped her find the buried treasure. She knew she might never have found the buried treasure, or found it before the two thieves had a chance to find it, if Holger hadn't followed her and eventually made his presense known to her.

"They had a happy trip back home together, lugging their treasure with them. Soon after, they were married. The treasures they had found together were as precious to them as children. The electrical charge the lightning strike had given Holger gradually diminished and he was eventually able to hold the metal treasures in his hands without receiving a shock. He and Tanja would sit together for hours on end stroking the treasures they may have never found it if hadn't been for a fortunate stroke of lightning."

∎

With perfect timing, a brilliant flash of lightning ripped across the sky and illuminated the inside of the cabin a fraction of a second after Guggle spoke the word "lighning" to finish the tale. Rott wondered if Guggle told them the tale because she suspected, or possibly even intuited, that Rott had followed Tala much like Holger followed Tanja. Had some of the glances Guggle gave him while telling the story been her way of letting him know she understood, or surmised, his conniving ways? Did she perhaps tell them the story as a way of letting Rott know love works in mysterious ways? He envied Holger's good fortune in winning Tanja's hand. For Holger, a thunderstorm had changed his luck for the better. For Rott, the thunderstorm hit so soon after he revealed himself to Tanja that it had not given him the time he expected to have to work at trying to make her like him.

As Guggle and her pop-in guests talked about nothing much in particular, the storm soon abated, with the brunt of it sweeping off to the south. The storm had not passed completely, though, so Guggle insisted that Rott and Tala spend the rest of the night with her, which they did.

51 ▪ Ort's Dream

There was rumbling within the tribe as work continued apace at the construction site. As much as most tribe members wrote off Old Fungus's grumbling and criticsm as the wild, scattershot rantings of someone who did not fully understand the situation because he hadn't seen the construction site with his own eyes, his point of view gradually seeped into the hearts and minds of some of the other trolls who couldn't help but wish people would leave the bottom of the mountain and wonder if there wasn't something more that could be done, or tried, to make that happen. Of course, none of them had any realistic ideas about what more they could do. Nonetheless, a pretty fair number of them began feeling that Ort should be coming up with ideas and doing more about the situation. After all, Ort had vowed that people would not force the trolls to leave their homes this time; he had drawn a line people would not be allowed to cross. With the exception of Old Fungus, who was not afraid to speak his mind to anyone, whatever his thoughts, no one confronted Ort directly, or even whispered their doubts and concerns very loudly to anyone else, for no one wanted Ort angry at him. Ort was ready to fight anyone, anywhere, for any disparaging, distrustful or skeptical remark, though he gave Old Fungus a pass on that because of his advanced age and was satisfied to wage word battles with him whenever that seemed necessary.

Ort was unaware of the level of unease, frustration and resentment within the tribe, at least as far as some of the frustration and resentment being aimed at him, when he had an exceedingly strange and disturbing dream.

In his dream, he was down toward the bottom of the mountain, by himself, to check out what was happening at the construction site. He arrived just in time to see an enormous yellow bulldozer rumbling and thundering up the mountain slope, trampling trees and tearing up a wide swath of earth. He was so astonished by the size of the machine and so insensed at what it was doing that he neglected to exercise his usual caution and remain concealed. Without considering the potential consequences, he rushed out into the bulldozer's path, exposing himself to the bulldozer operator. Instead of stopping the bulldozer, or veering around Ort, the operator aimed the machine directly at Ort, who ran to his right to try to avoid being squashed. The bulldozer operator steered the growling, smoke-belching machine toward Ort, though. Wherever Ort ran the bulldozer followed close behind. Whatever tangent he took the bulldozer was right on his heels, on the same tangent. Finally, after creating a destructive path far up the side of the mountain, the bulldozer made a U-turn and scraped the path twice as wide as it roared down the mountain slope.

Other members of the tribe heard the unusual commotion and rushed to see what was happening. They were enraged by the degree of destruction that people had done, and by how far up the mountain it extended. Soon eight or ten of those were plotting how they could overthrow Ort and install someone else as king. It didn't take long for the plotters to take action. Ort was pawing through one of his chests of treasures when they rushed into his sleep chamber, seized him and dragged him outside. They continued dragging him away from his cave, pulling on his feet so that Ort's upper back and the back of his head dragged and bounced on the ground. Soon they had Ort's arms and legs tied to ropes and they were using the ropes to stretch him between two trees, fifteen feet above the ground. "No!" Ort shouted, actually voicing the cry aloud, which caused him to awake, his entire body wet with perspiration.

"People!" he thought, after regaining his sense of the here and now. "They cause nothing but trouble."

52 ▪ Milo And The Magic Seeds

This is the next story Anders Branstad read to his son, Andrew, from *A Treasury of Troll Tales.* It is called *Milo And The Magic Seeds.*

▪

There was once a farmer who had a son named Milo. The farmer raised Milo by himself, with the help of a housekeeper when the boy was very young, because his beloved wife died giving birth to her only child. The farmer resented his son because his wife died giving birth to him, and so he treated him cruelly. He constantly criticized, reprimanded and scolded him in the bitterest, most caustic language imaginable, and punished him for his misdeeds with forceful swipes of a leather strap.

Having been deprived of sufficient oxygen at a critical moment of his birth, Milo was mentally deficient. As a result, he was slow to understand things and quick to make mistakes. His resentful father scolded him and punished him for every mistake he made, and Milo made many mistakes. The father did not understand that what Milo needed most was love, patience and understanding, not loathing and physical punishment.

Despite the meanness his father displayed toward him, Milo maintained a sweet, innocent, gentle disposition. He remained good-natured and kindhearted all the years his father treated him cruelly, and cursed him, and displayed unconcealed contempt for him.

One late summer day, when Milo was barely eighteen years of age, his father ordered him to take a prize cow to the annual local fair and sell it there. This was a larger responsibility than the farmer liked to delegate to Milo, but crops were ripening and the farmer could not afford to miss a single harvest day if he hoped to harvest all of the crops he had planted.

And so Milo set out in the morning for the nearest village, where the annual fair was being held. The village was a three-hour walk in each direction, so Milo carried along a lunch, which he stopped to eat after walking for two hours. He had taken only a few bites of his lunch before an ugly old woman happened along where he was seated beneath a tall birch tree. At least Milo thought it was an ugly old woman; in truth, it was a troll witch.

"I am so hungry and thirsty," the troll witch said. "Would you be so kind as to share your lunch with me?"

"Certainly," Milo said, knowing how it felt to be hungry and thirsty, for his father had often sent him to bed without a meal for some mistake he made, or for something he had said or done to displease his father. "You're welcome to everything I have. We'll divide it equally."

And so Milo divided his lunch with the troll witch, the two of them eating together in the shade of the tall birch tree.

"You're very kind," the troll witch said to Milo. "There aren't many people who would give a tro. . . an old woman half of their lunch."

"They wouldn't?" Milo said in amazement. "Why not?"

"Because most people are mean," the troll witch said, wrinkling her nose. "Haven't you found that to be the case?"

"My father is mean to me sometimes," Milo said, "but he says it's because I don't do things right and he's trying to teach me how to do things right."

The troll witch asked Milo where he was taking the cow. When Milo told her he was taking it to the fair to sell it the old troll said, "I would like to have the cow for myself, for it is as fine a cow as I've ever seen. Would you be willing to trade me the cow for a sack of magic seeds? Since you have shown me kindness, I would like to reward your kindness."

"What are magic seeds?" Milo asked her. "I've never heard of them."

"Magic seeds are just that—magic," the witch said. "You make a wish when you plant them and anything that you wish for will grow. The magic seeds would be far more valuable to you than whatever money you would be able to get from selling the cow."

Magic seeds did indeed sound as though they were much more valuable than money, so Milo quickly agreed to the trade. The troll witch took the cow and Milo returned home with the small leather pouch containing the magic seeds.

"You are certainly home early," Milo's father said when Milo arrived back home. "How much money did you receive for the cow?"

"Well, I didn't take the cow to the fair," Milo told his father.

"You didn't take the cow to the fair!" his father exploded in outrage. "You had strict orders to sell the cow at the fair. You left with the cow this morning and now you come home without it. What happened to the cow? Did it run away?"

"No, it didn't run away," Milo said.

"Did someone steal it from you?"

"No, no one stole it." ˙

"Well then, what happened to it?!" Milo's father said impatiently.

"Well," Milo explained, "I met an old woman in the forest when I stopped for lunch, and I traded her the cow for some magic seeds."

"You what?!" his father exploded.

"She said the magic seeds were much more valuable than money," Milo said.

"You dolt! You simpleton!" Milo's father stormed, and proceded to call him several even more insulting names, with vulgar language. "There is no such thing as magic seeds! You were tricked—and by an old woman at that. Do you realize what you've done? You've given away my best cow for a few worthless seeds!"

"But the old woman was very nice," Milo said. "I don't think she would try to trick me."

"You're going to be the ruin of me!" his father wailed. "Show me the seeds," he demanded.

Milo took the pouch of magic seeds from the pocket where it was and handed it to his father. Opening the pouch and seeing what appeared to be ordinary seeds, his father shook with anger, grabbed a handful of the seeds and tossed them into the wind with all his might, spitting "Sod it all!" as he did so. Then he

flung aside the pouch and gave Milo a swift kick on his behind.
"This is the final straw!" he thundered. "I want you out of my
sight. I want you out of my life." He picked up a handful of
small rocks and began throwing them at Milo, who ran to get out
of the way, snatching up the pouch of magic seeds as he ran. His
father continued shouting curses at him and flinging rocks at him
as Milo fled. His father also chased him, but Milo was a much
faster runner and was easily able to get away. Exhausted from
running, his father stopped and shouted "I never want to see your
face again!" as Milo became little more than a dot in the
distance.

When Milo's father went outside the next morning the ripening crop fields that had been there the day before were nowhere
to be seen. All of the cultivated and seeded fields were now
nothing but solid sod. The man was completely perplexed. He
didn't remember that he had said "Sod it all!" when he tossed a
handful of magic seeds into the wind. He didn't understand that
his wish had been fulfilled.

Meanwhile, Milo found that a few seeds remained in the
leather pouch after his father had carelessly tossed away most of
them. He planted one and wished for an apple tree so that he
would have something to eat. The following day an apple tree
loaded with crisp, sweet, large apples stood where Milo had
planted the magic seed.

Milo planted another magic seed and wished for new clothes.
The following morning a pile of new clothes stood on the spot
where he planted the seed.

With only three magic seeds left, Milo knew he must make
wise use of his remaining wishes. After thinking over the matter
for several days, he finally planted one of the three remaining
seeds and wished that he would meet a beautiful girl who would
instantly fall in love with him and be his companion for life, for
his heart ached for love. The following day, when he walked
into a small village, the first person he met was a beautiful girl.
It was love at first sight between the two of them. The beautiful
girl helped Milo secure a job in that village so that the two of
them could live near each other, spend a lot of time together, and
do things together.

Soon Milo told the beautiful girl, whose name was Anne, about how he had acquired magic seeds from an old woman and how three wishes he made had come true. He wanted Anne to help him decide what wishes he should make with the last two magic seeds, for he doubted he could make the wisest choices possible by himself.

After weeks of deliberation Anne decided how she and Milo should use one of their two remaining wishes. They selected a secret spot, planted one of the seeds and wished for a money tree. Anne reasoned that if they could harvest as much money as they needed from a tree anytime they wanted to do so they could buy whatever they wanted and live a life of leisure and not want for anything of a material nature.

Sure enough, a tree with money rather than leaves shot up in the spot where they planted the magic seed. Just as Anne had calculated, with a money tree they needed nothing more.

Soon they were married. They built the largest house in the village and had three children they loved dearly and who loved them equally in return. Whenever they needed money for anything they harvested some from their money tree and bought whatever it was they needed or wanted.

They kept the one last remaining magic seed in a safe place just in case they ever needed to use another wish.

53 ▪ Suspicion Swells

Ort's disturbing dream—his nightmare—haunted him as few dreams ever had. It made him moody and caused him to stay pretty much to himself for a couple of days. He spent an inordinate number of his waking hours fondling his treasures, as if to reassure himself that he was firmly ensconsed as king of the tribe and that his cache of treasures was material evidence of that fact. Still, he kept a wary eye on his fellow tribe members, for his dream made him suspicious of them. He even considered revealing his dream and his concern to either Kravig or Guggle, to see if either had any advice or potions to offer, but decided in the end that might be regarded as a small show of weakness on his part, and he wanted to display only strength.

On the second night after his dream, he awoke, ate a large meal Tattra cooked for him, and emerged from his cave energized for a night of adventure. As he rounded a bend in the trail that led past the larger of the two communal caves six male trolls not far from the cave entrance suddenly stopped talking when they caught sight of Ort—or so it seemed to Ort. That made Ort's blood boil as though someone had passed a blowtorch across his torso.

"Isn't this cute!" he spat, thundering toward the group of six, his dream about insurrection still very much on his mind. "You don't fool me for a minute. I know what you're up to."

"What are you talking about?" Traug said.

"You know as well as I do what I'm talking about," Ort seethed. "I'm not blind, you know. I can see that you're plotting against me, trying to figure out how you can overthrow me."

"Where did you get a crazy idea like that?" Grentd said. "We weren't doing anything of the sort, Ort."

"Oh, nooooo!" Ort said sarcastically. "And lightning doesn't cause thunder either, I suppose. I've seen how you all think that it's my fault that the destruction at the bottom of the mountain hasn't been stopped, and that Gangl got shot. So, which one of you thinks he would make a better king? Which one of you thinks he is strong enough to be king?"

None of the six said anything. Several of them looked down at the ground, avoiding eye contact with Ort.

"Well, which one?" Ort demanded. "I know that one of you has to be the ringleader in all of this."

"In all of what?" Grentd said.

"In all of this plotting—this plotting to overthrow me and make someone else king," Ort said. "I know that"s what you were talking about just now, until you saw me and stopped talking all of a sudden."

"We weren't talking about trying to overthrow you," Scurf said. "The thought never entered our minds."

Ort cursed and said: "That's my answer to that! I'd wager half the watches I own that you're behind everything, Scurf."

"There's nothing to be behind, I tell you," Scurf insisted. "Is there?" he asked the others for confirmation.

Before the others could say anything, Ort said to Scurf: "All right, if you think you would make a better king than me I'll give you your chance right now. Only, I'm not going to let you scheme behind my back; you're going to have to prove it out in the open by fighting me one-on-one, fair and square. Whoever wins the fight is king. Come on, right now! This is your chance."

"I don't want to fight you," Scurf said.

"I'm afraid you don't have any choice now," Ort said, whaling into Scurf like a hawk into a rodent.

Despite the fact that Scurf was a couple of hundred years younger, he was no match for Ort when it came to brute strength and anything-goes fighting savvy. Ort used his fists, elbows, feet, knees, and head to land four blows to every one of Scurf's. It was a short fight; Ort had Scurf thoroughly beaten in a matter of barely more than two minutes. The end came when Ort pressed Scurf's face against a lichen-covered boulder, set a foot on Scurf's back and asked boldly if anyone else wanted to take him on. No one did. "All right then," Ort said with a triumphant tone. "I don't want any more of this plotting behind my back. Is that clear to everyone?"

Everyone assured him it was.

54 ▪ The Splinter Cat Tale

"What would you do if you ever met a troll?" Andrew asked his father.

Anders chuckled and said, "Well, I don't think that's very likely, being that it seems like no one has seen a troll in decades."

"They haven't?" Andrew said, surprised.

"Not really," Anders said. "Some people claim they have, but it's rather doubtful they really did because people who have claimed to have seen a troll are pretty much kooks and crackpots, or maybe just someone looking for attention. People say that the trolls that used to live near people have all moved far to the north, to mountain caves, so it's far less likely anyone will see one, if they're still around."

"How about Troll Mountain?" Andrew said. "Don't trolls live there? Wasn't it named Troll Mountain because a lot of trolls lived there?"

"Well, it was said quite a few trolls lived there," Anders said. "But people say the ones who did live there have probably moved farther north too."

"So you don't think you'll ever run into a troll?" Andrew asked.

"Well, let's just say I don't stay awake nights worrying about it," Anders responded.

"But what if you *did* meet a troll somewhere?" Andrew persisted. "What do you think you would do? Do you think you would be scared?"

"Well, I suppose it might make me a little nervous," Anders said, "but I would hope I would be as quick-witted as the people in some of the stories we've been reading. I think I would try to fool him some way."

"Trolls spend a lot of time in the forests, don't they?" Andrew said.

"Well, yeah, quite a few stories about them are set in a forest," Anders said.

"Well, you cut down trees in forests," Andrew said, "so aren't you more likely than most people to meet a troll?"

"That does seem logical, doesn't it?" Anders said, rather proud of his young son for following that path of logical thought. "I should read you a story about a logger who encountered a rather nasty troll and had to do some creative thinking. Let's see here. . ." he said, scanning the table of contents until he came across *The Splinter Cat Tale*, which he proceeded to read aloud to Andrew.

■

Once there was a poor farmer with three ne'er-do-well sons. As the farmer grew older his stamina diminished, so he could do less and less work. As a result, he fell far into debt, for his three sons would do little of the work that needed to be done around the farm.

Finally, one day the farmer explained to his three sons that if they did not go out into a large patch of woods that was part of the farm and cut down some trees to sell for lumber, to help him pay his debts, they could no longer stay with him, but rather would have to go out and make their own way in the world. This they agreed to do.

The oldest son, Peter, was the first to go, that very day. He went deep into the woods, selected a mossy old fir tree, and began chopping at its trunk with an axe. He delivered only a half-dozen blows to the trunk before a big, beady-eyed, hideous, menacing troll suddenly appeared, as if out of thin air, and thundered, "Be gone from my woods. If you hew here I'll kill you."

Frightened from the top of his head to the tips of his toes, Peter tossed aside his axe and ran toward home as fast as his legs would carry him. He had never run so fast for so long in his life. By the time he reached home he was almost out of breath, his lungs heaving like a bellows. After his breathing rate slowed enough so he could speak he told his father and his two brothers what had happened.

"You spineless coward!" his father rebuked him. "If I were your age and had your strength no troll would ever stop me from cutting trees in my own woods, I can promise you that. You not only let a troll scare you out of doing what you should have done, but you lost a perfectly good axe on top of it."

The farmer turned to his middle son, Jesper. "Jesper, can I count on you to go into the woods tomorrow and cut down trees and stand your ground against the troll if you have to?"

"I'm not afraid of any old troll," Jesper said bravely, eager to prove himself more worthy than his older brother. "Yes, you can count on me."

The next day Jesper ventured into the large patch of woods to begin his logging operation. Just as had happened to his brother Peter, Jesper chopped into the trunk of a tree with only a few axe blows before the same troll who had threatened Peter suddenly appeared and growled, "Be gone from my woods! If you hew here I'll kill you."

Jesper's bold words of the day before melted in his mind like an icicle in direct sunlight. One look at the troll, and one listen to his voice, and Jesper was shaking with fear. He had no idea the troll would be so big, so hideous, or quite so menacing. Forgetting the resolve with which he promised his father he could be counted on to do the job, he dropped his axe, turned on his heels, and fled for home.

The father had harsh words for Jesper, just as he had for Peter the previous day, when Jesper told him and his two brothers about the troll he had encountered.

"Don't despair, father," the youngest son, Niles, said to the old farmer. "I'm still left to give it a try."

"You!" Peter exclaimed. "Don't make me laugh. Both Jesper and I are far bigger and stronger than you, and yet neither of us would be any match for this troll. How do you expect the troll to let you cut down trees if he wouldn't let either of us do it?"

"He would not only kill you; he might eat you alive as well," Jesper warned his younger brother.

"In one gulp," Peter added.

"Maybe you two just didn't go about it the right way," Niles said. "Maybe you just didn't say the right things to the troll."

"Say the right things!" Jesper sputtered, laughing at Niles' naivete. "This troll isn't exactly partial to standing around shooting the breeze. What he does is make threats, and if you don't do what he says he'll no doubt do exactly what he threatens to do."

Niles grinned enigmatically and said, "We'll just see about that, won't we?"

The next morning Niles set off for the patch of woods where a troll had scared away both of his older brothers. He left his axe at the edge of the woods and walked in empty-handed. It wasn't long before the ugly troll suddenly appeared in front of him, in his path.

"Be gone from my woods," the troll demanded. "If you don't leave I'll kill you."

"Are these your woods?" Niles asked with the most innocent tone of voice he could muster, managing to keep the fear he felt inside out of his speech. "You must be heartbroken about what a splinter cat is doing to the trees then."

"A what?" the troll asked.

"A splinter cat," Niles repeated. "Look at that tree over there, the one that is all splintered and dying. A splinter cat did that." Niles knew very well the tree had been struck by lightning, but he hoped the troll would fall for his fabrication. He pointed at two other trees that had been uprooted and felled by windstorms. "And look at those two over there. A splinter cat knocked down those too. Have you noticed any other damaged trees anywhere else in the woods?"

"Now that you mention it, I have," the troll said.

Niles shook his head sadly and scrunched his face into a grim expression. "That doesn't sound good," he said. "Once a splinter cat starts knocking down trees somewhere it doesn't stop until every tree in the woods is destroyed."

"What's a splinter cat?" the troll asked. "I've never heard of such a thing."

"You've never heard of a splinter cat?" Niles said, his voice full of surprise. "I thought everyone knew what a splinter cat is. A splinter cat is a ferocious animal with quills as sharp as needles all over its body. It has back legs longer than its front legs, and all of its legs are as strong as tree trunks. It has enormous claws that are as sharp as its quills, and a long tail with a thick nob at the end of it, which it uses as a weapon. The strangest feature of the splinter cat, though, is the shape of its head. It has a head that looks like a large maul and is harder than most types of rock. It uses its head to ram into trees, trying to find honey. Splinter cats love honey. They can't get enough of it. When a splinter cat can smell honey somewhere, but can't see it, it goes stark raving mad and starts ramming its head into trees and knocking them to pieces until it finds the honey."

"I've never seen any sort of animal you're talking about," the troll said.

"Of course you haven't," Niles said. "Very few people have actually seen a splinter cat, and most of them caught only a glimpse of one. First of all, splinter cats roam only at night or during heavy thunderstorms. And they're so wary and wily that they almost always see someone or something else first, before that someone or something sees them, and then they hide or run away. And can they run! They can run so fast that they can outrun the wind."

Niles looked around as though assessing the scene. "This is such a pretty woods too," he went on. "It will sure be a shame when it's all gone."

"All gone!" the troll exclaimed. "I won't let it happen! I'll stop that splinter cat somehow."

"Well, if you're really determined to save your woods there is one thing that just might work," Niles said to the troll. "It would take a lot of time and travel on your part, but it has worked for other people in the past."

"What?" the troll said eagerly. "What is it? I'll do anything to save my woods."

"Well, what a splinter cat wants more than anything else in the world is honey," Niles explained, "so if you want a splinter cat to leave your woods the only way to make it leave is to draw it away with honey. What you must do is collect a big jar of honey and carry it through the woods. The splinter cat will smell the honey and start following you. Then what you want to do is keep on walking—far, far away, toward the sea. I know it's a long way to the sea, and it will take you weeks to get there and return, but if you want to get rid of the splinter cat that is what you have to do. The splinter cat will keep following you, since it will want the honey you have. It's not likely that you'll see the splinter cat, or even hear it, but don't worry about that; it will be following you, you can be sure of that. Then once you reach the edge of the sea you want to find a high cliff and toss the jar of honey over the edge of the cliff. The splinter cat will go over the edge of the cliff to get the honey and not be able to climb back up the cliff, and you will be rid of it."

"But I don't know where I can find any honey," the troll said.

"That's no problem," Niles assured him, for he knew where there was a honey tree. "I will get you some and bring it to you. Then you can start your journey this very day."

Not by accident, or happenstance, Niles had a jar with him, so he went and gathered honey from the honey tree he knew about and brought the honey to the troll, in the woods. The troll took the jar of honey from Niles and started walking through the woods with it, toward the nearest seacoast.

Niles went home and told his two brothers that beginning the next day the three of them could hew in the woods in peace for several weeks without any worry that the troll would interfere with them.

"The troll has gone on a long journey and won't be back for quite some time," he assured them.

Niles's two brothers were skeptical that the troll had vacated the woods and would present no hindrance to their hewing. Nevertheless, at their father's insistence, they agreed to accompany Niles to the woods the following morning. There the brothers began chopping down trees, and cutting them up, and hauling the logs back home, all without any sign of the troll. They worked for several weeks, and in that time they harvested enough timber to pay off all of their father's debts. And from that time on none of them were ever lazy again, but did all of the farmwork that needed to be done so that the farm prospered, and neither their father or they were ever in debt again.

55 ▪ Stewing Over Stew

Utrud, Skimpa and Retta were cooking up a meal in the smaller communal cave, the main component of which was a large volume of stew bubbling in an iron caldron hanging above the fireplace fire. Inevitably, their conversation came around to the latest developments at the construction site at the bottom of the mountain, where work still proceeded apace. The prototype cabin was nearly complete and stonemasons were attaching fieldstones to the front of the lodge. Other workers were installing large windows on all sides of that structure, with the largest on the front side, which faced the mountain. Many men were working in the interior of the lodge.

"Llop told me the building is so big that a thousand people could live there," Retta reported.

"Does he think people are going to live there?" Skimpa asked.

"He's not sure," Retta answered. "I don't think anyone knows exactly what the building is for, do they?"

"Not that I know of," Utrud said. "It doesn't look like any barn anyone has ever seen. And it doesn't seem to be a church, thank goodness."

"That would be terrible," Retta said.

"What would be?" Utrud said, seeking clarification.

"If it was a church," Retta said.

"I sure would like to know what those people are up to," Skimpa remarked.

"We know what they're up to; they're up to no good," Utrud said. "People always are."

"You know what I mean," Skimpa said, stirring the stew with a de-barked branch about three feet long and more than two inches in diameter. "I mean: how are they going to use it? What's it for? And why are they tearing up the side of the mountain?"

"It's absolutely disgusting, that's what it is!" Utrud declared, never one to hold an opinion in check. "They're invading our territory, that's what they're doing. Well, if they want to invade our territory we should return the favor and invade their territory too. You know what we should do? We should take over one of their houses and live there for a while. Yeah, let's see how they would like that!"

"Aren't you forgetting that that's been tried?" Skimpa said.

"What do you mean?" Utrud said.

"Trolls have taken over human houses in the past, and that has always come to a bad end, as far as I know," Skimpa said.

"You know, I seem to have a vague memory of something of that sort," Utrud said. "It seems to me I *have* heard stories about that, but I can't remember any details."

"I've never heard any stories like that, that I can remember," Retta said.

"Well, I have," Skimpa said. "I can't really remember many details myself, but I know the stories always had a bad ending. I don't remember ever hearing about trolls taking over a human house and then living there for years and years, in peace. Besides, even if we wanted to take over a human house, there are no houses very close to us. The nearest ones are quite a ways away."

"Well, I'd be willing to go quite a ways to get back at people for what they're doing here," Utrud said.

"We all came here to get away from people, partly," Skimpa pointed out. "I, for one, would be happy to never see a person again, or have anything to do with people."

"Sure, that would be great," Utrud agreed. "But people keep crowding us everywhere we go. They won't *let* us get away from them, completely. I'm just saying it would be great to get back at them in some way."

"I agree with you there," Skimpa said. "I just don't think that trying to take over a human house is a smart thing to do. It sounds too risky. I wish I could remember one of the stories about what happened to other trolls who tried to do that, but it's been a long time since I've heard a story about that."

One of the stories both Skimpa and Utrud had heard but no longer could recall in any detail is the following one:

56 ▪ When Trolls Took Over A House

A farmer named Einar Hanson and his family once lived on a miserable little farm a mile and a half from the nearest neighboring farms. The land was laced with so many rocks that it would have taken a hundred farmers a hundred years to clear them all from the fields. Because of the lay of the land, much of what little good soil existed eroded every time there was a hard rain. Half of the seeds Einar planted produced nothing. Those that produced anything at all produced crops so poor that it would be a generous use of language to call them pitiful.

When a strong windstorm passed through one summer and flattened fields, uprooted large trees, knocked down the barn, and smashed several windows in the house the Hansons decided they had endured all they could of their hardscrabble life. Without regret, they abandoned the little farm and moved away, leaving behind their two-story fieldstone house without even attempting to sell it.

It wasn't long before a group of trolls that lived nearby, in mountain caves, discovered the house was abandoned. After the house remained empty for many weeks, one of the trolls came up with the idea that the trolls should move into the house and live there. As far as they knew, no troll had ever lived in such a large house. Many had lived in dingy, deteriorated little shacks and cabins deep in a forest, but none had ever lived in a many-room house built by and for people.

One of the trolls pointed out that for centuries trolls had moved from their homes to more secluded places when people moved in and crowded them out of areas. Wasn't it time, she reasoned, that trolls took a stand and maybe started pushing the line back a little bit the other way?

And so it came to pass that seven trolls took over the house Einar Hanson and his family abandoned. And what a grand time they had in their new living quarters! The three troll children chased each other around the house with delirious delight. They and the adult trolls alike slid down the stairway banister rail over and over again until the wooden rail was so warm it was in danger of catching fire. The trolls made music, of a sort, by banging on pots and pans they found in the house and danced wildly, spastically, to the music they made, whooping and hollering with glee all the while. The female trolls built blazing fires in the fireplace and pretended they were princesses when they cooked their meals there. All in all, they had a raucus, rollicking good time.

Living so close to people, of course, provided them a better opportunity to steal things from people. The house, nearly empty when they moved in, quickly began filling up with clothes, bedding, food, cooking utensils, dishes, furniture, books (the trolls couldn't read, of course, but they could at least look at pictures in some of the books), decorative objects, and other items.

The neighboring farm families suspected trolls of being responsible for the increased incidence of theft, for whenever anything is stolen people are quick to point a finger of blame at trolls. No one knew trolls lived so near, though, until a farmer saw trolls around the old Hanson place while out searching for stray cattle early one morning. The farmer watched from a concealed vantage point as one troll drew water from the outdoor well and carried a bucket of water into the house and other trolls gathered firewood and did various other things. Smoke rose from the house's chimney, and even from a distance the farmer could hear there was a din inside the house.

Alarmed by what he had seen, the farmer informed others of his observations. Over the next several days he and others kept the old Hanson house under surveillance fourteen to sixteen hours a day to try to determine if trolls were living there and, if so, what they were up to. It soon became obvious to them that trolls were indeed living in the house, but they couldn't fathom for a flat-footed second what diabolical reasons the trolls had for doing so.

Whatever the trolls' reasons were, the people obviously could not tolerate having trolls living so close—and in a house, no less! People knew trolls were not only inveterate thieves, but also mean, vile, dirty, nasty, scoundrelly creatures who spelled trouble for people in capital letters. At least that was their perception of them.

Given that all indications pointed to the conclusion that the trolls apparently intended to remain residents of the house indefinitely, and seemingly had no plans to move out of their own volition, the neighbors held a meeting to try to figure out a way to make the trolls leave. A number of proposals were made at the meeting. A consensus quickly developed that the best plan would be to try to make the trolls believe the house was haunted. Trolls being as gullible as they are, making them believe a house was haunted seemed an easy enough task. Suggestions about exactly *how* to do that flowed fast and furious.

First, of course, the idea of the house being haunted had to be planted in the trolls' minds so that the power of suggestion would take root and grow into a field of fear. The opportunity to plant that seed presented itself to Elsa Norquist one evening when she went walking near the old Hanson house and encountered one of the female trolls who lived in the house.

"You weren't going to that house, were you?" the troll said to Elsa, anxious to keep her and all other people away from the house.

"Not on your life!" Elsa said. "I wouldn't go in that house if you gave me a pot of gold. It's haunted, you know. That's why the people who lived there moved out. They heard such strange noises, and saw such strange things, and had such frightening experiences, that they feared for their lives."

"Is that so?" the troll said. "What sort of things did they hear and see and experience?"

"They heard noises like thunder coming from the attic," Elsa told her, almost whispering, as though afraid to say such things out loud. "They saw objects move by themselves, and strange, odd-colored lights, and strange shapes in the fireplace, and puffs of smoke rising between the floorboards. They experienced sudden chills and hot flashes and sensed eyes watching them when no one visible was there, and rain *inside* the house, and lots of other things. There are ghosts in that house all right; there's no doubt about that."

"Maybe the ghosts were just after that one family," the troll suggested.

"Not a chance," Elsa said. "Ghosts have control of that house, and they intend to keep control of it, at whatever cost. They may be quiet from time to time, but they always return, with more hate and harmful intent every time. And once they start in on whoever lives there they won't rest until they either kill who lives there or whoever is there leaves."

"Maybe they only mean to harm people," the troll said. "Maybe they have nothing against trolls, say."

"Ghosts will harm anyone or anything," Elsa said. "It makes no difference to a ghost if it's a person, a troll or a dwarf. If ghosts believe they belong in a house they will do whatever they have to do to keep the house all for themselves."

The troll who spoke with Elsa Norquist in turn told her fellow trolls what Elsa told her. After that the trolls kept their eyes open and their ears perked for any signs of ghosts. Several days passed and they saw or heard nothing that seemed like any sign of ghosts.

Then one night all of the trolls left their house to engage in their favorite pastime, thievery, leaving the house unoccupied. The neighbors, who had been watching the trolls' house so they could take advantage of just such an opportunity, sprang into action. Five people entered the trolls' house and made preparations for the trolls' return. After setting up things according to plan, two of the people hid in the cellar, two in the attic, and one in a large closet.

When the trolls returned the people hiding in their house heard them and started to cause seemingly strange things to happen. By pulling attached threads, making use of strong magnets, and pounding on walls, floors and ceilings, the people made bottles smash, metal objects move, chairs tip over, and pictures jump off of walls. The two people in the cellar lit a fire and collected smoke under a blanket, then sent up clouds of smoke through cracks in the floorboards while one of them repeated several times, in a spooky voice, "GET OUT!" The person in the closet let loose with an undulating "*whooo-ooo-oo-oooo!*" From the attic, a croaking forlorn call of "Lorna, get help!" echoed through the house over and over again, between shakes of a large sheet of metal, which sounded like eerie ripples of thunder from The Great Beyond.

These sound and sight effects had the trolls frightened out of their low-voltage wits. They rushed about the house, tripping over furniture and each other, emitting screams and shouting at each other about what they should do.

When an extraordinarily long and loud ripple of thunder boomed from the attic and the person hiding in the closet came out and rolled a large round rock down the stairway one of the trolls shouted "Let's get out of here!" and the trolls flung open the front door and ran for their lives, never to return and never again giving the least bit of consideration to living in a house again.

The trolls were frightened away so quickly that they had no time to think about taking any of the things they had stolen from the nearby farms. Except for a few pieces of jewelry, and food items, the people recovered everything the trolls had stolen from them.

57 ▪ Tucking In

Utrud cracked a stirring stick across the back of Traug's right hand as Traug reached into the caldron to pick out a hunk of meat, causing Traug's hand to plunge into the stew.

"Wait until it's dished out!" Utrud ordered.

"Ow, that's hot!" Traug cried, pulling back his hand.

"Of course it's hot!" Utrud said. "It's sitting over a fire. What did you think it would be?"

Traug and others had been drawn to the large front chamber of the communal cave by the aroma of stew that wafted both deeper into the cave and outside the cave. It was dusk, so the trolls were eager to bolt down some food and head out into the night for their various adventures and objectives. Bolt is the operative word when it comes to eating, for trolls are notorious for their voracious appetites and despicable table manners, at least from the point of view of people. "Table manners" is even something of a misleading term, for as often as not trolls eat standing up or seated on a rock ledge, a large log or even the ground rather than at a table. This night, as was often the case, more trolls than could fit around the cave's only table, which was constructed rather shoddily from logs, wanted to eat at the same time, so seven of them sat and stood wherever they could find a place to sit or stand.

Utrud dished up the stew onto pie tins stolen from various houses over the years. All of the tins were rather old, and most dented and crinkled. Except for a few strange ingredients, this was a stew even humans would find palatable, with meat, potatoes, onions, carrots and other vegetables in it. Given some of the nasty things trolls eat, the stew was quite a treat for them, so they tucked in to the food with relish. There was little conversation as they ate, but a lot of noise, since nearly all of them chewed their food with their mouths open, burped and belched, smacked their lips, licked their fingers, grunted, sniffed, snuffled, wheezed, moaned in ecstasy, scratched themselves, wiped their mouths with their forearms and their hands on their clothes and the walls of the cave. In short, it was a raucous, repellant scene. The female trolls displayed slightly better manners than the males, but the margin was minimal. While there were enough forks and spoons for everyone to have one, some ate entirely or mainly with their hands and drank the stew broth from their plates as though drinking broth from a mug. Several times a bug flew or dropped into someone's plate of stew and the troll eating from that plate ate the bug rather than pick it out and discard it.

What conversation there was centered mainly around what each of them had planned for the night. Some had no plans except to venture out and see where whim and instinct took them. There was a small amount of talk about what was happening at the construction site at the bottom of the mountain, but very little. None of them had been down the mountain for a look for several days, so no one had anything new to report. Still, there was some grumbling and ranting about what people were doing, of course.

"We need to catch another gnome to cheer us up, that's what we need," Old Fungus opined with his mouth half full of food.

"We might still have two as prisoners if you had been quicker on your feet and hadn't let those two escape," Rnobrna griped, without any allowance for Old Fungus's age.

"Don't go blaming me for that!" Old Fungus shot back. "There was nothing anyone could have done by himself."

"Gnomes are devilish," Skimpa declared.

"That they are!" Old Fungus said. "Oh, if only we could catch another one and have him as our prisoner. This time I would tease him as much as I wanted to, no matter what anyone said." That was a criticism of Ort, of course, but Ort wasn't there to hear it. Ort and Tattra rarely ate a meal with others; mainly they ate by themselves, in their own cave. Old Fungus was still lamenting the gnomes' escape, and the fact Ort had not allowed him to tease the two gnomes to his heart's content.

As soon as each male troll finished devouring his food he headed off into the night, with four of them pairing up. None of them went down to see what was happening at the construction site.

274

58 ▪ The Creative Cooks

Anders Branstad read his son, Andrew, a story called *The Creative Cooks* the following evening.

▪

Nils and Nina Hallstrom lived on a secluded farm far from the nearest village. All four of their children had married and moved away, leaving Nils and Nina all by themselves, with only each other for companionship most of the time. For the Hallstroms, a trip to the nearest village to stock up on groceries and other supplies was anything but an everyday occurrence, or something done on the spur of the moment. A trip to town was an infrequent event that required careful planning and more than half a day of travel. It was extremely difficult for them to get to the village during the winter, when ice, snow and bone-chilling temperatures made travel torturous and troublesome.

One particularly harsh winter, blizzard followed blizzard until the snow was so deep it was all but impossible for the Hallstroms to make it to the village. The snow was so deep and crusty that their horses could not walk through it. Even as their stock of food dwindled by the day Nils and Nina did not want to risk a trip to the village, for it would have been a hazardous journey. They rationed their remaining food carefully and prayed for a break in the weather that would allow at least Nils to get out for more food—if not to town, at least to the house of one of their distant neighbors.

Late one afternoon, when they had enough food remaining for only more more day, Nils and Nina were seated on chairs in front of their fireplace when they heard a knock at their front door. They would not have been more surprised if a wolf had climbed down their chimney into their parlor. Visitors were rare even in good weather. It was unheard of to have a visitor in this sort of winter weather.

"Was that a knock at the front door?" Nils asked his wife.

"It sure sounded like it," Nina said.

"It couldn't have been," Nils said. "Maybe the wind blew something against the door."

Three quick raps sounded on the outside of the door.

"*That* wasn't the wind!" Nina said. "There's somebody out there."

"Who could it be?" Nils said, realizing as soon as he spoke that Nina could have no more of a clue about that than he did.

"Open the door and find out," Nina said.

Nils did so. He opened the front door a few inches to see who was at the door. As the door cracked open a shaggy, stocky, powerful troll pushed the door open wider and stepped into the Hallstroms' home, followed closely by an equally shaggy, stocky female troll. Even bundled up in heavy clothing as the trolls were, both Nils and Nina instantly recognized them as trolls. Frightened by the presence of trolls in her home, Nina rose from her chair and said to the intruders: "Out of our house! You don't belong here! Out!"

The two trolls merely laughed at her.

"Who's going to make us leave?" the female troll, whose name was Gjerde, said defiantly.

"We aren't leaving until you give us something to eat," the male troll, Kjar, declared. "We haven't eaten for nearly two days, and we still have far to go before we reach home. We need food."

"And we mean a full meal," Gjerde added, "not merely a few crusts of bread and some water."

"But we have hardly any food for ourselves," Nils explained. "Because of all the snow and the bad weather we haven't been able to travel to the village for the food we need."

"You're lying," Kjar charged. "Close the door and rustle us up something to eat right now or we'll burn down your house."

"We'll warm ourselves by the fire while you two cook us up a good meal," Gjerde said. "And be quick about it."

Nils closed the front door and went over next to Nina. As he tried to whisper something to her, Kjar snapped: "Get busy now!

No more of this foolishness! Hurry up! Get into the kitchen and make us a meal."

Intimidated by the blustery, burly trolls, Nils and Nina went into the kitchen and held a hurried, whispered conference. They knew that trolls are far stronger than humans, so they knew it would be senseless to try to force the trolls to leave.

"What should we do?" Nina said. "I'm not about to give the last scaps of food we have to a couple of dirty, nasty trolls."

"But they'll burn down the house if we don't give them anything to eat," Nils pointed out.

"I know!" Nina said with a flash of inspiration. "We'll give them as big of a meal as they want and still be able to eat ourselves."

"How can we do that?" Nils said, puzzled by his wife's seemingly unrealistic statement. "You know how little food we have left. It's barely enough to stop our stomachs from grumbling, much less being enough to feed two greedy, hungry trolls."

"That's why we'll have to improvise," Nina said.

"Improvise?" Nils said. "What do you mean?"

"I mean we'll substitute whatever we can find for food," Nina explained. "We can cut up some twine and color it with something to make string beans out of it. We could cut tongues out of old shoes and fry them up like bacon. We could boil shoelaces as pasta."

"We can't do that," Nils protested. "If we try to feed them things such as that they're sure to become angry and burn down our house anyway—and do who knows what else."

"You're forgetting that they're *trolls*," Nina emphasized. "Trolls eat bugs and bat ears and roasted rats. Some fried shoe leather will seem like a delicacy to them."

"I don't know. . ." Nils said, not convinced the plan would work.

Kjar appeared at the kitchen door at that point. "What are you two whispering about?" he demanded. "Get busy and make us something to eat."

"We were just getting started," Nina said, scurrying to get out some pots, pans and bowls. Nils busied himself as well, despite the fact he felt about as much at home working in a kitchen as a snowman would feel at home on a South Seas island.

"We're going to keep checking on you," Kjar warned, "so you better be busy working all the time or you'll be sorry." With that he returned to the fireplace in the adjoining room.

Using their imaginations like a strongman strains his muscles to lift heavy objects, Nils and Nina searched frantically about the kitchen for items that could substitute for food, at least in appearance, when presented in the right manner. They cut up a green rag and boiled it as substitute cabbage. They made talclum powder into substitute biscuits. They tossed short lengths of twine—substitute string beans—into the pot with the green rag to give the twine a green tint. They fried shoe leather in lamp oil, boiled shoelaces and string as substitute pasta, shredded soap as substitute cheese, and used wet paper as mashed potatoes. Nina brewed a pot of "coffee" with some of Nils's tobacco.

The two trolls checked on the Hallstroms frequently during the meal preparation and were satisfied to see their hosts busy. They had no suspicion anything was amiss.

When Nina placed the substitute food on the kitchen table the two trolls dug in like two famished wolves. Although they made some derogatory remarks about the toughness of the meat, the stringiness of the string beans, the texture of the mashed potatoes and the bitterness of the coffee, they devoured all that was set before them.

When Kjar finished eating he belched loudly and said: "Well, it certainly wasn't the best meal I've ever had, but all in all it wasn't bad. We'll overlook the fact that you lied to us about not having much food. At least you gave us a meal, and for that we won't burn down your house."

Then, without a word of thanks, the two trolls took their leave. Nils quickly locked the front door behind them, then he and Nina crumbled onto chairs before the fireplace, heartily relieved they had managed to save their house by fooling two trolls with creative cooking.

The following day a warm front came through and Nils was able to ski to the Hallstroms' nearest neighbors and borrow enough food to tide them over until they were able to get to the village.

59 ▪ Curious Changes

"**D**on't you think it's about time you found out what's happening at the bottom of the mountain?" Tattra said to Ort as Ort ate his evening meal.

"Why, what's happening there?" Ort said, vigorously scratching the top of his head.

"Who knows," Tattra said. "That's why you should find out. Aren't you curious?"

"It's the same old thing, I suppose," Ort grumbled. "People being people."

"Yes, and they could be halfway up the mountain by now and you wouldn't know it," Tattra said.

"They're not halfway up the mountain," Ort said, though Tattra's statement made him wonder just how far up the mountain people might be cutting trees and digging up dirt by then. "But if you're so all-fired worried, I'll send someone down there to take a look."

"Why don't you go yourself?" Tattra said.

"I have other things to do tonight," Ort growled. "I'll send someone else."

"What's so important that you can't go?" Tattra asked.

"I said I'll send someone," Ort snapped, leaving Tattra's question unanswered. "Just let me eat in peace."

As he ate, Ort thought about who he should have go down the mountain to the construction site. He quickly decided on Haar, for Haar was not quite as dense as most members of the tribe, and he also was more careful than most others in situations of this sort. Then he decided it would be better to have two tribe members perform the mission, with Grentd going along with Haar.

Haar and Grentd took their sweet time making their way down the mountain. They foraged berries, mushrooms and a few edible plant leaves along the way, went out of their way to drink water from a stream, and stopped to rest a couple of times.

An overcast sky made the night quite dark, testing even the storied night vision of trolls, so the two needed to watch their steps so they didn't trip over protruding tree roots, get slapped in the face by low branches or venture into patches of brambly bushes. Even so, they stumbled and strayed from their path more often than usual. When the ski area construction site finally came into view they slowed their pace even more and zigzagged around until they found a good position, behind four large pine trees, to see most of what they wanted to see. Given the degree of darkness, they were able to sneak closer to the construction site than the trolls generally did. Haar and Grentd were as still as possible as they took in the scene. Two guards were on night duty, as usual, but both were slouched on chairs and so still themselves that Haar and Grentd weren't sure if they were asleep or awake.

"What are we looking for?" Grentd asked Haar after more than a minute, keeping his voice as low as he could, which was not as whispery as people would have spoken to each other in such a situation.

"Nothing special," Haar answered in a slightly lower volume. "We're just looking. For anything different, I guess. Whatever." He would have preferred to be somewhere else, so his heart wasn't entirely in this mission.

One of the security guards stirred a bit, but didn't look in their direction, so it didn't appear as though he had heard them speaking or sensed something.

Haar and Grentd continued scanning the construction site in silence for a couple of minutes before something clicked in Haar's mind. "Look at that line of tree trunks going up the hill," he pointed out. "They all have only one branch, right across the top. All of the other branches have been broken off, and the bark has been peeled off too, I think."

"I think you're right," Grentd said, staring at what Haar described.

"That's very strange," Haar said. "That's not natural. People must have done that on purpose. But why would they do that?"

"Look!" Grentd said, noticing something himself, and speaking louder than was prudent in his excitement. "It looks like there are ropes running from tree to tree. Can you see those?"

"You're right!" Haar said, squinting to see. "Those *are* ropes. Why are there ropes there? Who strings trees together with ropes?"

"People, I guess," Grentd said.

"But why?" Haar said, his brain feeling as though it was being squeezed from three sides.

"You know what Ort says about people," Grentd reminded him. "They have their own ways."

"We need to tell Ort about this," Haar said.

"So we're leaving already?" Grentd said.

"Not yet. I mean we'll tell him whenever we get back."

"Oh."

As he continued scanning the scene, something else suddenly dawned on Haar. "You know what?"

"What?" Grentd said.

"I don't see any big machines around here now. Do you think they're gone?"

"I don't see any either," Grentd said after doing more scaning of his own.

"Wouldn't it be great if they were gone for good?" Haar said.

"Maybe the people will go away soon too," Grentd said.

"I don't know about that," Haar said. "I wouldn't count on that. Once people start doing something somewhere they usually stay there for good, or at least for a long time."

"Why do you think the machines are gone, if they are?" Grentd asked.

"Who knows? Let's just hope they're gone for good. People are bad enough all by themselves, but look at what sort of damage they can do when they have big machines that run all over, even up the side of a mountain."

As Haar mentioned the side of the mountain, both trolls cast their eyes in that direction, where workers had cleared a wide swath for two fairly long ski runs. Though Haar and Grentd couldn't detect such a detail in the existing light condition, there was grass seed planted there, with grass already sprouting.

The two trolls remained there nearly another ten minutes before Haar decided they should leave and they stole away, taking a roundabout route back toward the caves.

"I was just thinking," Haar said when they were far enough away from the construction site to speak at normal volume. "If they don't have the machines there to use anymore maybe they've cleared trees as far up the side of the mountain as they're going to. Maybe our worries are over."

As on their way down the mountain, Haar and Grentd did not push their pace as they headed back toward the caves. There was plenty of night left for them to explore a bit, and that is what they intended to do. After about a half-hour they came upon a large berry patch and began picking berries and stuffing the plump berries into their mouths. Grentd preferred filling one of his cupped hands with berries and shoving a whole handful of berries into his mouth while Haar popped berries into his mouth as he plucked them, picking with both hands. A few minutes into their picking there was a primal roar behind them. Both of them swiveled their heads and found themselves face to face with a very large bear, which was reared on its hind legs so that it presented an intimidating appearance, even to trolls, particularly with its teeth bared and its eyes full of brute menace. The bear gave another roar and swung one of its front legs in the trolls' direction. At a distance of more than twenty feet, the bear had no chance of clawing either troll with its swing, though. Both Haar and Grentd were already running, straight through the berry thicket, as the bear plopped its front paws on the ground and started chasing them. Trolls are able to run at a rather speedy clip when the need or the inclination arises, and both Haar and Grentd recognized the need to run as fast as they possibly could in their present predicament. Of course, bears are no slouches at running either, so despite the trolls' best efforts to put distance between themselves and the large bear they widened the gap by only a few feet after several minutes of running. As Haar rounded a sharp angle of a rock ledge, with Grentd on his heels, he was so startled by what he saw that he pulled up short, which caused Grentd to smash into him from behind and nearly knock him over. The surprise was in the form of Kravig, who stood facing them on the trail, not ten feet in front of them, motioning for them to follow him into a large crack in the rock ledge wide enough for the three trolls to slip through sideways but not big enough for a bear—at least not one the size of the one chasing Haar and Grentd—to squeeze through. Grentd, the stoutest of the three, barely squeezed through the fissure himself, just as the bear came around the bend. The bear evidently did not catch a glimpse of Grentd slipping through the crack, though, for it did not go up to the crack and start sniffing and pawing and bellowing. Instead, it ran right past the spot where Haar, Grentd and Kravig were squeezed into an opening in the rock ledge barely large enough for the three of them.

"How did you get here?" Haar asked Kravig.

"You're just lucky I happened to be here," the wizard responded.

"There was a bear chasing us," Haar said.

"I know," Kravig said. "I saw it running after you when I was standing on top of the ridge here."

"What luck it was there was this opening in the rock here," Grentd said. "I don't know how long I could have kept running as fast as I was running."

"Luck?" Kravig said. "You think it was luck? Think again. I saw what was happening from some distance off, and saw that you were running this way, so I cast a quick spell on the rock to make it crack so that you would have a place to escape from the bear." It *had* been sheer luck, of course, but Kravig liked to seize every opportunity that presented itself to make the other trolls believe he possessed supernatural power.

"I wonder where the bear is," Haar said.

"He's no doubt quite a ways away by now," Kravig said. "It's awful cramped in here. How about we go sit outside where we can breathe better."

"You're sure the bear is gone?" Haar said.

"If it comes back, we'll be right next to the crack so we can slip in again," Kravig said.

And so the three slipped back out into the open air and sat on the ground.

"That's the closest I've been to a bear in quite a few years," Haar observed.

"That was a big one," Grentd said.

"If I had been with you I could have tried giving it the whammy," Kravig said.

"I didn't know any of us were still capable of doing that," Haar said. "I know I've heard it talked about, but I thought only trolls that lived a long time ago had that power."

"Well, I haven't tried it in quite a while," Kravig admitted, "so I don't know how effective I could still be with it. I could never do what Tebben could do, of course. He was a one-of-a-kind troll when it came to fixing a whammy."

"Tebben?" Haar said. "I've never heard of him. Where did he live?"

"I'm not sure, exactly," Kravig said. "It's hard to believe you've never heard of him, though."

"I've never heard of him either," Grentd interjected. "Did you know him?"

"No, I just know about him," Kravig said. "It's hard to believe you two haven't heard about him, as many stories as there are about him. The most famous one involves a big bear, which is why I thought of the whammy now. Tebben is the only troll I've ever heard of who could inflict a triple whammy."

"A triple whammy?" Haar said. "Is that better than just a plain old whammy?"

"Of course it's better," Kravig said. "There's the whammy, then there's the double whammy, which is rare, and then there is the triple whammy, which only Tebben managed to pull off, as far as I know."

"How come?" Grentd asked.

"How come what?" Kravig said.

"How come he was the only one who could do a triple whammy?"

"He just was," Kravig answered. "I don't know *why*. He just was. I think I better tell you two the bear story about Tebben."

"Right now?" Haar said.

"Now's as good a time as any," Kravig said. "We don't want to stray too far from our escape hole here for a while yet, just in case the bear comes back this way."

And so Kravig told Haar and Grentd the following tale, in considerably less detail than it is presented here.

60 ▪ Tebben's Triple Whammy

No other troll ever had eyes quite as potent as Tebben had. Down through history, a number of trolls have possessed the ability to put a whammy on both people and animals. Some have even been able to deliver an effective double whammy. But of all the trolls in troll history, a troll named Tebben is the only one capable of administering a true triple whammy—a hex of such strength that it inflicted the unfortunate recipient with months of misfortune.

Other trolls that tried to give a triple whammy failed miserably. For them, trying to put a triple whammy on someone, or some animal, was like someone trying to blow a hole in the side of a mountain with his breath. It is said that one poor troll was so determined to give a triple whammy that he subjected his eyes to such a prolonged strain that he went blind. Tebben's red eyes had such power that even other trolls, who were generally immune from the hexes of run-of-the-mill whammies, were afraid of his strong spells. No members of his tribe wanted to cross Tebben, lest he unleash a double or triple whammy on the one who offended him. As a result, few trolls have ever been treated so kindly by other trolls as Tebben was.

After he discovered he had the power to give a triple whammy Tebben used his full-force triple whammy at every opportunity, even when a simple one-eyed whammy would have sufficed. He would turn his head to the right, close his eyes and concentrate to focus energy into his eyeballs. Then he would twist his head back to its normal face-foreward postion, with the thumb and index finger of his left hand pressed against his closed eyelids, pull his left hand away as he opened his eyes, and fix the object of his wrath with a bug-eyed stare. He did this three times for the triple whammy, noticeably debilitating the person or animal by large degrees with each successive stare.

After a wizard warned Tebben he may well wear out his hexing powers by using the triple whammy too often, Tebben made more judicial use of his singular power. "We must use our gifts wisely," the wizard counseled, "or they will be taken from us. This is a truth I have learned from experience. When I was young like you I misused some of my powers, with bad results. I tell you this because some day the tribe may need your full powers, and if you do not guard your powers and use them wisely you might find that you will fail the tribe just when the tribe most needs you."

Tebben took the wizard's advice to heart and used the triple whammy sparingly from then on, only when it seemed truly necessary. He had such extraordinary strong power that he rarely needed to resort to a double whammy, though, much less a triple whammy. Even his simple single whammy was stronger than the whammy of others. When hunting, Tebben could immobolize most animals with a single whammy.

An enormously large and enormously fierce bear lived on a nearby mountain in Tebben's time. One autumn this gigantic bear, sensing that the coming winter would be extraordinarily cold and long, ate so much food to store up body fat to prepare for winter hibernation that it used up all the food on its home mountain and set out in search of more food to satisfy its voracious appetite. The bear soon found its way to the mountain where Tebben's clan lived.

At the first enticing sniff of food cooking, the large bear followed its nose to a spot where the trolls were cooking supper just outside the opening of one of their caves. The bear hadn't smelled anything so good in ages. Without hesitation the gargantuan animal tramped toward the kettle of food that was hung over a fire. All was chaos in the troll camp as trolls shrieked and fled every which way, terrified, as other trolls came running out of their caves to see what all of the commotion was about. A few of the boldest male trolls hurled rocks and sticks at the hairy intruder, but the rocks and sticks may as well have been cotton balls for all the effect they had on the big bear. Concerned with its single-minded mission of eating the trolls' food, the bear didn't even seem to notice some of the trolls were pelting him with rocks and sticks.

When the bear snatched the pot in its front paws, stood on its hind legs and dumped the pot of food into its enormous mouth one of the trolls became so enraged he found a jagged rock more than a foot long, ran under the bear and heaved the rock at the bear's head. A sharp edge of the rock caught the bear on the bottom of its snout, causing a cut. The bear felt that hit. It roared like a thundercrack, looked around to see what had caused its wound, and caught sight of the troll who threw the rock running away. It tossed aside the empty pot and snatched the fleeing troll with a swipe of one of its huge front paws. The poor, unfortunate troll was helpless in the bear's clutches as the bear lifted the troll to mouth level, growled so loud the ground shook, and opened its razor-toothed jaws to take a bite of the squirming troll.

Tebben, who had been in a cave a good distance from the scene of the disturbance, came running up just as the gigantic bear was about to have its first taste of troll. The bear glanced at Tebben, who launched into his triple whammy act without hesitation while he had the bear's eye, even as he wondered if even a triple whammy would be strong enough to work on such a huge, ferocious animal. This bear was far larger than any other animal he had ever encountered, after all. All he could do was give it a try and hope his powers were strong enough to subdue even such a savage creature.

Certainly a double whammy would not have been enough. Tebben's triple whammy, though, had just enough hex energy to debilitate the bear to the point where it dropped the troll it was holding.

"Go away!" Tebben shouted at the bear. "Get away from here! Go on!"

The big bear dropped its front paws to the ground and began ambling away, as Tebben had ordered. When it was nearly out of the trolls' camp the bear glanced up into a tree and spotted a troll named Ekre seated on a lower branch, where she had climbed to hide from the bear. For the bear, it was love at first sight. Even under the spell of a hex, such strong instant love is an extremely powerful force. Once again the bear reared on its back legs, a position that allowed it to stand tall enough to grab Ekre out of the tree. Ekre screamed for help as the bear held Ekre in its mouth and scrambled away with her.

Tebben was horror-stricken by this development, for he loved Ekre and wanted to marry her. He was so horrified that it took him several seconds to regain his senses. When he did, he set out in pursuit of the big bear that had his beloved Ekre in its wicked clutches. Several other trolls were close behind Tebben in his chase.

Tebben and the other trolls finally came close to the bear after it climed onto a rock ledge that overlooked a rocky ravine a couple of hundred feet deep. The bear, which now pressed Ekre to its side with one of its front legs, was about fifteen feet above the trolls, who were on a wider, less precarious rock ledge.

"Here's my chance," Tebben said to the other trolls. "I'm going to try to give him the triple whammy again."

"Give it everything you've got!" one of the trolls said in encouragement.

"I'll whammy him until my eyes pop out if I have to," Tebben vowed.

"That might be too dangerous," the wizard warned Tebben. "Putting so much energy into another triple whammy so soon after already giving one triple whammy could have bad consequences, even for you."

"But I have to save Ekre!" Tebben said, disregarding whatever risks might befall him in his reckless efforts to rescue his precious Ekre.

Catching the bear's attention, Tebben focused hex energy into his eyes with more intensity than he had ever before mustered. He whammied the huge bear once, he whammied it a second time, and then with a force of lightning-like intensity he whammied it a third time. He put so much force into his whammies that one of the trolls with him said he detected smoke coming from Tebben's eyes. Tebben felt power flow from his eyes as he directed his wrath at the bear. Shocked into limpness, the bear lost its balance and plunged from the ledge into the deep canyon, where it died instantly.

Freed from the bear's grasp, Ekre managed to reach her hand into a crevice between two slabs of rock and hold on until Tebben and other trolls rescued her.

Overwhelmed by Tebben's courage and the unshakable love he demonstrated by rescuing her from the bear, Ekre agreed to marry Tebben.

The wizard proved to be a prophet the day of Ekre's rescue, for Tebben invested so much energy in the final triple whammy he gave the bear to save Ekre that it was the final whammy of any strength he was able to perform. The all-out effort he gave to save Ekre completely sapped his whammy power. He never regretted the decision he made that day, though. To Tebben, saving Ekre's life had been worth any cost, however high that cost proved to be. His love for Ekre meant more to him than anything. Anyway, by using up his power in one last glorious gasp he was able to win Ekre's love in return, and he and Ekre were able to be with each other and love each other the rest of their days.

61 ▪ Brine's Dream

Autumn was sneaking into the landscape as subtly as an adroit thief in the night. Some trees were tinged with yellow, and some yellow leaves had already pulled away from the trees' tentacled branches and floated to the ground. Some nights there was a snap in the air that hadn't been there for nearly three months. The period of daily daylight had dwindled considerably in the more than two months since the Summer Solstice. While summer still held sway, an inevitable change of seasons was in its early stages, and Brine took notice as he and Llop hiked a switchback course down the mountain in the late afternoon to check out what was happening at the construction site.

They were making good progress until Llop stepped into an eight-inch-deep depression, lost his balance and twisted his left ankle.

"I'm going to have to stop and rest a while," Llop told his companion, rubbing his enormous, blocky chin with his closed right hand. Luckily, there was a convenient moss-covered rock ledge nearby, which provided a degree of comfort rarely found in a forest. The spongy moss did not completely cover the rock ledge, but there were large patches of it for both Llop and Brine to sprawl on.

"Are we still going to go down to the bottom?" Brine asked.

"Well, that's where we're going, isn't it?" Llop responded.

"I mean, are you still up to it?" Brine said. "Can you walk okay to make it?"

"I'll make it," Llop asserted, picking at his long rectangle-shaped nose, one of the tribe's longest noses. "Don't worry about me. Worry about yourself if you want to worry about someone. Ort wants us to go down and have a look, and that's what we're going to do."

"We could just not go and tell him everything's the same," Brine suggested.

"We could, I guess," Llop said. "But I want to see what"s going on there for my own self too. Don't you?"

"Do you think we might have to leave this mountain if too many people come?" Brine asked.

"You never know," Llop said. "I don't think it's likely. They're still quite a ways away from our caves, and there are only a few of them so far."

"Do you think more are coming?"

"I haven't really thought about that," Llop said, his voice scratchy. "I have better things to think about. If we do have to move I know where I'd like to move to; I'd like to live beside a fjord again. The older I get, the more I think that the happiest time of my life was when I lived next to a fjord."

"Is that so?" Brine said. "What's a fjord?"

"You must know what a fjord is," Llop said.

Brine strained his brain several seconds. "Not that I know of." While he had heard fjords mentioned in tales, he never really understood what they were, and didn't have any curiosity about them until that moment.

"You must have heard about fjords; you just don't remember. A fjord is like a finger of the sea that has steep cliffs along the edge of it. You know about the sea, don't you?"

"I've heard of it, but I've never seen it," Brine said.

"You should see it someday. There are fjords all along where the sea is."

"How many are there?" Brine asked.

"A *lot*. Everywhere you go along the sea there's a fjord. I don't know if anyone knows how many there are."

"How big are they?"

"What do you mean?"

"I mean how big are they?"

"Well, some are big and some are small. Some you can throw a rock across and see from one end to the other. Others are so wide you can barely see across from one side to the other, and so long that they look like rivers. The water is deep blue and you can see the reflections of the rock cliffs in the water. It's quite a thing to see."

"And you lived next to one?" Brine asked.

"A long while ago," Llop said. "I was much younger then. It was a wonderful place, until people came. People made it a bad place for trolls to be, of course. There got to be too many people there." He paused a couple of seconds before shifting gears. "Well, enough talk. We have to get going. Let me just test my leg to see how it feels."

Llop pushed himself to his feet, tested his sprained ankle, and pronounced himself fit enough to continue on down the mountain.

In part because of the delay caused by Llop's mishap, all of the workers were gone by the time Llop and Brine reached a place where they could see the construction site. Things looked pretty much the same as Haar and Grentd saw and reported. There were no large machines visible, work on the cabin was completed, the exterior of the lodge was almost complete, and a line of evenly spaced, T-shaped trees strung together with ropes climbed the scraped incline. With more light available, Llop and Brine could tell grass was growing on that scraped area of the lower mountain.

"What do you make of that?" Brine asked about the grassy slope and the line of T-shaped trees.

"It's hard to say," Llop said, as clueless as Brine was.

"Now what?" Brine said. "There's nothing going on here. Should we go back, or go somewhere else?"

"Let's stay here a while," Llop decided. "Maybe something will happen. I'm tired, though. I think I'm going to get some sleep. You watch and wake me up if you see anything going on." With that, Llop crawled beneath a large pine tree, lied down on a mat of orange-ish pine needles, used a protruding root as a pillow, and was soon asleep.

Brine quickly became bored with looking at the inert construction site, where he couldn't even see the security guards, and decided it was silly to keep looking at "nothing." Following Llop's example, he found his own pine needle mat and fell asleep himself.

Brine rarely dreamed, at least as far as he could remember when he woke up, but he had a vivid dream this evening. In the dream he was sailing through the air through a spectacular scene featuring a pearly blue stretch of water bordered by towering, steep-walled, misty mountains, which were covered by a velvety layer of green vegetation. He seemed to sail for mile upon mile, serene as a white, puffy cloud as he floated above the snaking waterway. Eventually a round, inviting cave entrance appeared high above where the waterway ended and Brine floated to the cave entrance and landed there like a bird. He was turning around to look back down the waterway when his dream ended abruptly as Llop poked him awake, none too gently.

"You were supposed to keep watch," the older troll scolded.

Still groggy, Brine asked: "What's going on?"

"Nothing," Llop said. "It's time to go. Let's go."

Brine told Llop about his dream as they hiked up the mountain, as best he could remember and describe it.

"It sounds to me like you saw a fjord in your dream," Llop said.

"Really?" Brine said. "You think so? That was a fjord?"

"It sure sounds like it."

"It was wonderful. Are they actually that pretty?"

"Well, I don't know what you saw," Llop said, "but most fjords are very pretty, yeah."

"I hope I get a chance to see one in person someday," Brine said. "Do you think I will?"

"I have no idea," Llop said, sounding indifferent, as he was.

"I bet that would really be something," Brine said.

62 ▪ Toller's Neighbors

"Let's see. . ." Anders said as he browsed the table of contents of *A Treasury of Troll Tales*, "what's a story we haven't read yet? Oh, here's a good one: *Toller's Neighbors.* I don't think we've read that one yet, have we?"

"I don't think so," Andrew said.

"Well, let's read it then," Anders said.

▪

Long, long ago a young man named Toller and a young woman named Inger fell in love with each other when they both worked as servants at the same mansion. And so they were married. Their master provided them with a sumptuous wedding dinner and gifted them a little stone cottage where they could live.

Their cottage was in the middle of a tract of open wasteland covered with heather and other low shrubs, and in fairly close proximity to a cluster of grave-mounds, which people in the region generally believed to be occupied by mound trolls. In this distant time, human beings had not yet learned that mound trolls were nowhere near as mischievous and evil-minded as mountain trolls and forest trolls. They lumped all branches of the troll species together when they thought of trolls. To human beings, trolls of all types were to be feared and detested.

Toller, however, felt not a fleck of fear living so close to mound trolls. He firmly believed that as long as he placed his trust in God and was just in his dealings with other men he had no reason to be afraid of anything.

One evening not long after they moved into their cottage Toller and Inger were sitting together talking over their future when there was a knock at their door. When Toller opened the door a short, hunchbacked figure with long hair and a long beard entered the cottage with a hearty "Good evening!" The visitor wore a red hat and a leather apron, which had a hammer hung on a loop on the front of it. While neither Toller or Inger had ever before laid eyes on a troll, they both knew immediately they were in the presence of one now. The troll seemed so friendly and good-natured, though, that neither was afraid.

"I see that you know who I am, do you not, Toller?" the visitor said, addressing the man of the house.

"Well," Toller replied, "my guess is that you are one of those who live under the grave-mounds nearby."

"That is an excellent guess," the little troll said. "Yes, I am one of the poor little mound dwellers who must live in old graves, forever hidden from the sun, because people have left no other place for us to be. We have heard that you have come here to live, Toller, and our king is concerned that you may try to harm us, or drive us away. He sent me here tonight to implore you to let us live in our mounds in peace. We promise that we will never steal things from you or cause you any aggravation or disturb you in any way as you go about your affairs."

"I assure you that you have nothing to fear from me," Toller responded. "I have never been a man of violence or animus. As long as you allow us to live in peace we will allow you to live in peace. I see no reason why we can't be good neighbors to each other. There is plenty of space so that each of us should be able to go about our own affairs without getting in each other's way or making mischief for each other."

"I am well pleased to hear you say that!" the troll said, dancing a little jig around the room. "You will find that if you keep your promise to let us live in peace we will not only return the kindness but also give you all the good it is our power to give."

"And what do you have the power to give?" Toller asked.

"You will come to know what that is in due time," the troll said. "For now, though, I must withdraw from your good company, for the king is anxious to hear my report of my visit to you. I don't want to keep him waiting a minute longer than necessary with the good news." With that, he departed.

True to their words, Toller and his mound troll neighbors lived in peaceful harmony with each other from that night forward. Indeed, in time they grew so familiar with each other that the trolls felt free to borrow a pot or a copper kettle from Toller and Inger anytime they wished. The trolls always returned the borrowed vessels promptly, and always cleaned and scrubbed. In return for such favors, the trolls voluntarily performed tasks to help Toller. In the spring, for instance, they would go out at night and gather up stones from the ground where Toller had plowed and pile the stones next to the furrows of soil. In the autumn they would harvest ears of corn so that Toller would not have to work to the point of weariness trying to finish all of the harvesting himself before winter set in.

Far from cursing and fulminating against trolls, as most people did, Toller thanked God with prayer for providing him with such agreeable and helpful neighbors as the mound trolls. At Christmas and Easter and other important feast days he left a large bowl of milk-porridge on one of the mounds for the trolls.

After the birth of their daughter, Inger became so ill that Toller was sorely afraid she would die. There was no doctor in that district, so expert medical care was unavailable. Toller asked a midwife what he could do and she was at a loss to make any suggestion. He sat beside his wife's bed many nights in a row so that he could give her whatever comfort he was able to provide, and to be there to get her whatever she wanted. One night his eyes drooped shut and he fell asleep and slept in his chair most of the night. When he awoke, very early in the morning, several mound trolls were in the bedroom. One was sitting in a rocking chair rocking the baby girl, another was busy cleaning the room, and a third was stirring a mixture of herbs into a glass of water, which she then gave Inger to drink. As soon as they saw that Toller was awake all three trolls hurriedly left the room. From that night on Inger's condition improved steadily. In a week she was on her feet again, as healthy as ever.

On another occasion Toller did not have enough money to have new horseshoes put on his horses. One night, when Toller and Inger were in bed but not yet asleep, they heard the horses making a disturbance in the stable.

"You better go out to the stable and check on them," Inger said. "There might be something wrong."

Toller quickly dressed, lit a lantern, and went out to the stable. When he cracked open the door he saw many of the mound folk inside, busily removing the horses' worn-out shoes and replacing them with new shoes. Not wanting to startle or disturb the trolls, he slipped away quietly.

When Toller took the horses out to water them in the morning he saw that the horses were shod as well as though the country's best blacksmith had done the work.

The relationship between Toller and his little underground neighbors continued in this reciprocal manner for many long years, with Toller and the mound folk doing whatever they could to be of service to each other.

As Toller and Inger grew older their investment of hard work paid dividends. What had been scrubby heath when they first moved in to their little cottage was transformed into fertile farmland. They were able to build a large, attractive house to replace their humble cottage.

One evening, just as they were preparing to go to bed in that house, there was a knock at the front door. The visitor turned out to be the same mound troll who had visited them so many years before, shortly after they took up residence in their little cottage. Instead of his usual garb, the troll wore a long sheepskin coat, a tattered hat and a woolen scarf, which was wrapped around his neck. His demeanor was also different. His usual peppiness was gone, replaced by a doleful expression.

The troll said that he brought greetings from the king, who requested that Toller, Inger and Inge, their grown daughter, join him in the trolls' underground cave that evening because of some important matter the messenger would not disclose. Tears rolled down the troll's cheeks as he choked out his message, but he would not say why he was so sad.

Toller, Inger and Inge followed the troll to the cluster of old grave-mounds, where the mound trolls lived. When they descended into the cave, where they had never been before, they saw that the cave was decorated with flowers from the heath and that a long table was set with dishes and food, as though in preparation for a feast. The three people were led to the head of the table, where they sat next to the troll king. The other mound trolls sat along both sides of the long table and began eating.

297

While the table seemed to be set for a feast, the dinner was anything but festive. There was little conversation. The trolls ate in sad-eyed silence, hanging their heads, sighing from time to time, and even sniffling away tears. It was evident to Toller, Inger and Inge that something was wrong, but they dared not ask any questions for fear of further upsetting the trolls.

When the dinner was over the king at last offered an explanation. Addressing Toller, he said: "I invited you here tonight because we all wished to thank you and your wife and your little daughter—who is no longer so little—for being so kind and friendly all the time we have been neighbors. I'm sure we could not have found better neighbors had we searched a thousand years. Now, though, sadly, the time has come for us to leave. Since the time you moved here, several churches have been built in the area, with loud church bells that ring out across the countryside, every morning and every evening. I'm afraid this is a situation we simply cannot tolerate, for the ringing of a church bell is so painful to our ears that it is nothing short of torture. Therefore, we must leave this good home."

"But where will you go?" Toller asked.

"Farther to the north, where most of our people have already gone," the king said. "We are told that we will be able to find a place to live far away from people there, and far away from the sound of any church bells. Few people are as friendly as you three are, unfortunately, and church bells are torture."

"Well, we will hate to see you leave, but I wish you good luck, wherever you may go," Toller said to the king.

"I wish you good luck as well, my good neighbor," the troll king said. With that, he shook hands with both Toller and Inger. When he came to Inge he said, "To you, sweet Inge, we will leave a remembrance so that you will think of us and remember us when we are far away." He then took up a small stone and placed it in Inge's apron. All of the other mound trolls did likewise, after saying their farewells to Toller and Inger.

Led by the king, they then left the cave, single file. Toller, Inger and Inge followed them out of the cave and stood on a grave-mound watching as the trolls, each of whom had a pack on his or her back and a walking stick in his or her hand, walked away. When the trolls reached the road, by which point they were barely visible to the three neighbors they were leaving behind, they all turned around, waved farewell one final time and turned northward. Tollelr, Inger and Inge watched the trolls until they disappeared from sight, then returned to their home, feeling an emptiness in their hearts for the loss of such good neighbors.

The next morning Inge discovered that all of the stones the trolls had dropped into her apron the previous night were precious stones that shined and sparkled. The stones were four different colors: blue, black, brown and green. Toller recognized that those were the four colors of the mound trolls' eyes, and he felt that was no coincidence. To him, it seemed obvious the mound trolls had imparted the color of their eyes to the stones so that Inge would remember them.

63 ▪ The Pull Of Place

Brine found himself haunted by his dream of a spectacularly beautiful fjord. He kept projecting the image in his mind's eye, both because it was such a pleasant image and because he felt that by keeping the image in his mind as much as possible the image would be less likely to fade from his memory. He wanted to hold the blissful image in his memory as long as possible, for it was so different from the reality of cave life on a mountain. Llop had said he thought his happiest days were when he lived beside a fjord, and Brine could understand why if all fjords were as beautiful as the one he envisioned in his dream.

His mind was so consumed with the fjord image that gradually he felt an overwhelming compulsion to have such an image right in front of him, to actually see a fjord with his eyes. He felt the compulsion was deeper than mere curiosity, that it went beyond his simply wanting to see one; he sensed his dream was meant as a message that he was supposed to visit a fjord and possibly even live beside one, that the dream dealt with his destiny, though he could not have defined destiny if spotted a twele-word headstart. But where were the fjords, exactly? In which direction did they lie? How long would it take to walk to one? He didn't know the answer to any of those questions. Given that Llop had not only seen at least one but actually lived beside one, he was the obvious tribe member to pump for information.

"Remember that dream I had about a fjord that I told you about?" he said to Llop when the two were alone, fishing for trout in the stream near the caves.

"What about it?" Llop said gruffly, far more interested in fishing than in anything Brine had to say.

"Well, I think I maybe had the dream because I'm supposed to go to a fjord," Brine said, slightly embarrassed by sharing such a thought with someone else. "Do you think that's possible?"

"What do you mean, go to a fjord?" Llop asked.

"I mean walk to a fjord, and maybe stay there and live there, I don't know," Brine said.

"Do you know how far it is to a fjord?" Llop said.

"No, I don't," Brine admitted. "That's why I'm asking you about them, because you've seen one. How long would I have to walk to see one?"

"I'm not sure exactly," Llop said. "It would take many, many, many days, I know that. I know it's a crazy idea."

"Why do you say that?"

"Because it is, that's why. You're actually thinking about doing this?"

"Well, it's just an idea," Brine demurred, not comfortable telling someone else how compelled he felt to do it. "I'm just curious about fjords since I dreamed about one, and where they are, exactly. Which direction are they from here?"

"Well, I'm not positive," Llop said. "I know they're in the direction where the sun sets."

"Where the sun sets, huh?"

"I don't know much else than that."

"But you lived by one, you said."

"That was a long time ago," Llop said.

"Have you wanted to go back and see another one since?"

"It would be nice," Llop said, remembering his years beside a fjord, "but this is our life now, here. You can't always have what you want."

"I guess not," Brine said, dropping the subject—with Llop, at least.

The desire to see a fjord still jangled in his mind, though. He felt as though the fjords were pulling at him with a powerful, invisible force that nonetheless was as perceptible as someone tugging on a rope tied around his torso. His urge to see a fjord was as strong as his urge to eat food when he was hungry.

And so he made up his mind to make the journey, with all of its mysteries, unknown factors and potential perils. One night he gathered some food, a blanket and a set of extra clothes into a burlap sack and set off toward where the sun disappeared every evening, on those evenings when the sun was visible.

Now that Brine's tribe lived in such a remote place, so far from the houses and farms of people, it wasn't unusual for a tribe member or two to be gone from home base two or three days at a time. Indeed, Brine had made quite a few such two- or three-day outings himself. So none of the other trolls took much notice of Brine's absence until no one had seen him for three days and three nights. At that point some of them began worrying and expressing concern about his welfare.

"I hope nothing's happened to him," Skimpa said during a morning mealtime, meaning of course she hoped nothing bad or fatal had happened to him. "I've always liked Brine."

"I bet he's actually gone and done what he said he was thinking of doing," Llop said.

"What's that?" his wife, Retta, asked.

"He told me he had a dream about a fjord that made him want to go see one," Llop said, sharing the information with others for the first time.

"When did he tell you that?" Retta inquired.

"A few days ago. I don't remember," Llop mumbled.

"Does he know how far away the fjords are?" Utrud said with a tone suggesting she blamed Llop for not doing more to discourage Brine.

"I told him they were a long ways away," Llop said.

"But he still decided to go?" Utrud pressed.

"I guess so," Llop answered. "I don't know. He didn't *tell* me he was going; he just said he was thinking about it."

"He just wants to *see* a fjord?" Retta said.

"I don't know," Llop said in his mumbly voice. "I think he said something about he might stay there if he likes it."

"Well, isn't that just dandy?!" Utrud said with a sarcastic tone. "That's just dandy, that is!"

Llop practically buried his face in his plate of food, wanting to put the entire subject out of his mind.

It wasn't long before Ort learned of what Brine may have done and gathered what information he could from Llop himself. Ort was fairly nonchalant about the situation. "Oh, well," he said. "I guess maybe he just craved some adventure. We don't get as much adventure here as we did way back in earlier days, in other places. If he comes back, he comes back; if he doesn't, he doesn't. We have bigger things to worry about."

64 ▪ Drawing Power

This evening, Anders happened to select a tale that featured a young girl rather than a young boy, which was unusual for a troll tale.

▪

Beginning at age three, Bertina Tollefson attended the annual local village fair with her parents, Iver and Hannah, every year. In time, her two younger brothers, Arthur and Henry, went along as well. The Tollefson family lived on a farm more than seven miles from the village, so the three children considered each trip to the village a treat, and the biggest treat of all in this regard was a trip to the annual fair, which brimmed with music, merriment and—so it seemed to them—a magical atmosphere.

When Bertina was ten she accidentally became separated from the rest of her family at the fair and found herself wandering about the fairgrounds all by herself. She was trying to find her parents and her brothers when a sorceress seated at a small round table in front of a colorful tent attracted her attention. The sorceress wore several layers of brightly colored, flowing clothing, including a long silk dress, silk scarves and a shoulder shawl, and was adorned with long, dangling earrings and other flashy jewelry hanging around her neck and slipped on her wrists and fingers. She had dark eyes and flowing black hair, which streamed from under a bright-orange scarf with yellow star shapes on it that covered the top one-third of her head. A black cloth with yellow star shapes on it covered the table, and a crystal ball sat in the center of the table.

Bertina quickly opened up her drawing book to a blank page, took a drawing pencil from a pocket of her light-blue dress, sat down on a patch of grass and started drawing a picture of the sorceress. Bertina loved to draw, and she had brought a drawing book and drawing pencils to the fair to draw pictures of some of the scenes there. To her, the exotic sorceress was a fascinating subject full of exceptional features and captivating flair. Several people stopped by the sorceress's table to have their fortunes foretold as Bertina drew her picture. After gazing in Bertina's direction many times, the sorceress eventually summoned Bertina with a hand motion just as Bertina completed the final few strokes of the drawing. Somewhat anxiously, Bertina walked over close to where the sorceress sat.

"May I be so bold as to ask what you're scribbling in your book?" the sorceress said to Bertina.

"I've been drawing a picture of you," the girl told her. "I just finished it."

"I'd love to see it," the sorceress said. "May I?"

Bertina held out the picture for the sorceress to see.

"That's wonderful!" the sorceress said with obvious sincerity. "You are a very talented little girl. Do you know that?"

"Thank you," Bertina responded, blushing a bit.

"I bet you will be a great artist when you grow up," the sorceress said.

"I hope so," Bertina said. "That's what I want to be."

"Maybe I can help you along," the sorceress said. "I happen to have a very special herb mixture that will give you amazing power as an artist, more power than you ever imagined."

"But I don't have any money," Bertina said.

"None is necessary," the sorceress said. "I will give it to you because of the talent you already possess. Call it my contribution to the world of art if you like." With that, she reached under the table and pulled out a large cloth handbag, from which she took a small cloth pouch tied up with some type of vine. "This is a very special herb mixture," she said almost solemnly, "so you must take extra special care of it. Do you promise that you will?"

"I promise," Bertina said in her most sincere voice.

"Very well then, here you are," the sorceress said, handing the pouch containing the herb mixture to Bertina. "Here are your instructions: You must place the pouch of herbs under your pillow and sleep on it for seven nights. After sleeping on the herbs for seven nights you must bury the pouch in a spot near the north side of a mossy tree and tell no one where the pouch is buried.

Follow those instructions to the letter and I promise you will find that your drawings have amazing power."

"What sort of power?" Bertina asked.

"It's best that you discover that on your own," the sorceress said. "The herb mixture works in its own way, differently for each person."

Bertina slipped the pouch into one of her dress pockets mere seconds before her father spotted her and Bertina was reunited with her family.

As the sorceress instructed, Bertina began sleeping on the pouch containing the dry herb mixture that very night, and then did so again the succeeding six nights before she buried the pouch in a secret spot near the north side of a mossy tree.

The first drawing she created after that was a drawing of a troll. Recalling some descriptions in troll tales she had heard and read, she used her imagination to draw a burly, grotesque, terrifying troll with long arms, vice-like hands, a projecting, pimply nose and evil evident in his bulbous black eyes. Bertina thought it was one of the best drawings she had ever done, and both her mother and father thought so too when she showed them the drawing.

"I'd hate to cross his path, I tell you that," her father remarked.

Two days later, late in the evening, between sunset and darkness, Bertina was sitting on a tree stump next to the family garden making a drawing of her father working in the garden when a rather formidable figure emerged from a nearby patch of woods. Given that Iver had his back to the stranger and was making noise scratching up dirt with a hoe, Bertina noticed the figure first. Even in the dusk she was able to discern it was not a person but a troll.

"Daddy!" Bertina managed to say as she pointed at the troll.

Iver looked at his daughter and then to where she was pointing. "Well, hello. . ." he started to say before he recognized the stranger was a troll. "We don't want any trouble here," he said, turning to face the troll as he held his hoe in front of him as though it was a weapon.

"Trouble?" the troll said. "I don't want any trouble either. I just want a few of your vegetables."

As the troll stepped toward Iver and Bertina had a better look at his face she was flabbergasted to see that the troll looked exactly like the one she had drawn in her drawing book. Iver seemed to sense that as well, for he said to the troll, "There's something familiar about you," even though this was the first troll he had encountered.

"I'll just help myself to some of the vegetables," the troll growled as he tromped into the garden.

Bertina flipped back to the troll drawing in her drawing book while trying to keep her eyes on her father and the troll. Sure enough, the real troll before her was the spitting image of her drawing.

"All right, I'll let you have a few," Iver said to the troll, thinking that he would be doing well if he got off with losing a few vegetables in this ticklish situation.

The troll proceeded to pick beans, cucumbers, tomatoes and other vegetables and put them in a burlap sack he carried. When he picked far more than a few, by Iver's definition of "a few," Iver felt compelled to say something. "That should be plenty for you," he said. "We need this food."

Ignoring Iver, the troll went right on picking vegetables, faster than ever.

"I said that's enough," Iver said sternly, stepping toward the troll and brandishing his hoe like a spear.

"I say it isn't!" the troll all but hissed, then swatted Iver's hoe aside with a quick swipe of his left arm.

"Daddy!" Bertina shouted, fearful of what the powerful troll might do to her father. Spittle flew from her mouth and landed on her drawing of the troll as she spoke. Noticing the spots on the paper, and acting on instinct, she tried to wipe away the moisture. As she did so, the troll was trying to grab her father's neck with his right hand when the troll's hand went misty and lost substance. Noticing that, the troll pulled back his misty hand. Looking at the drawing, Bertina noticed she had rubbed some lines into a blur where the troll's right hand was. As she rubbed another wet spot where the troll's lower left leg was the troll in the garden wailed in pain. Bertina looked at him and saw that the troll's lower left leg was but mist as well. In an instant she realized that the changes she was making to the drawing— the rubbings—were affecting the real life troll trying to harm her father. She literally seemed to have total drawing power over this particular troll.

Losing control of parts of his body incensed the troll, who tried to attack Iver more ferociously than ever. As Iver attempted to run, the troll sent him sprawling face down in the dirt with a well-aimed cabbage between his shoulder blades, then rushed over and planted his right foot on Iver's back.

Recognizing the power she possessed, Bertina spit on the troll's right foot in her drawing and frantically rubbed that part of the drawing to blurriness. Looking up, she saw the real troll's right foot go misty.

From that point, it was merely a matter of trying to keep up with the troll's attacks on her father as Bertina spat on the drawing and rubbed every part of it blurry until the real troll was nothing more than late-evening mist hanging over part of the garden.

"Where did he go? Where did he go?" Iver asked his daughter after scrambling to his feet.

"He's gone," was all Bertina said, not wanting to explain her interaction with the sorceress at the fair and how the sorceress seemingly had given her magical power to create and get rid of trolls—or at least one troll. She never drew a picture of another troll, so she never knew whether another drawing would create another real troll.

"That's strange," Iver remarked. "That's very strange. Come on, let's go get inside the house," he said as he and Bertina walked together from the garden to their house.

The next morning all of the garden mist was gone and sunshine reigned. The Tollefsons never saw that troll, or any other troll, ever again.

65 ▪ Resignation

"They *are* gone!" Ort said to Rott, his grandson, as he took in the construction site scene, which was shrouded in a soft orange mist created by fog and moonlight.

"Who?" Rott asked.

"The big, ugly, stinkin', rotten machines."

"Oh. No, I don't see any either."

"Let's hope they're gone for good," Ort said.

"Do you think they are?"

"You never know what people might do, you know that," Ort reminded Rott. "They're not here now, so that's a good turn of events."

Ort was out on a nightlong jaunt with Rott, with one of his main chores being checking out the construction site to see for himself if reports others had given him were accurate. While hearing from others that the big, noisy machines were gone was welcome news, he was not completely convinced the machines truly were gone until he checked out the situation himself. Seeing what was not there with his own eyes was more satisfying.

As others were, Ort was perplexed about the row of T-shaped trees with ropes running between them. He also was somewhat surprised others had described them so accurately, for the descriptions they gave seemed outlandish and exaggerated, as well as nonsensical. And while he was pleased to see grass growing where bare earth had been, he could no more understand why people had replaced trees with grass than he could comprehend the chemical properties of the natural environment.

Rott found himself fixated on the lodge. "Do you suppose it's a church?" he asked Ort. "Could it be a church?"

"No, it's no church," Ort said. "It doesn't look like any church I've ever seen, and I've seen a lot of 'em. It can't be a church." He added the last sentence as much for his own peace of mind as to reassure Rott, for having a church there seemed the worst possible scenario. Had religion been a part of his life he would have prayed it wasn't a church.

"A house?" Rott speculated. "It's a big house, if it is."

"It doesn't look like a house either," Ort said.

"Then what is it?" Rott said. "It can't be a barn, can it? I've never seen a barn like that."

"I can't imagine anyone trying to farm here," Ort said. "It's no barn, any more than it's a church."

"Then what is it?" Rott asked. "If it's not a church or a house or a barn, or a shed, what could it be?"

"I suppose we'll find out in time," Ort said.

"Aren't you dying of curiosity to know? I am."

"It would be nice to know," Ort admitted. "But like I've always said, trying to understand people could drive you batty. People do things it's impossible to understand."

"I'd sure like to have a look inside," Rott said. "Isn't there any way we can get closer, at least, and maybe look in the windows?"

"Not as long as men are sitting around with guns just waiting to shoot us," Ort said. "This is a dangerous place. Don't forget that. And if I ever find out that you came back here by yourself and tried a stunt like that I'll whip you every which way there is, and don't you forget it."

Ort and Rott remained near the ski area site for a half-hour before resuming their wandering. At one point, when they were walking side by side atop a long rock ledge, Rott found himself thinking about Brine.

"Do you think Brine's okay?" he asked.

"Why wouldn't he be?" Ort responded.

"I mean, if he's all alone. . ." Rott said. "He's been gone quite a few days now. Do you think he's ever coming back?"

"If he comes, he comes," Ort said. "If he doesn't, he doesn't. There's nothing we can do about that."

"I guess not," Rott said. "I just hope he's okay."

"Trolls have lived on their own ever since time began," Ort said. "I wouldn't worry about him. I'm sure he's fine. Anyway, he made up his own mind to leave; nobody forced him to leave. So let him do what he wants to do."

"I guess," Rott said, shrugging his shoulders.

Returning to the area of the caves as the lower eastern sky showed the first hints of a red dawn, Ort and Rott met a group of three male trolls—Haar, Traug and Drulle—returning to the caves from a different direction.

"Well, you were right about the machines," Ort said to Haar. "I didn't see them anywhere there either. They must be gone."

"You went there?" Haar asked.

"I just said I did," Ort said.

"And the trees with ropes running between them? Did you see those?" Haar asked.

"I saw them," Ort said. "I've never seen anything like that."

"What do you make of all that?" Haar asked. "Can you figure out why they're there and what they're for?"

"Who knows," Ort said. "People must have put them there for some reason, but I'm at a loss to even guess why."

"So what do we do next?" Traug asked Ort. "Do you have a plan?"

"We wait, and we keep checking on what's going on there," Ort answered.

"Just wait? That's it?" Traug said, obviously disappointed that Ort didn't have something up his sleeve. "How long?"

"As long as we have to," Ort said.

"But how are we going to make the people leave if all we do is wait and watch?" Traug said.

"Maybe we won't be able to make the people leave," Ort said. "Maybe there won't be enough people there, and they won't be nuisance enough, to make it worth the bother of trying to make them leave. As long as they stay where they are and don't advance up the mountain any further than they have they're far enough away to not give us any trouble."

"So we just let them stay there and do what they want?" Drulle said.

"Do you have a better idea?" Rott challenged, instinctively coming to his grandfather's defense.

"Trolls have lived much closer to people for a lot of years without people disturbing us much," Ort pointed out. "As long as the people stay where they are we can stay where we are and keep on living our normal lives."

66 ▪ The Shadow Troll

Retta was headed for a mountain meadow to help Elseth, her daughter, gather greens as the sun descended in the western sky. Elseth had hurried on ahead as Retta ambled along the path to the meadow, keeping an eye out for anything edible along the way. As she approached the meadow, Retta was taken aback by her daughter's peculiar behavior. Elseth, who did not know her mother was close enough to see her, was flapping and waving her arms, kicking out her legs, bobbing her head, and making other strange motions that didn't appear to be dancing. Both alarmed and mystified, Retta crept closer for a better view, using trees for cover. When she reached a spot where she could see most of the meadow she saw that Elseth seemed to be playing with her long shadow, which the slant of sunlight made three times as tall as her. Then Elseth began dancing with her shadow, frolicsome and freespirited as dragonflies. Retta couldn't have been more horrified if she had caught Elseth in a passionate embrace with a human being.

"Elseth!" she scolded, charging out into the meadow.

"Oh, you startled me!" Elseth said, clutching her right hand to her chest.

"I saw what you were doing just now," Retta said sternly. "You were playing with your shadow, weren't you?"

"I never really realized how fascinating shadows are," Elseth said matter-of-factly. "Your shadow is really remarkable when you really think about it and take time to look at it. Watch this:" she said, waving her left arm wildly about as she watched the arm's shadow mirror the wild movements.

"Elseth, stop that!" Retta snapped.

"What's wrong?" Elseth asked innocently.

"Shadows are nothing to play with," Retta said with a severe tone of voice. "Shadows are a product of sunlight, and you know how dangerous sunlight can be."

"But moonlight makes shadows too," Elseth pointed out, "so shadows can't be all that bad, can they?"

"Yes, they can," Retta said. "True, shadows made by moonlight won't hurt you. And even shadows made by sunlight won't hurt you by themselves, as far as that goes. But a troll should not even look at his own shadow much because it could lead to him, or her, spending more time in sunlight than is healthy. Haven't I ever told you the story of the shadow troll?"

"The shadow troll?" Elseth pondered. "No, I don't think so; not that I remember."

"Well, I think it's high time I tell you that story then," Retta said. "Come on, let's go sit on this log over there and I'll tell you the story."

Once both Retta and Elseth were seated on the large log, Retta told Elseth the following tale, in simpler form.

■

There was once a troll named Roo, who did not fully understand that while daylight delights people and makes them feel safer and happier than darkness does, daylight is displeasing and potentially disastrous to all right-thinking trolls, that trolls thrive on darkness. Roo was attracted to sunlight, not repelled by it. What he found particularly fascinating about sunlight was the shadows it created. He was fascinated with shadows from the time he could walk. As he grew, he was enthralled by the way his own shadow followed him around and grew longer and shorter at different times of the day. He sometimes played with his own shadow for hours at a time, waving his arms and jumping about to see how his shadow reacted.

Shadows on snow fascinated him most of all, for shadows on snow are the starkest shadows, the ones that are the easiest to see. He spent more time outdoors during the winter, watching shadows, than he did during the other seasons of the year.

When Roo tried to share his interest in shadows with other trolls they not only had very little interest in shadows, many warned Boo that anything to do with sunlight could only cause him grief. Boo's parents worried about him and asked themselves where they had gone wrong in bringing him up.

"Staying out in the sun too long will make you weak and helpless," his mother often warned him.

"Why can't you love darkness, as all normal trolls do?" his father said to him. "Darkness is what is good for trolls." They also are happiest in darkness. Indeed, the darker, murkier and mistier the night, the happier the troll. "Sunlight is not good for trolls, and you are a troll. Never forget that. Why all this weird interest in shadows, anyway?"

Try as they did, Roo's parents could not prevent him from frolicking about on sunny days, for while Roo was different than other trolls in that he liked daylight he was like other trolls in that he was unruly, disobedient and deceitful.

Roo tried to like darkness, he really did, but there was just something about shadows a sunny day produced that compelled him to leave his family's dank cave for bright, fresh air.

By the time he was thirteen Roo had spent so much time in sunshine—more time, in fact, than some trolls spend in sunshine their entire lives—that he sensed sunlight was sapping strength from him, just as older trolls had warned him it would. His mother noticed that his skin was growing paler, for unlike human beings, whose skin darkens the more it is exposed to sunrays, Roo's blotched skin grew paler and paler the more time he spent soaking up sunshine. Still, Roo could not resist exposing his weakened body to more sunlight, for the beguiling nature of shadows pulled him outside like a magnet pulls a nail.

One day while outdoors he fell asleep against a rock. The sun blazed across the cloudless sky for hour after hour as Roo slept. The strong sunlight was not only weakening him so that he could not wake up; it was actually making him fade away. As the day wore on the sunlight completely bleached away his body, leaving him only his shadow on the rock.

At last he did awake, and quickly discovered that his body had disappeared and that he was now literally a shadow of his former self. The sun had seared him into a shadow. He could no longer communicate with anyone, not even other trolls. In fact, even other trolls felt fear when they saw the shadow troll, for they believed the vision to be a bad omen.

Roo led a lonely existence from the day he was transformed into a shadow. Mercifully for him, he did not have to endure many solitary years as a shadow troll. A few short years after his transmogrification, overcast skies prevented the sun from making even the briefest appearance for more than three weeks and the shadow troll faded into the earth, never again to exist.

■

"Poor Roo," Elseth said when Retta finished telling the story.
"Poor Roo is right!" Retta said. "See what too much sunlight can do? I don't want you falling into the same trap. Sunlight is nothing to play with. It's dangerous."

67 ▪ Bitter Creek

Four days out, Brine had already wolfed through nearly all of the food he had taken from home—or possibly his former home, depending upon how things eventually played out. He had restocked his larder with juicy apples from someone's apple tree, tomatoes, green beans and other vegetables from someone else's garden, and a large batch of cookies and a sizeable hunk of cheese from a summer kitchen. He also had gathered some berries, and caught two trout in a stream very early in the morning.

He traveled by night and rested by day, of course, taking shelter wherever he could find it. He actually found a cozy little cave for one of those days. He spent another day in a seemingly abandoned, ramshackle little shack he guessed had been a shepherd's shelter. There were no sheep or any other species of animal in sight, so he concluded the overgrown pasture was no longer used for grazing. He spent the two other days concealed beside rocks and beneath bushes in a forest. Since he didn't feel shrouded enough by the natural vegetation, he gathered brush and created something of a cozy tent for himself right next to a rock cliff. Wanting to minimize his exposure to sunlight, he then placed his blanket over that brush and camouflaged the blanket with more brush. Nothing bothered him, as far as he knew, so he felt proud of his tent-like creations.

Given that life in the Troll Mountain caves was pretty much all he knew up to this point in his life, thoughts of what might be happening back at the caves dominated his mind. He missed having others to talk with every day; being all by himself every minute of the day wasn't as easy as he imagined it would be. Still, the dream image of a stunningly beautiful fjord continued to pull him onward. He felt confident he was traveling in the right direction. He was careful about taking notice of where the sun set and heedful to walk in that direction the following day. So if Llop had given him the correct information about the fjords being in the direction where the sun set, he was pretty sure he was going the right way.

So far he had been able to find water to drink quite easily, as he had crossed several clear streams. He even found a lidded glass jar in the summer kitchen where he helped himself to cheese and cookies. Having neglected to take a container for water with him from his cave, he was happy to now have a jar he could fill with water so he could have a drink of water anytime he wished rather than rely on the vagaries of the natural environment.

The jar was empty when he happened upon the next stream, a stream that averaged six feet in width and had a modest current, with small rapids at frequent intervals. The sight of running water sent a swell of relief through him, for he was quite thirsty by then. Approaching the stream, he selected a spot where there was nearly level land along the creek, knelt and used his cupped hands to scoop water into his mouth. The water had such a bitter taste that he immediately spit it out. In fact, he spit several times to try to get the acrid taste out of his mouth. Thinking he may have happened to drink from a bad spot, he walked upstream a short distance and tried the water there. The water tasted no better there; it was equally as bitter as at the first place he tried. He tried several more places by dipping a fingertip into the stream and touching his wet fingertip to his tongue. Each time the water remained bitter. Brine couldn't understand that, for every other stream he crossed had provided good-tasting water. He didn't know the stream was called Bitter Creek because its water was bitter, nor did he know the tale of how the water became bitter.

■

Tosnak was one very bitter troll. Life had not been kind to him, which embittered, angered and vexed him, and made him sour, resentful and surly.

Tosnak's wife caught a disease that caused her prolonged pain and an early death. He lost two fingers in one accident, broke a leg and cracked open his skull in another accident, and had his skin badly burned in a fire. Both of his children died horrible, excruciating deaths. Other trolls always seemed to have better luck than him when it came to hunting or fishing, or finding gold and other treasure, or almost anything else. A cave in which he lived sprang leaks and filled with water, making it uninhabitable.

Tosnak was so angry at fate that he resented anything good that happened to anyone else. Because of his own misery, he couldn't bear to see anyone else happy. He was always ready with a caustic comment, a snaggly snarl and a trip-wire temper whenver he met another troll. On those rare occasions when he happened to catch glimpses of human beings, their good looks and privileged positions made him so bitter that a thousand angry wasps could not have come close to matching the depth and intensity of that bitterness.

Eventually Tosnak went off all by himself to live as a hermit far from other trolls and—of course—any human beings. He lived in the hollow shell of an enormous tree trunk beside a mossy bog where hundreds of underground springs gave rise to a bubbling creek. The water in that creek was so sweet and pure that people who lived in villages and on farms far downstream from the creek's swampy source drew most of the water they drank and cooked with directly from the creek. They did, that is, until Tosnak began living in the hollow tree next to the bog.

Tosnak would stomp around the bog muttering epithets, spitting out curses and railing against all of creation. He was so infused with bitterness that he affected everything he touched. The bottomless well of bitterness he possessed seeped into the swampwater and was eventually carried downstream in the creek's current. People who drank water from the creek started detecting a bit of a bitter taste in the water.

Tosnak grew more and more bitter as the years passed. As a result, the water in the creek became more and more bitter tasting. People began calling the creek Bitter Creek. It had a different name originally, but that was so long ago that the name has been lost to the mist of time. Eventually the water in Bitter Creek was so bitter that no one except Tosnak could drink it. In fact, the water was so bitter that no one could even eat food cooked in that creek water.

Tosnak died several hundred years after he moved into the hollow tree trunk beside the mossy bog. By the time of his death he had so contaminated the source water with his bitterness that the water had a permanently bitter taste. To this day the water in Bitter Creek remains bitter because of how Tosnak affected it.

■

Tosnak may have been able to drink the bitter creek water, but Brine could not, even though he was a typical troll in that he could eat and drink substances most human beings would find unpalatable and nauseating. And so, heavy with disappointment, he continued on until he found another, smaller stream with sweeter water nearly an hour later.

68 ▪ Stream Of Consciousness

"So, how are things coming along with the lodge?" Emma asked Anders as the Branstad family ate supper.

"Good," Anders responded. "Everything seems to be right on schedule."

"So it's going to be open before Christmas?" Emma asked.

"It should be," Anders said. "It looks like it should open sometime in early December, as long as there's enough snow by then."

"I don't think that's much of a worry," Emma commented.

"Maybe not," Anders said. "We'll see."

"Can I ski there?" Andrew asked his father.

"We'll see," Anders said. "Probably, but I won't promise anything. Did you hear what the slogan is for the ski area?" he asked Emma.

"No. What is it?" Emma said.

" 'Ski with the trolls,'" Anders informed her.

"Clever," Emma said. "It *is* on Troll Mountain, after all."

"Can trolls ski?" Andrew asked his parents.

Anders and Emma looked at each other. "I'm not sure," Anders admitted. "I guess I never really thought about that. I'm not sure if they can or not."

"Can we read another troll story tonight?" Andrew asked his father.

"Oh, I guess so," Anders said.

"Haven't you read about every story in the book by now?" Emma said, posing the question to both her husband and her son.

"No, there are still quite a few more he hasn't heard yet," Anders said.

"It's a big book," Andrew pointed out.

Given that Anders was bouncing around the book with the tales he read to Andrew, it took him some time to find the title of one Andrew hadn't heard as he scanned the table of contents.

The first fresh title his eyes fell upon was *Stream Of Consciousness*, and so that was the one he read this evening.

■

Peter Evers was a rather impetuous young man, quick to act and react without clear thought or consideration as to what results or ramifications his actions might have.

Peter loved berries of every sort, and often he roamed the countryside in search of those delectable morsels of sweet succulence. One August day he was hunting for wild berries deep in a forest, following the course of an eight-foot-wide stream, when he came upon a large patch of lingenberries. He was in heaven as he picked and picked, dropping most of those he picked into a large pail, but also scarfing down many, for he couldn't wait to eat as many of the plump, blue berries as his stomach would hold.

Peter had ventured so deep into the forest, to a place he had never been before, that it was early evening when he came upon the lingenberry patch, and dusk was setting in by the time his pail was brimming with berries. Before starting for home, he walked over to the stream, thirty feet away, to wash his hands and drink water from the crystalline, fast-flowing stream, using his cupped hands to scoop up water. He was kneeling beside the stream, slurping water from his cupped hands, when he heard a rustling sound behind him, from where he had left his pail of berries. Turning his head, he saw a large, lumpy figure snatch the handle of the pail and start running away.

"Hey!" Peter shouted. "What are you doing? Stop! Put that down!"

The thief continued running, without even glancing back at Peter.

In a second, Peter was on his feet, running after the fleeing figure. After twenty or so strides he was not making up any ground on the thief; if anything, the distance between him and the thief had increased. Thinking the thief might be able to outrun him, and incensed someone would steal berries it took him so long to collect, Peter stopped, picked up a three-inch-diameter, two-foot-long weathered branch from the forest floor and hurled the stick at the thief. The stick spun in the air, glanced off a tree trunk and thwacked the thief on the back of the head. Staggered by the blow, the thief spun around and glared at Peter. Only then did Peter realize the thief was not a man but rather a grotesque troll—a troll who was now burning with a sulfurous fury and an overpowering impulse for retaliation. Knowing that trolls are much stronger than humans and seeing how the blow to the head enraged the troll, whose face displayed his ire, Peter knew he was in physical danger. He had thrown the stick out of instinct. Now his instinct was to run, to try to get away from the troll. And so he ran, and the troll ran after him, growling and roaring gutteral sounds.

The chase lasted but a short time before Peter tripped on an exposed tree root and fell flat on his face. The troll was quickly upon him, pressing him to the ground with a foot to the back, as Peter tried to get to his feet. The brawny troll jerked Peter upright by his shirt collar, pulling with such force that Peter nearly choked.

"Hit me in the head, will you?!" the troll growled, controlling Peter as easily as a girl controls a doll. "I'll show you!"

"I'm sorry! I'm sorry! Please forgive me!" Peter begged, frightened out of his wits. "I just lost my head for a second."

"I'll show you what I do to someone who attacks me!" the troll thundered. "I'm going to drown you in the stream!"

"Please, no!" Peter pleaded. "Please spare me! I'll do anything you ask. I'll give you anything you want. Don't kill me! I beg of you! Please don't kill me!"

Even as Peter pleaded, the troll carried him toward the nearby stream, with one hand. Peter's feet were off the ground most of the time, touching only briefly two or three times, as the infuriated, revenge-minded troll stepped toward the stream, intending to carry out his threat to drown his attacker. The troll waded into the stream, where the water was more than two feet deep in the center, and held Peter's head underwater until no more bubbles burped to the surface. Satisfied that the person who struck him in the head was dead, the troll left Peter's limp body lying in the stream, went back for the pail of berries, and set off for his cave.

Two figures—a man and a woman—were standing beside the stream, on the other side, as Peter opened his eyes.

"Are you alright?" the woman asked.

Bracing himself with his hands, Peter spun so that he was sitting up near the shallow edge of the stream, trying to take in how it was that he was alive and who the man and the woman were.

"Here, let us help you up," the man said, wading into the water to help Peter to his feet, and help him across the stream. "We heard a commotion over this way and rushed over to see what was going on."

"Berries. . . picking. . . lots of lingenberries. . . lingenberry pie. . . clouds of wonder reflecting. . . the most I've ever seen in one place. . . blue berries," Peter babbled. "Wonder how long I was unconscious. . . strange. . . wonder what time it is. . . time waits for no one, they say. . . I wonder what time it is. . . I was unconscious, wasn't I? . . . what a nightmare. . . how long have you two been here? . . . time flies. . . is it suppertime? Did all that really just happen? . . . it was terrible. . . what a nightmare. Could I be in a nightmare. . . wonder what time it is. . . is it still the same day? . . . What day is it? . . . thought sure I was dead. . . what's happening? . . . was I dead? . . . am I dead now? . . . that horrible face! . . . that face!. . . if only I had knocked him out. . ."

"There, there!" the woman consoled, trying to calm Peter. "Sit down and rest. We'll stay here with you while you regain your wits."

With the man and the woman helping him, Peter sat against the trunk of a large tree and let the fact that he was still alive sink into his consciousness.

"Where did you come from?" Peter asked the man and the woman.

"We live just across over there," the woman said, pointing in the direction she meant. "We were out checking a fence when we heard strange noises over this way. What happened to you anyway? Why are you out here in the forest all alone? What were those strange noises all about?"

Much calmer and more clearheaded by then, Peter recounted for them the series of events that led to them finding him lying in the stream.

"It was lucky for you that it happened to be this stream," the woman said when Peter finished his account.

"Why do you say that?" Peter asked.

"Well, because," the woman said. "You know the legend about this stream, don't you?"

"Not that I recall," Peter said.

"You don't?!" the woman said. "I thought everyone who lived around here knew about that. Well, the legend is that a long, long time ago a young woman was walking along the stream one day, by herself, and as she was crossing the stream by stepping on stones at the head of a rapids she slipped and cracked her head against a big rock, which knocked her unconscious, so she drowned. It just so happened that her best friend was a sorceress, and when the sorceress found out how her friend had drowned in the stream she was so distraught and angry that she came to the stream and put some sort of spell on it so that no one would ever again drown in the stream. That's why it's called the Stream of Consciousness."

"I didn't know that," Peter said.

"Now you do," the woman said. "And as far as I know, no one else has ever drowned in it since the sorceress put a spell on it. It's said it's impossible to drown in this stream."

Glad to be alive, and feeling extremely fortunate the body of water a troll tried to drown him in was where drowning was said to be impossible, Peter accepted the couple's invitation to spend the night at their house, for it was a long walk home and he had had more than enough adventure for one day.

69 ▪ A Rare Sight

It was a crisp, foggy, breezy autumn night. Haar and Scurf had walked for two hours when they came upon a hilly farm that seemed to be a good candidate for a vegetable raid. The two trolls stopped on a rise that provided a good overview of the farm landscape. A meandering ten-foot-wide stream passed the bottom of the hill on which they stood to study the layout of the farm. The farmhouse was a magnificent brick structure, three stories high, with many large windows, all of which were dark at that hour.

"Just look at the fancy house these people have," Scurf sneered. "Why should we have to live in caves and people can live in places like that? It's not fair."

"I'd like to spend just one day in a house like that," Haar said.

"When was the last time you talked to a person?" Scurf asked.

Haar scrunched his face, trying to recall. "I can't remember. It's been a long time, I know that. I really never talked to very many. I was never that interested in having anything to do with them."

"Me neither," Scurf said. "People are trouble. Ort is right about that. I remember the last person I talked to was someone I ran into by accident very early one morning. I was walking down a trail in a forest and I came around a corner and here was this man, who was pretty young, walking toward me from the other direction. He saw me and his eyes opened as wide as saucers and he turned around and started running from where he had come from. 'Yeah, you better run!' I shouted at him. 'I'm going to catch you and cook you in a big pot!' I didn't want to have anything to do with him any more than he wanted anything to do with me, of course. I just wanted to scare him a little."

"When was that?" Haar asked.

"A long time ago," Scurf said. "I can barely remember it. I know I scared him pretty good, though."

"That's one thing we can do to people is scare them," Haar said.

"So why are we the ones living in caves?"

Haar shrugged his shoulders and scanned the farm some more. "If what I'm seeing is a garden, we've come to the right place tonight. Look at the size of that! That *is* all garden, isn't it? On this side of the house?"

Scurf looked more intently. "I think you're right. Maybe we should have brought more sacks."

"We'll take as much as we can carry," Haar said. "Let's go." Scurf followed as Haar started climbing down the hill toward the stream. The stream was rather deep below the hill, so they walked along the side of the creek until they found a place where the water was a mere six inches deep and crossed there. Advancing cautiously but assuredly toward the garden, which was about forty feet from the house at its nearest point, Haar and Scurf made it to the enormous garden in a matter of minutes. Rows of tall corn stalks grew where they entered, so they broke off dozens of plump cobs of corn and slipped them into their burlap sacks. Then it was on to the melon path, and the gourd patch, and the potato patch. By the time they came to long rows of carrots, turnips and beets their sacks were so full they could cram in only a small portion of what they would liked to have taken of those delicious root vegetables.

Just as they were about to leave, a dog barked outside the house. The house was between the dog and the two trolls, so the dog could not see who or what was in the garden, but it knew something was up. "Let's beat it!" Haar said to Scurf as the dog continued barking, with no letup. The heavily laden sacks slowed them somewhat, but not much; Haar and Scurf were still able to beat a quick retreat, through the corn, across a hayfield and into the cover of woods. Since the dog didn't chase them, they assumed it was tied up. Had they been religious, they would have said a prayer of thanks for that. While it was never a good thing when there was a guard dog around, at least it wasn't nearly as bad when the dog was tied up rather than allowed to roam freely. Once they reached the woods, Haar and Scurf slowed to a walk and went a couple of hundred feet into the woods before they sat down to catch their breath.

"There are too many dogs around," Scurf remarked. "Those darn dogs always make things tougher."

"At least this one didn't start barking until we had our sacks almost filled," Haar pointed out. "We made a good haul tonight. I can't remember when I've had a better night rading a garden."

"It's easier than having a garden ourselves," Scurf said. "People are helpful in that way at least: they grow food for us, and all we have to do is go and get it."

Once suffifiently rested, Haar and Scurf started back home, passing through territory they rarely visited. Close to an hour into their walk home they came upon a flat open field where Haar pulled up short and held out an arm to stop Scurf as they reached the edge of a woods. "Look!" Haar whispered, wide-eyed, almost as though what he was seeing was so remarkable that a whisper was all he could muster. "A white buck!" he announced just as Scurf recognized what it was. Both of the trolls stood as still as possible, not wanting to spook the unusual deer, which was grazing in the field while remaining alert to any potential danger. Although Haar and Scurf were quiet and still, the white buck started doing more listening and looking around than eating, and it wasn't long before it bolted into woods on another side of the field and disappeared from view.

"Wow!" Haar said out loud when the white buck was gone. "This must be our lucky night. Seeing a white buck! You know what this means, don't you?"

"Of course," Scurf said. "It means good luck."

"Exactly!" Haar said, pumped with an adrenaline rush such as he hadn't felt since he couldn't remember when. "Seeing a white buck means good luck is coming."

Nearly all trolls believed that because of the story about what happened to a troll named Rintoul after he spotted a large white buck.

"Who's going to have the good luck?" Scurf asked Haar. "You, because you saw it first? Or both of us because we both saw it? Or our whole tribe? What do you think?"

"Well, I guess I'm not really sure," Haar said. "I would say you and me, since we're the ones who saw it. I don't know, though. Maybe this means good luck for the tribe."

"Maybe it means the people working at the bottom of the mountain will go away," Scurf said.

"Maybe," Haar said. "I wouldn't count on that, though. I think probably the luck will just come to us two."

"What do you think it will be?" Scurf said excitedly, sure in his mind that seeing a white buck meant good luck was on the way.

"I don't know," Haar said snappisly, annoyed that Scurf thought he knew all the answers, as though he could foretell the future.

"But we *will* have good luck, won't we?" Scurf said.

"We should," Haar agreed. "There's no question about that."

"Maybe we'll have such good luck that we'll become as famous as Rintoul," Scurf said.

70 ▪ Rintoul And
The Large White Buck

Rintoul seemed to be one of the unluckiest trolls ever born. His life was as full of mishaps and misadventures, calamities and catastrophes, frowns of fortune and lesions of luck, as the future is full of time. If bad luck was a bottle Rintoul would have had a bottle as big as a barn. If misfortune was a metal he would have had a house-sized block of gold. If adversity was an animal he would have had a huge bear as a pet.

Even when he was very young Rintoul was such a magnet for misfortune that his parents eventually took him into a deep forest and abandoned him there, fearing that if they allowed him to remain with them that tragedy would soon befall the entire family. Rintoul's mother felt a pang in her heart for this action, even though she believed her husband's assessment that Rintoul might well be the embodiment of evil who would call down a curse upon himself and all those near him. The troll king had more than hinted that Rintoul and his parents would be expelled from the tribe if Rintoul's string of bad luck did not end soon. Rintoul's mother and father did not want to be set adrift from the tribe to survive on their own. If their son was truly jinxed, as he appeared to be, they felt it would be best to sacrifice him for their own wellbeing. What good would it do to let Rintoul remain with them, they reasoned, if by doing so they were dooming themselves to disaster?

For years, Rintoul lived more like an animal than a troll. He roamed the countryside, sleeping under rock ledges he came upon and in crude shelters he constructed. He was nearly killed when the roof of a cave collapsed on him, and again when a loose ledge of rock gave out from under him and he slid down a hillside, and again when lightning struck a tree he was seated against, and again when he slipped off a windfallen tree that bridged a river and tumbled into a whitewater rapids, and again when a poisonous snake bit him and his neck muscles tightened like a vice.

Since his hunting trips were rarely successful, Rintoul survived mainly on berries, nuts, grass, dead bugs, and half-decayed animals he found dead. As a result, he grew up gaunt and sickly. He had a chronic cough and open sores on his body. His hair was matted with burrs and other sticky substances.

Once a small band of trolls took him in for several months. Rintoul's cloud of misfortune followed him, though, and it wasn't long before an unusual number of bad things began happening to the members of the tribe. The other trolls started blaming Rintoul for everything bad that happened. Eventually Rintoul was blamed for the least little thing that went wrong. If someone didn't sleep well he blamed Rintoul. If someone went out hunting and came back to camp empty-handed he blamed Rintoul for the lack of luck. If someone saw a cloud formation that seemed to portend trouble the others said that Rintoul was a walking curse.

One day Rintoul simply slipped away from the tribe before the others had time to order him to leave, or perhaps decided to take more drastic measures.

About a year after he left the small tribe, Rintoul was hunting one day when he saw the most remarkable animal he had ever seen. He was hiding at the edge of a forest when a large, all-white buck deer suddenly pranced across an adjacent meadow. Rintoul blinked at the brilliance of the animal, which moved with the regal bearing of a king. "Magnificent" is too meager a word to describe this large white buck; it was magnificence multiplied a hundredfold. When the white buck disappeared into towering trees Rintoul hardly believed his senses. He *had* really seen a large white buck, hadn't he? Or had he? Could such a splendorous creature actually exist, or had it been a hullucination? He concluded that it had certainly seemed real so it must have been real.

Rintoul ran to where the large white buck had disappeared into the trees and found hoofprints in the ground. So, he *had* actually seen a large white buck! His mind hadn't played a trick on him. Judging by the size of the hoofprints, Rintoul knew this was perhaps the largest buck that ever existed. Even from a distance he knew it was large when he saw it, but if its body were in any way proportional to the size of the hoofprints then this was indeed an extraordinarily large white buck.

Rintoul followed the deer's tracks as far as he could before losing the trail in a stream. He went upstream to see if he could pick up the tracks anywhere and noticed something flash in the sunlight on the streambed a few feet above a small rapids. Upon closer inspection, there appeared to be some gold coins laying there. Rintoul waded into the stream, reached into the water and picked up one of the gold objects. Indeed it was a coin! There were dozens of gold coins scattered about, many of them covered by sand.

Rintoul had never enjoyed such good luck. Giddy with joy, he gathered up all the gold coins he could find and set off through the forest. As dusk descended he happened upon a tidy cabin. He peeked in the windows and saw that the cabin was full of furniture and stocked with a supply of food. He also saw that no one was in the cabin, so he entered and made himself at home. He ate food until his stomach nearly burst, then lied down on a nice soft bed and went to sleep.

The next day, as he scouted the surrounding area, he came upon the largest berry patch he had ever seen, where he ate his fill. He also found a sharp axe someone had forgotten and came upon two stray goats, which he took back to the cabin.

Since no one showed up, he assumed possession of the cabin and lived there in luxury of a sort—at least it was luxury by his standards.

As he thought back on the events of the past several days, it occurred to Rintoul that good luck had practically overwhelmed him ever since he saw the large white buck. He now seemed to be as lucky as he had been unlucky before that sighting. As time went on, all of his hunting and fishing trips ended in success rather than failure. He found so many gemstones and pieces of lost jewelry that he filled a storage chest in the cabin with them. When he met a vicious bear on a trail and ran from it the bear stepped on a huge thorn while chasing him and had to give up its chase. He found a stray cow to go along with his two goats, which provided him with more milk than he could drink. He discovered gold nuggets in a nearby stream. Apple trees outside the cabin were weighted down with perfect, delicious red apples. Vegetables in his garden grew to such size that he could have kept three giants well fed. When he tried to analyze his reversal of fortune, the only explanation that made any sense to him was that seeing the large white buck had brought him good luck.

Tired of living by himself, Rintoul resolved to return to his native tribe for companionship. He wasn't sure where that tribe lived, but he reasoned that if he were truly charmed that luck would lead him home.

Along the path of his homeward journey, one day Rintoul heard what seemed to be a cry for help and headed in the direction from where the voice seemed to come. Guided by the sound of the voice calling out for help, he soon came to a cliff, looked down and saw a lovely troll maiden clinging precariously to the branch of a tree twenty feet below.

"Please save me!" the troll maiden wailed.

Rintoul quickly took a long rope off one of his goats, tied a loop at one end and lowered the rope to the troll maiden, who tied the rope loop around herself just as the tree branch broke away, leaving her dangling in the air high above a deep canyon. Rintoul pulled the maiden to safety with the rope.

"How can I ever thank you enough?" the maiden said. "I must be the luckiest troll maiden on earth to have you come along when you did. If you hadn't come along at just the right time I surely would have died."

"It is *I* who am the lucky one for having the opportunity to save such a beautiful maiden," Rintoul gushed. "I feel honored merely to be in your presence." Needless to say, Rintoul was head-over-heels in love with the golden-haired maiden, who had a garland of daisies in her hair.

It turned out that the maiden was a member of Rintoul's native tribe, so the two of them returned to the cave village together. Rintoul had a tearful reunion with his parents, who had thought they had seen their son for the last time many years before. The king was reluctant to let Rintoul rejoin the tribe, though, until the maiden told the story of how Rintoul saved her and Rintoul showed the king his chest full of treasures and offered to give all of the treasure to the king if the king would allow him to stay. Rintoul was confident that he was so charged with magical good luck because of seeing a large white buck that he would soon find even more and better treasures.

And, indeed, in very little time Rintoul proved to everyone that he was as full of good luck as he fromerly had been full of bad luck by finding and easily stealing enough gleaming treasures to fill three chests.

What made Rintoul feel luckiest of all, though, was that the golden-haired maiden he saved agreed to marry him and be his wife.

After learning about Rintoul's sighting of a large buck and his subsequent reversal of fortune, no one had any doubt that seeing a large white buck was what caused Rintoul's seemingly permanent streak of good luck. Ever since Rintoul's sighting, good luck has come to any troll who has seen a large white buck. No one else has had quite as large of a windfall of good luck as Rintoul had, but seeing a large white buck never fails to bring the fortunate observer some good fortune.

71 ▪ The Albino Troll

"**A**h, here's one I know we haven't read yet," Anders Branstad said as he skimmed the book's table of contents. "*The Albino Troll.*"

"What's an albino troll?" Andrew asked.

"Well, I'm sure the story will no doubt explain that," Anders said, "but an albino is a person or an animal—or in this case a troll—that doesn't have the normal coloring that most people or animals do. An albino person has whitish skin, white hair and pink eyes."

"Pink?"

"That's right," Anders said.

"Are there really albino people?" Andrew asked, skeptical.

"Yes, there are," Anders assured him.

▪

Long ago a troll named Edda bore an albino son, who was given the name Alrik. The boy had white hair, pink eyes and pale skin. Since most trolls have black hair and a general swarthy appearance, an albino troll looked startlingly different than the other trolls in his small tribe.

All of the other trolls, children and adults alike, made fun of Alrik because he looked so odd to them. The other children picked on him and beat him up. Even many of the adult trolls would stretch out a leg to trip Alrik when he walked past, or push him from behind, or kick him behind a knee to cause him to fall down.

The troll who was king of Alrik's tribe noticed that most of the people who lived nearby had blond hair. He pointed out that fact to Alrik's father, Nedja, and questioned whether or not Nedja was Alrik's father. Given that Alrik's white hair and pale skin made him look much more like the many blond-haired men in the area than like Nedja, the king suspected it was likely Edda had consorted with one of the blond-haired men and that Alrik's true father was actually a human being.

The more Nedja tought about what the king said the more likely it seemed to him that he was not Alrik's real father, but that Alrik's real father was a human.

Edda denied having cheated on Nedja and the accusation that Alrik's true father was a person, but the more vehemently she denied those rumors the more Nedja believed them to be true. After all, both he and Edda were dark-haired. He didn't see how it was possible that two black-haired parents could produce a white-haired child. He was not a genetics expert, by any means, but even trolls think logically at times.

Not wanting to live with the stigma of having his fellow trolls suspect that Edda had produced a child with a human father, Nedja ordered Edda to take Alrik and leave the tribe. "Go far away and never return," Nedja told his wife, "or I will drown Alrik so that I will not have to live in shame all the rest of my days."

Knowing that Nedja would indeed carry out his threat to drown Alrik, who was then eight years old, Edda went away with her albino son, whom she loved despite his unusual appearance. The two of them walked for weeks before Edda decided they would live at the edge of a large, remote bog. There they built a hut for themselves and lived in peace.

Edda resented how Nedja had treated her. He thought she had lied to him and deceived him, did he? She vowed that, in due time, she would get back at him somehow for casting her and Alrik into exile. And the other members of her tribe were no better. They deserved her scorn as well. Not a single one of them had spoken up in her defense, and probably not one of them would have raised the meekest peep if she had stayed and let Nedja drown Alrik.

She knew the sweetest sort of revenge would have to involve Alrik in some fashion, since Alrik's appearance was at the heart of why Nedja and the other trolls distrusted her and believed she had disgraced herself by consorting with a person. Without having a precise plan plotted, Edda decided she would do everything within her power to turn Alrik into one of the strongest, toughest trolls that ever existed. She figured that by the time Alrik was grown up and supernaturally strong she would have some revenge strategy cooked up that would make use of Alrik's great strength.

Edda fed Alrik as well as or better than any troll had ever been fed. She made him do many hard chores to build up his muscles. She had him lift progressively heavier rocks and boulders. With all of this exercise and fortifying nourishment, in ten years' time Alrik was more than a match for the fiercest cave bear that ever lived. He had arms of iron, a granite-like chest, and legs like tree trunks.

The time was right for Edda to retaliate against Nedja and the other trolls who had treated her so shabbily. She and Alrik journeyed back to where their home tribe had its caves and began building a stone cabin for themselves within sight of the caves.

Feeling he had to do something about this if he was to maintain any respect, Nedja walked over to where his wife and son were building their cabin and said sternly to Edda: "I thought I told you to never come back. Didn't I tell you that I would drown Alrik if you two ever returned?"

"Now that you mention it," Edda said nonchalantly, "it seems to me I do remember you saying something like that. Well, if you must you must. Alrik," she called to her son, who was busy carrying large rocks for the cabin walls, "come here a minute. Your father wants you for something."

Alrik heaved aside the rocks he was carrying, creating large dimples in the ground where the rocks landed, and strode over to where his mother and father were. For the first time, Nedja saw just how muscular and strapping Alrik had become.

"What is it?" Alrik asked his mother.

"Your father wants to drown you," Edda informed him.

Alrik grabbed Nedja around his neck with one hand and lifted him off the ground. "You do, do you?" he growled, and spit in Nedja's face. "Maybe I should drown you by spitting on you. That sounds like a better idea to me."

Nedja begged for mercy and Alrik set him down, none too gently.

"Get away from us," Edda said to Nedja. "The mere sight of you makes both of us sick. If you ever take a step this close to our cabin again we *will* drown you, I promise you that."

When Nedja returned to the caves some of the other trolls gathered around, wanting to know when Edda and her albino son were leaving.

"I don't think they are leaving—at least not anytime soon," Nedja said.

"You mean you didn't tell them they *had* to leave?" one of the trolls asked.

"Well, not exactly," Nedja said.

The others couldn't understand that. For years after he sent away Edda and Alrik, Nedja boasted of how decisively he had acted and blustered about how the two of them would never dare to show their faces within a hundred miles of the caves because they understood how tough Nedja was and feared what he would do to them.

"What harm are they doing?" Nedja said, trying to save face. "If they want to build a cabin there, so what?" He didn't want to admit to the others that he was afraid of his rock-ribbed albino son.

After hearing such bombastic bluster for so long, this sort of conciliatory talk caused the other trolls to ridicule Nedja mercilessly. His respect within the tribe drained away like water in a tub that has a large hole punctured in it.

A few of the other trolls soon discovered why Nedja was now so willing to leave Edda and Alrik alone when they made the mistake of making fun of Alrik, as they had in the past. This time Alrik gave them painful first-hand demonstrations of his incredible strength. One troll had a sore arm for a month after Alrik twisted it as though he was twisting a rope. Another troll found out how painful it is to have most of the hairs on your body plucked out by hand. Another ended up with one leg several inches longer than the other as a result of Alrik's selective limb stretching.

None of the trolls had softened their feelings toward Alrik during the ten years he had been away. They still regarded him as odd, freakish, and possibly even cursed. In fact, an albino troll of his size and strength seemed even more freakish than a child-size albino troll. No one liked the idea of having him so near, so the troll king told Nedja he would have to make Edda and Alrik move again. Nedja responded that such banishment seemed to be something the king should do.

"It is a husband's job!" the king thundered, since he had no desire to confront Alrik. "Either you make them leave or you will be cast out of the tribe."

Nedja promised he would take care of the matter the first thing the following morning. Fearing for his very life, though, that night he slipped away, never to return.

So the king and his tribe still had the problem of the albino troll. By then Edda and Alrik had long since completed construction of their tidy stone cabin, with a thatched roof, and seemed to have settled in for a long stay.

Three days after Nedja disappeared the trolls of the tribe were seated in a circle outside, eating supper, when the side of the mountain suddenly shuddered and rumbled, causing a rockslide. As fast as a flash of fire, a raging flood of rocks and dirt flowed down the mountain and trapped all of the trolls in their tracks. All of them cried for help. The only ones close enough to hear them, of course, were Edda and Alrik. Despite how the other trolls had treated him, Alrik didn't hesitate for an instant in running to their aid. As he ran toward the trapped trolls, with Edda trailing behind, he looked up when he heard more rumbling on the mountain and saw a half-dozen or more huge boulders tumbling toward the other trolls. Seeing those breakaway boulders as well, the other trolls shouted out for help all the louder, for it appeared certain that the boulders would roll over them and squash them dead as easily as they squashed bugs with their feet.

Running like a blast of hurricane-force wind, Alrik reached the trapped trolls two seconds before the first boulder was about to roll over a troll buried up to his chest in rubble. Hitting the boulder from the side with the force of four falling trees, Alrik altered the boulder's course so that it rolled harmlessly past the trolls. Using both his powerful legs and his brawny arms, Alrik mustered up every ounce of his strength to steer aside the enormous boulders as they tumbled down the mountain directly toward the partially buried trolls. He pushed every boulder out of its deadly path, and the boulders eventually crashed into a deep river gorge.

As soon as the rockslide ended Alrik quickly dug out the trolls who had been trapped. Relieved to be rescued, they all had kind words for Alrik, for they knew that if he hadn't been close by, and if he hadn't been so supremely strong, most of them—or maybe all of them—would have been killed or severely injured by the barrage of big boulders.

Suddenly the others viewed Alrik as just a troll—and a beloved one at that—rather than as a strange and peculiar troll. Now none of the other trolls objected to Edda and Alrik living so close to their caves. In fact, the king invited Edda and Alrik to build a cabin closer to the caves. Edda and Alrik said they were content where they were, though.

Alrik did eventually build another stone-walled cabin, a few steps from the cabin he and his mother constructed. The second cabin was for Alrik and his wife, the fairest troll maiden of the tribe. She and Alrik had two fair-haired children and lived a long, happy life together.

72 ▪ Brine's Progress

Brine was able to travel a considerable distance one night by riding a horse he borrowed without the owner's knowledge, as he was raised to regard such a circumstance. The horse was cinnamon-colored with white in its tail, on its right foreleg and along the top of its head. It had been a good many years since Brine had ridden a horse, so it took him a little time to be able to make the horse go where he wanted it to go. For the first hour or so the horse was more in charge of the route than he was. Fortunately the horse went in the general direction Brine wanted to go.

Unfortunately for Brine, he tied the horse to a tree rather carelessly the next morning, when he went to sleep beside a river, and the horse was able to free itself and wander away, back toward its home. At first, when he awoke, Brine was puzzled by where the horse was when he didn't see it where he had tied it. Then he was hopping mad when he realized the horse was nowhere in sight, meaning it had become untied. He looked around a little before soon accepting the reality that the horse was gone and he would have to walk that night, unless another opportunity arose where he could borrow another horse. That didn't happen that night.

Although he didn't know it, Brine was now traveling in a general northwesterly direction, so he was still headed toward the sea and the fjords of his wonderful dream. Most often he walked more west or north than northwest, but the sum result was a northwesterly route. At least he hadn't become disoriented and started walking eastward, or southward, where more people lived. While his survival was made easier by taking what he could get from farms and country houses, he didn't want to venture into an area where a lot of people lived. As it was, he felt a bit nervous being so close to people, for he was not used to such proximity. He and the others in his tribe were well isolated from people in their Troll Mountain caves, which was why the construction at the bottom of the mountain that had been going on for several months so alarmed the trolls there. Brine wondered what was happening at the construction site and if he would ever go back and be able to see for himself what in the world people were building there, and for what purpose.

A couple of days after he lost the horse Brine found a rickety wooden bridge across a forty-foot-wide river where he could sleep—under the bridge, that is. About an hour after he went to sleep, quite early in the morning, he awoke to what to him was an excruciatingly painful sound. If he had known about particles he would have thought every air particle around him was vibrating with tiny screeches, creating unbearably intense screeching. What he did quickly realize was that a church bell was producing the piercing sound. The fact that he hadn't heard a ringing church bell in many years made the sound seem all the more piercing to him. He covered his ears with his hands to dull the sound. Still, it felt as though each overlapping peal was shooting pins into his head. By chance, the bridge where he stopped to sleep was only about five hundred feet from a country church, and this was a Sunday morning. While the bell sounded only a half-dozen times, the ringing was torturous to Brine. He wished he were back in his Troll Mountain cave, where no nerve-jangling church bells violated the peace. For the first time during his journey he considered abandoning his quest and returning to Troll Mountain. His dream vision of the glorious fjord had faded and he wondered if he had acted foolishly in trying to find one. Deciding such thoughts were for later, and conscious that hearing the church bell had his mind in a dither, he tried to sleep again, now that the church bell had stopped ringing. While he needed sleep more than ever, he kept re-hearing the horrible church bell in his mind, and fearing it might peal again at any moment, so it was more than an hour before he managed to doze off.

That evening, after eating, he set off before the sun sank below the western horizon. Knowing he was so near a church made him edgy as a knife blade, so he wanted to put distance between himself and the church, even if that meant traveling in unfamiliar territory in daylight. By instinct, he found himself climbing a mountain, which made him feel more at ease. His sure-footed hiking took him to a broad plateau as the daylight dimmed. Gazing ahead, he could see the far portion of a placid tarn, which is to say a small mountain lake. Then a movement to his left, up ahead, caught his attention. Looking that way, he saw a person seated cross-legged near the edge of a cliff staring down into the lake. Curious as to what the person was doing, Brine ducked behind some nearby rocks, from where he could see the person through a convenient small opening between two rocks. With a more prolonged look, Brine judged the person to be a teenage boy. The boy simply sat there, still and silent, as far as Brine could tell; at least he could hear no sound except natural sounds of birds and insects. Brine wondered what in the world the boy could be doing. Why would someone just sit at the edge of a high cliff doing nothing? Was he one of those soft-in-the-head humans he had heard about, the sort who did crazy, inexplicable things? He wondered if he should show himself and demand to know what the boy was doing there, or demand that he leave. He remained still and silent himself as waves of thoughts washed across his mind, too curious about why the boy was just sitting there as darkness set in to take any action to alter the normal course of events.

As it turned out, nothing eventful happened. The boy merely sat there, still and silent, looking out over and into the tarn until a mere hint of daylight remained, then he rose to his feet and walked away, making his way down a mountain path as Brine held his position for a time, thoroughly perplexed by the boy's strange, passive action—if sitting still for a long time can be called action—and wondering what was so special about the tarn to make someone sit beside it and look at it for such a stretch of time. Given that it appeared as though the boy had left for good, Brine went over to where the boy had sat and looked down into the tarn himself. It looked like a normal, ordinary tarn to him. He couldn't detect anything so special about it that it would cause someone to act as the boy acted. Shrugging his shoulders, he walked on. After all, it was fjords he was interested in, not lakes.

73 ▪ The Transformation Tarn

Next up for Anders and Andrew was a tale entitled *The Transformation Tarn.*

▪

Carl Engstrom had traipsed about Gundy's Mountain since he was a young boy. He knew every crack and crevice on the mountain. He knew where every loose rock was located and where every nature-sculpted rock formation could be found. He was familiar with every tree and every tarn, or small mountain lake.

One day when he was sixteen and brooding about his father's stubbornness, Carl went for a long walk up on Gundy's Mountain and wound up contemplating his sixteen-year-old situation on a rock ledge overlooking a calm, seemingly bottomless tarn. The deep lake was such an extraordinary shade of blue that it was as though the lake had sucked extra color from the sky. Carl sat on the rock ledge hurling stones into the tarn as though the surface of the water was a pane of glass covering a portrait of his father.

"I don't want to be a stupid farmer!" he muttered as he threw rocks into the water with vengeance.

"Then don't be," he heard a voice over his shoulder say.

Feeling embarrassed, Carl swiveled his body to see who had snuck up behind him without his being aware of it. There was no one in sight, however. He wondered what in the world was going on. Had his father made him so muddled with resentment that he was beginning to hear strange voices in his head? He turned back toward the tarn.

"Be whatever you want to be," the same voice spoke.

Carl swiveled around even quicker this time. Still, there was no one in sight. There *was* a blue bird perched on a lower branch of a pine tree about ten feet behind him. Carl thought he detected a peculiar glint in the bird's eyes, so he looked at the bird at length.

"Why are you staring at me?" the bird said.

Carl was so astounded that he nearly fell off the rock ledge. A talking bird?! "You can talk?" he said excitedly.

"I can," the bird said. "I can talk because I'm really a man in a bird's body."

Carl was more than a little skeptical. "Is that so?" he said. "How did you get to be a bird?"

"Because of this tarn," the bird answered. "This is no ordinary tarn you have come to sit beside. This is a transformation tarn."

"A transformation tarn?" Carl said. "What do you mean?"

"The water in this tarn has a magical quality," the bird explained. "A person can bathe in this tarn and transform himself into anything he wishes to become, if his desire is great enough."

Carl wondered if the bird was hoodwinking him. If, however, he could converse with a bird, then what, after all, was so far-fetched about a transformation tarn?

"You mean that I could dive into this tarn and be changed into a wolf?" Carl asked.

"If you wanted to be a wolf strongly enough you could," the blue bird said. "The proper desire is an essential component of the magic."

"And you changed yourself into a bird here?" Carl asked.

"That's right," the bird answered.

"Are you a bird forever?" Carl asked.

"Only if I want to be," the bird said, flying down to the rock ledge to perch beside Carl. "I can change myself back into a man the same way I changed myself into a bird. In fact, I've done just that several times, more to assure myself that I can do so if I really need to than anything else. I prefer being a bird, though, for the time being."

Carl considered that at least ten seconds. "How long have you been a bird?"

"Almost three years," the bird told him. "The transformation occurred quite by accident, actually. For as long as I can remember I always envied how birds soared through the sky, sailing on the wind wherever they wanted to go. Often I wished that I were a bird so that I could be as free and could fly above the earth looking down on everything. One day I was swimming here when a flock of birds flew overhead. 'I wish I was with them instead of down here,' I thought. Suddenly—*zap!*—I *was* with that flock of birds, flapping wings of my own and flowing with a warm breeze. My wish had been granted by this transformation tarn."

"That's amazing!" Carl said.

"That it is," the bird agreed.

Carl thought about this, trying to puzzle out the wondrous, extraordinary possibilities this transformation tarn presented to the world.

"Could a bird lturn itself into a person here if it wanted to?" Carl asked.

"No, the tarn works magic only for people," the bird said. "Only people have the necessary desire and the necessary intellect and the necessary makeup to transfigure themselves here."

"Could I become a metalsmith if I swam here?" Carl asked.

The bird chuckled at the innocence of youth. "I'm afraid not. This works only for *physical* transformations. You can change your appearance, or your species, but there are limits as to what the water is able to do. You want to be a metalsmith, do you?"

"More than anything," Carl said. "My father won't let me become one, though. He insists that I have to be a farmer, like him, and help him run the farm. He doesn't care anything about what I want to do. If he wants to be a farmer, that's fine, but I just know that farming isn't for me. He's going to make me be a farmer, though, and I'll be miserable all of my life because of his bullheadedness."

"Do you mind if I give you a bit of advice?" the bird said.

"Go ahead," Carl said. "After all, I get nothing but 'advice' from my father. I'm used to it."

"I've thought a lot about transformation since I've become a bird," the bird said. "The water in this tarn changing me into a bird taught me something that I should have realized a long time ago: A person is capable of being whatever he wishes to be, if his desire is strong enough. While you can't jump into this tarn and become a metalsmith in an instant, like you could change yourself into being six inches taller, or being a fish, you can become a metalsmith someday if that's what you truly want to be and you have enough determination to become one. You could say that every person possesses the power of magic, in that way. The world is full of magic. The trick is to learn how to make use of your own magic to achieve your goals in life."

"That's easier said than done," Carl responded, "especially when you have a father as stubborn as mine."

"That may be true enough," the bird conceded. "But it's also true that nearly nothing is impossible. If you want something strongly enough you can find a way to get it, or do it. Think about it. You'll come to see that I'm right."

With that the bird flapped its wings and sailed out over the tarn. It circled the lake once and flew away.

Over the course of the next several weeks Carl returned to the rock ledge next to the transformation tarn many times to contemplate his life. He hoped to encounter the man-turned-bird once more, but he never did. On a number of occasions he was on the brink of diving into the water to try to change himself into something else. He never dove into the water, though, because deep in his heart he knew he didn't want to be anything other than what he was, or alter his appearance. The idea of changing himself into something else for a matter of minutes, or maybe an hour or so, was almost too tempting to resist, but Carl did manage to resist the urge, for he feared he may not be able to transform himself back into a human being again, and he liked being a human being; he could think of nothing better to be. The only thing he was truly unhappy about, as a person, was that his desire to be a metalsmith seemed to be an unattainable goal, given his father's insistence that he be a farmer.

Late one afternoon Carl fell asleep on the rock ledge and dozed for hours. A noise awoke him, and Carl immediately sensed danger. Then he saw a stout, wide-bodied form shuffling toward him in the dusky, mist-shrouded halflight. His first thought was that it was an animal of some sort—a bear cub, perhaps. As his mind focused more sharply, as he became more fully awake and aware, he discerned that the intruding creature was not an animal but a hairy, hideous troll. Judging by its corrugated skin, the sag of its face, and its stooped posture, Carl thought the troll must be at least three hundred years old if it was a day.

"You don't belong here!" the troll grunted, brandishing a long, rusty chain. "I'm going to whip you with this chain and take you back to my cave and keep you as a prisoner."

Carl was too frightened to speak. The troll had him trapped. His only escape route was to jump into the tarn and try to swim away. His only other option seemed to be to try to fight his way past the old troll. Despite the troll's obvious advanced age, Carl knew the troll was still undoubtedly much stronger than he was, for trolls are by nature much, much stronger than people. Given the additional fact that the troll had a heavy chain to use as a whip, Carl had an easy decision to make.

And so Carl dove headfirst off the rock ledge as the troll swung the rusty chain at him. As his hands, held out in front of him in a V formation, began slicing into the water, Carl thought to himself: *It would be easier for me to escape if I were a bird. I want to be a bird.*

The troll watched Carl's body disappear into the transformation tran. He saw a seagull emerge from the water, but the person never surfaced. The troll scoured the surface of the tarn intently with his eyes, watching for Carl to reappear, as the seagull, which actually was Carl in the form of a seagull, flew up and circled over the troll's head.

"I'm up here!" Carl said teasingly. "Try and catch me now!"

The troll couldn't believe his eyes and ears as he stared at Carl the seagull.

"Pretty neat trick, huh?" Carl said, cackling with laughter. "I bet you didn't know I could change myself into a bird, did you?"

"How did you change yourself into a bird?" the troll growled.

"Well," Carl said, "it just so happens that this tarn is a transformation tarn where people can change themselves into whatever they want to be."

The troll looked down at the water, then back at Carl the seagull. Suddenly, a smirk creased his face as an idea struck him. "Then I'll lturn myself into a bird too, and catch you anyway."

The troll leaped over the edge of the rock ledge and splashed into the water on his back. When he floated back to the surface he was still a troll; there wasn't a single feather on his body.

Spitting out water as he swam clumsy dog-paddle strokes, the troll headed for shore. Carl the seagull was waiting there, perched on a rock, to mock the troll some more.

"It's kind of late to be swimming, isn't it, troll?" Carl taunted. "You still *are* a troll, you know."

"What's going on here?" the troll demanded, standing in foot-deep water a few feet from shore. "How is it that you can change yourself into a bird and I can't?"

"That's because you're a troll and I'm a person," Carl said. "Only people can change themselves into whatever they wish to be. Trolls are destined to remain trolls forever and always. A troll can be only one thing. People, on the other hand, can advance and change and grow and become anything they wish to be, if their desire is great enough. That is one of the things that sets people above trolls."

As he spoke, finding himself echoing the talking bird's words, Carl truly understood his own unlimited potential for the first time. Becoming a bird made it much easier for him to believe that he could become a metalsmith if he wanted to be a metalsmith, despite his father's feelings on the matter. After all: where there was a will there had to be a way. He now had no doubt of that.

Carl flew away, waited until the old troll left the transformation tarn, then went back and turned himself back into his own sixteen-year-old human self and returned home.

From that day forward Carl never wavered in his resolve to become a metalsmith rather than a farmer. Eventually he became an apprentice metalsmith, and then a master metalsmith in his own right.

Perhaps recognizing that Carl was satisfying an inner need by becoming a metalsmith, even his father, in the end, came to accept Carl's occupational choice.

Carl was happy as a metalsmith, for he felt he had become what he was meant to be. Still. . . he had to admit that life was even more fun and fulfilling for him because of the pleasure he took in returning to the transformation tarn now and again to see what it was like to be other things for short periods of time.

74 ▪ Abandoned

With Ort not pushing or prodding anyone to make the long trip down the mountain to check on developments at the construction site, none of the trolls had been within sight of it since Ort, accompanied by Rott, made the trip himself and concluded there seemed to be no reason to monitor developments as often as they had been monitoring them. Trolls are lazy by nature, after all, and so are inclined to do nothing as much of the time as possible. As long as no noises disturbed them and the people seemed to have worked as far up the mountainside as they planned to go Ort and all of the other members of the tribe were content to live and let live. At least, none of the trolls openly complained that the tribe should be doing more to either keep an eye on the tricky, unpredictable people or try to force them to abandon the site. Indeed, by this time most of the trolls gave scant thought to what was happening at the bottom of the mountain, if they thought of it at all. After all, most trolls, by nature, have limited attention spans and are easily distracted by other events, concerns and considerations. A magician would find an audience of trolls ridiculously easy to deceive and misdirect.

At this period of the year, in autumn, the trolls were most concerned with storing up a supply of food for the winter. This is when they did their heaviest raiding of farms and gardens that were within a reasonable walking distance of their caves. Not many people lived near Troll Mountain, so the raids required some rather long, arduous walks and took all night; sometimes there were two-day outings to reach a greater population density. That was one of the disadvantages of being so isolated from people. Still, considering their history with people, which was rife with crowding and flight, the trolls preferred needing to travel some distance to take what they could get to living so close to people that they would always be on edge, anxious as to what the people might do next, or where they might spread and build, annoy and destroy.

One night Haar, Scurf and Rnobrna headed for a place where the trolls had had good luck in previous years, for there was a king-sized garden there replete with a wide variety of large vegetables. It was a small farm with a rather rundown house and a rotting barn with a sagging roof, but the vegetable garden was a jewel of abundance. Adding to the garden's attractiveness, the trolls had rarely encountered a dog there.

"It looks nice and quiet," Haar said as the farm came into view and the three trolls stopped to look and listen for any movements or sounds.

"I don't hear a thing," Rnobrna said. "That's good."

Even so, the three trolls approached the farm cautiously, alert for any sounds, lights or movements. They drew nearer and nearer until Haar stopped, scratched his head and said, "There's something strange here. I thought the garden was right here." Having been there the previous autumn, as Scurf and Rnobrna had not been, he thought he remembered where the garden was situated. "Maybe they put it in a different place." Even as he spoke, he had an empty feeling in the pit of his stomach, for he knew the garden had been in the same spot every year he had been there, which was quite a number of years; he sensed something was not right.

"Where did it go to?" Scurf asked.

"How should I know?" Haar snapped. "Let's split up and look for it. Hoot like an owl if you find it."

With that, Rnobrna veered to the left, Scurf to the right, and Haar continued on a middle course. After several minutes of fruitless searching, Haar hooted so the other two would come to him.

"Did you find it?" Scurf asked excitedly, even though it was obvious Haar was not standing in any garden, but in an overgrown field of weeds.

"Does it look like I found it?" Haar said. "There's no garden anywhere. I don't think there is one."

"So what does that mean?" Rnobrna asked.

"It means there's no garden," Haar said, exasperation in his voice.

"No garden?" Rnobrna said. "You mean the people here didn't grow one this year?"

"It looks like it," Haar said. "In fact, I'm wondering if there are still people living here. Maybe they left."

Scurf and Rnobrna looked at each other, as though the concept of people abandoning a place was too great a notion to comprehend.

"Let's have a look inside the barn and see if there's anything in there," Haar went on.

The three trolls walked to the barn, peered in windows, then entered through the main door, which they found partially open. There were no animals in the barn, and little else except for old, damp hay on the floor and more than a few cobwebs scattered about.

"Let's check the house," Haar said to the other two.

They approached the house more carefully, and spent more time looking in windows before they entered. As soon as they stepped inside it was obvious no one lived in the house anymore, for it was barer than the inside of the barn, and also decorated with cobwebs, mice droppings and other signs of negligence.

"I don't think there's anyone here," Rnobrna said in little more than a whisper.

"You don't need to be quiet," Haar said to him in a normal tone of voice. "There's no one here. Obviously no one has lived here for a while."

"Is this the good luck we're getting from seeing the large white buck?" Scurf asked Haar.

"What do you mean?" Haar said. "How is this good luck?"

"Well," Scurf said, "it's an empty house. We could move in and live here."

"Why in the world would we do that?" Haar said. "Why would we want to live here when we have nice safe caves? Finding no one here is not a lucky thing because it means there's no garden to get stuff from anymore. That's an *unlucky* thing!"

"I guess maybe you're right," Scurf conceded.

"Now what?" Rnobrna said. "Should we look for another farm?"

"Let's look around here a little more first," Haar said. "I've never had a chance to look around before; I always just came right to the garden, took what I could get, and left."

With Haar leading the way, the three trolls left the house through the outside kitchen door and followed a path that grass and weeds only partially obscured. Less than a hundred feet away the path passed a well.

"A well!" Rnobrna said excitedly, pointing out the obvious. "And look, there's still a rope and a bucket here!"

The rope and the bucket were attached to a windlass, which indeed was good fortune, though neither Scurf or Haar recognized that fact and wondered if that was some of the good luck they had coming to them as a result of their seeing a large white buck.

"Maybe we can pull up some water," Haar said.

"Let's do it!" Rnobrna said, still animated with excitement. "I'm thirsty."

"So am I," Scurf said.

With Haar and Rnobrna doing the work, the three trolls found a sizeable rock to place in the bucket so it would be sure to sink below the surface of the water, lowered the bucket and drew it up, finding it half full of brownish water. The water was a bit bitter, but not nearly as bitter as the water Brine found in Bitter Creek, so they scooped it into their mouths with cupped hands and again lowered the bucket down the well shaft for more, for all three of them were very thirsty.

75 ▪ Else And The Wishing Well

This evening Anders read Andrew a tale called *Else And The Wishing Well.*

▪

One day a pretty eighteen-year-old girl named Else Winberg went into the woods near her village in search of wild strawberries. After finding a large strawberry patch, Else picked berries until her large basket was filled. The long walk into the woods and the work of picking the berries made her hungry, so she sat down against the trunk of a tree and ate wild strawberries until her stomach could hold no more. Feeling lethargic from eating so many strawberries, she learned back against the tree trunk, closed her eyes and fell asleep, intending to take a short nap before making the long walk back home. She was so tired and languorous from stuffing herself with strawberries, however, that she slept on and on, all through the afternoon.

When she awoke she was startled nearly out of her wits by the sight of a grotesque, smelly troll, who was crouched a few feet in front of her, staring at her. The troll had long, stringy, mangy black hair, a snout of a nose, deep-set red eyes, a misshapen mouth containing only a few brown teeth, and stubby fingers and toes that looked as though they had been chiseled from blocks of wood. Else was too shocked and terrified to scream. Instead, she gasped, emitting a mouse-like squeak.

"You're beautiful," the troll said to Else. "I've been watching you sleep."

Else wondered how long the troll had been watching her. The mere thought of such a grotesque creature watching her sleep gave her the creeps and made her squirm emotionally, as though she had been tied down and several poisonous spiders had been allowed to crawl freely about her body.

Sitting up straight, Else tried to prepare herself as best she could for the possibility that the troll might physically attack her.

"Why have you been doing a thing like that?" she asked, in response to the troll's declaration that he had watched her sleep.

"Because you're so beautiful," the troll said in a slow, gravelly voice. "I could watch someone as beautiful as you sleep all day."

Else didn't like the tenor of this conversation. The fact that the troll thought she was beautiful was much more frightening than it was flattering.

"I feel as though I *have* slept all day," Else said. "I must be getting home."

"Here's your basket," the troll said, holding out Else's woven basket, which was now empty.

"What happened to all of the strawberries?" Else asked.

"I ate them while I was watching you sleep," the troll said. "They were delicious, I must say."

Else wanted to scold the troll for eating the berries it took her so long to pick, but under the circumstances she let that matter pass without comment, for her most pressing concern was getting away from the troll and returning home safely.

"I'm glad you liked them," she said.

When Else stood up and reached out to grab the handle of her empty basket the troll suddenly gave the basket a fierce jerk, causing Else to stumble into the troll, who grabbed the pretty young woman in a vice-like grip and said, "You're coming home with me tonight."

Else screamed for help and begged her kidnapper to let her go as the troll dragged her away. Her screams went unheard, and the smitten troll ignored her pleas for freedom. Eventually Else's screams gave way to deep sobs. Thoughts of what the troll might do to her sent icy shivers down her spine and made her mind swirl with kaleidoscopic images of horror and dread.

After what seemed like a nightmarish eternity to Else, she and the troll came upon a covered well with a winch and a bucket. They were crossing a large farm where more than one well was necessary, which is why there was a well so far from any buildings.

"Please let me stop for a drink of water," Else pleaded with the troll.

The troll grunted and said, "Why should I? You've been nothing but trouble for me. If I let you drink water you'll just refresh your strength and shout and cry even more than you've done until now."

"No, I won't," Else said. "I promise I won't. If you let me stop for a drink of water I promise I won't shout anymore. Besides, you must be thirsty yourself, aren't you? We've been walking quite a long time."

The troll couldn't deny that. It was true that he was thirsty and could use a drink of cold water himself.

"Just think of how good it will feel to have a long drink of cold, sweet water," Else said as enticingly as a silver-tongued peddler.

"All right, we'll stop for a drink of water," the troll relented.

The troll kept a close watch on Else as she lowered the wooden bucket into the well and cranked the winch to lift the filled bucket. While engaged in this activity, Else noticed a couple of dozen coins scattered about the bottom of the well. The sight of the coins made her heart skip with hope. *I wonder if this is a wishing well*, she thought. *If it is, I know what I'll wish for.*

As soon as the thought crossed her mind, though, hope fizzled like a spark in a wet fuse, for she didn't have a coin to toss into the well. Anyone old enough to tie his or her own shoes understands that a wishing well can make wishes come true only if someone drops a coin into the well while making a wish, and Else was well aware of this basic rule of wishing wells.

As she slowly swallowed a ladleful of water while trying to think of a solution to her dilemma, a thought struck her with the brilliance of a lightning bolt: Her shoes! Why hadn't she thought of her shoes immediately? Her mother, a superstitious woman of the highest order, had sewen two "lucky coins" into the lining of Else's shoes when the shoes were new. That way, Else's mother said, Else would always walk with luck. Well, Else thought, if ever she needed luck now was the time. As the troll gobbled water in big, sloppy slurps, Else leaned over to remove her shoes.

"What are you doing?" the troll demanded, suspicious that his captive might be up to some sort of trick.

"I'm just taking off my shoes for a minute," Else answered. "My feet are very tired from walking and I want to massage them."

That answer satisfied the troll, who resumed his slurping. The cold water gurgled down his thick throat as though his throat contained several frogs.

As soon as she removed both shoes, Else tossed them into the well. As they fell through the air toward the water at the bottom of the well she closed her eyes tightly, crossed fingers on both of her hands, and said to herself: "I wish the troll would fall into the well so that I could escape."

Else's shoes barely touched the water before a small swarm of more than a dozen angry bees came along and all stung the troll simultaneously, on various parts of his head and neck. Flinching with pain, the troll lost his balance and tumbled into the well, where he became wedged in an awkward position at the bottom. Else glanced quickly down the well shaft before fleeing as fast as her shoeless feet would carry her. She ran for what seemed like an hour before she came to a familiar road, which she followed to her home village.

Never again did Else venture so far into the forest alone, and never again did she wear a pair of shoes that did not have lucky coins sewn into them.

76 ▪ Snozzle

Although he didn't know it, Brine was halfway to the sea when he came to the bank of a raging thirty-foot-wide river that cut through a moderately dense forest. The river was too deep to wade across and too dangerous to try to swim across, even had he been an experienced swimmer, which he was not, so he had no other choice but to walk either upstream or downstream to try to find someplace he could cross. He hated having to make such choices, for he was always apprehensive he would choose the wrong option and end up in an even worse situation, and waste time retracing his steps back to where he made the wrong choice. It was at moments such as this he felt loneliest and wished he had a companion to share the worry and the decision-making responsibility. He was alone, though, so the weight of responsibility was entirely on his shoulders; it was up to him to decide. After stewing for several minutes about which direction he should go he started walking upstream, for no particular reason; it just seemed to be the way his feet wanted to go, so he let his feet do his thinking.

As the river grew wilder, with swifter rapids, more boulders and more violently turbulent dropoffs, Brine second-guessed his decision to head upstream and thought about turning back and walking downstream instead, for he feared it might be a long while before he found a place he could cross with any confidence of safety. Each time he thought of turning back, though, he decided to go just a little further to see what was up ahead, around the next bend or above a stretch of powerful rapids.

After a half-hour's walk a glorious sight presented itself a short distance ahead: a bridge across the river. Energized by the sight of this structure, which would afford him the opportunity to cross the river, Brine had a fresh spring in his steps as he tramped toward the bridge. As he drew nearer he saw that the wooden bridge had seen better days. It was rotting, sagging and moss- and lichen-covered. Even so, it was the sweetest sight

Brine had experienced in some time, for it was still plenty strong enough to walk across. On his side of the bridge—that is, the side of the river he was on—forest gave way to meadow some twenty feet from the bridge, which was more than ten feet above the river's rippling surface. Forest still prevailed on the opposite side of the bridge, with a five-foot-wide path leading through the trees from the other end of the bridge. Glancing behind him, Brine detected a hint of dawn in the eastern sky as he stepped onto the bridge and made his way across. Before he reached the other side a voice boomed out demandingly from under the bridge, as gruff-sounding as gravel is coarse: "Who goes there?" Brine stopped in his tracks, wondering exactly where the voice came from and who had spoke. Those questions were quickly answered when first a head and then a body emerged from under the bridge, to Brine's left. Even more astonishing than hearing a voice in such a remote spot at such an hour of the day was the fact that the figure that emerged from beneath the bridge was a troll. Both Brine and the other troll obviously thought they would see a human being rather than a troll, for they looked at each other, and looked each other over, for a full ten seconds before either of them spoke. The other troll, who had a broad, lizard-like nose, pointed ears that stuck out straight from his head, a mop of tangled, shoulder-length black hair, and long, thin arms and fingers, broke the silence. "Who are you, and what are you doing on my bridge?"

If Brine had been thinking, as he had been, that a troll would treat him better than a person would, this gruff, confrontational opening disabused him of that notion. The other troll was a stranger to him, and seemingly as crotchety as Old Fungus, or even more crotchety, judging by first impressions. While he obviously wasn't nearly as long in the tooth as Old Fungus, or even as old as Ort, he was quite old.

"I'm Brine," Brine told him. "I'm crossing the bridge to get to the other side of the river."

The other troll lumbered up onto the bridge deck, with some effort, and planted himself in front of Brine. "No one crosses this bridge unless Snozzle says they can cross it," he declared, his voice still gruff and menacing.

"Who's Snozzle?" Brine asked.

"*I* am Snozzle!" the other troll said with a haughy air, eyeing Brine suspiciously. "What do you want on the other side of the river anyway?"

"I just want to get across the river so that I can continue my journey to the sea," Brine said.

"To the sea!" Snozzle said with disdain, and spat. "Why are you going to the sea?"

"I want to see a fjord," Brine divulged.

"What for?" Snozzle said, still obviously suspicious.

"I've never seen one, and I hear they are wonderful," Brine said, thinking it best not to tell this grumpy stranger about his dream vision and his sense of destiny. "Have you ever seen one?"

"Of course," Snozzle replied.

"Are they wonderful?" Brine asked, interested in the opinion of anyone who had seen a fjord.

"They're okay," Snozzle answered. "Frankly, I prefer living here under this bridge."

"You live under the bridge?" Brine said.

"That's what I just said, isn't it?' Snozzle snarled. "Where do you live?"

"Well, I've been living in a mountain cave on a mountain far from here," Brine told him.

"By yourself?" Snozzle asked.

"No, I'm part of a tribe," Brine answered.

"Maybe I've met some of them," Snozzle said. "Tell me some of their names."

"Well," Brine said, "there's Ort. He's king of the tribe."

"Never heard of him," Snozzle said, with a tenor that implied Ort couldn't be much of a king if he had never heard of him.

"Haar?" Brine offered, to which the other troll shook his head and said no. "Rnobrna? Scurf? Kravig? He's a wizard." The other troll said "no" to each name. "Guggle? She's a witch. She's not a member of the tribe, really. She lives off by herself, but not too far away."

"It seems to me I may have heard of her," Snozzle said. "Yeah, I think maybe I have heard of a witch named Guggle. I remember that because her name is sort of like my name. Who else is in your tribe?"

"Let's see. . ." Brine thought. "Old Fungus."

"Fungus?" Snozzle said.

"Yeah—Old Fungus," Brine said.

"I don't know any Old Fungus, but it seems to me that I did run into someone named Fungus a time or two, quite a ways back."

"Well, he wasn't always Old Fungus; he used to be just Fungus. That was long before I ever knew him. He's the oldest member of the tribe, by quite a few years."

"Old Fungus, huh?" Snozzle said. "Maybe it's the same Fungus I met."

"Maybe," Brine said.

"What's in your sack?" Snozzle asked, as though noticing it for the first time.

"Oh, this and that," Brine said. "Things I need for traveling—food and clothes and. . ."

"Food?" Snozzle said, brightening. "What kind of food?"

"Oh, apples and carrots, and turnips, and potatoes, and cheese, and other things I've been able to pick up along the way."

"Cheese?" Snozzle said with obvious relish. "You have cheese? I love cheese, and I don't get to eat it very often. Tell you what: You seem like a good enough fellow. I'll let you cross my bridge if you share your food with me, especially the cheese."

Though not keen on sharing his food, Brine quickly calculated that doing so may well be the most prudent course of action, for despite the fact that Snozzle was much older he was still in fit condition, and Brine knew it would not be easy to fight his way past him. Also: until now it had been fairly easy for him to restock his food supply at farms and country homes, so it seemed a good bet his luck would hold and he would continue to be able to find all the food he needed along the way. And so he agreed to share his food with Snozzle.

"Do you have any bread to go with the cheese?" Snozzle asked.

"Two loaves of it," Brine told him. "Well, more like a loaf and a half now; I ate nearly half of the one loaf."

"I was just about to catch a couple of trout when you came along," Snozzle said. "Let's start a fire so we can cook them right away. Along with what you have, we'll have a feast."

"I have gear along for catching trout myself," Brine said.

"No need of that," Snozzle said. "All I need to catch trout is my hands. I'll catch an extra one or two for you."

Snozzle told Brine to watch from the bridge as he went a short distance upstream and used protruding rocks to make his way out into the river, walking with a pronounced limp that favored his left leg. Brine thought of running, particularly when he noticed Snozzle's limp, but decided to stay. For one thing, he had never seen anyone catch a trout by hand, and he was curious to see if Snozzle was capable of such a rare feat. He quickly found out he was, as Snozzle snatched first one, then a second, then a third and a fourth good-sized trout from the river in no time at all. Snozzle quickly brought back the trout and summoned Brine beneath the bridge, where he uncovered embers from the bottom of a firepit just off the lower edge of the bridge and soon had a fire blazing in the pit and the trout cooking in a frying pan over the fire. Then Snozzle and Brine feasted on the food Brine carried in his sack as the trout fried. Snozzle was amazed at the amount of food Brine had.

"I thought sure you were a human being when I heard someone crossing the bridge," Snozzle confided as they ate.

"I thought maybe you were a person when I heard someone speak," Brine said. "You're the first troll I've met along the way, since I left home."

"Is that so?" Snozzle said. "Have you met any people?"

"I haven't met any, no," Brine said, noticing for the first time, because of the way the firelight illuminated their faces, that Snozzle had a long scar down his left cheek and onto his neck. "I've been taking what I can get from farms and houses along the way. And I heard a church bell one morning. It nearly drove me wild!"

"A church bell!" Snozzle said, shivering at the thought. "I haven't heard one of those in a long, long while, and I hope I never hear one again."

"I'm with you," Brine said. "I hope I never hear another one either. It was torture, pure torture. Do people ever cross your bridge here?"

"They used to," Snozzle answered, "but I can't even remember the last time one did, it's been so long."

"But people built the bridge, didn't they?" Brine asked.

"I take it they did," Snozzle said. "I didn't build it, I know that. I have a cozy home here, in the bank. I'll show it to you when we're done eating. I built *that* all by myself, by digging into the bank and making a nice snug cave for myself. I just keep making it bigger and bigger over the years so that now I have even more room than I need."

"You say people used to cross the bridge?" Brine said.

"All the time," Snozzle said, though in fact that was always a fairly rare occurrence, for few people lived anywhere near the bridge by the time Snozzle took up residence beneath it. "And I always made them pay me to cross my bridge, you can bet I did! I made it clear to every one that there was a price to pay for them to cross the bridge."

"What did they pay you?" Brine asked.

"Usually food of some sort," Snozzle said, "but sometimes it was other things—coats and boots and shovels and whatever."

"I'd rather stay away from people, if possible," Brine offered. "Just going into their barns and gardens and sheds sort of gives me the creeps sometimes."

"People are rotten creatures," Snozzle agreed. "They're sneaky and conniving and crafty; I know that. That's why I always let them know who was in charge of this bridge."

77 ▪ Two Versions Of One Story

"See this scar here?" Snozzle said, pointing to his facial scar. "Know how I got that?" Brine shook his head as Snozzle went on, not really looking for an answer to what was more of a rhetorical question. "That happened when I made a person give me a ham to let him cross the bridge. When he came back again he had a huge pet bear with him because he thought the bear would scare me into letting him cross the bridge without having to give me anything. Well, I told him I still wouldn't let him cross the bridge unless he gave me something, so he ordered the bear to attack me, and me and the bear had quite a tussle—quite a tussle, I can tell you that. The bear scratched me all over and tried to throw me around, and I slipped and nearly fell off the bridge, but I managed to push back and get the upper hand and push the bear off the bridge—off the end of the bridge, not into the water—and prevent the person from crossing the bridge. But it was a tough fight, and it left me with a limp leg and this nasty scar on my face and neck."

"You hurt your leg while fighting the bear too?" Brine asked.

"When I slipped off the bridge," Snozzle said. "I twisted it something fierce. It's never been the same since. I've had to live with it this way all these years. So you can see why I'm not fond of people, not to mention bears."

In reality, Snozzle's account of how he sustained the scar and came to walk with a limp was no closer to the truth than moths are to having the multiplication table memorized. The actual events that occurred are as follows:

▪

Snozzle took up residence beneath one side of the bridge when few people used the bridge any longer. A farmer who owned land on both sides of the river built the bridge—not by himself, of course, but with the help of several other men—quite a few years earlier to allow himself and his livestock a convenient crossing point between the two parcels of land. None of the land was productive farmland, though, so the farmer could not make a decent living farming there, and he and his family moved to a different area, which left the bridge unattended as far as maintenance and upkeep were concerned. Few people used the bridge after the farmer and his family left, for few people lived within ten miles of it.

One person who knew about the bridge and decided to use it was a young man named Jesse Nilsson, who worked as a hired hand at a farm about three-and-a-half miles from the bridge, which is to say the farmhouse was that far from the bridge. Under the terms of his employment Jesse was allowed several days off each autumn to attend the annual harvest festival in the nearest village, which was fourteen miles from the farm by road. Since the trip was two miles shorter if someone took a route that included crossing the bridge where Snozzle lived, Jesse followed the shortcut route the first year he worked at the farm.

Jesse was less than halfway across the bridge when a voice thundered "Who goes there?" and an ugly old troll—Snozzle— emerged from under the other end of the bridge. The young man backed away slowly as the troll stomped toward him and said in a gruff, raspy voice, "Who are you and why are you crossing my bridge?"

Jesse stopped retreating and answered, "My name is Jesse and I'm on my way to the annual harvest festival in Eskerheim."

"You are, are you?" Snozzle said in a sneering tone. "Well, if you want to cross my bridge you have to give me something for allowing you to cross."

Jesse was in no position to protest, for he knew trolls were much more powerful than humans, which would leave him on the short end of any physical confrontation. "I don't have much of anything to give you, I'm afraid," he said.

"What's in your sack?" Snozzle asked, his demeanor still as gruff as gravel. By "sack" he meant the knapsack Jesse was carrying.

"Those are my provisions for my trip," Jesee said.

" 'Provisions!'" Snozzle sneered, not understanding the word. "What do you mean, provisions?"

"My supply of food for the trip," Jesse explained. "But I need every bit of that."

"Let's see it," the troll demanded, and the frightened young man removed his knapsack and spread out the food it contained. "Yes, this will do nicely," Snozzle said, grabbing dried meat, pieces of fruit, a hunk of cheese, and some bread, leaving a small portion of the food for Jesse. "I'll let you cross the bridge with this small payment this time, but if you ever want to cross my bridge again you need to bring me more than this pittance. You may be on your way now."

Jesse needed no further encouragement to leave. He quickly gathered the food the troll left for him into his knapsack and stepped across the bridge and off into the wood as quickly as he could walk, without running, for a sixth sense told him that running away might provoke the troll. He was dejected about the stolen food, but relieved he had survived an encounter with a gruff, nasty troll with life and limb intact. After the harvest festival he returned home by the long route rather than re-cross the bridge where Snozzle lived.

The following autumn Jesse again wanted to attend Eskerheim's harvest festival, and he wanted to get there by the shortest route possible, so he took the shortcut, hoping the troll had moved and no longer lived under the bridge. In the event the troll was still there, he took along a smoked pork roast to buy his way across the bridge. And, indeed, Snozzle still lived under the bridge Jesse needed to cross, and demanded payment for letting Jessee cross the bridge, so Jesse offered him the smoked pork roast, which Snozzle accepted as full fare.

After attending the festival Jesse again took the long way back to the farm where he worked, for he had nothing but the clothes he was wearing to offer to the troll if he wanted to try to cross the bridge along the shortcut route. First of all, he didn't want to give the troll any of the clothes he was wearing. Secondly, he didn't know what the troll would do if he had nothing to give him to gain his permission to cross the bridge. If the troll prevented him from crossing the bridge he would need to retrace his steps for quite a distance to return home via the long route, and he didn't want to face that prospect.

The third year Jesse worked at the farm and attended Esker-heim's harvest festival he brought sufficient food to buy safe passage across Snozzle's bridge in both directions. While he hoped the troll no longer lived under the bridge, he accepted the likelihood that he did and prepared himself for that probability. Indeed, Snozzle was still there, still claiming he owned the bridge and demanding some sort of payment from anyone who wanted to cross the bridge. Jesse gave Snozzle a brick-sized hunk of cheese, a loaf of bread and a smoked sausage so that Snozzle would allow him to cross the bridge on his way to Eskerheim.

At the harvest festival Jesse met two fellows close to his own age he had become acquainted with the previous year and steered his conversation with them to the subject of trolls, without saying anything about his three encounters with the bridge troll. Neither had encountered a troll personally, as Jesse had, but each told a tale about how humans had hoodwinked dimwitted, gullible trolls with superior savvy and intelligence. Jesse kept thinking about those tales, and remembered other such tales he had heard, as he wandered about the festival grounds. The more he thought about them, the more ashamed he felt for allowing a troll to bully him three years in a row. Human beings were far superior to trolls, after all, particularly when it came to intelligence, so he figured he should be able to outwit a troll as easily as a rabbit could outrun a turtle. Various schemes simmered in his mind until one boiled up as a brilliant idea, or so Jesse hoped. At least the idea was the one he thought would provide a satisfying measure of revenge. And given that he knew this was the last year he would work at this particular farm, it wouldn't matter if he burned bridges behind him, so to speak.

As expected, Snozzle confronted him on his return trip and demanded some sort of payment for the privilege of crossing the bridge. "What goodies do you have for me this time?" Snozzle wanted to know.

"You know what?" Jesse responded. "This time I would like to give you something far more valuable than food."

"Gold?" Snozzle guessed.

"No, to you this would be far more valuable to you than gold," Jesse said. "I'm sure that as well as you guard the bridge to make sure no one crosses it without your permission there are times when you need to sleep, or are away from the bridge, and no doubt some people slip past you when you are sleeping or are away from the bridge and cross your bridge without paying you anything for the privilege. I can set up something for you that will prevent that from happening anymore. I happen to be an expert carpenter, and I will create a trap door in the bridge that will allow you to make anyone who tries to cross your bridge without paying you anything drop into the river as a punishment. No one will ever again be able to cross your bridge without you knowing about it. How does that sound to you?"

"You can do that?" Snozzle said excitedly.

"I can and I will," Jesse said. "Do we have a deal then? I'll set up booby trap if you let me cross the bridge for doing it."

"Okay!" Snozzle said. "It's a deal!"

Jesse persuaded Snozzle to stand at the other end of the bridge so the troll could watch for anyone approaching, then he went to work with items he had picked up at the harvest festival. He was able to set up things as he wanted them set up in a mere ten minutes. Then he called Snozzle over to show him what he wanted Snozzle to believe would happen. He showed the troll the thin rope with bells attached he had stretched across the bridge, side to side, that would alert Snozzle to anyone's presence on the bridge. Then he pointed to where a trap door supposedly was that would send someone crashing into the river when Snozzle stomped on a certain plank of the bridge that was near the end of the bridge where Snozzle lived. Jesse had scratched several "X" marks into that plank to that Snozzle would know what plank it was.

"You have to stomp on it really hard to make the trap door open," Jesse told him. "And I mean *really* hard, like you're trying to kick in a locked door. Understand?"

"Yeah, yeah, really hard," Snozzle assured him.

"All right," Jesse said. "Let's give it a try. You stay here and stomp on the trip-board while I go over and stand next to the trap door."

When he was in place Jesse told Snozzle to stomp on the marked plank, which was one of several planks Jesse had loosened With Snozzle stomping on one end of the plank, the other end of the plank shot up and hit Snozzle's cheek and neck as he fell through the bridge deck, his arms and legs flailing as he attempted to prevent himself from falling into the rocky river. And while he did manage to avoid falling into the river, he was clinging to the bridge largely from under the bridge, through the jagged hole, pain shooting through several parts of his body, especially his left leg.

Jesse ran away as fast as he could as soon as Snozzle plunged through the bridge deck. He glanced back only once, and smiled with satisfaction when he saw Snozzle's hands gripping the deck through the hole in the bridge.

With his immense strength, Snozzle managed to pull himself back up onto the bridge deck, where he sat and massaged his left leg and other scraped and sore spots as he tried to spot Jesse, who was far out of sight. He directed a long string of curses in Jesse's direction, even though he couldn't see him, as well as curses aimed at human beings in general.

Snozzle was never quite the same again. Jesse's trick left him with a nasty scar on his cheek and neck and a permanent limp to his walk. It didn't make him leave the bridge, though. He continued living under the bridge, protecting it as though he was a sentry at a particularly significant post.

78 · Arvin's Tale

"Look at the size of those squash!" Emma Branstad marveled as she toured vegetable exhibits at an annual harvest festival with her husband, Anders, and her son, Andrew.

"Why don't ours get that big?" Andrew asked his parents.

"I guess we just don't have the magic touch," Emma said.

"Or the right soil," Anders added, then pointed out some huge pumpkins. "Do you think you could lift that biggest one?" he asked Andrew.

Andrew laughed and said, "No! Could you?"

"I doubt it," Anders admitted.

"Just think of all the pies you could make from just one of those huge pumpkins," Emma said. "Of course, I don't know how good the meat would be when they're that big. I'm sure the ones we raise are much tastier."

"I think you're right," Anders said. "You know," he went on, addressing his son, "seeing all of these huge vegetables reminds me of one of the troll tales in the book that we haven't read yet. Maybe we should read that one this evening."

Anders did indeed read that story to Andrew that evening, though it took him some time to find it in the book, given that the title offers no hint that it involves vegetables in any fashion.

■

One day when he was fifteen years old Arvin Sundquist was walking through a forest, taking a shortcut to the annual village fair, when he heard—faintly—a woman's voice calling out for help. Arvin stopped and looked around. He couldn't see anyone. Again the voice called out: "Help!" Arvin walked in the direction from which the voice seemed to emanate, and the cries of "Help!" grew louder and more frantic as he drew nearer to the person in trouble.

Arvin ran toward the sound of the voice. Soon he was on the rim of a large hole about eight feet in diameter and fifteen feet deep. A hook-nosed woman wearing a long black dress was at the bottom of the hole, clinging to the clay sides of the hole with long, bony fingers. In fact, the woman was a witch, though Arvin neither recognized or sensed that.

Hearing the rustling Arvin made, the witch looked up and saw the boy. "Save me!" she pleaded. "I fell into this hole and now the quicksand is pulling me under!"

"What should I do?" Arvin asked.

"Cut a long vine and use it to pull me up," the witch instructed. "You will find many strong vinces nearby. But hurry! I am being sucked under more and more every moment!"

Arvin turned away from the witch to look for a vine long enough to reach the witch. Just as the witch had said, there were many strong vines growing nearby, wrapped up onto tree limbs like enormously long, leafy snakes. Arvin found one that appeared to be long enough for his purpose and proceeded to pull its roots from the ground and its tentacles out of a tree. He lowered the vine to the witch, who grabbed it and ordered Arvin to pull for all he was worth. It took all the strength he could muster, but Arvin was able to pull the witch out of the quicksand hole. Covered with mud nearly to her waist, and exhausted from the frightful experience and the physical effort required to escape from the hole, the witch sat back against a large tree trunk, breathing laboriously. "Thank you, thank you, thank you!" she panted to Arvin. "I could never have gotten out of that quick-sand by myself."

"You're lucky I came along," Arvin said.

"Indeed!" the witch said. "I'm lucky that someone as kind as you came along. Many people would have done nothing to save a witch from certain death."

"Are you a witch?" Arvin asked, backing away.

"You needn't be afraid of me," the witch said. "I will do you no harm. In fact, I want to give you a reward for saving my life."

"You're really a witch?" Arvin said, amazed that he had encountered a real witch.

"Yes, I really am," the witch said, her breathing more regular by now. "Come back to my cabin with me and I will give you your reward."

"But I'm on my way to the village for the fair," Arvin said. "I want to get there as quickly as I can so that I can spend as much of the day there as possible."

"But I must reward you," the witch said. "And the gift I want to give you is back at my cabin. My cabin is less than a mile from here. It will not take you so very long to come with me to allow me to reward you. I assure you that the time it takes will be more than worth your while. You have a garden, of course?"

"My family does, yes," Arvin answered.

"Then you will find my gift *most* useful," the witch said. "Come"

Although he was still not entirely confident that the witch had nothing nefarious in mind for him, Arvin went with her, for she seemed sincere and he was curious about what gift she had in store for him. When the two of them reached the witch's small cabin Arvin was bug-eyed by what he saw in her garden: some of the largest vegetables he had ever seen; they were absolutely gigantic.

"What a garden you have!" he marveled.

"Stay here," the witch instructed. She entered her cabin and emerged two minutes later with a small bottle of gingery liquid. "How would you like to grow vegetables as large as the ones in my garden?" she asked.

"Boy, I wish I could!" Arvin said. "That would really be something."

"Well, you *can* with this," the witch said, handing Arvin the liquid-filled jar.

"What do you mean?" Arvin asked.

"This is a special potion I brew that makes things grow very large," the witch explained. "Place a drop of this in the roots of a plant and it makes things grow like crazy. You must be very careful to use *only* one drop at a time, though, because the potion is so powerful that if you used even a few drops more than you should you would have pumpkins the size of houses."

Since Arvin had never been in that particular part of the forest, the witch gave him directions for reaching the village and

Arvin set out on his way again. This route took him up and over a large hill. A small stream flowed down that hill, and the witch had told Arvin to follow that stream, which he did. After walking a couple of miles he detected the sound of something crashing through the forest toward him. He wondered if it was a wolf, or a bear, or possibly something even more ferocious. Whatever it was, he wasn't anxious to meet it, so he found a tree he could climb easily and shinnied up to a heighth of some twenty feet off the ground.

A minute later a hairy, glowering troll with red eyes and reddened ears came into view beneath Arvin's tree. There it stopped, sensing the whiff of Christian blood. The black-haired troll muttered and looked about, then circled the base of the tree, still muttering and looking daggers in all directions. It sniffed the air, raising its head a little higher with each deep sniff.

Fearing the troll might spot him, Arvin leaned back in an attempt to hide himself better. As he did so the bottle of magic potion he was holding tipped downward. Before he could right the bottle one-third of the liquid spilled onto the troll's head and shoulders. The troll looked up into the tree and caught sight of Arvin, who was fear-stricken that the grouchy troll would climb the tree and do who knew what horrible things to him.

Then something even more terrifying happened: The troll started growing. The magic potion Arvin received from the witch and spilled on the troll was causing the troll to grow to giant size. Arvin could do nothing except sit in the tree and watch in horrified fright as the troll grew to ten feet tall, then twenty feet tall, and finally to thirty feet. The troll's chin was now above Arvin. The giant troll growled, muttered, scowled and threatened Arvin with various acts of torture as he snatched poor little Arvin in one of his beefy hands and squeezed the breath from him. The troll's actions caused Arvin to lose his grip on the bottle of magic liquid. The bottle slipped from his hand and smashed against a rock in the stream below.

All at once the small mountain stream boiled with foam, swirled like a maelstrom, and grew much wider and deeper. The current raged, sweeping large rocks and small boulders along in its course. What had been a slow-moving stream only seconds before was now a torrent of swift, strong water ten times wider than it had been. The current was so strong that not even a thirty-foot-tall troll could stand still in it. The raging water swept the troll off his feet. Interested only in saving himself, the troll released his grip on Arvin, who managed to cling to a branch of a tree to save himself from falling into the raging river.

Arvin felt a mixture of horror and relief as he watched the river carry away the giant troll. He was able to climb down from the tree and find his way safely out of the forest, and eventually home. While he missed the village fair that year, he was happy to be alive.

As for the stream transformed into a river by an accident of fate, it still rages down the mountainside to this day.

79 ▪ Every Which Way

Fog was forming in the foothills and on the lower parts of Troll Mountain, the air was full of a drizzly mist, and an overcast sky helped produce a murky atmosphere. This was the sort of fabled "troll weather" people talk about when they talk about what trolls like. And, indeed, trolls regard these atmospheric conditions as their favorite conditions. They thrive in fog, murk and mist as much as most plants do with sufficient water and a flood of sunlight. Add the chill of an October night, and a lengenthed period of darkness, and the Troll Mountain trolls were as wrought up as a five-year-old boy on the eve of his sixth birthday. Just as an unobstructed full moon is said to affect both animals and humans in a primordial fashion, inducing strange, unusual behavior, drizzle, murk and fog seem to stimulate trolls to instinctual action. Those soupy conditions make trolls want to ramble, roam, and raid, though what human beings regard as their raiding is simply taking what they can get to them.

With everyone sensing the night would become deliciously foggier, mistier and murkier as the night rolled on, they all ate even more rapidly than they usually did, for they were eager to ramble, roam and raid in the murk and the mist. Keyed up to something approaching a fever pitch, they talked excitedly as they ate their evening supper, many announcing where they planned to go and what they planned to do. They had it in mind to go every which way, either by themselves or with a companion or two.

"I don't hear any of you saying anything about trying to catch another gnome," Old Fungus grumbled. "We need another gnome around here that we can tease. Why doesn't someone catch another gnome? *That's* what someone should be doing!"

"Why don't you catch one yourself if you want one so bad?" Traug shot back, not granting Old Fungus a sliver of slack for his advanced age and limited physical ability.

"Yeah, and we might still have those two here to tease if you hadn't let them escape," Dau added, even more coldly. "So don't go complaining that you don't have a gnome around to tease now."

"Ah, you two probably couldn't catch a gnome if your life depended on it anyway!" Old Fungus said. "I bet I could catch one before either one of you."

"Then do it, if you think you can!" Traug snapped.

"Yeah, why don't you just shut up and eat," Dau said.

The perfect weather, in the trolls' view, had Old Fungus as keyed up as it did the others. Unlike the others, though, he was not able, because of his physical condition, to venture a long distance from the caves to explore the countryside and simply wallow in the impulsive experience that is so natural and necessary to trolls. That frustrated him something fierce on such nights, and he wasn't one to hold in his frustration or hold his tongue when he had something to say—or even when he didn't have much of substance to say but felt like venting his frustration nonetheless. His engine was revved, but he had no wheels. So he grumbled to himself as he ate, and the others pretty much ignored him as they bolted their food and set out every which way into the murky, misty night.

Ort and Llop ventured out a considerable distance together, and made a nice haul at a farm they visited, taking all sorts of small metal objects—mainly scrap metal—and food items, as well as a few items of clothing. Their burlap sacks sagged like bunches of soggy seaweed when they left that farm and started back toward their mountain caves. Simply walking about in the murk, the mist and the fog was so invigorating and pleasant—as pleasant as sailing on a lake on a warm day beneath a sunny sky is to humans—that they were in no hurry to return home. Since Ort was curious about what was happening at the construction site, they veered from the natural course—the shortest route—to have a look. They approached from the side where there was a gravel road, and where the ski resort entrance road met that public road. All at once Llop stopped and held out his left arm in front of Ort to force him to stop as well, for he saw something alarming near where the entrance road met the public road. He was so startled he couldn't speak, only point. Looking to where

Llop pointed, Ort's eyes widened with amazement, for there was a troll frozen in time, standing on skis. "What. . ." Ort muttered softly. "Who is it?" Even with their great night vision, the thick fog didn't allow Ort and Llop to see the figure clearly.

"Why doesn't he move?" Llop said to Ort. "Is he dead?"

"How can he be dead if he's standing up?" Ort responded.

"Then why doesn't he move?" Llop asked.

"Maybe the people captured him and turned him into stone somehow," Ort speculated.

"I can't tell who it is," Llop said. "Can you? Is it one of us?"

"I can't recognize him from this far away," Ort said. "Let's get a little closer." With slow, deliberate steps, Ort and Llop approached the stationary troll figure until they were near the edge of the other side of the road. "He's not from our tribe," Ort pronounced.

"No, he's not," Llop agreed. "But who is it then? I've never seen him before. Have you?"

"No," Ort answered, then asked the stationary troll: "Who are you?" There was no response.

"He seems to be frozen," Llop said. "I don't see him moving at all."

"Let's go across," Ort said, leading the way across the road and walking to within a few feet of the figure, which was standing on a slab or granite two feet high. "Why, it's not stone at all; it's wood!" Ort declared.

"I think you're right," Llop agreed.

Ort felt of a leg. "It *is* wood."

Following Ort's lead, Llop felt the life-size statue as well. "You're right! Did people turn one of us into wood?"

"It looks like it's been carved, that somebody carved it," Ort said, inspecting it closer. "I don't think this is a real troll at all."

"What's it doing here?" Llop asked.

"How should I know?" Ort said. "It's probably one of those things that people do that doesn't make any sense."

"What's this here?" Llop said, pointing to a large sign next to the troll statue that had the words "Ski With The Trolls" on it in large letters. The two trolls could not read the sign, of course, so they had no idea of its message. And neither knew the tale of *The Wooden Troll*, which may have helped them recognize that the stationary troll was a wood statue sooner than they did.

80 ▪ The Wooden Troll

One day a gifted woodcarver named Lute Soderberg decided he would use his artistic talent to carve a life-size troll out of a beautiful block of wood. He was determined to make the most lifelike troll statue anyone had ever carved, so he took great care in his carving so that all of the features of the troll figure would be exactly right, as he imagined them in his mind. The woodcarver's attention to detail made the troll statue a painstaking project of the highest order. When he had shaved away the last flakes of wood and blew away the last specks of sandpaper dust the old woodcarver was mightily proud of his creation. It was, without question, his life's masterpiece. The wooden troll looked even more lifelike after he painted it.

After devoting many months to the carving and being so pleased with the result, the woodcarver felt attached to the wooden troll. He hated the thought of selling it, but he and his wife were in great need of the money the wooden troll would bring, and so when a nine-year-old boy came into his shop with his wealthy mother and immediately fell in love with the wooden troll and begged his mother to buy the wooden troll for him the woodcarver was able to negotiate a very handsome price for himself.

Using a horse-drawn wagon, two deliverymen delivered the wooden troll to the estate where the boy's rich family lived, on the outskirts of the village.

At the time the men were delivering the magnificent statue a troll maiden named Chirre was tramping around the mountainside near that village. When she saw what appeared for all the world to be a troll riding in a wagon Chirre's curiosity clutched her like the hand of a fearful child and she made her way closer to the rolling horse-drawn wagon. She wasn't able to get as close to the wagon as she would have liked, for she would have exposed her presence to people by doing that, but she was able to get near enough to determine for certain that there was a troll riding in the wagon. He appeared to be a handsome troll, from Chirre's perspective, and a troll she had never seen before. The troll was lying down in the wagon, which greatly puzzled Chirre. Was he asleep? Had people given him a potion to put him to sleep? Was he dead? Was he being kidnapped? Where were the men driving the horse-drawn cart taking him?

Careful to remain screened behind trees and bushes, Chirre followed the horse-drawn wagon carrying the supine wooden troll to find out where it would go. She didn't need to follow for very long before the wagon turned in at the gate of a fenced estate where a brick mansion was situated atop a grassy knoll overlooking a winding, fast-flowing stream. Chirre watched in fascination as the deliverymen unloaded the wooden troll from the wagon and stood it on a large flat rock near the mansion. Then she watched as the boy who lived at the estate played around the wooden troll, punching it and kicking it and tying ropes around various parts of it. Chirre had never in her life seen a human being act so strangely. And why did the troll just stand there doing nothing? Why didn't he fight back? Surely something extremely strange was at play here.

Chirre waited until the veil of darkness fell over the face of the Earth, then ventured all the way to the estate fence to have a closer look at the troll in the yard. Her excellent night vision allowed her to see that the troll in the yard was even more handsome than he had appeared to be from a greater distance, and her heart fluttered with instant love.

Suddenly a door of the mansion opened and part of the yard was illuminated by a lantern held by a young man emerging from the house with three other people—his wife and a couple visiting that night. The four people walked to the troll statue and stood there admiring it.

"You would hardly know it was made of wood, if you didn't know, would you?" one of the women remarked.

"The woodcarver certainly did a wonderful job," the man holding the lantern said. "Of course, it's mainly a toy for Nils. Look at that nose, would you! And those arms!" He and the others laughed at the troll's features and made more comments about how the woodcarver had captured the charming ugliness of trolls.

Wood?! Chirre said to herself. The troll was made of wood? A woodcarver had carved it? As the people returned to the mansion Chirre fled to the safety of the forest and looked at the wooden troll from a distance. She had felt love when viewing the wooden troll from a relatively close distance. How could people laugh at the troll and say such nasty things about it?

While her anger over what she had overheard simmered, a freezing drizzle began, for fall gripped the countryside and winter's icy fingers were already reaching out to stroke the skin of a new season. The more Chirre thought about the wooden troll left outside in the freezing drizzle at a place where people laughed at it derisively, and a little boy mistreated it, the angrier she became. From her perspective, people such as that didn't deserve to have a troll statue. While the troll may have been carved from wood, Chirre couldn't escape the fact that she loved the troll all the same, nor the feeling that the wooden troll belonged with trolls, not with people. She resolved she would rescue the wooden troll from the clutches of people.

When she told Ekre and Ullda, who were married to each other, about what she had seen, and about her desire to rescue the wooden troll, Ekre and Ullda agreed to go with her that night to help her take the wooden troll from people.

Fog almost as thick as whipped cream was spread over the ground that night, giving the three trolls a welcome protective cover for their daring rescue attempt. Chirre, Ekre and Ullda made their way down the mountainside, crossed fields, and snuck up close to the mansion where the wooden troll stood in the yard. Unable to contain her love, Chirre hugged the wooden troll and kissed one of its cheeks as tears of happiness welled in her eyes at the realization that she and her friends were actually taking the troll away from people, where he didn't belong, and home with them, where he belonged.

As Chirre's lips touched his cheek the wooden troll suddenly was no longer an immobile wood carving but a flesh and blood troll who could move and speak and feel. Chirre's great love had brought him to life, and this magical development made Chirre deliriously happy.

All four of the trolls ran for the forest, where the troll carved by a woodcarver was as free as any other troll. Before long he acquired a name, Tosnak, and came to love Chirre as much as she loved him. The two were married and lived a long, happy life together, and Tosnak was always particularly fond of carved wooden objects.

81 ▪ Another River To Cross

In exchange for more food from him, Snozzle allowed Brine to sleep under his bridge for one day. Given that Snozzle was a voracious eater, that bargain depleted Brine's food supply more rapidly than he had expected and left him in need of more food to maintain the level of energy necessary to complete the journey he was on. He had no idea how many more days he would have to walk to reach the sea, but he was as determined as ever to reach it, even though the dream-image of a magnificent fjord that inspired him to make the journey was by now but a foggy memory, like a picture bleached by sunlight to such a degree that it was faint and whispery. Luckily for Brine, autumn was the best season of the year to find food; it was everywhere, practically, if one knew where to look. As a well-trained troll, Brine knew where to look, and how to take things he found without being found out or disturbed. He came upon quite a few objects he normally would have taken—non-food items—while gathering food and left them behind, though it often pained him to do so, because even with his great troll strength he didn't want to carry the extra weight for he wasn't sure how long. And so his journey continued, as he made steady progress each night, found somewhere to sleep each day and ate well on what he managed to find and take along the way.

Toward morning the night he left Snozzle's bridge he happened upon an elevated salt block in a field. This was akin to a chocoholic with a breadboard-size block of chocolate. Brine licked at the salt block for a half-hour, until he rubbed his tongue almost raw and felt as thirsty for water as a large river drinking in the current of feeder streams. After gulping down what remained in his water jar, which was slightly more than half full, his thirst was not close to being satisfied, so he set out in search of a river, a lake, a spring, a well, or whatever source of drinking water he could find. Twenty minutes of walking brought him to the edge of a stream, where he scooped water directly into his mouth for a while before he realized it would be easier to drink water from a jar, since he had one.

Rivers and streams were as plentiful as wrinkles on Old Fungus's skin. While the streams were easy to cross, the rivers offered more of a challenge, particularly given that Brine, like all trolls, could not swim. That inability to swim is one of the reasons trolls are averse to taking baths, even a bath in the form of a river soaking. Of course, that disinclination to bathe is due mainly to indifference and natural slovenliness. Brine wondered how much further he would had needed to walk to find a safe crossing point it he hadn't happened upon Snozzle's old, deteriorated bridge. It wasn't simply his imagination that the farther he walked the more rivers he encountered that were difficult to cross, for he had entered a region where the mountains were steeper and the rivers that ran down them more tumbling, turbulent and intimidating. The mountains he then traversed also had more bare rock and less vegetative cover than his home mountain, Troll Mountain. While he took note of that fact, he didn't understand that indicated he was closer to reaching his goal.

As he came to another wide river, in the deepest recess of the night, he groaned with weariness, not so much because he was up against another landscape barrier that would cost him travel time as that the stretch of river before him presented a dangerous crossing point, which meant he again would have to choose between heading either upstream or downstream to try to find a better place to cross. He hated these headache-inducing decisions more and more all the time; each new upstream-or-downstream option seemed more difficult than the last until by this time the need for a decision nearly paralyzed his mind.

This time he decided to head downstream, for no particular reason; there was no logic, or even intuition, involved. The river sang its flowing rhythm as Brine followed the river's edge as closely as possible, while arcing around patches of brush and boggy areas. He came to a tiered waterfall, where the river tumbled over four rock cliffs and thundered with gravity's harmony, and wondered if he had made the wrong decision to walk downstream, and if he would ever find a place to cross, for the river flared wider and grew wilder beneath the falls. Nevertheless, he continued his downstream exploration.

Twenty minutes downstream of the tiered waterfall he came to a rock-strewn rapids where the river appeared to be shallower than anywhere else he had seen. Protruding rocks extended all the way across the river, from bank to bank, and Brine tried to plot out, in his mind, how he might be able to step and leap from one rock to another to reach the other side. Given the kinetic briskness of the current, he knew it would be a dangerous risk to try to walk across the river, even if the water was no deeper than chest-high in the middle, and for all he knew it might be quite a bit deeper than that. Judging by the roar ahead, there was either another waterfall or a humongous rapids a short distance downstream. This rock-step route appeared to be the best crossing point Brine was likely to find, unless he continued walking downstream for who knew how long. So with a larger-than-usual knot of nervousness in his stomach he steeled himself and jumped from the bank to a flat-topped rock three feet from shore, gained good balance there, then stepped to two smaller rocks, with one foot on each rock, and on to another larger rock. On he went, stepping and jumping from rock to rock, wobbling and swaying now and then before regaining his balance. It occurred to him that the crossing would have been easier if he had a long, stout stick to help balance himself. But he wasn't about to return to the shore he had left to look for one at that point.

Slightly more than halfway across he leaped to a wet, moss-covered rock from four feet away, with his right foot first, then his left foot, and found himself tottering like an off-balance tightrope walker. His feet slipped, his arms flailed, and he found himself falling headfirst toward the swift, foamy current. . .

82 ▪ The Promise

This is the next tale Anders read to Andrew from *A Treasury of Troll Tales*—a tale entitled *The Promise*:

▪

Einer Soderbeck was cutting firewood in a far-off parcel of woods one day when his axe glanced off a knot in a tree he was chopping down and opened a nasty gash on the calf of his left leg. As he was tending to that severe cut, trying to stench the bleeding, a gust of wind toppled the twenty-inch-diameter tree he had been working on. The tree crashed to the ground, with the trunk landing across Einer's upper legs, pinning him to the ground. As hard as he tried, he couldn't budge the heavy tree trunk a single inch. And as much as he shouted for help, no one heard his plaintive cries.

Einer remained in this predicament for three days, without food and water the entire time, for he was unable to reach the food he had brought to the forest for a lunch. Without food and water, he grew weaker each day. Dehydration made him hallucinate. He was losing hope that his life would be saved. He feared he would die where he was, trapped beneath a fallen tree.

As if in a dream, he at last heard voices. Forcing the grogginess from his brain, he raised his head and started shouting—as much as he could shout in his weakened condition—the word "Help!". The plea trailed off mid-word, though, for Einer saw not people but a family of grotesque trolls approaching—a father troll, a mother troll, and a baby troll. He watched as the trolls drew nearer.

"My, my, look what we have here!" the father troll said. "It looks like you had a little accident," he said to Einer.

"You have to help me," Einer said. "Try to get the tree off of me."

"Don't do a thing to help him," the mother troll said to her husband. "What have human beings ever done for us? Do you think that he would help one of us if we were in the same situation? Not on your life!"

The father troll spotted the finely honed axe lying on the ground several feet from Einer. "Look at that shiny axe!" he said, his eyes widening to the size of saucers. "I could sure use an axe like that. I think I'll take it."

"And look—he has food too!" the mother troll said, pawing through Einer's three-day-old lunch.

"Please give me a drink of water," Einer said. "I've been trapped here for three days and haven't had anything to eat or drink in all that time."

The troll woman sampled some of Einer's food and handed some to her husband. As much as Einer pleaded for help, the trolls paid him no more attention than they would have a grasshopper. Instead of helping Einer, the trolls searched the pockets of his clothing and took the few items they found there. Then they started removing his boots, intending to take those as well.

"Please help me!" Einer pleaded. "I'll die if you leave me here! I'll do anything to repay you if only you'll free me from under this tree."

That statement caught the troll woman's attention. "Do you have a wife?" she asked Einer.

"Yes, I have a wife and two children," Einer told her, hoping that fact might elicit a spark of sympathy from her. "I'm sure my wife must be sick with worry about me."

The troll woman took her husband aside to speak with him out of Einer's earshot. After a minute the two trolls walked back over to Einer and presented a proposal. "We have decided that we will move the tree off of you if you will make us a promise," the troll woman said.

"Anything!" Einer said, his heart racing with excitement. "If it is in my power to give you what you want I will give you what you want, I promise you."

"This is something well within your power to give us," the troll woman said.

"What is it you want?" Einer asked.

"We want you," the troll woman said, "to take our baby and raise it as your own. We want our baby to live as human beings live. We want our baby to have a better life than the life that awaits him as a troll."

Einer hadn't anticipated such a strange request. The thought of raising a troll baby, and then a troll child, made his skin crawl.

"Do you think that you could bear to give up your child?" Einer asked, hoping to make the trolls reconsider.

"It is what would be best for him," the troll woman said. "We want him to have the best life possible. Will you promise us this—that you will raise our baby as your own child if we set you free?"

Einer swallowed hard. He was in no position to try to bargain with the trolls. Given that no person had crossed his path in three days, it seemed unlikely anyone would find him anytime soon if the trolls did not free him. As he saw it, he would be left there to die unless he agreed to the trolls' condition. It seemed an either/or choice to him, and he didn't want to die.

"You have my promise," he said.

Immediately the trolls, who of course are much stronger than humans, lifted the trunk of the large tree off of Einer, gave him food and water, and helped nurse him back toward health. Einer then kept his word by taking the baby troll home with him.

Einer and his wife cared for the baby troll as if he were their own, even though the baby seemed to grow uglier by the day and the two of them couldn't look at the baby without cringing. By the time the troll child was six years old Einer wished that he had chosen to die in the woods rather than promise to raise a troll child. There were times when the sight of the troll child made him so queasy that he couldn't even eat. He hated the troll child as he had never before hated anything. He knew he could never grow to love this child. He knew his loathing for the child would only intensify as the child grew older. He also knew his loathing for the troll child was making him a bitter man who was starting to have contempt for even his wife and his two human children. He began to rationalize that the promise he made to the troll couple to raise their baby shouldn't be binding because he made the promise under duress. He began to tell himself that a person did not need to keep a promise to trolls because trolls do not have the same moral and ethical code human beings have, and that the situation had changed now that the troll baby was a troll child.

One day Einer took the six-year-old troll child fishing with him. They fished in a section of a river where the water was deep and a boulder-strewn rapids presented a hazard. The troll child drowned that day. Einer told everyone it was an accidental drowning, but it wasn't. Einer pushed the child off a bridge and into the rock-strewn rapids and the little troll died.

Einer wasn't the least bit sorry about what he had done, though—not at first, at any rate. When the melons and gourds in his garden all grew into the likeness of the troll child's head, though, or so they appeared to Einer, Einer was frightened as to what it meant. That's when guilt began creeping in. As quickly as the melons and gourds grew, Einer stacked them on a wagon, carried them some distance from his farm, and hurled them into a ravine. Week after week, new melons and gourds appeared on the vines in his garden, all of them resembling the head of the troll child he pushed to his death. Einer couldn't escape thinking about what he had done. He couldn't go into his garden without having to face the dark secret of his tormented soul.

He knew he could no longer stay where the troll child had lived, knowing his guilt would overwhelm him there, so he and his family fled the farm he had worked so hard to develop into something productive and protective. And while he managed to get away from ghostly gourds and morbib melons by moving, guilt clung to him like a birthmark.

Einer came to understand that when a person makes a promise to someone else he makes a promise to himself at the same time. He learned that when someone breaks a promise he makes to someone else he also breaks a promise to himself, which is even a more solumn pledge. He learned that while trolls may have a looser moral code than human beings have, even a promise made to trolls should be kept because a promise is alwlays first and foremost a promise to oneself. He learned that breaking that promise to oneself is what haunts a person the most.

83 ▪ Twists Of Fate

Unable to regain his balance as he wobbled on the rock, Brine tumbled face-first toward another large rock, this one jagged as a shark's teeth. Instinctively, he thrust out his left arm so that his face wouldn't be the part of his body to smash into the rock first. By pushing against the rock as his arm hit it he was able to prevent his head from hitting the rock at all. That maneuver did cause him to roll in the river, though, and various parts of his body hit various rocks, resulting in numerous bruises and punctures. Luckily, he didn't seem to have any broken bones, at least any major ones, for he managed to stand in the river and hold his own against the powerful current as he regained his bearings and figured out which shore he had started from and which one he was headed for. The water reached his chin where he stood, and the current ran deep, so there was a terrific force against his legs and his body. Once oriented correctly, he knew his only hope of reaching the other side of the river was to walk, rather than try to climb onto a rock and continue his rock walk. And so he started moving his feet along the bottom of the river. He quickly discovered it was more difficult to hold his own against the current when he lifted a foot than when he stood still, so he adjusted his foot movements to a shuffle. Even at that, the current swept him downstream a bit as he shuffled along slowly. As he advanced toward the shore, at little more than a snail's pace, the water became shallower and the force of the current diminished. Still, he was pretty much exhausted by the time he pulled himself up onto the riverbank and flopped on his back in long grass, breathing heavily and glad to be alive, for he understood that if he had cracked his head on the jagged rock he easily could have been knocked unconscious and drowned. He didn't even want to think about that narrow escape, so he let his mind go blank, which is something trolls are able to do far more easily than most human beings, with their intellectual superiority and restlessness, are able to manage.

After resting for a half-hour he continued on his journey while wishing he were back at Troll Mountain with other trolls, dry and content. Wet and bruised and battered, as he was, this was his longest night, in terms of being uncomfortable, forlorn and lonely. His soaked clothes seemed to grow heavier on him with each step he took, and some of his many bruises and wounds ached more by the minute.

He hurt so much that he stopped walking far earlier in the morning than he generally did when he came upon a place in the forest that seemed to be a good place to sleep that day. He needed sleep more than anything else at the time. While sleep worked wonders for him as far as recovering his strength and lessening his pain, he was unlucky that the sky remained overcast the entire day, so there was no sunshine to dry his wet clothes. The extra clothes he carried in his burlap sack were of course soaked as well, so he had to wear wet clothes, which made the air temperature seem quite a bit chillier than it actually was to someone wearing dry clothes.

That night, having slept more than twelve hours and gobbled up much of his remaining food before setting out again, his luck began to turn. He came upon another horse to borrow, without the owner's knowledge or consent, and gained back some of the distance he had lost the previous night by riding the horse for a couple of hours. As with the other horse he borrowed earlier on his journey, this horse fled when Brine stopped for a break and neglected to tie up the horse. His attempt to call back the horse was futile, so he spat curses at the horse, and his bad luck, and went on alone, on foot.

A couple hours of walking found him at an attractive farm where there seemingly was no nuisance of a dog—unless, perhaps, it was sleeping in the farmhouse—and outbuildings were situated well away from the house, which trolls like. Brine slithered about in the darkness, investigating each building, large and small, except for the house, with the intention of restocking his food supply. And what a supply of food he found—dried sausage, smoked fish, cheese, potatoes, beets, carrots, cabbage, apples, and other fare. He helped himself to enough food to eat well for the next week, as well as a tan winter coat, and set off down a wagon path that led away from the buildings—in the opposite direction from which he approached the farm, that is.

That wagon path was about one-third of a mile long, ending at the shore of a large lake. Brine looked both left and right and couldn't see land in either direction. There was land straight ahead, but it was barely visible in the dark, even for a troll. He wondered if he had reached a fjord. Had he reached his goal? While this body of water didn't look like the fjord in his dream, or fjords as Llop sketchily described to him, for there were no steep-walled cliffs on its banks, he supposed there might be different sorts of fjords. He thought there might be cliffs he couldn't see from where he was standing. If this was only a large lake, and not a fjord, being at the spot where he was was as confounding as running into a wide river and not knowing whether it was best to walk upstream or downstream—and even more difficult to cross to the other side. Brine wondered how far he would have to walk to get around the lake, if it was a lake. He had no idea. Nor did he have any idea whether it would be a shorter distance to the left or to the right. As he swept his head from side to side, looking left and right and trying to determine which direction to take, he glimpsed a bulky object in tall weeds about thirty feet off to his left. Curious as to what the object was, he walked toward it. Halfway to it he realized it was a turned-over rowboat. Excited by the discovery, he ran toward it and touched it, as though the boat was a sacred object. He knew a boat wouldn't do him much good without oars, though, and he couldn't see any oars. Flipping the boat over with one hand, so that the bottom of the boat was on the ground, he discovered a pair of oars on the ground where the overturned rowboat had been. Eureka! That meant he could row the boat across the water. While he hadn't rowed a boat in many years, he *had* done it, so he knew he could do it.

Brine soon had the rowboat on the water, and was soon seated on the middle seat. It took him some time to figure out how the oars should be placed in the oarlocks, and how to work the oars, but before long he was headed across the large, glassy lake in his borrowed boat. While his rowing strokes were far from efficient—indeed, he never figured out that a synchronicity of movement between the two oars produced the best results—he was able to row the boat all the way across the lake, his path decidedly a "drunken sailor's" erratic path if there ever was one.

84 ▪ The Fisherman And The Trolls

Anders scoured the book's table of contents for a considerable period of time, looking for tales he had not yet read to his
son, and wondering whether or not he had read some of them,
when his eyes fell upon the title *The Fisherman And The Trolls.*
He couldn't remember reading that one to Andrew, and Andrew
couldn't remember hearing it, so they settled on this one as their
tale for the evening.

▪

Once there was a fisherman named Olaf who lived with his
wife and five children in a remote house beside a long fjord.
One late-summer morning Olaf discovered two of his chickens
were missing. The next morning half of the vegetables in his
garden had disappeared. Two mornings later he found that his
best cow had been stolen during the night.

That night he was awakened in his upstairs bedroom by
noises downstairs. Fearing that the burglar, or burglars, had
returned, and were in his house, Olaf slipped out of bed and crept
slowly down the stairway, stopping on each step to listen. He
knew someone was downstairs all right, for he heard voices and
other sounds—sounds people make when they move. Halfway
down the stairs, he called out as forcefully as he could: "Who's
down there?" The sounds ceased. "Who's down there, I say?"
Olaf demanded. "You better leave right now, whoever you are.
I've got a gun, and I'll shoot!"

Enraged by the audacity of the crooks, Olaf charged down the
remainder of the stairway, took down his rifle from its hanging
place in the parlor and started loading the gun. There was a
commotion in the kitchen as Olaf readied his rifle. Once he had
the gun loaded with bullets he strode into the kitchen, which he
found empty. The outside kitchen door was wide open, though.

Looking through the door opening, Olaf saw two bulbously featured figures, illuminated by a half moon, running outside. If the two figures weren't trolls, he thought, then fish don't like to swim.

Bracing his body against the frame of the open door, Olaf fired at the two trolls—or what he felt certain were trolls—just as they were about to round the corner of the barn. They were already behind the barn, out of sight, when he fired a second shot, more to scare them than hit them.

"I'll be waiting for you next time!" Olaf shouted into the darkness.

After reloading his rifle, he went outside to have a look around, to make sure the trolls were gone. With lantern light, he could see that the trolls' footprints led away from his property.

That was the last of the nighttime raids.

A year later Olaf was bringing his boat ashore after a day's fishing when all at once he was surprised to see two trolls—a male troll and a female troll—near his landing area. The male troll carried a sack that sagged with heavy objects that clinked when he tugged on the sack to balance it better on a shoulder.

"Could you carry us to the other side of the fjord in your boat?" the male troll said. "We're willing to give you something for your trouble."

"I'm afraid I'm awfully tired," Olaf said, wanting to avoid becoming involved with trolls in any way. "I've been out rowing all day, for I went a long ways away to fish today."

"We would give you this if you would take us across," the male troll said, holding up a copper amulet of a Viking ship.

"Let me see that," Olaf said.

"I'll show it to you," the troll said as Olaf took a couple of steps in his direction, "but I can't let you touch it unless you agree to give us a ride to the other side of the fjord."

Olaf took a good look at the amulet. It was exactly like one stolen from his house the night he chased away the two trolls—quite possibly these very two trolls.

"I bet this is something a fisherman like you would like to have, isn't it?" the troll said, with as much silvertongued enticement as he could muster.

"That *is* mine!" Olaf roared. "You stole it from my house a year ago. And now you're going to give it back!"

"That's what you think!" the male troll thundered back as Olaf snatched at the amulet and grabbed the troll's arm as he tried to wrestle away the stolen trinket. The troll pushed him away and slipped the amulet back into his bag as Olaf charged at him like a battering ram. With one mighty uppercut of his right forearm, the troll laid Olaf out cold.

When Olaf regained consciousness the trolls were nowhere in sight. He had a swollen jaw, a hammering headache, and a metallic taste in his mouth. Luckily, his boat was still there; at least the trolls hadn't taken that. He had tied his boat to a tree before his encounter with the trolls, and obviously the trolls had been unable to untie the intricate knot, if they had tried to do so. Losing his boat would have been almost as devastating as losing a leg. Not only was the boat necessary for him to make a living, but the boat was almost as precious to him as a child, for he built the boat with his own hands, lovingly and painstakingly.

Fearing the trolls *would* return and try to steal the boat, that night Olaf tied the boat to bolders with metal chains, and used locks to tie the chains together for extra security.

In the morning, when he carried his fishing gear to the landing area to go out fishing for the day, those chains secured nothing more than a heap of hot ashes and some charred boards. Olaf was as sure the trolls had burned his boat as he was that the fjord he fished in led to the ocean.

Olaf and his family lived through thin times for several weeks while Olaf built himself a new boat, as fine a craft, and as lovingly constructed, as the other.

About a year later Olaf was fishing far up the fjord one day, more than two miles from home, when two trolls appeared on the shore near where he was. Olaf knew immediately this was the same troll couple that had burglarized him several times and burned his boat.

"How would you like to earn some easy money?" the male troll called out to Olaf.

Olaf rowed closer to shore. "Doing what?" he asked.

"By taking us across the fjord in your boat," the troll answered. "It takes far too long to walk all the way around the fjord. We'll give you these coins if you will take us across." He displayed a palmful of coins to Olaf, who rowed still closer to shore.

Olaf felt like pummeling the two trolls for what they did to him in the past, particularly for burning his beloved boat. If he had had a gun along he might have shot them both on the spot. He didn't have a gun with him, though. And he knew he was no match for the trolls, even the female troll, in a physical fight, as strong as they were. Still, he couldn't let this opportunity for revenge pass without taking advantage of it. The trolls seemed not to recognize him. He was more than two miles from home, after all, so they probably didn't expect to see him there. And the large brimmed hat he wore shadowed his face. Suddenly, a scheme filled his mind. It was all he could do to refrain from chortling, the scheme seemed so clever, if only he could pull it off. And he was confident he could, for he knew how gullible trolls are.

"That seems like a good deal," Olaf said to the trolls. "Sure, I'll give you a lift to the other side."

Olaf brought his boat very near to the shore to allow the two trolls to climb in. The male troll still carried the same sack, which still clanked when the sack swayed.

"This is awful kind of you," the male troll said as Olaf pulled the boat out into deeper water.

"I'm happy to do it for that much money," Olaf said, careful to keep his face concealed by his hat lest the trolls should recognize him and either suspect something shady was afoot or attack him again. As long as they believed he was doing what they asked he didn't think they would harm him.

Noticing that Olaf wasn't rowing straight across the fjord, the female troll said, "Why aren't you taking us straight across? That's where we want to go." She pointed to the nearest spot on the opposite shore for emphasis.

"There's nowhere to pull close to the shore there," Olaf said. "It's too dangerous. We have to go across at an angle to find a safe place to pull in."

That explanation seemed to satisfy the two trolls, who sat back and said nothing the rest of the ride. After nearly a half-hour of rowing Olaf steered the bow of his boat onto a gravel beach to allow the two trolls to step out.

"Where's my money?" Olaf asked as the trolls started walking away.

"What money?" the male troll growled. "We didn't promise you any money."

"You mean you're not going to honor your promise?" Olaf said.

"There was no promise, we tell you!" the male troll growled again. "Be gone with you or we'll give you a beating and take your boat."

Olaf wasn't about to press his luck. He pushed his boat away from the landing and started pumping the oars as fast as he could to get as far away from the trolls as quickly as possible.

The two trolls laughed at Olaf as he made his hasty retreat. Olaf, though, allowed himself to smile now, and then to laugh when he knew the trolls could not hear him, for he felt certain it would be a long, long time before the two trolls managed to get off that desolate, uninhabited island, if they ever did.

85 ▪ Cheese And Chocolate

Jirik sniffed the air. "Do you smell that?" he asked his two companions, Gangl and Scurf.

The other two sniffed as well, almost as loudly as pigs snorting, as determinedably as dogs on the trail of a scent. "It's food," Gangl said, "but I can't tell for sure what it is."

"It smells good, whatever it is," Scurf said.

"It's coming from that direction," Jirik said, pointing with one of his slender fingers and starting to walk in that direction as the two others followed the younger troll. The three were at a farm, looking for food and treasure, which is to say anything trolls would regard as treasure, though humans may not necessarily value the objects as highly.

"I know I've smelled that smell before," Gangl said. "You know what I think it might be? I think it might be cheese."

"Cheese!" the other two chirped in unison. Most trolls love cheese, and few have the opportunity to eat as much of it as they would like to eat.

"I think it might be," Gangl repeated.

"I hope you're right!" Scurf said. "The smell is getting stronger, whatever it is."

Following their noses, the three trolls came to a small hill, where the odor was quite strong. "The smell almost seems to be coming from inside the hill," Jirik observed. "How can that be? How can a hill smell so good, like food?"

"Look! A door!" Gangl said to the other two, having ventured ahead a bit to see what was around a corner. "Maybe it's some sort of cave," he went on as Jirik and Scurf joined him.

"A cave?" Jirik said. "You think so? It must be a pretty small cave if it is one."

"Let's have a look," Gangl said, taking the lead role in this investigation. Having discovered the door, he thought that was appropriate. Anyway, Jirik was younger and Scurf wasn't as smart as he was, he thought, so it seemed natural and right to him that he would act as leader. "I don't see any lock. I don't think the door is locked; I think we can just walk right in."

Which is what the three trolls did after Gangl pushed open the door of the small hillside cave and the pungent odor of aging cheese blasted them like a gust of wind.

"It *is* cheese!" Gangl said in a triumphant tone, having had his guess confirmed. "More cheese than I've ever seen in one place in my life!"

Indeed, the three trolls could not have raided a better farm to find cheese. They had happened upon a motherlode of the delicacy, for the owners of this farm made cheese not only for themselves but also to sell to neighbors and several stores. The small cave was crammed with shelves of aging cheese wheels, from floor to ceiling, all the way around the walls as well as in the middle of the cave. While the trolls experienced the redolent emanation as one odor, cheese afficianadoes would have detected a dozen subtly different odors, for the cave held a dozen varieties of cheese.

"Just look at it!" Scurf marveled.

"Smell it!" Jirik said, breathing in the odor as some people do fresh air after spending hours in a stuffy building.

"I'm going to eat some!" Gangl said, breaking a piece from a nearby wheel of cheese with a pinch of a thumb and index finger and stuffing it into his mouth. Following his lead, Jirik and Scurf broke off pieces and ate as well.

"I bet this is the good luck I had coming for seeing a large white buck," Scurf said. "Do you think so?"

Busy eating, and moaning with delight, the two others ignored Scurf's question, if they heard it at all.

The three trolls feasted on several wheels of cheese, unaware that the cheese they were eating was not yet aged to its prime taste point, before they started stuffing some of the wheels into their sacks to carry home. They took note of various landscape features on the walk back in the hope they would be able to find this particular farm, and its cheese cave, again.

At the same time Jirik, Gangl and Scurf were at the cheese cave, Ort and Haar were making quite a delightful discovery of their own, at a lakeside property many miles away. Like the others, Ort and Haar made their discovery through scent. In this case the odor was chocolate. People had made chocolate fudge and chocolate brownies and left the fudge and the brownies on a porch to cool overnight. Naturally, trolls hold chocolate in even higher regard than they do cheese. And chocolate being an even rarer treat, Ort and Haar weren't about to pass up the opportunity to take some fudge and some brownies. Ort did the actual taking as Haar hid himself a hundred feet away to act as a lookout. The two were so atwitter at finding chocolate that they forgot about trying to find anything else at that place. They took the fudge and the brownies off a ways and ate some when a thought occurred to Ort.

"We better not eat too much of it," he said to Haar. "We better save it for the wedding. This stuff will be perfect to have at the wedding feast."

Ort's grandson, Rott, was to marry Tala, Kravig's daughter. The stormy night they spent together at Guggle's shack of a cabin had lit a romantic flame between the two, and Rott had courted Tala since that night. Tala had recently agreed to be Rott's wife, so there was to be a wedding. The wedding was to take place soon, but it was not yet scheduled for any particular day—or, more accurately, night, for of course the wedding would be held at night, as most troll activities occur at night. While not exactly spontaneous, troll weddings are not the long-planned and long-anticipated events people plan when they marry. Once two trolls decide to marry each other a wedding generally takes place in short order. Once Guggle, who would preside at the wedding, did what preparation work she needed to do the wedding would take place within a day or two.

86 ▪ The Shepherd's Stone

On this particular evening Anders selected a tale entitled *The Shepherd's Stone* to read to Andrew.

▪

When two sheep strayed from a flock and wandered into the edge of a forest, the young shepherd tending the flock, Lars, left his two dogs to control the flock and went off to retrieve the two stray sheep.

A troll named Dorak happened to come upon the two stray sheep as they wandered in the woods. "My, my, what have we here?" Dorak said, licking his thick lips with his thick, coarse tongue. "Two little lost sheep that I can take home for myself," he said, answering his own question. Then the troll found a whip-like branch and began driving the sheep back to his mountain cave.

It wasn't long before Lars heard the troll and the two sheep moving through the forest. Running to where they were, he said to the troll, "I see that you found my sheep."

"*Your* sheep?!" Dorak said. "What do you mean *your* sheep? These are *my* sheep."

"But these two sheep strayed from my flock," Lars insisted. "I've been looking for them."

"I'm afraid you're mistaken," the troll said. "If you lost two sheep they must be somewhere else. These two are *my* sheep, I tell you."

"But I'm sure these are mine," Lars said. "A shepherd always knows his own sheep."

"It seems to me that it is a poor shepherd who would lose his sheep in the first place," the troll said with a sneer. "It seems to me that a shepherd who would lose any of his sheep is not a good enough shepherd to know what sheep are his and what are not."

"I must insist that you give me back these two sheep," Lars said bravely, for he knew trolls are tremendously stronger than humans.

"And what if I don't?" Dorak challenged.

That was a good question, Lars admitted to himself. He knew he had no chance of getting the sheep back through physical force, for it is well known that the average troll is seven times stronger than the average human. It is also well known, of course, that trolls are greedy and gullible. Lars knew he would need to use cunning, to take advantage of the troll's greed and gullibility, in order to take back the two sheep. Thinking fast, he hit upon a scheme.

"I have an idea," he said to the troll. "Since I say these two sheep belong to me and you insist they belong to you, I propose we settle the matter with a contest of strength. Both of us will squeeze a stone, and whichever one of us squeezes more water from the stone wins the contest. If I win I get to take these two sheep. If you win you get to keep these two sheep and I will also give you two others from my flock. Are you willing to agree to that?"

Dorak looked the slight young shepherd up and down. "You are a fool to propose such a contest," he said. "It is not possible you could win any contest of strength against me. If you want to do that, though, I will gladly agree to it."

"Fine," Lars said. "I'll let you go first. There are some nice white stones right over there that will do nicely."

Lars and the troll went over to where a number of stones lay scattered about. Lars selected one of them and handed it to the troll, saying, "Here, let's see how much water you can squeeze out of this."

The troll took the stone and squeezed it with his powerful, leathery hands. He grimaced and grunted as he managed to squeeze out three drops of water. As Lars watched, he slipped an oblong-shaped white cheese from his knapsack and placed it on the ground without the troll noticing. When it was his turn, Lars picked up the cheese and squeezed it between his hands for all he was worth. Liquid squirted out in every direction, with some even pelting the troll in an eye.

"It looks like I'm the clear winner," Lars said. "I squeezed out much more water than you did. I'll be taking my two sheep back to my flock now."

"What if I still refuse to give them to you?" the troll said defiantly, for as a rule trolls are anything but gracious losers.

"In that case," Lars said, "I'm afraid I would be forced to squeeze your head just like I squeezed water from this stone."

"No, no, don't do that!" the troll pleaded. "You can have the sheep. I'm leaving."

With that, the troll quickly departed and Lars escorted the two sheep back to rejoin the rest of the flock.

87 ▪ Bergthor Of Black Mountain

Brine trudged on, not knowing how far he had traveled from Troll Mountain, or how near he was to reaching the sea, or even if he was still headed in the right direction. Rather remarkably, perhaps, his journey had followed a fairly straight course, given the landscape barriers such as lakes, rivers, swamps, mountains and other features he had to either cross or get around, and the fact that he had no map, compass or specific directions to help guide him, only Llop's vague shared knowledge to head in the direction where the sun set. Which is what he had been careful to try to do. And that simple strategy had served him well, for by this time he was within a night's walk of the sea, with its long series of coastal fjords reaching inland like hundreds of extended fingers of a giant hand. Being clueless about how near he was, though, he felt exhausted rather than exhilarated that his goal was close at hand.

He had been through a lot. Nearly every person—every human being—would have looked back at the journey and thought of it as an unfinished adventure. Most trolls don't think in those terms, though, and Brine was like most trolls in this regard. Trolls think in utilitarian terms, concerned mainly with the here and the now, not the past or the future. Brine no more thought of his journey as an adventure than commuters think of their daily commutes as adventures. He was simply taking actions to try to reach a goal, no more or no less. Adventure was as far from his mind as the appreciation of art, literature and music. So while he was having quite an adventure, to him the journey was no more exciting or stimulating than normal day to day life had been before he left Troll Mountain.

Brine reached the foot of Black Mountain as dawn drew near one morning. He didn't know the name of the mountain, of course, or know the sea was visible from its upper sections. With dawn approaching, it was time to look for a place to sleep for the day, so he started hiking up the mountain in search of a safe, dark, comfortable spot. To his delight, he happened upon the entrance to a cave in barely more than an hour's time. While the average person would have been hard-pressed to spot the small cave entrance, trolls, with their vast experience with caves, have the ability to detect such things. Entering the cave cautiously, Brine was even more delighted to discover that the cave was roomy, smooth, and just the right temperature for sleeping. Indeed, it was one of the best places Brine had found for sleeping on his entire journey. So after devouring some food he quickly curled up in a rounded corner and fell asleep, unaware of the famous tale associated with another cave on Black Mountain.

■

A long, long time ago a troll named Bergthor married a wife and moved into a cave on Black Mountain. While people widely believed Bergthor was a skilled sorcerer, he was not malevolent by nature. Indeed, he was mild-mannered and harmless most of the time. The only time anyone had any reason to fear him was when he was provoked.

An old man and several servants lived on a farm near the foot of Black Mountain. One day Bergthor showed up at the farm and said to the old man: "When I die, I wish to be buried where I can hear the sound of running water. Therefore, if you promise to bury me beside the river that runs through your farm you may take what you find in the kettle beside my body as a reward."

"I would gladly make you that promise," the old farmer said, "but how am I to know when you die?"

"You will find my large staff standing at your cottage door as a sign of my death," Bergthor said, holding out his distinctive staff to let the farmer have a good look at it.

"In that case, you have my promise," the farmer said.

Several years later the farmer's servants were leaving the farmhouse early one morning when they noticed a large wooden staff leaning against the house, near the door. The servants took the staff inside the house and showed it to the farmer, who recognized it as Bergthor's the instant he saw it.

Knowing this meant Bergthor had died, the farmer ordered a few of his men to construct a large coffin. He and those servants then rode up onto Black Mountain until they found Bergthor's cave. Inside the cave, they found Bergthor lying dead. They brought the coffin inside and lifted the body into it, all of them amazed by how light the large corpse seemed to be. With Bergthor's promised reward on his mind, the farmer looked for a large kettle, which he found next to Bergthor's bed. With his hands shaking with excitement, the old farmer lifted the lid off the kettle, expecting the kettle to be full of gold and other treasure. There was no gold in the kettle, though—or treasure of any sort. The kettle was filled with nothing but dry, dead leaves. The farmer frantically raked his hands through the dead leaves, hoping to find at least a few coins buried within the leaves. But he felt nothing but leaves. That made the farmer as angry as an enraged bull, for he believed the troll had lied to him. He was so insensed that he was tempted to leave Bergthor's body where it was and not bury it beside the river, as he had promised to do. Being he was a man dedicated to keeping his word, though, he felt obligated to honor his promise even if someone else did not honor a promise made to him.

Before the group left the cave one of the servants stuffed some of the dead leaves into his gloves to help insulate his hands, for there was a deep chill in the air and the man's gloves were thin and threadbare. When the group carrying the coffin stopped to rest, after going a good distance, the man who had stuffed leaves into his gloves removed his gloves and discovered the gloves were full of money rather than leaves.

"If the leaves turn into money there must be a fortune in that kettle!" the farmer said. "I have to go back and get them."

While three servants continued down the mountain with the coffin, the farmer and one servant backtracked up the mountain to retrieve the rest of the dead leaves. Search as they did, though, they found absolutely no trace of Bergthor's cave, much less the leaf-filled kettle. It was as though the cave had never existed. As darkness started falling the disappointed farmer abandoned hope and headed home. "What a fool I was," he said to the servant with him. "If only I had trusted that the old troll wouldn't cheat me I would be a rich man right now. Let that be a lesson: what you see is not alwlays what it seems to be."

88 ▪ A Talk And A Tale

Prickly snowflakes peppered the air as Ort and Tattra made their way toward Guggle's cabin. Winter was on the way, but it had not yet arrived. These snowflakes didn't constitute an actual snowstorm, as measured by North Country standards. Most of the snowflakes melted upon contact with the ground. Those that survived the landing produced nothing more than a patchy dusting of white.

Guggle was knitting in front of the fireplace when her visitors arrived and knocked at her cabin door.

"Well, well. Come in, come in," the witch said upon opening the door. "This is an unexpected surprise." Once Ort and Tattra settled into chairs and Guggle was back in her own chair she asked what brought them to her cottage this night, for while Ort paid an occasional visit it was unusual for Ort and Tattra to call on her together, so she suspected they were there for a specific, special purpose.

"We need you to do a wedding," Ort said, getting straight to the point.

"Ah, a wedding!" Guggle said, obviously pleased by the news. "And who's getting married?"

"Rott and Tala," Tattra informed her.

"Ah, I should have guessed!" Guggle said. "I had a feeling something might happen between the two when they came here for shelter one stormy night this past summer."

"That's when it all started," Tattra said. "That was the start of it."

"What's that?" Ort asked, unaware that Rott and Tala sought shelter with Guggle one stormy night. "What happened?" Guggle filled him in on what Tattra already knew.

Ort was at Guggle's cabin to ask her to preside at the wedding not because he was Rott's grandfather but because he was king of the tribe. As king, it was his responsibility to arrange such matters.

"Let's have the wedding tomorrow night," Guggle said, for it was pretty much up to her when the wedding would take place. "How does that sound?"

"Whenever you want," Ort said. "If you want it to be tomorrow night, then it will be tomorrow night."

"Fine," the witch responded. "The wedding will take place tomorrow night then. I must select the proper bones and the right potions."

"I and the others will prepare a feast," Tattra said, meaning her and the other female trolls.

"I think I'll get out my Viking goblet and use it in some fashion; I have to decide just how," Guggle said.

"I have a Viking helmet, you know," Ort said in a prideful tone.

"I know. You've showed it to me," Guggle said.

"Well, it's a rare thing to have a Viking helmet," Ort said with pride.

"Do you think Viking goblets grow on trees?" Guggle said. "Do you know anyone else who has a Viking goblet? Do you? It's one of my most prized possessions. You know, in a way I wish I had lived back in the Viking times. I've heard many tales about what Vikings did. Vikings thought more like trolls than people do these days. They took what they could get. You have to admire them for that."

"I wonder if trolls ever had much to do with the Vikings," Tattra pondered.

"Of course we did!" Guggle said. "There are tales about that. My favorite is the one about Semolina and the Vikings, maybe because Semonlina was a witch, like me."

"I don't think I've heard that one," Tattra said.

"You haven't?!" Guggle said, surprised. "Then I must tell it to you.

■

"Long, long ago, back in the Viking era, a band of Vikings got wind of a rumor that an elderly troll witch named Semolina had managed to amass a spectacular hoard of treasure. And, indeed, the rumor was true. Except for a few troll kings, Semolina was the wealthiest troll alive, in terms of treasure, much of which she acquired in payment for spells, potions, curses and other witchcraft. Other trolls, and people, were more than willing to give her objects of great beauty and great value for services she could provide.

"Vikings, of course, were attracted to treasure like bees are attracted to flowers. Indeed, their thirst for treasure was as great as a giant troll's appetite for food and drink. No matter how much treasure they acquired they always wanted more. They could never have enough treasure to be satisfied with what they had. And they were always ready and eager to travel as far as necessary to find and take treasure by whatever means necessary. So when this one particular band of Vikings heard about Semolina's hoard of treasure they were intent upon taking her treasure away from her and adding it to their own wealth of treasure, especially since they thought they could do so by staying in their own land rather than sailing to some far-off land, as they usually had to do. Semolina's treasure was all the more attractive to the band of Vikings in that it was believed Semolina lived by herself in a labyrinthine cave high on a steep cliff beside a certain fjord. To their way of thinking: How much could one old woman do to stop them from taking whatever they wanted to take, even if that woman was a witch with who knew what sort of magical powers, when ranks of palace guards, whole towns of angry men and organized soldiers hadn't been able to stop them elsewhere? It didn't matter to them in the least that they wanted to take things from an old woman; Viking warriors took whatever they could get from whoever they could get it from. That was their way. To them, whatever they wanted rightfully belonged to them, if they could get it, no matter who happened to have possession of it for the time being.

"And so the small band of Vikings, which consisted of seventeen men, set out up the seacoast in a longboat, with its high, pointed front, which looked like the neck and head of a horse, in search of the fjord where Semolina had her cave. It took them several days to find the right fjord, as they explored several long fjords without success and passed by the fjord where Semolina lived twice without realizing they were at Semolina's doorstep, so to speak, before two fishermen they happened upon told them exactly where they could find Semolina's cave.

"The band of Vikings swarmed into Semolina's cave, which had many pathways and chambers, in the evening, when Semolina was still asleep. She quickly woke up, though, as the Vikings probed every nook and cranny of the cave, making enough noise to wake a dead goat. All of the Vikings had long beards and long hair, and they carried big battle-axes and metal shields, and wore metal helmets on their heads. While Semolina had heard of Vikings, these were the first ones she had seen. She had no doubt they were Vikings, though, as soon as she saw one with a burning torch tromping toward her as she came out of her bedroom chamber, which was far back in the cave.

" 'What are you doing in my cave?' Semolina demanded. 'Be gone with you!' she said.

"The bearded Viking merely laughed at her and said, 'We're here to take your treasure. Try to stop us and we will kill you.' Then he turned and walked toward another part of the cave as Semolina followed him. She was about to kick the man from behind when three others appeared alongside the first one. Old as she was, Semolina knew she was stronger than any one of the Vikings, or possibly any two of them, but she knew she could not out-fight four of them, especially since they had heavy battle-axes and strong shields. And she could hear others in other parts of the cave, so she knew it would be useless to fight all of them.

"The Vikings ordered Semolina to go to the large front chamber of the cave, where she stored her food and cooked her meals. There two of the intruders guarded her while all of the others spread through all the other parts of the cave in search of the treasure. Semolina had hidden much of her treasure well, but Vikings were like bloodhounds when it came to finding treasure, and eventually they found all of it and brought it back to the large front chamber, where they piled it up and stuffed it into sacks.

" 'I see you have barrels of mead!' one of the Vikings roared while others were still deep in the cave looking for more treasure. 'We will have some!' he said.

"Semolina told him it was actually wine.

" 'That will do just as well,' the Viking said. 'Draw us all a goblet full, and be quick about it!'

"None of the Vikings knew that by ordering Semolina to serve them wine they were giving her an opportunity to foil their raid. On her way to the two wine barrels, Semolina was able to swoop up a container of a very special potion and conceal it in the folds of her dress. Then she was able to put some of the potion into each of the two barrels of wine without any of the Vikings noticing, for they were so preoccupied in looking at and caressing their newly acquired treasure that they neglected to watch Semolina's every move, as would have been wise. Snickering to herself, Semolina served goblets of wine to each Viking, for of course not one of the Vikings was satisfied with only one goblet of the drink when there was more to be had.

" 'You may think that I live here all alone, but you are mistaken in that belief,' Semolina said to the Vikings when all of them had drank at least two goblets of the strong wine laced with the special potion. 'There are many other trolls, much bigger and stronger and more dangerous than me, all around.'

" 'What are you talking about?' one of the Vikings scoffed. 'There are no other trolls here! We've been in every part of the cave, and you are the only one here.'

" 'The others are much too large to fit into this cave, for they are giants,' Semolina said. 'But they live all about. You can see their faces in big trees, and their forms in rocks and clouds and mist, and in the water. Beware of them, for they will not let you get away with the treasure you are trying to take, for part of it belongs to them as well. You may be able to take the treasure from this cave, but you won't get it past the giant trolls who are all around, for they will kill you if you try to take the treasure from this place.'

"Semolina could tell by the expressions on many of their faces that her words had hit their mark and frightened many of the Viking plunderers. A few suspected she was bluffing, though. 'You're a liar,' one of those who was not convinced said to her. 'You're lying, and we're taking all of your treasure, and that's all there is to it.'

" 'I have tried to warn you,' Semolina said. 'It is up to you to believe me or not, but I say truly that you ignore my warning at your own peril. Some advice: If you do see any of the giant trolls, the only way to save your life is to immediately put down not only the treasure you take from this cave but also anything else of value in your possession, including your weapons and your shields. Then the giant trolls will spare your life and allow you to leave.'

" 'Enough of this crazy talk!' one of the Vikings declared. 'Let us take what we have gathered and leave this crazy old woman to her madness.'

"Apparently the one who said that was the leader of the group, for that is precisely what the Vikings did. As they began following the winding path leading to the place where their long-boat was anchored near the shore of the fjord, though, some of them started seeing faces and forms of giant trolls all around them, in rocks, in trees, in clouds above and in the water below, for the potion Semolina poured into the barrels of wine was a potion that caused people to have hallucinations, especially when the power of the potion was combined with the power of suggestion. Those who saw faces and forms of trolls were frightened out of their wits, for none of them wanted to deal with angry giant trolls, and they dropped the stolen treasure they were carrying, as well as their shields and their weapons, and ran toward their boat as though their lives were at stake. Some of the others gathered up some of the abandoned treasure before they too started imagining they were seeing giant trolls all about and fled for their lives as well after leaving Semolina's treasure and other valuable items they were wearing and carrying. Within minutes the Vikings had left behind all the treasure they had taken from Semolina's cave, and nearly all of the battle-axes and shields, and were scurrying down the cliff-side trail toward their boat.

"Semolina couldn't help but chuckle out loud as she watched all of this amusing activity from her cave entrance. The loss of so much wine was almost worth such an entertaining show. The Vikings who had raided her cave were not yet out of the fjord before Semolina started gathering up all of the treasure the Vikings had taken and then left behind, as well as the weapons, shields and other items of treasure they had discarded to get away from giant trolls that didn't exist."

89 ▪ Completion
And Commencement

Brine was not far from the west side of Black Mountain when he started noticing something different about the air. It had a certain vaporous quality that made it thicker than the air on Troll Mountain, or the air he had breathed from there to where he was. He wondered if it indicated snow was approaching, for it was chilly enough for snow. He had no idea it was the scent of the sea. He had no idea how close he was to reaching the destination he wanted to reach. For all he knew he was still hundreds of miles from his goal. And so he trudged on, a weary traveler unaware of his proximity to some of his dreamed-of fjords.

He walked through the night, using dazzling pale-green Northern Lights for orientation, knowing that celestrial illumination should be to his right. The Northern Lights stretched so far into the heavens that they encased him in a half-dome and aided his ability to see. The more he walked the more he noticed a difference to the air. Unintentionally, his pace perked up; without understanding, he sensed something in the offing.

And then it happened. As he made his way up a long incline of exposed bedrock he caught sight of a sliver of silvery water beneath a sheer, mossy cliff. More and more water became visible as he walked up the incline. From the crest, the land sloped toward a body of water no larger than a modest lake, at least from what Brine could see. A hill to the left , as he looked at the scene, blocked his view of some of the water, so he knew there was more water there, but he didn't know how much. Instinctively, he believed this was a fjord. While he couldn't quite put a finger on why, this seemed different than the tarns and other lakes he had passed and crossed, crossing one large lake in a borrowed skiff. But was it or wasn't it a fjord? He had expected to be sure when he saw one, not confounded and unsure. While the sheer cliff directly opposite and the less severe cliff to the right matched his dream image of a fjord, the scene before him differed from the fjord he dreamed about as well. First of all, he envisioned lusher, greener surroundings, save for the sheer cliff section. Secondly, Llop's description and his dream led him to believe fjords were much larger than the body of water he saw before him. Of course, he couldn't tell how large a body of water it was because of the obstructive hill to the left. He decided to walk to his right so he could hopefully get a better view. After but a short distance he looked down and saw a small fishing village on a flat area next to the fjord. From what he was able to see, the village consisted of no more than twenty-five to thirty main buildings. Still, that distressed him. If this was a fjord, it was a fjord with people living next to it. If he decided he wanted to live beside a fjord he wanted it to be one he didn't have to share with people. Having lived on Troll Mountain, so isolated from people, all of his life, he wasn't keen on the prospect of living close to human beings. So if this were a fjord, it wouldn't be one where he would want to live. From what Llop had told him, though, there were more fjords than one could count, so he knew, or at least felt confident, there were some fjords without people.

As Brine walked, more and more of the fjord became visible. Without the large hill blocking his view, he could see that the body of water was quite long, and relatively narrow. He wasn't sure how long, for he couldn't see the other end of it. At this hour of the morning even a troll's keen night vision couldn't see all the way to the sea, a body of water so large Brine could not even imagine how large it was.

Not sure what to do, but knowing this wasn't the place for him because people were present, Brine walked on, northward. It was ingrained in trolls: north was the best direction for them to go, for that generally meant getting away from people, or at least a greater number of people. About a mile away he came upon another fjord, pretty similar in size and character to the first one. He couldn't see a village beside this one, but he did spot a few scattered farms. Again, he wasn't sure if it was a fjord or not. He sat down on a rock ledge for a while and gazed at the fjord, trying to decide if it was or wasn't a fjord. He had expected to be filled with joy when he saw a fjord for the first time. Here he was filled with uncertainty rather than delight. He had reached his dreamed-of destination, but it was an anticlimactic completion to his long journey. He didn't even know his journey was practically complete, that he had found fjords, if not a people-free one where he might want to live.

Brine stood up and continued on, for it was still dark and not yet time to look for a place to sleep and wait out the day. After ten minutes of walking he was rounding a protruding rock formation when suddenly a figure leaped from above and landed in his path. Startled, Brine pulled back, thinking it must be a large and possibly dangerous animal. To his astonishment, the figure standing before him was another troll—a female troll with dark, penetrating eyes, a thick-lipped watermelon slice of a mouth, an almost-human-sized nose, and long, chocolate-colored hair decorated with pins, ribbons and several flowers. She was slightly shorter than Brine and approximately the same age, as far as Brine could tell. The lavender dress she wore had billowy sleeves and a skirt that nearly touched the ground.

"Who are you?" the other troll asked in such a manner that the question carried both fascination and demand.

"I'm Brine," Brine answered. "Who are you?"

"We'll get to that," the other troll said. "First: What are you doing here?"

"What do you mean?" Brine asked.

"I mean: What are you doing here?" the female troll repeated. "I've been following you since I saw you sitting on a rock ledge back there. It almost seems like you're looking for something. Are you?"

"As a matter of fact, I am," Brine said. "I'm looking for a fjord."

"What do you mean you're looking for one?" the other troll responded. "You were looking at one when you were sitting there."

"I was?!" Brine said, excited to know he had reached his goal.

"You mean you didn't know that?" the female troll asked.

"No," Brine said. "I thought it might be one, but I wasn't sure."

"Why were you looking for one?"

"Well, I had a dream about one, and I was at a fjord, and I got this feeling deep inside of me that I should go and find one."

"Where did you come from?" the female troll asked.

"From that way," Brine said, pointing to the northeast when actually Troll Mountain lay to the east/southeast. "I've come a long way."

"Just to see a fjord?"

"I guess so," Brine said, the "just" in the question making him feel a little foolish, for it made it seem as though the female troll thought traveling a long distance merely to see a fjord was sort of silly. "I had never seen a fjord," he went on, trying to justify his action, "so I just wanted to see one, and maybe stay and live beside one if I liked it well enough." Brine had never felt so attracted to a female troll as he did to this one. Once past the shock of her surprise appearance, he was instantly infatuated with her.

"I'm Piela, and I live beside a small fjord not far from here," the female troll said by way of introduction. While she wasn't about to reveal it at the moment, she fell in love with Brine at first sight, when she saw him seated on the rock ledge, and wanted to get to know him.

"You do!" Brine said. "How many others do you live with?"

"I live alone," Piela revealed.

"You're not part of a tribe?"

"No, I'm alone," Piela said. "Are you part of a tribe?"

"I was," Brine said. "I guess I'm not if I decide to stay here."

"Do you think you will stay?"

"I don't know yet. The two fjords I've seen aren't exactly what I expected."

"What did you expect?"

Brine told her his dream vision and how the reality he saw didn't quite match that.

"That's because it's nearly winter," Piela said. "What you saw in your dream is what you see during the summertime. You should stay until at least then before you make up your mind about whether or not you want to stay."

"Maybe I will," Brine said. "Do you know if there are other fjords around without any people beside them? I'm not used to living close to people, and I don't want to start that now."

"You could stay with me if you want," Piela offered. "That way you wouldn't have to look for a place to stay along another fjord. My cave has plenty of room for two."

"Are there any people around, in your fjord?" Brine asked.

"None," Piela said. "I have it all to myself. It's close enough to other fjords where people *do* live, though, that I don't have any problem keeping myself well fed and well clothed."

"I like your dress," Brine complimented her. "It's very pretty."

"I like it too," Piela said. "So, what do you say; do you want to come and live with me?"

"That would be great, if you'll have me," Brine said, his mind racing at his good fortune.

"I'll have you," Piela said. "Come on. The sky is already turning light in the east. We need to get home and get into the cave. Then you can tell me all about where you came from, and your tribe, and everything."

Side by side, Brine and Piela walked off toward Piela's fjord-side cave, both of them thrilled the night had delivered a partner they could love and cherish.

90 ▪ The Twins And
The Two-Headed Troll

"**M**y friend Charley says there are two-headed trolls," Andrew said to his parents at the supper table. "Is that true?"

"Well," his father said, "there are tales about two-headed trolls, and three-headed trolls, and even ones with more heads than that."

"Wow!" Andrew marveled. "More than three?!"

"They're just stories," his mother cautioned. "People may have been exaggerating. And if there were trolls with more than one head, there probably aren't now." She didn't want Andrew having nightmares about multi-headed trolls. He already was so enamored of trolls that she feared his interest might lead to bad dreams and unhealthy fantasizing.

"There must be stories in the book about trolls with more than one head," Anders said to his son.

"Can we read one tonight?" Andrew said excitedly.

"Oh, I guess so, if I can find one," Anders said.

Later in the evening, he did find one in the book, a tale entitled *The Twins And The Two-Headed Troll*. As he read the opening paragraph to Andrew he was tickled to discover one of the tale's characters was named Anders.

▪

Anders and Asgard Holmgren had strict instructions from their mother. The thirteen-year-old twins were to take two freshly baked pies to their grandparents' place, stay there overnight, then return the next day, following the main, well-trod path through the forest.

This was the first time the lads had been allowed to travel to their grandparents' house alone. Always before one or both of their parents accompanied them. Now that they were thirteen, though—their birthday having passed ten days earlier—their parents believed they were old enough and responsible enough to make the five-mile journey by themselves. Indeed, Anders and Asgard felt so grown-up and self-assured, now that they were thirteen, that they saw no reason to follow their mother's instructions *explicitly*. It seemed pointless to stick to the main trail the entire way when there was a shortcut through the forest that would save them at least a mile of walking each direction. They had been along several times when their father took the shortcut. While they knew the shortcut had more twists and turns than the main path, it seemed to them it wouldn't be all that difficult to follow the shorter path. And so Anders and Asgard veered from the main trail and ventured into a thicker part of the forest, taking the shortcut to their grandparents' place.

It wasn't long before they were totally confused as to where they were. The granite-grey sky, which blocked the sun, provided no clues, and they couldn't determine which direction was east, which was west, which was north, and which was south. They tried to retrace their steps to the spot where they had left the main trail, but they couldn't find any path of any size. So they kept walking, first this way and then that, growing more frightened and confused by the minute.

"If you hadn't wanted to take a shortcut we would have been at Grandma's and Grandpa's a long time ago," Asgard accused Anders. "We would have eaten supper and now be as cozy as cats in front of a fireplace."

"You wanted to take the shortcut as much as I did,"Anders shot back, "so don't go trying to blame me for us being lost."

The darkening forest assumed an even more frightening atmosphere as fog formed and dusk gave way to a gloomy darkness. The sky was still heavily overcast, so there were no stars twinkling on Earth's ceiling to provide any light. In no time at all the fog clinging to the forest floor was as thick as a creamy soup. Combined with the darkness, the fog didn't allow Anders and Asgard to see more than a couple of feet in front of them. Even so, they continued stumbling through the thick forest, desperate to spot a dim light, a house, or a path—anything that would give them a spark of hope that they weren't hopelessly lost forever.

The twins were so caught up in their own concerns, concentrating on thoughts of finding safety, that they failed to notice there were other sounds in the forest, not far away. Gradually, though, that realization soaked through Asgard's subconscious and penetrated his conscious mind. He stopped, and motioned for Anders to stop as well.

"What is it?" Anders asked.

"Listen," Asgard said.

The two boys remained absolutely still, with their ears perked for any sound.

"I don't hear anything," Anders said.

"I thought I heard footsteps," Asgard said.

"You probably only imagined it," Anders said. "Your mind is playing a trick on your ears. Come on; let's go."

Anders started walking again. Asgard joined him, looking around nervously. Anders took only ten or twelve steps before he stopped again. Asgard followed suit.

"I think you're right," Anders whispered. "I thought I heard footsteps too."

"Do you think maybe it's a bear?" Asgard whispered back.

"I don't know," Anders said. "It could be."

"What should we do?" Asgard said.

"Let's take a few more steps," Anders suggested, "and see if whatever it is keeps following us."

The two boys took a few more steps, then suddenly stopped simultaneously. Not far away there was a delayed echo of the same sound pattern. Unmistakably, something or someone was following them.

"Maybe we can scare it away," Anders said, feeling fairly certain that either a bear or some other large, wild animal had made the noise. "Who's there?" he demanded, calling into the soupy fog.

"Who's *there*?" a voice replied.

Obviously it wasn't a bear or any other species of wild animal behind them. And the fact there was a voice offered hope for rescue and deliverance.

"My name is Anders," Anders said, wanting to cry for joy, he felt such relief. "And my brother's name is Asgard."

"I'm Holger," the other voice said in introduction. And then, after a pause: "What are you doing out here?"

"We're lost," Anders admitted. "Can you help us?"

"Stay right where you are," Holger said. "I'll come to you."

In a couple of minutes Holger was only a few feet from Anders and Asgard. Even at that close proximity Holger was no more than a shadowy shape to them because of the thick fog and the inky darkness.

"We're trying to get to our grandparents' place," Anders explained.

"What's their name?" Holger asked.

"Holmgren," Anders told him.

"I know where they live," Holger said. "Would you like me to take you there?"

"Would you?" Anders said.

"I would be happy to," Holger said.

Rejoicing at their extraordinary luck in encountering someone deep in the forest, amidst the fog and the darkness, Anders and Asgard followed Holger through the forest for a couple of miles. Anders and Asgard may as well have been blind for all they could see. They placed their trust in Holger, hoping he knew where he was going. He seemed to know, for he never hesitated or seemed uncertain as to which way to go. It seemed to Anders that they were walking uphill more than they had on previous trips to their grandparents' place, though. When he commented about that Holger explained that was because they were approaching from a different direction. When Asgard noticed his footing was different he asked Holger if they were walking on bare dirt. Instead of answering, all at once Holger turned around and shoved Anders and Asgard to the ground.

"What's going on?" Anders said, trying to get up.

Holger kicked him in the stomach and growled "Shut up!" as Anders fell back against a rock wall. Then Holger lit a large candle, which made his features distinguishable for the first time. Asgard screamed when he saw what Holger looked like, for the sight the candlelight illuminated would have terrorized a tree. For the first time in their lives Asgard and Anders understood exactly what the term "as ugly as sin" meant. Holger was undeniably as ugly as sin, for he was not a man but a two-headed troll—a bushy, bug-eyed, blotchy, black-haired, barbarous, baboonish, two-headed troll. The two heads branched from a single neck like two trunks of a tree sprouting from one trunk.

Anders, Asgard and the two-headed troll were now in a dank cave chamber, which the twins found as eerie as the feel of bloodsucking leeches on one's skin. Anders and Asgard looked at each other open-mouthed, both as terrified as trapped rats cornered by a mountain lion.

"You should be nice and tender to eat," one of Holger's heads said.

"I'm not going to eat them yet," the other head said. "I want to have some fun with them first."

"What sort of fun?" Anders asked, his voice shaking like a tree branch in a strong wind.

"Ah, you shall find out soon enough," Holger said.

"We trolls have very special ways of having fun, especially when humans are involved," the other head said.

"You probably won't have nearly as much fun as I will, I admit," the first head said. "In fact, some of the things I have in store for you will be downright painful for you, I'm afraid. But that's just the way things have to be. The more pain you feel the more fun I have. That's the way things work."

Anders and Asgard shuddered to think what the sadistic troll had in mind for them.

"First, I'm going to tie you up and drip hot wax on your faces," Holger's first head said.

"No, no," the second head rejoined. "First I have to do some stretching." Of course, he meant stretching Anders and Asgard somehow.

When the first head tried to argue for its preference the second head interrupted with arguments of its own. With both heads talking at the same time, Anders and Asgard could not understand Holger's babble. The two heads argued ferociously for a couple of minutes before there was any letup. When the heads finally ceased arguing, apparently with nothing resolved, one of the heads noticed the sack near Anders and said, "What's in the sack?"

"Just a blueberry pie," Anders answered.

"A blueberry pie!" Holger's head said. "That's my favorite! Bring it to me."

As Anders was removing the pie from the sack Holger's second head noticed a similar sack near Asgard and asked him what was in that sack.

"A strawberry pie," Asgard told the second head.

"A strawberry pie!" Holger's second head said, wide-eyed. "That's my favorite! Bring it to me."

As Asgard started taking the strawberry pie out of his sack Anders quickly whispered something to him. Asgard gave a quick nod to indicate he understood.

"Bring me my blueberry pie!" Holger's blueberry pie-loving head demanded of Anders. "And be quick about it!"

"And bring me my strawberry pie!" Holger's second head demanded of Asgard.

"Here you are," Anders said, walking toward one side of the cave chamber. "I'll set it right over here."

"And I'll put your strawberry pie right over here," Asgard said to the other head, walking to the opposite side of the cave chamber.

"This way!" Holger's first head said, trying to move toward the blueberry pie.

"No, this way!" the other head argued, trying to make Holger's body move toward the strawberry pie.

With the two heads giving the body diametrically opposite instructions, Holger's body was in a tug of war with itself. As a result, it went in neither direction; it remained where it was, its two halves struggling against each other as equally as two men well-matched in strength armwrestling each other for long minutes with neither able to overpower the other.

With Holger's two heads loudly arguing with each other and the two pairs of eyes focused in opposite directions, on the two different types of pies, Anders motioned toward the cave entrance with a jerk of his head. Asgard followed Anders's lead in backing toward the opening. Holger's heads didn't notice Anders and Asgard slip out the cave opening and start running away. Miraculously, moonlight now flooded the forest. The fog had lifted, making it possible for the twins to see where they were going. By sheer luck, in only five minutes' time they came upon the main trail, which they followed directly to their grand-parents' house. It was shortly after dawn when they reached that house. Their grandparents were in the kitchen, where their grandmother was preparing breakfast. Anders and Asgard had never been so happy to see their grandparents—or any other person, for that matter.

91 ▪ Wedding Bones

A bonfire blazed on a rocky plateau nearly half a mile from the troll caves. With the exception of the bride, the groom, and Guggle, who would preside at the wedding ceremony, all of the Troll Mountain trolls were standing in two lines, with all of the males in one line and all of the females in the other. All of the trolls in the two lines held torches, for while trolls dislike sunlight, for practical reasons, torchlight is an entirely different matter. Torchlight does not debilitate them, or drain strength and energy. Even with their acute night vision, torchlight helps them see better at night.

By coincidence, this was All Hallow's Eve, though not one of the trolls, even Guggle, a witch, was aware of the fact. From a human point of view, non-believers, as trolls are, could hardly have selected a more appropriate date for a wedding. All Hallow's Eve held no special significance for these trolls, however. To them, October thirty-first was no more special than April twenty-second or November eleventh.

With everyone in place, Guggle called for Rott to be summoned. He and Tala were waiting in different places, and tradition, such as it was among trolls, was for the groom to be summoned first, the bride last. In truth, trolls didn't have much tradition when it came to weddings, and what tradition existed was a patchwork of invention, imitation and expediency. For ages, trolls had no wedding tradition at all. Those times could be classified as the "me like, you come" era. A male troll who saw a female he liked simply picked up the female, slung her over a shoulder and took her back to his cave, unless the female didn't want to go with him and overpowered him, which was not all that uncommon. Gradually families arranged marriages between their male and female offspring. In the sweep of time, it has been but a blip during which young males and females decide for themselves who they will marry, with the female having as much of a say as the male in the matter. This evolved marriage process developed as a result of what trolls learned about what human beings were doing, of course. The fact that most human weddings took place in churches, structures trolls loathed and dreaded, did not deter trolls from imitating the human practice.

"Rott, we are ready for you," Ort, who was wearing his battered Viking helmet for the occasion, bellowed. "Come forward and walk the line!"

Rott, dressed for the occasion in his usual dirty, ragged attire, appeared and began walking past the line of his fellow male tribe members. Each troll he passed gave his tail a playful tug. All of the tugs were playful, that is, until he reached Drulle. Drulle yanked Rott's tail so viciously that Rott was sent stumbling as he tried to maintain his balance. "You can't have her!" Drulle seethed as he attacked Rott. "I want her!" Forced to defend himself, Rott found himself in a fight with the physically stronger Drulle, who was jealous that Tala was about to marry Rott instead of him. The two young trolls punched, pinched, pulled hair and limbs, squeezed, bit, spit, kicked, and attacked each other every other way imaginable. There was such a ruckus that Tala emerged from her waiting place to see what was going on. The fight continued for a couple of minutes before Ort said, "Alright, that's enough! Break it up!," and ordered several tribe members to separate the two combatants.

"Control yourself!" Ort barked at Drulle. "This is a wedding, not a time for fighting."

"I'm leaving!" Drulle spat. "I'm not staying here and watching this!"

"Good!" Ort shot back. "Go. The sooner the better. That means more food and drink for the rest of us."

"Maybe I'll go and never come back," Drulle threatened.

"Suit yourself," Ort said emotionlessly. "Leave or stay. Do whatever you want. You attack Rott again, though, and I will personally wring your neck."

"I'd like to see you try," Drulle said defiantly.

"You'd better leave," Rnobrna advised him before Ort could respond.

"I'm going!" Drulle said, massaging a particularly painful bruise as he walked away.

With Drulle gone, the proceedings resumed, with the rest of the male trolls giving Rott's tale a tug as he made his way toward Guggle, who stood close to the bonfire. Tala was then summoned, and she walked past the line of female trolls as she made her way to Guggle's side. Unlike Rott, Tala was dressed up for the occasion. She wore her best dress, which had a blue print pattern, had a wreath of holly in her hair, and carried a bouquet of plants her wizard father, Kravig, had selected and gathered for her. Each female troll she passed on her way to the bonfire slapped her back with a pine bough, as Guggle had instructed them to do.

Once both Rott and Tala were in place next to the bonfire Guggle had all of the others form a semi-circle for the actual wedding ceremony.

"Gather," the troll witch intoned solemnly when everyone was in place and quiet. "Gather in the night, with good spirit and torchlight, for the time is now right for two hearts to unite. Two into one, this shall be done. Love burns like fire, the flames of desire licking the air with magic and care. This fire in our midst we see and we feel; we know it is here, we know it is real. And so, like the fire, Tala and Rott stand here before us on this special spot. Let everyone now raise a glad voice. Let us exalt and let us rejoice. Let us say 'cheer!'"

All of the other trolls echoed the encouraging word, chorusing "cheer!"

"And let us all say 'happiness!'" Guggle orchestrated.

"Happiness!" all of the others belted out.

"And let us all say 'good fortune!'" Guggle said.

"Good fortune!" the others echoed.

"And now for the Ceremony of the Bones," Guggle announced, picking up a small burlap sack containing various types of animal bones, of various shapes and sizes, and shaking it with her right arm, the top of the sack at shoulder height. Solemn as stone, she intoned the following, while shaking the bag of bones at frequent, appropriate intervals:

Rattle, rattle, bag of bones,
Rattle the air and shake the stones.

Rattle the ages, rattle the earth,
Rattle the night for all it's worth.

Bones of every sort and kind,
Rattle in our hearts and minds.

Work your magic spell this night,
Make this marriage start off right.

Rattle the sky and rattle the ground.
Rattle loudly, all around.

Rattle, rattle, bag of bones,
Rattle the air and shake the stones.

Rattle the ages, rattle the earth,
Rattle the night for all it's worth.

Guggle then gave the bag of bones one long, final flourish before setting the sack back on the ground and picking up a different, smaller bag, this one made of leather. She extracted two bones from the leather bag and held them out in front of her. "First, wolf bones for Rott," she announced, and proceeded to place the two legbones on Rott's shoulders, as she held them. "May these bones, from a wolf so wild, impart to you and any child a life of health and happiness, as well as help you love your wife, for the spell of time is in our bones, its endlessness it does intone. O bones of wolf, so fierce and fast, help this marriage force to last."

Guggle paused as she put away the wolf bones and brought out a long necklass made of small bones and feathers. "And now," she announced, "swan and hawk bones and feathers for Tala. Bone and feather, mixed together, are what is needed for any weather. Bones are hard, feathers fair. The first is earth, the second air. Swans are sleek and hawks soar high; they represent both earth and sky." Guggle then placed the necklass around Tala's neck before continuing. "May these bones and feathers you now wear remind you you are part of a pair. Hawk and swan, feather and bone, lightness and firmness, dirt and stone, give this union a life of its own."

With the Ceremony of the Bones complete, Guggle had everyone, herself included, circle around the newlyweds and the bonfire. Many danced, in the crazy, cavorting sort of way trolls dance, and many whooped, hollered, whistled crazily and uttered nonsense sounds like so many Holy Rollers speaking in tongues. Soon Tala was dancing as well, and eventually she persuaded Rott to try a few dance-like moves too as their fellow tribe members continued circling.

Ort called an end to all of this after a few minutes by stopping and holding up his hands, indicating he was about to speak. "It is time to feast!" he announced. "Bring out the food!"

Most of the female trolls uncovered piles and pans of food on the backside of the bonfire from where Guggle had performed the wedding ceremony and all of them dug in with ravenous delight, with the males ignoring suggestions from some of the females that Rott and Tala should be allowed to be first in line. Most trolls are not accustomed to standing on ceremony when it comes to eating. The brownies and chocolate fudge Ort had insisted on saving for the wedding feast disappeared quickly. Plenty of apple cider and wine was available, and the trolls lapped it up like thirsty horses at a trough. They rarely had alcohol to drink, so a modest amount made most of them quite tipsy. Trolls that had found musical instruments over the years pulled out harmonicas, a battered, three-string fiddle, and a wheezy squeezebox for music-making. With no knowledge of how to play any of the instruments, they created a din, which a couple of others contributed to by banging spoons on their metal plates. A few sang as well, if squeals, screeches and other primal sounds can be considered singing. Wild, disjointed dancing matched the tenor of the cacophonous music. And so things continued for several hours. At one point Drulle, who had disappeared to a spot from where he could see what was going on, reappeared to try to get his fair share of the food and drink.

92 ▪ The Boy Who Wanted
To See A Troll

"**I** wish I could see a troll just once," Andrew Branstad said one evening at the family supper table.

"You do, do you?" his father said. "You don't think you would be afraid?"

"I don't know," Andrew replied. "Maybe, if he was close like this. But maybe I could just see one from quite a ways away. Then I don't think I would be afraid. If I could do that, then I would want to see one."

"You know," Anders said, "I just remembered that there's a story about a boy like you who wanted to see a troll in the worst way."

"What happened?" Andrew asked. "Did he ever see one?"

"I'm pretty sure the story is in the book," Anders said. "How about if we try to find that and read it later on?"

"Yeah!" Andrew said.

Which is what they did later that evening.

▪

Niles Okerlund had heard tales about trolls ever since he first learned to talk. His parents told him a troll tale many nights just before his bedtime. By the time he was six he was hoping to see a troll with his own eyes, for while he knew trolls were ugly, meanspirited, scary creatures, his curiosity about them glowed like hot coals and he wanted to experience the thrill of seeing one. "If only I could see just one I would be happy," he thought to himself.

Alas, young Niles was doomed to disappointment when it came to his desire to see a troll. By the time he turned seven he still hadn't seen a troll. He turned eight and *still* hadn't seen one.

He couldn't understand it. Many nights he looked out his bedroom window for an hour or two trying to spot a troll sneaking around the Okerlund barn or stealing vegetables from the family garden. There were no trolls there to be seen, though, at least while Niles was watching.

Then one night—or one early morning, if you will, for it was four o'clock in the morning—Niles awoke, felt compelled to go to his bedroom window and look out, and thought he caught a glimpse of a troll-like form slipping behind the barn. Bolting from the window, he ran to his parents' bedroom and shook his father awake.

"There's a troll behind the barn!" Niles said.

"What?" his dazed father said. He was still half asleep, trying to regain his waking senses.

"There's a troll behind the barn!" Niles repeated, this time loud enough to wake his mother, who raised her head, saw Niles by the side of the bed, and said, "What's going on?"

"There's a troll behind the barn!" Niles said yet again, almost as though his brain had been sent into such a state of shock that he could speak only that one sentence. "I saw it from my window."

"What!" his mother said. "You saw it?"

Niles nodded his head vigorously and pleaded, "Come and see!"

The two adults climbed out of bed and followed Niles into his bedroom, where all three looked out the window.

"I don't see anything," the father said.

"I saw it go behind the barn," Niles said, pointing to where he meant.

"Maybe you should go out and have a look around," Mrs. Okerlund said to her husband. "If it is a troll it's probably trying to steal something."

Wearing only bedclothes and boots, Mr. Okerlund ran downstairs and went outside. He grabbed a pitchfork that was leaning against the near side of the barn before creeping around the far side of the barn as his wife and son watched from Niles' bedroom window. He circled the barn, searched inside the barn and part of the pasture behind the barn, then returned to the house, none too happy that Niles had awaken him from a sound sleep an hour before his usual waking time to walk around in the chill morning air in his bedslothes.

"There's nothing there," he announced to his wife and son. "I looked all over and I couldn't see any strange tracks or any signs of anything being gone or out of place."

Mrs. Okerlund assured Niles that he must have been mistaken, that he didn't really see a troll. Then all three of them returned to bed, but none of them could sleep anymore that morning after so much excitement.

The following week, as a thunderstorm that held more wind than rain raged one night, Niles was again looking out his bedroom window when he again thought he saw a large troll prancing about the yard. Actually, it was nothing but the play of lightning and swaying pine branches producing flickering shadows. Niles's imagination, and his overpowering desire to see a troll, caused him to see what he wanted to see, though.

As he had the previous week, he dashed into his parents' bedroom to let them know there was a troll in the yard. This time his parents were awake, for they couldn't sleep with the thunderstorm raging outside. "Again?!" Mr. Okerlund said when Niles blurted out that there was a big troll in the yard. "Are you sure you aren't just seeing things again?"

Niles insisted that he *knew* there was a troll this time. He was so insistant that his mother and father go to his room to have a look at it that Mrs. Okerlund said to her reluctant husband: "We better go have a look." With a heavy sigh, Mr. Okerlund got out of bed and followed Niles and his wife to Niles's bedroom.

Once again the three of them crowded together at the window.

"There it is!" Niles fairly shouted when a streak of lightning torched the sky, pointing at the place where he thought he saw a troll.

"That's nothing but the shadow of a tree branch," his father said, none too kindly. "The only trolls around here are the ones in your head."

"You saw it, didn't you, Mom?" Niles asked, seeking support for his vision.

"I'm afraid not, dear," his mother said consolingly.

At that instant, another bolt of lightning struck. All three of the Okerlunds were staring at the right spot to clearly see that the troll of Niles's imagination was in reality nothing more than a dancing shadow.

"See there?" Mr. Okerlund pointed out triumphantly. "It's nothing but a shadow. Now are you satisfied?"

"It *is* a shadow," Mrs. Okerlund said kindly. "You see that it's only a shadow, don't you, Niles?"

"Yeah, I see," Niles said, dropping his head in disappointment, for he still hadn't seen a troll.

"Get back into bed now," his mother said as she and her husband went to the bedroom doorway and Niles crawled back into his bed.

"And we don't want to hear another peep out of you tonight," Mr. Okerlund admonished. "Understand?"

"Yes," Niles said.

Two weeks later Niles again imagined he saw a troll. Once again he woke his parents, who investigated Niles's supposed sighting and concluded he had had another flight of fancy.

The following day Mr. Okerlund decided it was time to lay out the facts of life to his son, as they applied to trolls. "This business about you imagining that you see trolls in the middle of the night has to stop," he said as matter-of-factly as he could, not angrily. "Maybe it's the fault of your mother and me for telling you so many tales about trolls over the years. You have to understand that you may live your entire life and never see a troll. Most people do; most people never see a troll. *I've* never seen a troll. Your mother has never seen a troll. In fact, despite all the stories about people who have seen trolls, there are a lot of people who think that trolls don't really exist. To tell you the truth, I'm skeptical about them myself. There may very well be trolls, but there might not be too. Maybe all of the stories about trolls are just stories that people made up. Or maybe the trolls that used to live around here have moved away, farther north. I guess what I'm saying is: if trolls *do* exist, very few people ever get to see one, so you shouldn't expect to see one in your own yard every week, because it is highly improbable that you will ever see a troll, much less see one looking out your bedroom window."

No trolls? Niles contemplated that possibility in the following days. How could anyone believe trolls did not exist?, he concluded. Certainly trolls existed. Niles was as sure of that as he was of the fact that he didn't like the taste of cooked peas. Nothing would shake him of that belief—not the disbelief of others, not his father's skepticism, not his own mistaken visions.

Less than two weeks after his father's lecture Niles was looking out his bedroom window one night when he was so sure that he saw a troll outside, after watching what he thought was the troll for nearly half an hour, that he felt compelled to wake his father and ask him to go to his bedroom and look at it. His father was more than merely reluctant to get up this time; he was perturbed that Niles had woken him. He was so annoyed that he scolded Niles and ordered him back to bed. Niles was so persistent, though, that Mrs. Okerlund eventually persuaded her husband to go and have a look. This time even Mr. Okerlund had to admit the "troll" Niles pointed out did vaguely resemble a troll. But if it was a troll, why was it just sitting in one spot, seemingly motionless? "Wait a minute!" Mr. Okerlund remembered. "Isn't there an old stump there?"

"It *has* to be a troll," Niles said. "I just know it is."

"Well, I'll just go have a look then," his father said.

Mr. Okerlund did just that, with his wife and son tagging along behind him. It was, indeed, an old stump—a burled old stump that sort of resembled a troll shape in dim light.

"That does it!" Mr. Okerlund exploded. "I'm going to put a stop to all of this nonsense right now. Niles, come with me into the barn. You're going to get a whipping."

Using a leather strap, Mr. Okerlund gave Niles three lashes across his bottom and told him that if he ever again reported seeing a troll he would receive an even worse whipping.

"I don't care if you think you see a dozen trolls," Mr. Okerlund said. "I don't ever again want to lose any sleep because of what you *think* you see."

Five nights later Niles was lying in bed, with a soft breeze stirring through his partially opened bedroom window, when he heard an odd sound in the barnyard outside. He went to the window and looked out. There he saw, unmistakably, a troll in the horse corral, bathed in the pumpkin light of a half moon. He almost called out for his mother to come, but then quickly remembered his father's warning and his threat of a more severe whipping. So he remained silent, almost afraid to breathe. He watched in wonder, wide-eyed, as the squat, stringy-haired troll opened the corral gate, mounted the horse and rode away into the night.

Niles resolved that he would say nothing to his mother or his father about what he had seen. If his father asked him if he had heard or seen anything unusual in the night he would tell him he had been sound asleep all night. He would not say a word about what he knew about the horse being stolen. He would say nothing about finally having seen a troll.

93 ▪ Winter Arrives

A ferocious snowstorm struck Troll Mountain two nights after the wedding. Given the depth of the snow, all of the trolls remained close to home for several days. Indeed, they spent most of the time in their caves, sleeping, eating, roughhousing, and tending their fireplaces to keep the caves as warm as possible. Severe cold had not yet arrived, but it was cold enough that they wanted the warmth, especially when they were not yet used to the sting of winter's icy whip. Then some of them started venturing out nights, for male trolls are anything but homebodies by nature; they like to be on the move—to get out and roam. Still, they roam far less during the wintertime, in terms of both frequency and distance, than during the other seasons of the year.

As the days passed, and some days brought more snow flurries, it become more and more evident that winter had arrived for a long stay, that the ground would be snow-covered until Spring—until deep into April, if not into early May. A leaden sky prevailed most days, which of course did not affect the trolls as long periods of cloudiness affect people, since trolls have a nocturnal lifestyle. Recognizing the probability that winter would rule the mountain for the coming several months, the trolls settled into their winter patterns, which included a reduced level of activity, more sleep, even greater than usual food consumption, and increased concern about simple survival. They wore heavier clothing and built hotter fires. With the cave entrances closed off with boulders, the temperature in the caves remained tolerable even when the outside air temperature plummeted far below the freezing point. With fireplaces blazing, the caves generally were quite comfortable, particularly in the chambers where the fireplaces were located. Indeed, at times the caves became so toasty that some of the trolls, most often the males, complained of the heat. The temperature level within the caves caused many sputtered curses, outbursts of irritation, prickly exchanges and heated arguments.

The buildings at the bottom of the mountain were rarely on their minds anymore. There was very little talk about them. Occasionally one or two of them passed within sight of the buildings and glanced at them, but no one watched them for hours, as the trolls had during the summertime, to see if there was any activity there. Given that Ort seemed unconcerned with the structures by that point, none of the other trolls saw any reason to worry about them either. If the king was no longer obsessed about them, why should they be? And so the trolls were completely oblivious to the fact that people finished construction of the ski lodge in late November and that there was a well-attended grand opening for the ski area the first weekend of December. Only the prototype cabin had been built; other cabins were projects for the following year, and years to come. And only two runs were open, one scaled for beginners, the other for experienced skiers. All three members of the Anders Branstad family skied there the first day of the open house weekend, the Saturday. As a member of the construction crew, Anders received free passes for himself and members of his immediate family. At age ten, for he was ten by this time, Andrew was already experienced enough to ski the steeper slope. Despite the "ski with the trolls" motto and his desire to see a troll in the flesh, he did not expect to actually ski with trolls. The ski area did, however, have two experienced skiers wear troll masks and ratty wigs that grand opening weekend. They spent time skiing on the slopes and mingling with others inside and outside of the lodge, which contributed to the festiveness of the occasion.

After that first weekend there was light attendance at the ski area for the following couple of weeks, what with people so busy with Christmas preparations—buying and making gifts, cooking and baking special goodies, decorating their homes, churches and public areas, rehearsing musical performances, and so forth. The Troll Mountain trolls were not doing anything to prepare for Christmas, of course, for Christmas meant no more to them than a pair of skis does to a goat. While they were aware Christmas came fairly early during the winter season, none of them knew how many days remained until Christmas, or if the most festive human holiday was ahead or had already passed.

94 ▪ The Troll Who Was Curious About Christmas

Trolls have always abhorred the Christian religion, or any sort of religion, and thus consider Christmas as loathsome, despicable and contemptible as most people do trolls. While trolls know nothing of the biblical forbidden fruit story, some have fallen prey to the penchant to wonder about what is so special about something regarded as off-limits to them and, spurred by curiosity, even tempted to cross a line into a forbidden realm. The most famous tale trolls tell each other about a troll who crossed such a line, as it concerns Christmas, is one involving a troll named Leik.

▪

As a troll, Leik knew Christmas was something he was supposed to hate and detest. His parents and other trolls impressed upon him from an early age that anything that brought as much joy and happiness to people as Christmas did obviously was something accursed and abhorrent to all right-thinking trolls. Still, in the most secret, innermost chamber of his heart Leik couldn't help but feel a little envious of people who seemed to reap such joy and pleasure during the Christmas season. Eventually he found himself wondering if it might be possible for a troll to draw as much joy and pleasure out of Christmas as people did.

"Why should trolls take pleasure only from stealing from people, and causing people misery, and making mischief?" he asked himself. "Why can't trolls take pleasure from singing and giving gifts and doing good to others?"

Overwhelmed by such curiosity, Leik slipped away by himself one Christmas Eve. He headed for a church in a small nearby village and hid among the tombstones in the graveyard next to the church as people arrived and entered the church for a Christmas Eve service.

The churchgoers sang Christmas carols while waiting for the service to start. Leik found himself enjoying the singing, which came to him muffled at his hiding spot in the church cemetery. "I can't believe that anything that involves such beautiful music can be all bad," he thought to himself.

Precisely at midnight the bell in the church belltower rang out loudly, proclaiming the arrival of Christmas Day. To Leik, the pealing bell was the sound of doom. He was instantly turned to stone, for trolls, as Leik found out tragically, are not meant to participate in the Christmas celebration in any fashion, however far out on the edge of it they are.

To this day, the troll-shaped stone that was once Leik still stands in that church graveyard, a lesson to trolls and people alike that Christmas is for people, not trolls.

95 ▪ The Bewildered Trolls

There are many Christmas Eve tales better known to humans than to trolls, one of the most delightful being the following, which Anders Branstad read to Andrew one evening:

■

It is well known that trolls detest Christmas as much as nature abhors a vacuum.

Five trolls who lived on Moss Mountain hated Christmas so much that one year they decided to spoil Christmas for as many people as they could by going around to farmhouses on Christmas Eve and stealing all of the presents from under the Christmas trees so that people would have no presents to open Christmas morning.

When they came to the first farmhouse where they intended to steal presents the trolls were surprised to find that the farmhouse was not yet dark for the night and that the members of the family who lived there were not yet asleep. Light poured from every ground-floor window of the house, and the sound of song shook the walls with a joyful noise, as if the house itself was celebrating the occasion. The five trolls—two troll men, two troll women and one troll girl—snuck up to the side of the house and peeked in one of the windows. Seventeen people were gathered around a glowing Chrismas tree singing Christmas carols. Besides the farmer and his family, there were grandparents, brothers and sisters, uncles and aunts, and cousins, all singing with such fervor and appearing so happy that it made the trolls want to retch.

"Did you ever see anything so disgusting in all your life?" one of the female trolls said.

"Look at all of the presents under the tree!" the troll girl exclaimed.

"Look at them indeed!" her mother said. "They will be extremely miserably unhappy when they wake up tomorrow morning and discover all of their presents gone. I only wish I could be here to see the looks on their faces when they find nothing under the Christmas tree."

"When are they going to sleep anyway?" one of the troll men said, irritated and impatient. "Aren't most people usually asleep by this time of night?"

"I suppose it must have something to do with it being the night before *Christmas*," his wife said, spitting out the word Christmas as though the mere act of speaking the word left an unpleasant taste in her mouth.

The trolls watched and listened as the people inside the farmhouse began singing "Deck The Halls." When the people sang the line "troll the ancient Yuletide carol, fa-la-la la-la, la-la, la-la," the trolls grimaced and looked at each other to make sure they had all heard what they thought they heard.

"Did everyone hear that?" one of the woman trolls said. "Did they actually just sing something about trolls?"

"It sure sounded like it to me," the other woman troll said.

"Me too," one of the man trolls added.

"And what is it with all the 'fa-la-la-la-la?'" the other male troll said. "It seems to me I remember there once having been a troll named Fa-la. Do you suppose they're singing about her?"

"Why would people sing about some old troll who's no longer even around?" his wife said.

"And why at Christmas?" the other female troll asked.

"Why would people sing about trolls at all at Christmas?" her husband said. "Everybody knows that us trolls all *hate* Christmas and don't want anything to do with it."

"We must find out what this is all about," one of the women said. "I think I have a plan. We'll hide somewhere until these people are asleep, then we'll sneak into the house and kidnap one of them and take him somewhere and force him to tell us why they were singing about trolls in a Christmas song."

And so that was the plan the trolls followed. They hid in a shed, from where they could see the house, until some of the visitors left and the lights went off inside the house. After giving the people plenty of time to fall asleep, they pried open a bedroom window, kidnapped a teenage girl sleeping in one of the beds, and took her a short distance into a patch of woods near the farm.

"Why were you singing about us?" the trolls demanded.

"What do you mean?" the girl asked, her voice shaky with fright. "We weren't singing about you."

"Don't lie to us!" one of the women said. "We heard you ourselves. You sang about trolls in one of your disgusting songs."

"Tell us or we'll torture you without mercy," the other female troll threatened.

The poor girl didn't doubt for a moment that the trolls would follow through on that threat. "Believe me, I would tell you if we sang about trolls in any song," she said with a quivering voice, growing more frightened by the minute. "But I swear to you that there is no Christmas carol that has anything about trolls in it—not any that I know of, at least."

"It's that one with all the 'fa-la-las' in it," one of the male trolls said.

The girl thought for a minute. "You mean 'Deck The Halls'?" she asked.

"I don't know what it's called," the troll answered, "but if that's the one with the 'fa-la-la-la-las' in it then that's the one."

"Sing it," one of the female trolls ordered the captive girl.

"Now?" the girl said. She was in no mood to sing.

"Of course now," the troll said.

Knowing she would be wise to do what the trolls asked her to do if she hoped to escape from them unharmed, the girl took a deep breath to try to calm her nerves, then began singing "Deck The Halls" in a soft, wavering voice. As soon as she sang "troll the ancient Yuletide carol" all of the trolls showed signs of recognition. A couple of them pointed at her, as if accusing her of lying. "Aha!" one of them exclaimed triumphantly. "There it is! And you said there was nothing about trolls in any of your songs, you liar! What do you have to say for yourself now?"

"I've never heard of any ancient troll named Yuletide Carol," one of the trolls said.

"But that's not the name of a troll," the girl explained. "Yuletide carol means Christmas song. Yuletide is another name for Christmastime, and carol is a certain type of song."

"But you said 'troll,'" one of the trolls said. "You can't deny that you said 'troll.' We clearly heard you say 'troll.' What about that?"

"Yeah, what about that?" the others chimed in.

"But the word 'troll' in the song doesn't mean troll as in trolls like you," the girl said. "In this case 'troll' means to sing in full voice."

"Do you really expect us to believe that?" one of the woman trolls said.

"It's the truth," the girl insisted. "I swear it is," she pleaded.

The trolls talked things over amongst themselves and decided the girl was probably telling the truth, so they let her go, much to the girl's relief. If the girl had told the truth, it was bad enough news to them that the word "troll" could also mean singing to people, but at least that was preferable to being connected with Christmas in any way. Indeed, they were so relieved that they completely forgot about stealing presents from under Christmas trees that night. All of the presents the trolls had intended to steal were still under Christmas trees, in their bright, colorful wrappings, when Christmas morning dawned.

96 ▪ Fear For Old Fungus

Early on Christmas Eve—in fact, so early that it was not yet evening, as perhaps most people define that period, but rather late afternoon—Old Fungus was shambling about, for no particular purpose, following some of the trails not far from the two communal caves. Hundreds of footprints had packed and crystalized the snow, turning the snow to ice and making the trails as slick as seal skin. More snow was falling, a wind blowing it horizontally and making the trail surfaces even slipperier. Because of the trail conditions, Old Fungus was walking at an even slower than usual pace, and putting more weight on his walking stick than he generally did. He hated staying in his cave for days on end, as weather conditions sometimes forced him to do at his advanced age during the wintertime, and was determined to be out and about as much as possible, even if he no longer could contribute much to the needs of the tribe.

Old Fungus had no idea that it was Christmas Eve, nor could he have cared less had he known. Unlike Leik, the troll who befell a tragic end because of his curiosity about Christmas, Old Fungus was never the least bit intrigued by Christmas. He had no more interest in Christmas than he would have had in calligraphy or oceanography, had he had any idea those disciplines existed. Christmas was as far from his thoughts as philosophical musings about the nature of beauty. Needless to say, he never contemplated such things as beauty, character and ethics, as human philosophers do. As far as he was concerned, given that Christmas is a human holiday he knew it was something he, a troll, should not care about or concern himself with.

Old Fungus was making his way along a well-trod trail, walking away from the caves, when his left foot slipped out from under him and he found himself falling backwards. He tried to right himself, but he was far too off-balance to check his fall. As he fell, like a toppled tree trunk, the back of his head bounced on the rock-hard ground, which sent him into a state of unconsciousness. When he regained consciousness, more than a minute later, his head throbbed, his back hurt and his right knee felt as though someone was pounding spikes into it. Dizzy and confused as he was, it took him several seconds to realize where he was and what had happened. He lied on his back for a couple of minutes as he assessed his situation, then attempted to get to his feet. His back and his knee ached so much that he was unable to do so. Indeed, he could barely move anything other than his arms and his left leg. His head ached most of all, but that particular intense pain was not what was preventing him from getting to his feet.

A layer of snow collected on him, like dust on a jar cover, as he lay there for something on the order of forty-five minutes before Skimpa happened along the trail and nearly tripped over him. By then the cold ground had transferred much of its coldness into Old Fungus's body and he was shivering like a brittle leaf in a breeze and breathing in an odd, jerky fashion.

"At last!" Old Fungus said when Skimpa appeared. "I can't get up."

"You can't get up?" Skimpa said. "Why not?"

"I slipped and fell," Old Fungus barked. "My back hurts, my knee hurts, my head hurts. You have to help me."

"I'll see what I can do," Skimpa said. As it turned out, there wasn't much she could do by herself. "I better go and get some help," she said at last. "You wait here." With that, she headed off toward the caves. "Old Fungus has fallen and can't get up," she announced upon entering the larger of the communal caves, where a half-dozen tribe members were eating. "Two or three of you need to come with me and carry him back here."

"Let me finish eating first, then I'll help you," Scurf said, as others nodded and expressed agreement.

"He needs help right away, not an hour from now," Skimpa said in no uncertain terms. She went over and slapped her husband, Traug, on the back of the head. "You're coming with me right now," she announced. Then she flicked a finger into Dau's right temple and told him he was coming too. Seeing how serious and determined Skimpa was, Traug and Dau, as well as Rnobrna, left their meals unfinished, for the time being, and

441

followed Skimpa to the spot where Old Fungus had fallen and was waiting for help.

The four of them found the tribe's oldest member seemingly asleep when they reached him. He wouldn't wake up when they poked and shook him, though. They knew he wasn't dead, for he was breathing quite laboriously. Dau and Traug carried him back to the communal cave where he lived and plopped him on his bed in his private chamber before returning to the other communal cave to finish eating supper. Retta joined Skimpa in looking after Old Fungus, who by then was in a semi-conscious state part of the time and out like a switched-off light part of the time. He complained of having the chills, so they rounded up extra blankets and coats from other parts of the cave to add to his covering. Retta felt his forehard and found it to be fiery.

Most of the female members of the tribe took turns keeping watch over Old Fungus as he slipped in and out of consciousness and moaned from his pain. One or two of them remained in his candlelit room at all times, while those finishing their stints reported his status to other tribe members. By contrast to the women, none of the male trolls displayed much worry or concern, even though Old Fungus's condition apparently was worsening by the half-hour.

"I don't know if he's going to make it," Frel reported to others after an hour at his bedside. "He's in mighty bad shape. I'm afraid he might die." Frel, Dau's wife, had smallish ears, for a troll, but a big mouth, from a physical standpoint, and the sort of big hair both Jompa and Retta had as well. Her dark eyes seemed to penetrate whoever or whatever she was looking at.

"Well, no one lives forever," Scurf said evenly, with no hint of emotion.

"I'm just glad it's not me," Rnobrna commented.

Utrud, Rnobrna's wife, insisted that Rnobrna walk to Guggle's cabin to let her know what had happened to Old Fungus and ask if she could provide some sort of medical help. Reluctantly, for he didn't feel like making such a trip this night, Rnobrna agreed to fulfill Utrud's "request." Drulle, who was feeling frisky that night, went with him. Despite Old Fungus's precarious condition, the two of them took their sweet time in walking to Guggle's place, for Rnobrna considered such lassitude to be push-back against his wife's domineering demeanor.

97 ▪ Hildur And The Giant Troll

Andrew Branstad wanted to hear another troll tale on Christmas Eve, so his parents obliged him. Emma suggested that Anders read *The Trolls And The Pussycat*, a chestnut about a band of trolls that takes over the same human house every Christmas Eve until a visitor to that house frightens the trolls away by making them believe his large pet bear is a cat. Anders considered the tale too farcical, however, and so selected a different tale with a Christmas Eve setting, *Hildur And The Giant Troll*, he thought was far superior.

▪

Long, long ago a well-to-do sheep and cattle farmer named Gunner Hobert and his wife, Hildur, lived on a remote farm situated on a firth, which is to say a river estuary. It was commonly believed that a giant female troll lived in the mountains on the opposite side of the firth. This troll was thought to have a mild temperament, for she had never caused any mischief.

One Christmas Eve Gunner went out after dark and never returned. A full-scale search mounted in an attempt to find either him or his body proved futile.

Hildur asked one of the farm's hired hands to assume management of the farm after her husband's disappearance. The following Christmas Eve that man disappeared in the same manner Gunner had the previous year. As with Gunner, there was no trace of him ever found.

After two such mysterious Christmas Eve disappearances, Hildur was so fearful of what would happen the next Christmas Eve that she decided she would no longer spend winters at the farm. Her plan was to live there only during the spring, summer and autumn months and leave shepherds and herdsmen in charge of the sheep and cattle during the winter while she took up seasonal residence elsewhere, taking household possessions and four cows she kept for home use with her.

As winter approached and she prepared to leave the farm a woman wearing old-fashioned garments appeared to her in a dream.

"One of your cows has just calved," the woman said—as, indeed, one of Hildur's cows had. "I, however, have no hope of providing my children with any nourishment unless you put out a jug of milk for me in your dairy each day when you measure out your rations. I know that you intend to move to another farm in two days because you dare not stay here over Christmas after what happened to your husband and your servant the past two Christmas Eves. I must tell you that a giant woman troll lives in the opposite mountains. While she herself is of mild tempera-ment, several years ago she gave birth to a baby boy who has a heinous disposition. Now that the boy is old enough to talk and have his own thoughts, he insists that his mother bring him a human being he can have to torture each Christmas. If she doesn"t do that the boy becomes even more ill-tempered and unruly than he normally is. I will strike a bargain with you: If you remain here and provide me with fresh milk each day, as I have asked, I will give you good advice as to how you may rid yourself of these trolls in your neighborhood." With that, the woman vanished.

In the morning Hildur recalled the dream as vividly as she remembered what she had done the day before. Had a woman actually visited her during the night, while she slept? Feeling a little foolish, she set out a wooden jug of fresh milk in the dairy that morning, as the woman in her dream instructed her to do. When she went into the dairy again a few minutes later the jug of milk wasn't there. That evening she found the empty jug exactly where she had placed the full jug that morning. This was a most curious development.

The following day the same sequence of events took place: Hildur left a jug of fresh milk in the dairy in the morning and found the empty jug in the same spot in the evening.

With her dream seemingly coming true, Hildur abandoned her plan to move to another farm over the winter, for the woman in her dream had promised to give her good advice on how to get rid of the trolls in the neighborhood, and if she could get rid of the troublesome trolls there would be no reason for her to move, if what the woman told her in the dream was true.

Day after day Hildur refilled the wooden jug with fresh milk, wondering all the while when the woman who spoke to her in the dream would live up to her end of the bargain and advise her as to how she could get rid of the trolls.

The night of December twenty-third, the same woman who appeared to Hildur in the earlier dream appeared to her again. After a friendly greeting, the woman said, "You have no doubt wondered to whom you are giving milk each day. I will tell you: I am an elf woman. I live in a little hill not far from your house. You have treated me well by providing me with milk for my children, as I requested of you. Your obligation in this regard is now completed. Yesterday my cow had a calf, so now I am able to provide fresh milk to my children myself. You will find a gift for yourself on the shelf where you are accustomed to leaving the jug of milk for me. I also intend to deliver you from the danger that awaits you tomorrow night.

"At midnight you will awake and feel an irresistible urge to go outside, as though you are being drawn to a magnet. Do not resist this urge. Get up and leave the house. There will be a giant waiting for you outside. She will seize you in her arms and carry you across your grassy field, over the river, and toward the mountains where she lives. At that point, this is what you must do: . . ."

Here the elf woman explained to Hildur what actions she must take in order to escape the cluthes of the giant troll.

When she awoke in the morning Hildur recalled her dream in detail. When she went to the shelf where she was accustomed to leaving a jug of milk she found a large bundle containing a beautifully embroidered dress and cap.

That night, she awoke at midnight with an irresistible compulsion to get up and go outside. As the elf woman had advised, she did not struggle against this urge, but rose from her bed and left the house. As soon as she stepped outside a giant female troll seized her, lifted her high in the air and stalked off with her across the grassy field and over the river. A short distance from the river Hildur cried out "What did I hear then?" exactly as the elf woman had instructed her to do.

"What did you hear?" the giant troll asked.

"I heard someone cry 'Momma Gellivor! Momma Gellivor!'" Hildur said, using an answer the elf woman provided in the dream.

This stunned the troll, for she knew that no human being had ever heard her name spoken.

"Oh, I suppose it is that naughty child of mine," the troll said, setting Hildur on the ground and running toward the mountains in long, loping strides.

As the elf woman had directed, Hildur headed in the opposite direction, running as fast as her legs would carry her along the riverbank. If all was proceeding as planned, Hildur knew that at that very minute the elf woman was up in the mountains giving the giant troll's wicked child a merciless thumping.

As the elf woman had predicted, when the giant troll saw that Hildur was attempting to escape she turned around and overtook her.

"Why did you not stand still, you wretch?" the troll demanded. Once again she seized Hildur and headed toward the mountains with her. After only a few steps, Hildur, following the script the elf woman wrote for her, again called out, "What did I hear then?"

"What did you hear?" the troll asked, posing the question exactly as she had previously.

"I thought I heard someone calling out 'Momma Gellivor! Momma Gellivor!'" Hildur said.

Again the giant troll tossed Hildur aside, as though she were an unwanted ragdoll, and took off running toward the mountains. Mustering every ounce of her strength and every iota of her desire, Hildur ran in the direction of the nearest church. As she ran, she had the distinct sense that someone took ahold of her hand and helped her along, although no one was visible.

Suddenly the thunderous rumble of a rockslide was audible in the mountains. Hildur turned around and saw the giant troll striding furiously toward her across the bogs and marshes, which were bathed in moonlight. She thought it likely that the giant troll had returned to her mountain cave to discover her child had been thumped to within an inch of his life and was now out to exact a horrible revenge on Hildur. The thought made her woozy. Somehow, though, she found herself lifted up and gliding over the ground almost as though her feet were not even touching the ground. She wondered if the elf woman was helping her reach the church, as she had promised to do if such assistance became necessary.

As soon as Hildur stepped inside the church the door closed behind her, though she had no recollection of closing the door herself when she later went over in her mind what had happened, and the churchbell began ringing. Many people were in the church to celebrate an early morning Christmas service.

As the churchbell rang, all the people inside the church heard the crash of a heavy fall outside. Hildur and the others looked out the windows and saw the giant troll scramble to her feet and scurry away from the sound of the churchbell, which is a torturous sound to trolls. In her haste to get away, the giant troll stumbled on a fieldstone wall, ripping a large hole in it.

That was the last time anyone in that vicinity ever saw the giant troll Gellivor. It was generally believed she moved to a different mountain in some other location.

When Hildur Hobart returned home after the Christmas Eve church service she had the most joyous experience of her life, for both her husband, Gunner, and the servant who had disappeared were waiting to greet her. As tears of joy streamed down Hildur's cheeks, Gunner explained that a giant troll woman had kidnapped them and held them cavtive in a deep, dingy cave so her vicious young son could torture them until an elf woman appeared to thump the giant troll's wicked child and free them.

98 ▪ Fever Dreams

Delirious, Old Fungus dreamed of gnomes. He found himself with two gnomes in a field, and the two gnomes were trying to convince him that he had a skewed impression of gnomes, that he would like gnomes if he got to know a few. The two gnomes seemed so friendly and genial that Old Fungus wondered if he had perhaps judged the entire species unfairly. When the gnomes suggested playing on what they call a balance board, also known as a seesaw, or a teeter-totter, Old Fungus happily agreed to play with them. In the next instant Old Fungus was sitting on one end of a balance board, the two gnomes at the other end, and they were going up and down in turn. Old Fungus was thinking gnomes weren't so bad, after all, when suddenly the two gnomes made their end of the board go down so fast that Old Fungus was sent airborne, like an arrow from a deeply drawn bow. "Look! A flying troll!" one of the gnomes quipped, and both of them chortled. Their echoing laughter shrieked around Old Fungus as he soared into the sky, and awoke as he was still soaring.

His shirt had a patch of perspiration at the front of the neck. He was shivering with chills even as it seemed his head was directly over a hot fire. He turned from his right side to his left side and pulled his covers tighter, trying to warm his quivering body. Soon he was asleep again, and into another nightmare.

Gnomes featured in this dream as well. This time he was walking along a forest trail in the daytime, minding his own business, when suddenly he found himself trying to dodge dozens of pointed gnome caps. These were not the red felt caps male gnomes generally wear (female gnomes wear green caps), but copper-colored caps made of actual sheets of copper. And the gnomes were using them as weapons, like swords, pricking and prodding Old Fungus all along his sides, from his shoulders to his feet, darting out like wasps to sting him, then disappearing into the forest again, seemingly invisible. Old Fungus tried to run, but at his age, for he was his actual age in the dream, his running was no more than a brisk walking pace, and so he was a sitting duck for the persistent, pestiferous, copper-capped gnomes. "This is a nightmare!" Old Fungus thought in his dream. He was incapable of catching even one of the gnomes, or of evading a single copper-cap thrust, for the gnomes' actions were so lightning quick that he clutched nothing but air when he tried to grab one. After being pricked, prodded and poked dozens of times, Old Fungus found himself being attacked on both sides simultaneously as two gnomes, each with his head lowered, like a battering ram, speared him with the points of their caps just below his ribcage, at the same time. Old Fungus stiffened in his bed as he felt the imaginary pain, and the jolt of his body movement awakened him back to semiconsciousness, still in delirium. In his state, he didn't realize there were others—Frel and Jompa—in the chamber with him. Nor was their conversation anything but mumbling to him.

"He must have felt a pain," Jompa said. "Did you see how he jerked?"

"Maybe he was having a bad dream," Frel guessed. "Look how he's sweating. I better change the cloth on his head." She soaked an absorbant piece of cloth in a pail of cold water, wrung out most of the water, then removed an almost-dry cloth from Old Fungus's deeply-lined forehead and replaced it with the cold, wet, folded cloth.

By the time Frel and Jompa were talking about whether or not Old Fungus would make it through the night Old Fungus had drifted off to a shallow sleep again, and into another nightmare. An old gnome was blowing glass against a sun-bright yellow background that Old Fungus found so painful to look at that he was squinting. As the red-capped gnome blew on the blowpipe—Old Fungus had a side view of the gnome, but wasn't part of the scene himself—the marble-like red and yellow ball at the end of the blowpipe expanded in size and suddenly Old Fungus recognized his distored face in that hollow glass sphere. When the gnome stopped blowing and the glass sphere stopped expanding, the glassblowing gnome held out the ball, which still contained the image of Old Fungus's distorted face, and all at once about twenty gnomes were dancing about and chanting "We have you trapped, you wicked troll" over and over. Then some of the other trolls called for the glassblower to "blow some more," which he did, the result being that the glass sphere again expanded until it burst like a pyrotechnics shell, sending an explosion of glass shards into the air. As with fireworks, the glass shards literally disappeared into thin air and all burned up before falling to the ground.

Once again the tensest part of the nightmare jolted Old Fungus out of his sleep, though not into clear consciousness. He was still perceiving the real world as though through wavy glass. Everything looked blurred, distorted and perplexing. He heard mumbling—or what sounded like mumbling to him—that seemed to bounce around the chamber like a fly inside a jar. He had the sense that he was hearing backwards talk, which caused him to think time itself was moving backward and forward at the same time, each force of time pulling him in a different direction and stretching him every which way. He thought that he would fall through time, into oblivion, if the opposite time forces continued pulling at him much longer. He felt sick and ached all over, and seemed incapable of moving any part of his body except his eyes, as though some invisible force had him pinned down as surely as if rope straps held him to his bed.

Soon he was into another dream. A long line of gnomes was running across his chest as he lied on the snowy ground, as unable to move a muscle in that situation as he was in his bed this night. He actually thought of the similarity in his dream. Or was he awake and thinking of that? He wasn't sure. The gnomes started using his chest as a trampoline, jumping onto it and off of it, one after another after another. Suddenly, like a jump cut in a movie—though Old Fungus certainly didn't think in those terms, since he had never seen a movie—he was in a different place, all alone. The setting was a rocky plateau, with vistas in every direction. He wasn't alone for long, though. All at once giant gnomes beset him on all sides. At least he took them for giant gnomes, though the possibility occurred to him that the gnomes were their usual stature while he had somehow been transformed into a tiny troll who had the same proportion to gnomes as gnomes do to average trolls. The gnomes quickly had him in their clutches. In the next instant—another movie-like jump cut—one of them was holding him against a revolving grindstone while the others hooted and mocked him as they looked on, as entertained as Old Fungus had been watching gnomes undergo similar torture over the years.

Mercifully, the nightmare ended. Old Fungus's bedding was disheveled, bunched up and damp with perspiration. Recognizing that he seemed to be awake, though in a groggy state, the two female trolls keeping watch over him at the time, Feirn and Elseth, did what they could to straighten the bedding and wash Old Fungus, to try to make him cooler. In his delirious condition, Old Fungus thought two people—two human beings—were hovering over his bed with evil intentions. He wanted to shout, but found he couldn't make a sound of any sort come out of his mouth, which made him think the two women in his room had placed a spell on him so that he couldn't speak. He continued to feel that some invisible force had him pinned to the bed, for he seemed to be unable to move his arms or his legs, or even raise his head. He thought it must be morning, but it wasn't even midnight yet. He began wondering if he was dead, if this was what death was.

And so the night continued, with Old Fungus in piercing pain and delirious, addled and disoriented, by turns hallucinating and dreaming, and having some of the weirdest thoughts that had ever seared his mind. Gnomes and people featured in most of his nightmares. Malicious gnomes chased him and pelted him with small rocks they shot from blowguns, and he was helpless to do anything about it. He chased gnomes that were seemingly impossible to catch, which had him on the brink of mental madness. People fooled him into falling into a trough of blue-died water, which turned him blue. He envisioned himself in places and situations he hadn't seen or been in for hundreds of years in some cases. Gnomes again talked him into playing with them, a game of tug-of-war this time, and then somehow wrapped ropes around him until he was trussed up like a beef roast ready for the oven. Immobilized in his bed by the invisible force as he was, gnomes took advantage of the situation by sticking him all over his body, including his eyes and ears, with gold and silver needles. He was about to snatch a gnome, after jumping out of a hiding place, when all at once skis appeared on the gnome's feet and he skied away over the snow, leaving Old Fungus holding a handful of air. Then, as he stood there, a group of other gnomes skied past him, going as fast as a brisk wind. All the while, past, present and future were all wrapped up in a single package, with time sometimes going backward rather than forward, or backward from some future time. So much happened in his nightmares, and they embraced such a wide swath of time, that every five minutes of actual time seemed like an hour or two to Old Fungus, which made the night seem endless.

The female tribe members keeping watch over him had their own anxieties and distressed thoughts as Old Fungus's condition appeared to worsen hour after hour. Old Fungus had been part of the tribe for as long as most of them could remember, so the possibility of him dying and no longer being around was almost unimaginable to them. Except for keeping cold cloths on his fiery forehead, trying to keep his body as warm as possible and toweling him off occasionally, they had no idea what they could do to ease his pain or reverse his decline, though. That's why Utrud wanted Guggle there; she thought Guggle would know what, if anything, could be done, if anyone would. She couldn't understand why it was taking Rnobrna so long to fetch her. The reason was that, besides Rnobrna and Drulle taking their sweet time in walking to Guggle's cabin, Guggle wasn't home when they arrived. After waiting there a while, wondering if they should return to the caves or what, they decided to search the vicinity for her. Being illiterate, they couldn't simply leave a written message at her cabin letting her know that Old Fungus was gravely ill and needed her help. After searching for Guggle for nearly two hours, without success, Rnobrna and Drulle returned to her cabin and found her there this time. Guggle asked the two some questions to try to determine exactly what was wrong with Old Fungus. The scant information Rnobrna provided was so skechy—Drulle wasn't able to provide any information at all—that it was of little use to Guggle. Using instinct and common sense more than the scraps of information Rnobrna provided, the witch quickly gathered some ingredients for a tea potion and headed out to the caves with Rnobrna and Drulle.

Guggle arrived at Old Fungus's cave chamber just minutes after Elseth said to her mother, Retta, who was also in the chamber, that she thought Old Fungus might be dead. Retta felt his forehead and sensed an almost-imperceptible pulsing of blood. "I don't think he is yet, but I also don't think he has long to live," she said to her daughter. "He seems to be fading fast." Elseth's eyes welled with tears at the thought, and she fled from the chamber, with Utrud taking her place by Old Fungus's side.

While relieved to see Guggle, both Retta and Utrud feared she had come too late to be able to do anything to save Old Fungus from a fate of death. Guggle determined for herself that Old Fungus was still breathing and assured them she would do everything in her power to save him. As the three women talked, Retta and Utrud provided Guggle with much more information than Rnobrna was able to do. What they told her made her confident that she had brought the right potion for the situation. In a few minutes, Skimpa brought Guggle the tea potion Guggle had asked her to heat when she entered the cave's large front chamber.

"Is it hot enough?" Skimpa asked. "You said you didn't want it too hot."

Guggle took the mug of tea from Skimpa and put her nose close to the tea. "It's just right," she said. "He'll be able to drink it right away."

Shaking Old Fungus from the midst of a nightmare, Guggle had Utrud hold up the patient's head as she tried to get him to open his mouth and swallow the tea potion. Although Old Fungus's eyes remained shut, he was awake enough, though in an extremely groggy, hazy state, to allow Guggle to pry open his mouth and get some of the tea down his throat, though much of the tea ran down his chin and onto his chest.

"You can put his head back down," Guggle said to Utrud when it appeared Old Fungus was again asleep and she would not be able to get him to swallow any more of the tea. "About all we can do now is wait and hope," she said to the others.

Which is what they did—waited and hoped. From then on the watchers could tell he was less agitated and that he was in a constant state of sleep. His breathing was so shallow at times that they worried he was no longer breathing. At other times he gasped for air, as if suffocating, and they wondered if he was taking his last breaths. He continued to perspire effusively, make faint gurgling sounds in his throat and run a dangerously high fever. The women came and went into and out of the chamber throughout the long hours. Some knitted and sewed while others simply sat there watching him or staring into space. There was little conversation.

Mid-morning, Tattra and Feirn happened to be talking to one another when Old Fungus opened his eyes. Given that they were looking at each other while engaged in conversation, they failed to notice that Old Fungus was awake and alert. They quickly found out he was awake, though, when Old Fungus growled, "What's going on here? What are you two doing in here?"

The voice startled them. "You're awake!" Feirn said. "How do you feel?"

Tattra felt his forehead and reported to Feirn: "His fever's gone."

Old Fungus pushed away Tattra's hand and said, "How long have I been asleep? I feel like I've been sleeping for days."

Feirn and Tattra had a difficult time convincing him he experienced so many dreams and nightmares in only one night. Old Fungus thought they must have come to him over the course of at least three or four nights and days. He didn't remember slipping and falling, and may not have believed he actually did had his wounds and pains not offered evidence of that.

"Did someone catch a gnome?" Old Fungus asked excitedly, for his best remembered, most lifelike dream of the night was about someone in the tribe capturing another gnome, giving him another opportunity to tease one of the little creatures. "Do we have a gnome around to tease?"

"I'm afraid not," Tattra told him. "You must have dreamed that."

"No gnome?" Old Fungus said, crestfallen.

"Not right now," Tattra said.

While the female trolls were thrilled about Old Fungus's recovery, seemingly from the brink of death, most of the men were as indifferent as rocks. When Tattra shared the exciting news with Ort that "Old Fungus is going to be okay!," Ort mumbled, "Oh." He was much more concerned about what there was to eat.

99 ▪ Revelation

Haar was happy to find Ort chopping wood near his cave when he returned from an outing shortly before sunup, for he had what he thought was significant information to share with him.

"I think this might be Christmas," he said to Ort.

"So what?" Ort snapped. "We don't give a fig about Christmas. That's not for us; that's for people."

"That's my point," Haar said. "I got to thinking about it, and it came to me that if that big building at the bottom of the mountain is a church then people will probably go there on Christmas morning. I've heard that people go to churches on Christmas morning, for some reason. And a bell will ring. We should be able to find out once and for all whether or not it's a chuch, if we do a little investigating. Wouldn't you like to know whether or not it's a church?"

"Yeah, I guess that would be nice to know," Ort concurred. "But what makes you think this is Christmas? I know it has to be sometime around now, but what makes you think it's today?"

"Because I heard people singing outside a house last night," Haar said. "And I'm almost sure they were singing Christmas songs."

"That doesn't sound like much fun," Ort commented.

"Singing Christmas songs, you mean?" Haar said.

"I mean hearing people singing Christmas songs," Ort said. "Though I can't imagine it would be any fun to sing them either. Nothing about Christmas is any fun, that I can see."

"No, it was painful to my ears," Haar said. "I'm not *sure* they were Christmas songs, but I'm pretty sure they were. But I remember hearing somewhere that groups of people go around and sing outside other people's houses the night before Christmas. So if they were singing Christmas songs, which they probably were, then last night was probably the night before Christmas, which would make today Christmas. It makes sense, doesn't it?"

"Not to me," Ort grumbled. "I can't see that anything about Christmas makes sense."

"No, no, I don't mean that," Haar hastened to clarify. "I mean it makes sense that if last night was the night before Christmas then today must be Christmas."

Ort considered that logic a few seconds. "I suppose so."

"What do you say then?" Haar said. "Should some of us go down the mountain and try to find out if that big building is a church?"

"I'm not stopping you," Ort said. "Go ahead if you want."

"Well, I'm not crazy about going all alone," Haar said. "I thought maybe you would be interested in going with me, and maybe a few others too." When Ort displayed no enthusiasm about taking part in such a mission, Haar appealed to his vanity. "Wouldn't you like to be one of the first ones to know what that big building is for?"

That hooked Ort. He agreed to accompany Haar down the mountain. The two took Jirik along as well.

"**W**hat was that?" Haar asked Ort, pointing to his left as the three trolls neared the bottom of the mountain. "Something moved."

"An animal?" Ort said. "I didn't see anything."

"No, it couldn't have been an animal," Haar said. "It was a blue color, just whoosing between the two trees over there." He meant two large pine trees graced with generous dollops of immaculate snow. "Did you see it?" he asked Jirik.

"I didn't see anything," Jirik answered. "I was looking straight ahead."

"Is that the building down there?" Ort said. "I think it is."

"It looks like it," Haar said.

"Come on, let's get closer," Ort said to the other two.

With Ort leading the way, they made their way toward the ski lodge.

"Whoa!" Jirik said suddenly as he looked to his left. "I just saw a person over there."

"Where?" Ort asked.

"Right over there," Jirik said, pointing. "He was moving fast. I barely saw him and then he was gone."

"That sounds like what I saw," Haar said. "Maybe I saw a person too. Was the person you saw wearing something blue?"

"I don't think so," Jirik said. "I'm not sure what color clothes he had on. I just saw a flash and looked and he was gone."

The three descended further, looking for a screened spot that would give them a good view of the big building.

"Well, it makes sense we would see people. . ." Ort was saying, trailing off as he and the two others simultaneously saw something that stopped them in their tracks: people skiing down the bottom part of the mountain where workers had cut trees, graded the ground and planted grass months earlier. "What in the world?!" he said. "Do you see that? People are skiing down the mountain!"

"They *are* skiing, aren't they?" Haar said, almost too astounded by the sight to squeeze out any words. As noted, trolls were accustomed to seeing people getting around on skis, which sometimes involved skiing up and down slopes, rises, mounds and small hills. Skiing down a steep mountainside was something else entirely, though. That was something new to them, and peculiar. The towline carrying skiers back to the top of the ski runs was even stranger to their sensibilities. Haar was the first to notice that. "Look at that!" he said. "People are riding through the air!"

"What's going on here?" Ort said with an equal measure of puzzlement and disgust. "I've never seen anything like this, and I've been around more than a little and seen a lot of things. Let's find a good spot and watch this a while."

Selecting a spot where they had good views of both the ski lodge and the ski hill, and where pine trees, boulders and brush screened them well, the three trolls watched the human activity in fascination as people skied, talked, drove cars into the parking lot, went in and out of the lodge, and appeared to be enjoying themselves immensely. They could see forty to fifty people at any given time, ranging in age from six or seven to the sixties and seventies. Haar's conjecture that it was Christmas Day was not correct. This was not Christmas morning but the day after Christmas. The carolers he had heard the previous evening had done some of their singing on Christmas Day. So, had the large building been a church the trolls would not have found out it was that day, for no bells would have rung out.

"I don't know if I should say this, but that looks kind of fun," Jirik said about the skiing, worried that Ort might think he was reverting to past thoughts and wanting to emulate human beings.

"It does, doesn't it?" Haar said. "I can't quite understand it, though. I've been watching, and people will ski down the hill, then ride back up to the top on one of those flying benches and ski down the hill again. What's the point? Every other time I've seen people skiing they've obviously been going somewhere; there was some purpose to it. What's the point of going down the same hill over and over again?"

"Don't try to understand people," Ort advised. "You're liable to get your brain all tied up in knots if you do. People do a lot of things that don't make much sense, or any sense. And I'd say this is probably one of them."

"Maybe the point is to just have fun," Jirik surmised, drawing on the period when he appreciated nature for its own sake, and his conversations with his human friend, Sten. "Maybe people like to do things sometimes just because they have fun doing them, or it makes them feel good."

"I suppose that makes about as much sense as any other explanation," Haar remarked. "I can't think of any other reason for all of these people doing what they're doing."

"One thing for sure: this big building isn't a church," Ort said. "I never thought it was, myself."

"Well, that's something," Haar said. "At least we won't be tortured by the horrible clang of a bell then. I'd like to get inside once, though, and have a look around, to see what the people are using it for."

"It's strange alright," Ort said. "I've never seen a building so big that wasn't a church or a barn or something like that."

"Why do people keep going in and out of it?" Jirik asked his two more experienced companions.

"Maybe they think it's fun," Ort needled, throwing Jirik's supposition about the reason for skiing back in his face.

"Do you suppose people come here and do this every day, or is it just because it's Christmas?" Haar wondered aloud, still under the impression it was Christmas Day.

"Why would they just do it on Christmas?" Jirik asked. "What does skiing have to do with Christmas? Is skiing a part of Christmas?"

"I keep telling you: people do things that make no sense," Ort said. "They always have and probably always will. That's just the way they are."

The three trolls continued observing without any further conversation for a while. Ort found it very amusing every time one of the skiers took a tumble. The more spectacular the spill, the harder he laughed. Not being what anyone would characterize as a jolly bunch, trolls are not given to laughing much in the normal course of their lives. It felt good to Ort to laugh so much, particularly at human follies, but at the same time it pained him a little to make muscles stretch that were not accustomed to stretching so much. Haar and Jirik laughed and chuckled whenever Ort did, though not as long or as loudly. Ort laughed so loud on occasion that Haar cautioned him people might hear him if he was too loud.

"It looks dangerous," Haar commented after one skier took a particularly nasty spill that sent him swirling down the slope, completely out of control. "That can't be any fun."

"Serves him right, for coming here in the first place," Ort said with a snarl.

"Remember when we first came here, back in the spring?" Haar said. "I never imagined then that this is what would go on here. It could be worse, I guess."

After observing a short while longer the three trolls grew bored watching the same action over and over and headed back up the mountain. All three were quite tired, for it was far past their early morning bedtimes.

100 ▪ A Lark In The Dark

Fun? Was that the key? Could Jirik be on to something with that appraisal of why people were risking falls and fractures to shoot down a steep slope for no apparent practical purpose? Ort couldn't help but dwell on that possibility, the thought tumbling in his mind like a small rock caught in a river eddy, keeping him awake and disturbing his sleep. After all, Jirik had had a closer relationship with a human being than any other tribe member, so maybe he possessed more insight into the minds and motivations of people than he and the others did. Still, Ort couldn't shake the deep-seated conviction that people did many things that made absolutely no sense, at least to trolls. Trolls did things for fun too, but every such activity had a practical component as well, as far as he could see. To him, it made no more sense to do something strictly for fun than it did to build a fire on a hot day if you didn't intend to cook something over the fire. At the same time, he knew that people's brains seemed to work differently than trolls' brains in many respects. So maybe fun *was* the answer. On the other hand, even if people did some things strictly for fun, where was the fun in zipping down a hill over and over and sometimes falling down, or even crashing, sliding or tumbling downhill and potentially injuring oneself quite severely? Using skis to go across snow, from one place to another place, made sense; there was practicality to that. Skiing down a steep slope a relatively short distance, over and over, made no practical sense.

An image of himself cross country skiing suddenly flashed into his mind that night, when he was out and about and not even thinking of people skiing down the Troll Mountain ski runs, or even of people cross country skiing. It just popped up out of the blue, out of nowhere. The misty image was that of himself as a boy, approximately twelve years of age. It was as though he was seeing it in peripheral vision, in his memory, not clearly and fully. Had he actually skied when he was that age, or was he remembering a dream image from sometime during his long life? He wasn't sure. It seemed to him that he had actually skied or that he dreamed of himself skiing, though. This was not an entirely new image, but an image from his memory. He knew he was envisioning either an actual event or a snippet of a distant dream. He wasn't sure which it was, since either way he was straining his memory to recall something from hundreds of years in the past. As he tried to focus his concentration on the image to have a clearer, longer look at it, which he thought would help him remember if he had actually skied or merely dreamed about skiing, the image slid to the side of his mind and faded at the same time, like a ghost that didn't want anyone living to see it distinctly. The more Ort tried to concentrate on the image and have a distinct, prolonged vision of it, the more difficult it was to conjour up the image, however fractured or fuzzy, and in fairly short order he no longer was able to fix the image in his memory at all.

The image continued reoccurring in his mind, though, and every time it was off to the side, as it were, rather than in his direct line of sight. And each time Ort tried to fix it more clearly and for a longer length of time the image slipped away, as though teasing him like some creature with the ability to make itself invisible at will. It was as maddening as having a feast of food in front of him and having the table full of food slide just out of his grasp every time he reached for something, which was part of several dreams he had had.

Whether the image was a memory of a dream scene or some-thing he had actually experienced, the vision of himself skiing flooded him with a warm, pleasant feeling each time it entered his mind. That made him wonder if he—and all trolls, for that matter—was missing the boat by shunning skiing. Why was it that trolls didn't ski? Was it just because people skied and trolls did not want to be like people? If he was honest with himself, he had to admit, that was a big part of it, probably the major part of it. But now he began questioning if it was always wise to avoid an activity simply because people engaged in that activity. Trolls, after all, did a lot of things people did. Trolls and people both ate food, wore clothes, cut and gathered firewood, made music, told tales, and had many other commonalities. Was skiing so different that it was something trolls should cede to people just because they viewed it as a people activity? Besides, people were getting a foothold on Troll Mountain, on *his* mountain, by using a bottom section of it for skiing. Trolls had more of a right to use the mountain—all of the mountain—than people did. Didn't it make sense to show people who belonged on the mountain, and who the mountain belonged to? Not that he had any intention of skiing there in the daytime, when people were skiing there. Nighttime was the right time for trolls, so that is when he would ski there. He would ski there for his own self-esteem, to go where human beings no doubt did not want him to go. People wouldn't see him skiing, and so wouldn't know he was sending them a message by skiing there, but he and the other trolls would be able to take pride in the defiant action. They hadn't been able to prevent people from building structures at the bottom of the mountain, and going there to ski, but at least they could demonstrate to themselves that people not only had not driven them from the mountain but that they still had at least partial control of the small portion of the mountain people had invaded.

"We're going skiing," Ort announced to a group of fellow tribe members who were eating supper in the large communal cave three evenings after Christmas Day.

"We're what?!" Scurf fairly yelped, thinking he either had misheard or that Ort had gone off the deep end, that he had a loose screw.

"Going skiing," Ort repeated.

"What are you talking about?" Gangl said. "Trolls don't ski. People ski. We've never skied."

"Well, that's about to change," Ort responded. "We're not going to let people come here and use part of our mountain without doing something about it. We're going to ski right where they ski to show them who belongs on the mountain."

"Are you talking about skiing down the slope where we saw people going down?" Haar asked, close to incredulous. "Is that what you're talking about?"

"That's what I'm talking about," Ort confirmed.

"But you said it made no sense for people to do it," Haar pointed out. "And now *you* want to do the same thing? That doesn't make any sense either."

"I got to thinking: If people can do it, trolls can do it," Ort said. "Don't you see? We'll defy people by skiing there. We'll take back what is rightfully ours. We'll prove that we have control of the whole mountain."

"How about just tearing up their little ski hill instead, so they can't use anymore?" Gangl suggested.

"That sounds like a better idea to me," Scurf said.

"We tried that with their machines, and it didn't work," Ort said. "If we did that they would probably just fix it up and continue to ski there. That won't work. What will work is to use their little ski hill for ourselves, to do something they don't want us to do. That way we beat them at their own game."

"Well, if you want to go, go," Scurf said. "I'm not interested in trying to ski."

"Me neither," Dau said.

"If I go, we're all going," Ort said sternly. "Anyone who refuses will have to deal with me. I think you know what that means."

"Aren't you overlooking one pretty important fact?" Haar said to him. "We don't have any skis. How are we going to ski when we don't have any skis?" Others chattered in with supporting comments.

"I'm guessing there might well be skis in that big building," Ort said. "When I was there watching, people would come empty-handed and go into that big building, then be wearing skis on their feet when they came out the other side of the building. So I'm thinking there are skis in that building all the time."

"But what if there aren't? Dau asked.

"Then we won't have any skis, and probably won't be able to ski," Ort said.

"When were you thinking about doing this?" Haar asked Ort.

"Tonight," Ort answered. "Right now."

Ort beat down further questions and objections until the other trolls could think of no more ways to try to talk him out of what most thought was a crazy, potentially dangerous plan.

And so it was that Ort led a group of fourteen trolls down Troll Mountain that cold, late-December night. The group consisted of ten men and four women, the women being Jompa, Tala, Retta and Elseth, Retta's daughter. Some of the tribe's males were already out and about by the time Ort made his announcement, and Ort excused the older female members from going along if they didn't want to go. Anyway, it was necessary for at least a couple to stay behind to look after and wait on Old Fungus. While no longer in grave danger of passing away, he continued to be bedridden and unable to move about. Many of those in the group headed down the mountain hoped they would not find any skis in the big building so they wouldn't have to risk life and limb skiing down a steep slope. They would have considered a visit to a haunted house less frightening.

The trolls *did*, however, find skis in the lodge, which they were able to break into easily, using their great strength to push open a locked door. There were no people around, not even guards, as they had expected there would not be, given the night-time looks of the site they had had in recent weeks. So they had the run of the place, and Ort resolved they would make the most of the opportunity. They explored the rest of the lodge and discovered a large kitchen, where they were able to grab some food, a large dining area, a bar area, a ticket area, which baffled them, for they didn't know what it was, and other rooms and sections before returning to the ski storage area on the lower level of the two-story structure.

From watching people ski, they knew they were supposed to wear one ski on each foot and carry a stick in each hand long enough to reach the ground. Other than that, they knew about as much about skiing as they did about the Bible, which is to say practically nothing. It even took some doing for them to understand what ends of the skis were the front and which the back. The foot bindings were like mind-boggling puzzles. Eventually, by trial and error—a lot of error—many of them managed to strap on skis. A few put theirs on inside the building, others outside. Gangl had two left-foot skis, Rott two right-foot ones, for the subtlties of ski shape escaped their recognition. One of Drulle's skis was shorter than the other.

"How do we get up there to ski down?" Jompa asked after Ort explained they were going to ski down the slope.

Ort had overlooked that rather important detail. How *were* they going to get up there? Seeing the towropes, he had an inspired thought. "We'll get up there the same way people do— with that rope contraption."

Those who had not seen the towropes in action had no clue as to how they worked, while Ort knew they moved somehow but could not have explained how if his life depended on that knowledge.

"Those things, you mean?" Retta said.

"Sure," Ort said. "The benches move."

"How?" Retta asked.

"I'm not sure," Ort admitted. "But we saw them move, with people sitting on them, so it shouldn't be too hard to figure it out."

"I bet if someone pulled on a rope from the top they would move," Haar offered. "I'll volunteer to go up and try to make the ropes and the benches move."

"Go ahead," Ort said. Having the sense it might take a lot of muscle power to make that happen, he assigned Drulle, the tribe's strongest member, the job of going up with Haar to help him.

As Haar and Drulle made their way up to the top of the ski runs, going through the edge of the forest rather than up the bare slope, the others headed over to the base of the slope. Some of those wearing skis lost their balance and fell while others took to skiing, at least on level ground, like thoroughbred colts take to running. Ort was one of those who seemed to have a natural aptitude for the activity, even though his body shape hardly suggested such would be the case. Gangl, on the other hand, did the splits right away, as he made his first movement, and snapped a pole by putting too much weight on it as he tried unsuccessfully to remain upright.

Soon Haar and Drulle emerged into the open on the shelf of land at the top of the ski runs. Haar looked over the towrope setup, concluded it seemed to operate mechanically, and started pulling on a rope to see if it moved. "It's moving!" Retta shouted from below, as it did. It was moving rather slowly, though, so Haar asked Drulle to help him tug on the rope. With the two of them pulling, the towrope was fairly singing in the night, the attached benches flying through the air at the same speed.

"I think this will work!" Haar called down to the group gathered at the base of the ski slope.

"Let's try it!" Ort shouted back to him. "I'll get on one of the benches, and you two pull me up."

When Ort was seated on one of the benches Haar and Drulle hauled him up with ease. Ort was giddy with excitement as he slid off and looked down. The slope seemed much steeper from that vantage point than it did when he watched people ski, or even from the bottom of the slope, which gave him second thoughts about this whole adventure. Maybe this sort of skiing *was* too dangerous to try, and better left to human beings if they were foolish enough to do it. He wished he had held steady to his long-held conviction that there were some things people did that trolls should not do rather than waver from that for reasons he was having a hard time remembering just then.

"Are you really going to ski down the hill?" Drulle asked him. "It's awful steep."

Having put himself in this position, he saw no way to back away now. And his reasons for wanting to do it came back to him as clearly as his image in a mirror: It would be an act of defiance, a way for him and his fellow tribe members to assert their right to use the entire mountain. It was something important to them. Besides, he had done much riskier, more dangerous and more stomach churning things over the course of his long life. "Of course I am," he answered Drulle, with strengthened resolve.

Once in position to start, he hesitated only a second or two before setting his two poles into the hard-packed snow and shoving off. He felt a rush such as he had never felt before as he headed straight down the slope, making it seem as though wind was whistling past his ears as he cut through the still air. The noise those at the bottom of the slope were making—cheering him on, shouting advice, and laughing gleefully—was but white noise to him as he concentrated on trying to avoid taking a nasty tumble, as had happened to so many of the human skiers he had watched. He nearly made it all the way to the bottom without falling. Forty feet from the bottom, though, he leaned back too far and his skis ran out ahead of him, causing him to land on his backside and slide down the remainder of the slope in that position, with the back ends of his skis digging ruts through the snow. The others rushed around him as he slid to a stop, congratulating him and asking if he was all right.

"I'm fine," he assured them, sitting up. "That was fun! Even falling down and sliding across the snow was kind of fun."

He was unaware of the irony of describing the experience as fun, having flayed people for skiing down a mountain slope over and over merely for fun, if that was why they did such a thing.

With Ort encouraging all of the others to give skiing a try themselves, and several of the male trolls wanting to ski down the slope to show everyone else they were just as brave as Ort, the trolls were soon frolicking on the ski slope three and four at a time. Even Haar and Drulle were able to participate in the festiveness as others relieved them of the rope pulling duty. Amazingly, most of the trolls turned out to have natural skiing ability. Even a couple of them who could barely stand up on level ground showed remarkable balance on the slope. Rott, Tala, Jirik and Elseth, who were the four youngest trolls there, proved to be the most adept skiers. Even at his rather advanced age, and with his lumpy body type, which would seemingly work against him, Ort demonstrated extraordinary athletic ability for someone new to alpine skiing. Not surprisingly, the trolls had just as much fun, if not more fun, riding on the flying benches as they did skiing down the slope, so much so that sometimes someone would take two or three roundtrip rides before getting off.

"I'm glad you thought of this," Haar said to Ort when the two of them found themselves near each other when they finished runs down the slope within seconds of each other, more than an hour into the skiing. "I never would have thought of doing this myself."

"It's *our* mountain," Ort said. "We have more right to use it than people do. And I promise you this: We're coming back to do this again."

Other Books By Buz Swerkstrom

Sgt. Pepper's Inner Groove (novel)

Golfing With Grace (novel)

Alison's Adventures (fantasy novel)

In The Time of Twelve (fantasy novel)

Born To Coast And Other Stories (humor)

Swanberger's Song (play)

Polk County Places

Infinity On Trial (essays)

**Did Adam And Eve Live In Wisconsin?
(Pieces of Wisconsin History)**

**Profiles In Passion Vol. 1:
Artists & Artisans**

**Profiles In Passion Vol. 2:
Musicians & Other Entertainers**

With the exception of Polk County Places,
all titles are available from Amazon.com